Won from the Waves

by

William Henry Giles Kingston

Won from the Waves
by William Henry Giles Kingston

ISBN: 978-93-69072-69-9

Published by

DOUBLE 9 BOOKS

2/13-B, Ansari Road
Daryaganj, New Delhi – 110002
info@double9books.com
www.double9books.com
Tel. 011-40042856

ABOUT THE AUTHOR

William Henry Giles Kingston (February 28, 1814 – August 5, 1880), also known as W. H. G. Kingston, was an English author best remembered for his boys' adventure stories. Born in Harley Street, London, Kingston was the eldest child of Lucy Henry Kingston and Frances Sophia Rooke, the granddaughter of Sir Giles Rooke, a Court of Common Pleas judge. His paternal grandfather, John Kingston (1736–1820), was a Member of Parliament who, despite owning a plantation in Demerara, was a strong supporter of the abolition of the slave trade. Kingston's father, Lucy, ran a successful wine business in Oporto, Portugal, and spent much of his life there, making frequent trips to England. This international background sparked Kingston's lifelong love of the sea, which would become a central theme in many of his novels. As a writer, Kingston produced numerous adventure novels, filled with daring exploits and moral lessons. His works, such as The Three Midshipmen and Villegagnon: A Tale of the Huguenot Persecution, reflect his deep appreciation for exploration, courage, and the complexities of history. Kingston's stories remain popular for their exciting plots, inspiring young readers to embrace adventure and integrity.

CONTENTS

Chapter One
On the Pier

It was a gloomy evening. A small group of fishermen were standing—at the end of a rough wooden pier projecting out into the water and forming the southern side of the mouth of a small river. A thick mist, which drove in across the German Ocean, obscured the sky, and prevented any object being seen beyond a few hundred fathoms from the shore, on which the dark leaden-coloured waves broke lazily in with that sullen-sounding roar which often betokens the approach of a heavy gale.

On the north side of the river was a wide extent of sandy ground, where the vegetation consisted of stunted furze-bushes and salt-loving plants with leaves of a dull pale green, growing among patches of coarse grass, the roots of which assisted to keep the sand from being blown away by the fierce wintry gales which blew across it. On the right hand of the fishermen as they looked seaward, and beyond an intervening level space, rose a line of high cliffs of light clay and sand extending far to the southward, with a narrow beach at their base. Parallel with the river was a green bank, on the sides of which were perched several cottages, the materials composing them showing that they were the abodes of the hardy men who gained their livelihood on the salt deep. The palings which surrounded them, the sheds and outhouses, and even the ornaments with which they were decorated, were evidently portions of wrecks. Over the door of one might be seen the figure-head of some unfortunate vessel. An arbour, not rustic but nautical, was composed of the carved work of a Dutch galliot; indeed, the owners of few had failed to secure some portion of the numerous hapless vessels which from time to time had been driven on their treacherous coast.

On the level ground between the cliff and the river stood two or three other cottages. One, the largest of them, appeared to be built almost entirely of wreck wood, from the uneven appearance presented by the walls and roof, the architect having apparently adapted such pieces of timber as came to hand without employing the saw to bring them into more fitting shape; the chimney, however, and the lower portions of the walls, were constructed of hewn stone, taken probably from some ancient edifice long demolished.

Though the exterior of the cottage, with its boat and fish sheds, looked somewhat rough, it had altogether a substantial and not uncomfortable appearance.

The most conspicuous object in the landscape was a windmill standing a little way to the southward on the top of the cliff. Its sails were moving slowly round, but their tattered condition showed that but a small amount of grist was ground within.

Such was the aspect of the little village of Hurlston and its surroundings towards the end of the last century. It was not especially attractive—indeed few scenes would have appeared to advantage at that moment; but when sunshine lighted up the blue dancing waters, varied by the shadows of passing clouds, the marine painter might have found many subjects for his pencil among the picturesque cottages, their sturdy inhabitants, the wild cliffs, and the yellow strand glittering with shells.

Farther inland the country improved. On the higher ground to the south were neat cottages rising among shrubberies, the parish church with its square tower, and yet farther off the mansion of Sir Reginald Castleton, in the midst of its park, with its broad lake, its green meadows and clumps of wide-spreading trees, surrounded by a high paling forbidding the ingress of strangers, and serving to secure the herd of graceful deer which bounded amidst its glades.

The fishermen—regardless of the driving mist, which, settling on their flushing coats and sou'-westers, ran off them in streamlets—kept turning their eyes seawards, endeavouring to penetrate the increasing gloom.

"Here comes Adam Halliburt!" exclaimed one of them, turning round; "we shall hear what he thinks of the weather. If he has made up his mind to go to sea to-night, it must come on much worse than it now is to keep him at home."

As these words were uttered, a tall man a little past middle age, strongly-built and hardy-looking as the youngest, habited like the rest in fisherman's costume, was seen approaching from the largest of the cottages on the level ground. His face, though weather-beaten, glowed with health, his forehead was broad, his bright blue eyes beaming with good-nature and kindly feeling. He was followed by a stout fisher-boy carrying a coil of rope over his shoulders, and a basket of provisions in his hand. Two other lads, who had been with the men on the pier, ran to meet him.

"They are doubtful about going to sea to-night. What do you think of it, father?" said the eldest.

"There is nothing to stop us that I see, Ben, unless it comes on to blow harder than it does now," answered Adam, in a cheery voice. "The *Nancy* knows her way to our fishing-grounds as well as we do, and it must be a bad night indeed to stop her."

"What do you think of it, Adam?" asked two or three of the men, when he got among them.

Halliburt turned his face seaward, sheltering his eyes with his hand from the thick drizzle which the mist had now become.

"If the wind holds from the south-east there will be nothing to stop us," he answered, after waiting a minute. "It is likely, however, to be a dirtier night than I had thought for—I will own that. Jacob," he said to his youngest boy, "do you go back and stay with your mother, she wants some help in the house, and you can look after the pigs and poultry before we are back in the morning."

Jacob, a fine lad of ten or twelve years, though he looked older, seemed somewhat disappointed, as he had expected to have gone to sea with his father and brothers. Without attempting, however, to expostulate, he immediately turned back towards the cottage, while the rest of the party proceeded to the *Nancy*, a fine yawl which lay at anchor close to the pier.

She was quickly hauled alongside, when some of the men jumped into her. Before following them, Adam Halliburt took another glance seaward. The wind drove the rain and spray with greater force than before against his face.

"We will wait a bit, lads," he said. "There is no great hurry, and in a few minutes we shall make out what the weather is going to be."

His own sons and some of the men remained in the boat, knowing that he was not likely to give up his intention unless the weather speedily became much worse. Others followed him back to the pier-head, over which the spray beat in frequent showers, showing that the sea had got up considerably, even since they had left it.

They had retreated back a few paces to avoid the salt showers. Adam still seemed somewhat unwilling to give up putting to sea, when the dull sound of a gun from the offing reached their ears. Another and another followed.

"There is a ship on Norton Sands," observed one of the men. "Those guns are too far off for that," answered Halliburt. Two others followed, and then came the thunder-sounding reports of several fired together.

"I was sure those were not guns of distress. They come from ships in action, depend on that; and the news is true we heard yesterday, that the French and English are at it again," exclaimed Adam. "I thought we shouldn't long remain friends with the Mounsiers."

"Good luck be with the English ships!" cried one of the fishermen.

"Amen to that! but they must be careful what they are about, for with the wind dead on shore, if they knock away each other's spars, they are both more than likely to drift on Norton Sands, and if they do, the Lord have mercy on them," said Adam, solemnly. "Whichever gets the victory, they will be in a bad way, as I fear, after all, it will be a dirty night. The wind has shifted three points to the eastward since I left home, and it's blowing twice as hard as it did ten minutes ago. We may as well run the *Nancy* up to her moorings, lads."

As one of the men was hurrying off to carry this order to the rest, a heavier blast than before came across the ocean. It had the effect of rending the veil of mist in two, and the rain ceasing, the keen eyes of the fishermen distinguished in the offing two ships running towards the land, the one a short distance ahead of the other, which was firing at her from her bow-chasers, the leading and smaller vessel returning the fire with her after guns, and apparently determined either to gain a sheltering harbour or to run on shore rather than be taken. The moment that revealed her to the spectators showed those on board how near she was to the shore, though evidently they were not aware of the still nearer danger of the treacherous sandbank. An exclamation of dismay and pity escaped those who were looking at her.

"If she had been half a mile to the nor'ard she might have stood through Norton Gut and been safe," observed Halliburt; "but if she is a stranger there is little chance of her hauling off in time to escape the sands."

While he was speaking, the sternmost ship was seen to come to the wind; her yards were braced up, and now, apparently aware of her danger, she endeavoured to stand off the land before the rising gale should render the undertaking impossible. The hard-pressed chase directly afterwards attempted to follow her example. She was already on a wind when again the mist closed over the ocean, and she was hidden from sight.

"We will keep the *Nancy* where she is," said Halliburt; "we don't know what may happen. If yonder ship drives on the sands—and she has but a poor chance of keeping off them, I fear—we cannot let her people perish without trying to save them; and though it may be a hard job to get alongside the wreck, yet some of the poor fellows may be drifted away from her on rafts or spars, and we may be able to pick them up. Whatever happens, we must do our best."

"Ay, ay, Adam," answered several of his hardy crew, who stood around him; "where you think fit to go we are ready to go too."

The party had not long to wait before their worst apprehensions were realised. The dull report of a gun, which their practised ears told them came from Norton Sands, was heard; in another minute the sound of a second gun boomed over the waters; a third followed even before the same interval had elapsed. That the ship had struck and was in dire distress there could be no doubt, but when they gazed at the dark, heaving waves which rolled in crested with foam, and just discernible in the fast waning twilight, and felt the fierce blast against which even they could scarcely stand upright on the slippery pier, hardy and bold as they were, they hesitated about venturing forth to the rescue of the hapless crew. Long before they could reach the wreck darkness would be resting on the troubled ocean; they doubted, indeed, whether they could force their boat out in the teeth of the fierce gale.

Adam took a turn on the pier. His heart was greatly troubled. He had never failed, if a boat could live, to be among the first to dash out to the rescue of his fellow-creatures when a ship had been cast on those treacherous sandbanks. The hazard was great. He knew that with the strength of his crew exhausted the boat might be hurled back amid the breakers, to be dashed on the shore; or, should they even succeed in reaching the neighbourhood of the wreck, where the greatest danger was to be encountered, they might fail in getting near enough to save any of the people.

Every moment of delay increased the risk which must be run.

"Lads, we will try and do it," he said at length; "maybe she has struck on the lowest part of the bank, and we shall be able to cross it at the top of high water. Come along, we will talk no more about it, but try and do what we have got to do."

Just at that instant the words, uttered in a shrill, loud tone, were heard: —

"Foolish men, have you a mind to drown yourselves in the deep salt sea! Stay, I charge you, or take the consequence."

The voice seemed to come out of the darkness, for no one was seen. The men looked round over their shoulders. Directly afterwards a tall thin figure, habited in grey from head to foot, emerged from the gloom. Those who beheld it might have been excused if they supposed it rather a phantom than a being of the earth, so shadowy did it appear in the thick mist.

"The spirit of the air forbids your going, and I, his messenger, warn you that you seek destruction if you disobey him."

The men gathered closer to each other as the figure approached. It was now seen to be that of a tall, gaunt woman. Her loose cloak and the long grey hair which hung over her shoulders blew out in the wind, giving her face a wild and weird look, for she wore no covering to restrain her locks, with the exception of a mass of dry dark seaweed, formed in the shape of a crown, twisted round the top of her head.

"I have seen the ship you are about to visit. I knew what her fate would be even yesternight when she was floating proudly on the ocean; she was doomed to destruction, and so will be all those who venture on board her. If you go out to her, I tell you that none of you will return. I warn you, Adam Halliburt, and I warn you all! Go not out to her, she is doomed! she is doomed! she is doomed!"

As the woman uttered these words she disappeared in the darkness. The men stood irresolute.

"What, lads, are you to be frightened at what 'Sal of the Salt Sea' says, or 'Silly Sally,' as some of you call her?" exclaimed Adam. "Let us put our trust in God, He will take care of us, if it's His good pleasure. It's our duty to try and help our fellow-creatures. Do you think an old mad woman knows more than He who rules the waves, or that anything she can say in her folly will prevent Him from watching over us and bringing us back in safety?"

Adam's appeal had its due effect. Even the most superstitious were ashamed of refusing to accompany him. When he sprang on board the boat his crew willingly followed. He would have sent back his second boy Sam, but the lad earnestly entreated to be taken.

"If you go, father, why should I stop behind? Jacob will look after mother, and I would rather share whatever may happen to you," he said.

Adam and his men were soon on board the boat: the most of them had shares in her, and thus they risked their property as well as their lives. The oars were got out, and the men, fixing themselves firmly in their seats, prepared for the task before them.

Shoving off from the shore, Adam took the helm. The men pulled away right lustily, and emerging from the harbour, in another minute they were breasting the heaving foam-crested billows in the teeth of the gale. Sometimes, when a stronger blast than usual swept over the water, they appeared, instead of making headway, to be drifting back towards the dimly-seen shore astern. Now, again exerting all their strength, they once more made progress in the direction of the wreck.

All this time the minute guns had been heard, showing that the ship still held together, and that help, if it came, would not be useless. The sound encouraged Adam and his crew to persevere. The reports, however, now came at longer intervals than at first from each other. Several minutes at length elapsed, and no report was heard. Adam listened—not another came. The crew of the *Nancy*, however, persevered, but even Adam, as he observed the slow progress they had made, became convinced that their efforts would prove of no avail.

The gale continued to increase, the foaming seas leaped and roared around them more wildly than before. Even to return would now be an operation of danger, but Adam with sorrow saw that it must be attempted. For an hour or more no headway had been made. He waited for a lull, then giving the word, the boat was rapidly pulled round, and surrounded by hissing masses of foam, she rapidly shot back within the shelter of the harbour. The sinews of her crew were too well strung to feel much fatigue under ordinary circumstances, but the strongest had to acknowledge that they could not have pulled much longer.

"We must not give it up, though, lads," said Adam. "I am sure no beachmen will be able to launch their boats to-night along the coast. If the wind goes down ever so little, we must try it again; you will not think of deserting the poor people if there is a chance of saving them, I know that."

His crew responded to his appeal, and agreed to wait for the chance of being able to get off later in the night.

Looking towards the landing-place, the tall figure of Sal of the Salt Sea was seen standing on the edge of the pier gazing down upon them.

"Foolish men! you have had your toil for nought, yet it is well for you that you could not reach the doomed ship. I warned you, and you disregarded me. I commanded the winds and waves to stop your progress; they listened to my orders and obeyed me. You will not another time venture to disregard my warnings. Now go to your homes, and be thankful that I did not think fit to punish you for your folly. Again I warn you that yonder ship is doomed! is doomed! is doomed!"

While the old woman was uttering these words in the same harsh, loud tones as before, Adam and his crew were making their way to the landing-place. Before they reached it, however, the strange being had disappeared in the darkness, though her voice could be heard as she took her way apparently towards the cliffs.

"Again, lads, I say, don't let what you have heard from the poor mad woman trouble you," exclaimed Adam. "Come to my cottage, and we will have a bite of supper, and wait till we have the chance of getting off again."

Dame Halliburt, expecting them, had prepared supper. The sanded floors and rough chairs and stools which formed the furniture of her abode were not to be injured by their dripping garments. During the meal Adam, or one of the men, went out more than once to judge if there was likely to be a change. Still the gale blew as fiercely as ever. Some threw themselves down on the floor to rest, while Adam, filling his pipe, sat in his arm-chair by the fire, still resolved as at first to persevere.

Chapter Two
At the Wreck

Thus the greater part of the night passed by. Towards dawn Adam started up. The howling of the wind in the chimney and the rattling sound of the windows which looked towards the sea decreased.

"Lads!" he shouted, "the gale is breaking, we may yet be in time to save life, and maybe to get salvage too from the wreck. We will be off at once."

The crew required no second summons. Telling his dame to keep up her spirits, and that he should soon be back, he led the way to the pier.

Some of the men, hardy fellows as they were, looked round nervously, expecting the appearance of Sal of the Salt Sea. She did not return, however, and they were soon on board. The poor creature, probably not supposing that they would again venture out, had not thought of being on the watch for them.

Once more the *Nancy*, propelled by the strong arms of her hardy crew, was making her way towards Norton Sands. It was still dark as before, but the wind had gone down considerably, and the task, though such as none but beachmen would have attempted, seemed less hopeless. After rowing for some time amidst the foaming seas, Adam stood firmly up and endeavoured to make out the ship. At length he discovered a dark object rising above the white seething waters: it was the wreck. Two of her masts were still standing. She was so placed near the tail of the bank, where the water was deepest, that he hoped to be able to approach to leeward, and thus more easily to board her if necessary.

"We shall be able to save the people if we can get up to her soon, lads," he exclaimed. "Cheer up, my brave boys, it will be a proud thing if we can carry them all off in safety."

The wind continued to decrease. As they neared the bank, the force of the sea, broken by it, offered less opposition.

Just then amidst the gloom he caught sight of another object at a little distance from the wreck: it was a lugger under close-reefed sails standing away on a wind towards the south. "Can she have been visiting the wreck?" thought Adam; "it looks like it. If so, she must have taken off the people. Then why does she not run for Hurlston, where she could most quickly land them?"

As these thoughts passed through his mind, the lugger, which a keen eye like his alone could have discerned, disappeared in the darkness.

"I wonder if that can be Miles Gaffin's craft," he thought; "no one, unless well acquainted with the coast, would venture in among these sandbanks in this thick weather; she is more likely to be knocking about here than any other vessel that I know of. She has been after her usual tricks, I doubt not."

Adam, however, did not utter his thoughts aloud. Indeed, unless he had spoken at the top of his voice he could not have been heard even by the man nearest him, while all his attention was required in steering the boat.

The crew had still some distance to pull, and their progress against the heavy seas was but slow. At length dawn began to break, and the wreck rose clearly before them. She was a large ship. The foremast had gone by the board, but the main and mizzen-masts, though the topmasts had been carried away, were still standing.

With cool daring they pulled under her stern. To their surprise, no one hailed them—not a living soul did they see on the deck.

As a sea which swept round her lifted the boat, Adam, followed by his son Ben and another man, sprang on board. A sad spectacle met their sight. The sea had made a clean sweep over the fore part of the ship, carrying away the topgallant, forecastle, and bulwarks, and, indeed, everything which had offered it resistance, but the foremast still hung by the rigging, in which were entangled the bodies of three or four men who had either been crushed as it fell or drowned by the waves washing over them. The long-boat on the booms had also been washed away—indeed, not a boat remained. The guns, too, of which, though evidently a merchantman, she had apparently carried several, had broken adrift and been carried overboard, with the exception of the aftermost one, which lay overturned, and now held fast a human being, and, as her dress proved her to be a woman. The complexion of the poor creature was dark, and the costume she wore showed Adam that she was from the far-off East. Ben lifted her hand; it fell on the deck as he let it go; it was evident that no help could be of use to her. Her distorted countenance exhibited the agonies she must have suffered.

"She must have been holding on to the gun," observed Adam, "when it capsized; and if I read the tale aright, she was standing there calling to those in the boats to come back for her as they were shoving off. If the boats had not been lowered, we should have seen some of the wreck of them hanging to the davits. See, the falls are gone on both sides."

Having made a rapid survey of the deck, Adam looked seaward.

"We have no time to lose," he said, "for the sky looks dirty to windward, and we shall have the gale down on us again before long, I suspect. We must first, though, make a search below, for maybe some of the people have taken shelter there. I fear, however, the greater number must have been washed away, or attempted to get off in the boats."

Adam, leading the party, hurried below.

The water was already up to the cabin deck, and the violent rocking of the ship told them that it would be dangerous to spend much time in the search. No one was to be found.

"Let us have the skylight off, Tom, to see our way," said Ben.

Tom sprang on deck and soon forced it off, and the pale morning light streamed down below. Everything in the main cabin was in confusion.

"This shows that the people must have got away in the boats, and have carried off whatever they could lay hands on, unless some one else has visited the wreck since then," remarked Adam; and he then told Ben of his having observed the lugger in the neighbourhood of the wreck.

"She looks to me like a foreign-built ship, although her fittings below are in the English fashion," he observed, examining the cabins as far as the dim twilight which made its way through the open hatch would allow.

"As we came under her stern I saw no name on it; I cannot make out what she can be."

The lockers in the captain's state cabin were open, and none of his instruments were to be seen. Two or three of the other side cabins had apparently been searched in a hurry for valuables. The doors of the aftermost ones were however still closed. The violent heaving and the crashing sounds which reached their ears, showing how much the ship was suffering from the rude blows of the seas, made Adam unwilling to prolong the search. He and his companions secured such articles as appeared most worth saving.

"Let us look into the cabin before we go," exclaimed Ben, opening the door of one which seemed the largest. As he did so a cry was heard, and a child's voice asked, "Who's there?" He and Adam sprang in.

Chapter Three
Safe to Land

As Adam Halliburt and his son sprang into the cabin, they saw in a small cot by the side of a larger one, a little girl, her light hair falling over her fair young neck. She lifted her head and gazed at them from her blue eyes with looks of astonishment mingled with terror.

"Is no one with you, my pretty maiden?" exclaimed Adam; "how came you to be left all alone here?"

"Ayah gone. I called, she no come back," answered the child.

"This is no place for you, my little dear, we will take care of you," said Adam, lifting her up and wrapping the bed clothes round her, for she was dressed only in her nightgown.

"Oh, let me go; I must stay here till my ayah comes back," cried the child; yet she did not struggle, comprehending, it seemed, from the kind expression of Adam's countenance, that he intended her no harm.

"The person you speak of won't come back, I fear; so you must come with us, little maid, and if God wills we will carry you safely on shore," answered Adam, folding the clothes tighter round the child, and grasping her securely in his left arm as a woman carries an infant, and leaving his right one at liberty, for this he knew he should require to hold on by, until having made his way across the heaving, slippery deck, he could take the necessary leap into the boat.

"It is wet and cold, we must cover you up," he said, adding to himself, "The child would otherwise see a sight enough to frighten her young heart."

The little girl did not again speak as Adam carried her through the cabins.

"I HAVE A LITTLE MAID HERE, MY LADS."

"You must let go those things, lads, and stand ready for lending me a hand to prevent any harm happening to this little dear," he said, as he mounted the companion-ladder.

Before reaching the deck he drew the blanket over the child's face, and then, with an activity no younger seaman could have surpassed, he sprang to the side of the ship and grasped a stanchion, to which he held on while he shouted to the crew of his boat, who had for safety's sake pulled her off a few fathoms from the wreck, keeping their oars going to retain their position.

"Pull up now, lads! We have got all there is time for," he cried out. "Ben and Tom, do you leap when I do. I have a little maid here, my lads, and we must take care no harm comes to her."

While he was speaking the boat was approaching. Now she sank down, almost touching the treacherous sands beneath her keel—now, as the sea rolled in, part of which broke over the wreck, she rose almost to a level with the deck. Adam, who had been calculating every movement she was about to make, sprang on board. Steadying himself by the shoulders of the men, he stepped aft with his charge. Ben and Tom followed him.

The men in the bows, immediately throwing out their starboard oars, pulled the boat's head round, and the next instant, the mast being stepped and the sail hoisted, the *Nancy* was flying away before the following seas towards the shore. Adam steered with one hand while he still supported the child on his arm.

"You are all right now, my little maid," he said, looking down on her sweet face, the expression of which showed the alarm and bewilderment she felt, he having thrown off the blanket.

"We will soon have you safe on shore in the care of my good dame. She will be a mother to you, and you will soon forget all about the wreck and the things which have frightened you."

As Adam turned a glance astern, he was thankful that he had not delayed longer on board the wreck. The wind blew far more fiercely than before, and the big seas came hissing and foaming in, each with increased speed and force.

The *Nancy* flew on before them. The windmill, the best landmark in the neighbourhood, could now be discerned through the mist and driving spray. Adam kept well to the nor'ard of it. The small house near the pier-head, which served to shelter pilots and beachmen who assembled there, next came into view, and the *Nancy* continuing her course, guided by the experienced hand of her master, now mounting to the top of a high sea, now descending, glided into the mouth of the harbour, up which she speedily ran to her moorings.

Adam, anxious to get his little maid, as he called her, out of the cold and damp, and to place her in charge of his wife, sprang on shore. Jacob, who had been on the look-out for the return of the *Nancy* since dawn, met him on the landing-place.

"Are all safe, father?" he asked, in an anxious tone.

"All safe, boy, praised be His name who took care of us, and no thanks to that poor creature, Mad Sal, who would have frightened the lads and me from going off, and allowed this little maid here to perish."

"What! have you brought her from the wreck?" inquired Jacob, eagerly, looking into the face of the child, who at that moment opened her large blue eyes and smiled, as she caught sight of the boy's good-natured countenance.

"Is she the only one you have brought on shore, father?" he added.

"The only living creature we found on board, more shame to those who deserted her, though it was God's ordering that she might be preserved," answered Adam. "But run on, Jacob, and see that the fire is blazing up brightly, we shall want it to dry her damp clothes and warm her cold feet, the little dear."

"The fire is burning well, father, I doubt not, for I put a couple of logs on before I came out; but I will run on and tell mother to be ready for you," answered Jacob, hastening away.

Adam followed with rapid strides.

The dame stood at the open door to welcome him as he entered.

"What, is it as Jacob says, a little maid you have got there?" she exclaimed, opening her arms to receive the child from her husband.

The dame was an elderly, motherly-looking woman, with a kindly smile and pleasant expression of countenance, which left little doubt that the child would be well cared for.

"Bless her sweet face, she is a little dear, and so she is!" exclaimed the dame, as she pressed her to her bosom. "Bless you, my sweet one, don't be frightened now you are among friends who love you!" she added, as she carried her towards the fire which blazed brightly on the hearth, and observed that the child was startled on finding herself transferred to the arms of another stranger.

"Bring the new blanket I bought at Christmas for your bed, Jacob, and I will take off her wet clothes and wrap her in it, and warm her pretty little feet. Don't cry, deary, don't cry!" for the child, not knowing what was going to happen, had now for the first time begun to sob and wail piteously.

"Maybe she is hungry, for she could have had nothing to eat since last night, little dear," observed Adam, who was standing by, his damp clothes steaming before the blazing fire.

"We will soon have something for her, then," answered the dame.

Jacob brought the blanket, which the dame gave Adam to warm before she wrapped it round the child.

"Run off to Mrs Carey's as fast as your legs can carry you, and bring threepenny-worth of milk," she said to her son. "Tell her why I want it; she must send her boy to bring in the cow; don't stop a moment longer than you can help."

Jacob, taking down a jug from the dresser, ran off, while the dame proceeded to disrobe the little stranger, kissing and trying to soothe her as she did so. Round her neck she discovered a gold chain and locket.

"I was sure from her looks that she was not a poor person's child, this also shows it," she observed to her husband; "and see what fine lace this is round her nightgown. It was a blessed thing, Adam, that you saved her life, the little cherub; though, for that matter, she looks as fit to be up in heaven as any bright angel there. But what can have become of those to whom she belongs? Of one thing I am very sure, neither father nor mother could have been aboard, for they would not have left her."

"I'll tell thee more about that anon," observed Adam, recollecting the poor coloured woman whose wretched fate he had discovered; "I think thou art right, mother."

The child had ceased sobbing while the dame was speaking, and now lay quietly in her arms enjoying the warmth of the fire.

"She will soon be asleep and forget her cares," observed the dame, watching the child's eyelids, which were gradually closing. "Now, Adam, go and get off thy wet clothes, and then cut me out a piece of crumb from one of the loaves I baked yestere'en, and bring the saucepan all ready for Jacob when he comes with the milk."

"I'll get the bread and saucepan before I take off my wet things," answered Adam, smiling. "The little maid must be the first looked to just now."

Jacob quickly returned, and the child seemed to enjoy the sweet bread-and-milk with which the dame liberally fed her.

A bed was then made up for her near the fire, and smiling her thanks for the kind treatment she received, her head was scarcely on the pillow before she was fast asleep.

Chapter Four
May's New Home

"What are you going to do with her?" asked Jacob, who having stolen down from his roosting-place after a short rest, found his father and mother sitting by the fire watching over the little girl, who was still asleep.

"Do with her!" exclaimed Dame Halliburt, looking at her husband, "why, take care of her, of course, what else should we do?"

"No one owns her who can look after her better than we can; we have a right to her, at all events, and we will do our best for the little maiden," responded Adam, returning his wife's glance.

"I thought as how you would, father," said Jacob, in a tone which showed how greatly relieved he felt. "I knew, mother, you would not like to part with the little maid when once you had got her, seeing we have no sister of our own; she will be a blessing to you and to all of us, I am sure of that."

"I hope she will, Jacob; I sighed, I mind, when I found you were not a girl, for I did wish to have a little daughter to help me, though you are a good boy, and you mustn't fancy I love you the less because you are one."

"I know that, mother," answered Jacob, in a cheerful tone; "but I don't want her to work instead of me, that I don't."

"Of course not, Jacob," observed Adam; "she is a little lady born, there is no doubt about it; and we must remember that, bless her sweet face. I could not bear the thoughts of such as she having to do more work than is good for her. Still, as God has sent her to us, if no one claims her we must bring her up as our own child, and do our best to make her happy, and she will be a light and joy in the house."

"That I'm sure she will," interrupted Jacob; "and Ben and Sam and I will all work for her, and keep her from harm, just as much as if mother had had a little maid, that we will."

"Yes, yes, Jacob, I am sure of it," exclaimed the dame, smiling her approval as she glanced affectionately at her son.

So the matter was settled, and the little girl was to be henceforth looked on as the daughter of the house.

"Of course, dame, I must do what I can, though, to find out whether the little maid has any friends in this country," observed Adam, after keeping silence for some minutes, as if he had been considering over the subject; "she may or she may not, but when I come to think of the poor dark woman who was on board, and who I take to have been her nurse, she must have come from foreign parts. Still, as she speaks English, even if her fair hair and blue eyes did not show that, it is clear that she has English parents, and if they were not on board, and I am very sure they were not, she must have been coming to some person in England, who will doubtless be on the look-out for her. So you must not set your heart on keeping the little maiden, for as her friends are sure to be rich gentlefolks she would be better off with them than with us."

"As to that Adam, I have been thinking as you have; but then you see it's not wealth that gives happiness, and if we bring her up and she knows no other sort of life, maybe she will be as happy with us as if she were to be a fine lady," answered the dame looking affectionately at the sleeping child.

"But right is right," observed Adam; "we would not let her go to be worse off than she would be with us, that's certain; but we must do our duty by her, and leave the rest in God's hands."

Just then the child opened her large blue eyes, and after looking about with a startled expression, asked, "Where ayah?" and then spoke some words in a strange-sounding language, which neither the fisherman nor his wife could understand.

"She you ask for, my sweet one, is not here," said the dame, bending over her; "but I will do instead of her, and you just think you are at home now with those who love you, and you shall not want for anything."

While the dame was speaking the two elder lads came downstairs, and as the appearance of so many strangers seemed to frighten the little girl, Adam, putting on his thick coat and sou'-wester, and taking up his spyglass, called to his sons to come out and see what had become of the ship.

They found it blowing as hard as ever. The sea came rolling towards the shore in dark foaming billows. The atmosphere was, however, clear; and the wreck could still be distinguished, though much reduced in size. While Adam had his glass turned towards it he observed the mizzen-mast, which had hitherto stood, go by the board, and the instant afterwards the whole of the remaining part of the hull seemed to melt away before the furious seas which broke against it.

"I warned you that the ship was doomed, and that no human being would reach the shore alive," shrieked a voice in his ears; "such will be the fate, sooner or later, of all who go down on the cruel salt sea."

Adam turning saw Mad Sally standing near him, and pointing with eager gestures towards the spot where the wreck had lately appeared.

"Ah, ah, ah!" she shouted, in wild, hoarse tones, resembling the cries of the sea-gull as it circles in the air in search of prey.

"Sad news, sad news, sad news I bring,
Sad news for our good king,
For one of his proud and gallant ships
Has gone down in the deep salt sea, salt sea,
Has gone down in the deep salt sea."

"Yonder ship has gone to pieces, there is no doubt about that, mother," said Adam; "but you were wrong to warn us not to go off to her, for go off we did, and brought one of her passengers on shore who would have perished if we had listened to you, so don't fancy you are always right in what you say."

"If you brought human being from yonder ship woe will come of it. Foolish man, you fought against the fates who willed it otherwise."

"I know nothing about the fates, mother," answered Adam; "but I know that God willed us to bring on shore a little girl we found on board, and protected us while we did so."

"Think you that He would have protected you when He did not watch over my boy, who was carried away over the salt sea?" she exclaimed, making a scornful gesture at Adam. "He protects not such as you, who madly venture out when in His rage He stirs up the salt sea, salt sea, salt sea!" and she broke out into a wild song—

"There were three brothers in Scotland did dwell,
And they cast lots all three,
Which of them should go sailing
On the wide salt sea, salt sea;
Which of them should go sailing
On the wide salt sea;"

and, wildly flourishing her arms, she stalked away towards the cliffs, up which she climbed, still making the same violent gestures, although her voice could no longer be heard, till she disappeared in the distance.

A number of people had collected along the beach, eagerly looking out for any portion of the wreck or cargo which might be washed on shore, but they looked in vain; the sands swallowed up the heavier articles, while the rest were swept by the tide out to sea. Nothing reached the shore by which the name or character of the vessel which had just gone to pieces could be discovered.

Adam Halliburt, finding that there was no probability of the weather mending sufficiently to enable the *Nancy* to put to sea, returned home.

"Look you, lads," he observed, calling his sons to his side; "you heard what that poor mad woman said. You see how she was all in the wrong when she told us not to put off to the wreck, and warned us that we should come to harm if we did. Now, to my mind, she is just a poor mad creature; but if she does know anything which others don't, it's Satan who teaches her, and he was a liar from the beginning, and therefore she is more likely to be wrong than right; and when you hear her ravings, don't you care for them, but go on and do your duty, and God will take care of you; leave that to Him."

"Ay, ay, father," answered Jacob; "she would have had us leave the little maiden to perish, if we had listened to her; I will never forget that."

While the elder lads went on board the *Nancy* to do one of the numberless jobs which a sailor always finds to be done on board his craft, Jacob and his father entered the cottage.

The little girl was seated on the dame's knee, prattling in broken language, which her kind nurse in vain endeavoured to understand. She welcomed the fisherman and his son with a smile of recognition.

"Glad to see you well and happy, my pretty maiden," said Adam, stooping down to kiss her fair brow, his big heart yearning towards her as if she were truly his child.

"Maidy May," she said, with an emphasis on the last word, as if wishing to tell him her proper name.

"Yes, our 'Maiden May' you are," he answered, misunderstanding her, and from that day forward Adam called her Maiden May, the rest of the family imitating him, and she without question adopting the name.

Chapter Five
Dame Halliburt

Dame Halliburt was a good housewife, and an active woman of business. Every morning she was up betimes with breakfast ready for her husband and sons waiting the return of the *Nancy*, and as soon as her fish-baskets were loaded, away she went, making a long circuit through the neighbouring country to dispose of their contents at the houses of the gentry and farmers, among whom she had numerous customers. She generally called at Texford, though, as Sir Reginald Castleton lived much alone, she was not always sure of selling her fish there, and had often to go a considerable distance out of her way for nothing. If Mr Groocock, the steward, happened to meet her on the road he seldom failed to stop his cob, or when she called at the house to come out and inquire what was going on at Hurlston, or to gain any bits of information she might have picked up on her rounds.

Maiden May had been for upwards of a year under her motherly care, when one morning as she was approaching Texford with her heavily-loaded basket, she caught sight of the ruddy countenance of Mr Groocock, with his yellow top-boots, ample green coat, and three-cornered hat on the top of his well-powdered wig, jogging along the road towards her.

"Good-morrow, dame," he exclaimed, pulling up as he reached her. "I see that you have a fine supply of fish, and you will find custom, I doubt not, at the Hall this morning. There are three or four tables to be served, for we have more visitors than Sir Reginald has received for many a day."

As he spoke he looked into the dame's basket, turning the fish with the handle of his whip.

"Ah, just put aside that small turbot and a couple of soles for my table, there's a good woman, will you? You have plenty besides for the housekeeper to choose from."

"I will not forget your orders, Mr Groocock," said the dame; "and who are the guests, may I ask?"

"There is Mrs Ralph Castleton and her two sons, the eldest, Mr Algernon, who is going to college soon, and Mr Harry, a midshipman, who has just come home from sea; a more merry, rollicking young gentleman I never set eyes on; indeed, if the house was not a good big one he would turn it upside-down in no time. There is also his sister, Miss Julia, with her French governess, and Sir Reginald's cousins, the Miss Pembertons. One of them, the youngest, Miss Mary they call her, is blind, poor dear lady; but, indeed, you would not think so to see the bright smile that lights up her face when she is talking, and few people know so much of what is going on in the world, not to mention all about birds, and creeping things, and flowers. The other day she was going through the garden, when just by touching the flowers with her fingers she was able to tell their colour and their names as well as the gardener himself.

"Then there is a Captain Fancourt, a naval officer, a brother of Mrs Ralph Castleton, and Mr Ralph Castleton himself is expected, but he is taken up with politics and public business in London, and it is seldom he can tear himself away from them."

"I suppose Mr Ralph, then, is Sir Reginald's heir," observed the dame.

"That remains to be seen," answered the steward. "You know Sir Reginald has another nephew older than Mr Ralph, who has been abroad since he was a young man. Though he has not been heard of for many years, he may appear any day. The title and estates must go to him, whatever becomes of the personalty."

"You know when I was a girl I lived in the family of Mr Herbert Castleton, their father, near Morbury, so I remember the young gentlemen as they were then, and feel an interest in them, and so I should in their children."

"Ah! that just reminds me that you or your husband may do Master Harry a pleasure. He has not been on shore many days before he is wanting to be off again on the salt water, and who should he fall in with but Miles Gaffin, who came up here to see me about the rent of the mill. Master Harry found out somehow or other that Miles had a lugger, and nothing would content him but that he must go off and take a cruise in her. Now, between ourselves, Mrs Halliburt, I do not trust that craft or her owner. You know, perhaps, as much about them as I do; your husband knows more, but I think it would content the young gentleman if Halliburt would take him off in his yawl, and he need not go so far from the shore as to run any risk of being picked up by an enemy's ship."

"Bless you, Mr Groocock, of course Adam will be main proud to take out Sir Reginald's nephew, and for his own sake will be careful not to go far enough off the land to run the risk of being caught by any of the French cruisers," answered the dame. "When would the young gentleman like to come? He must not expect man-of-war's ways on board the *Nancy*, and it would not do for Adam and the lads to lose their day's fishing."

"As to that, he is not likely to be particular, and the sooner he can get his cruise the better he will be pleased. It seems strange to me that any one, when once he is comfortable on shore, should wish to be tumbling about on the tossing sea. Though I have lived all my life in sight of the ocean, I never had a fancy to leave the dry land. Give me a good roof over my head, plenty to eat and drink, and a steady cob to ride, it's all I ask; a man should be moderate in his desires, dame, and he will get them satisfied, that is my notion of philosophy."

"Ah! and a very good notion too," said Mistress Halliburt, who had great respect for the loquacious steward of Texford. "But you will excuse me, Mr Groocock, I ought to be up at the Hall. I will tell Adam of Master Harry's wish, and he will be on the look-out for him."

"Here comes the young gentleman to speak for himself," said the steward.

At that moment a horse's hoofs were heard clattering along the road, and a fine-looking lad in a midshipman's uniform cantered up on a pony, holding his reins slack, and sitting with the careless air of a sailor. He had a noble broad brow, clear blue eyes, and thick, clustering, brown curls, his countenance being thoroughly bronzed by southern suns and sea air. His features were well formed and refined, without any approach to effeminacy.

"Good-morrow, Mr Groocock," he exclaimed, in a clear voice, pulling up as he spoke. "Good-morrow, dame," he added, turning to Mrs Halliburt.

"I was just speaking to the dame here about your wish, Mr Harry, to take a trip to sea. Her husband, Adam Halliburt, has as fine a boat as any on the coast, and he is a trustworthy man, which is more than can be said, between ourselves, of the tenant of Hurlston Mill. Adam will give you a cruise whenever you like to go, wind and weather permitting, though, as the dame observed, you must not expect much comfort on board the *Nancy*."

"I care little for comfort—we have not too much of that sort of thing at sea to make me miss it," answered Harry, laughing. "If the dame can answer for her husband, I will engage to go as soon as he likes."

"Adam will be glad to take you, I am main sure of that, Mr Harry," said the dame. "But as the *Nancy* will be ready to put off before I get back, I would ask you to wait till to-morrow afternoon, when she will go out for the night's fishing."

Harry, well pleased at the arrangement, having wished the dame good-bye, accompanied Mr Groocock on his morning's ride.

Chapter Six
Lord Howe's Victory

Harry got back at luncheon time to Texford, where the family were assembled in the dining-hall. Sir Reginald—a fine-looking old man, the whiteness of whose silvery locks, secured behind a well-tied pig-tail, was increased by the hair-powder which besprinkled them—sat at the foot of the table in the wheel-chair used by him to move from room to room. His once tall and strongly-built figure was slightly bent, though, unwilling to show his weakness, he endeavoured to sit as upright as possible while he did the honours of his hospitable board. Still it was evident that age and sickness were making rapid inroads on his strength.

He had deputed his niece, Mrs Castleton, to take the head of his table. She had been singularly handsome, and still retained much of the beauty of her younger days; with a soft and feminine expression of countenance which truly portrayed her gentle, and perhaps somewhat too yielding, character—yielding, at least, as far as her husband, Ralph Castleton, was concerned, to whose stern and imperious temper she had ever been accustomed to give way.

"My dear Harry, we were afraid that you must have lost your way," she said, when the young midshipman entered the room.

"I rode over to the post-office at Morbury for letters, and had to wait while the bag was made up. I slung it over my back, and I fancy was taken for a government courier as I rode along. I have brought despatches for every one in the house, I believe; a prodigious big one for you, Uncle Fancourt, from the Lords Commissioners of the Admiralty, I suspect, for I saw the seal when it was put into the bag," he said, addressing a sunburnt, fine-looking man, with the unmistakable air of a naval officer, seated by his mother's side. "Mr Groocock, to whom I gave the bag, will send them up as soon as he has opened it. There is something in the wind, I suspect, for I heard shouting and trumpeting just as I rode out of the town. Knowing that I had got whatever news there is at my back, I came on with it rather than return to learn more about the matter."

"Probably another enemy's ship taken," observed Captain Fancourt.

"Are the Admiralty going to send you to sea again, Fancourt?" asked Sir Reginald, who had overheard Harry's remark.

"They are not likely, during these stirring times, Sir Reginald, to allow any of us to remain idle on shore if they think us worth our salt, and I hope to deserve that, at least," answered Captain Fancourt.

"You are worth tons of that article, or the admiral's despatches greatly overpraise you," observed Sir Reginald, laughing at his own joke. "I remember reading with great delight the gallant way in which, after your captain was wounded, you fought the *Hector* on your voyage home from the West Indies, when she was attacked by two 40-gun French frigates. You had not, I fancy, half as many men, or as many guns mounted, as either one of them, while, in addition to their crews, they were full of troops, yet you beat them off when they attempted to board; and though they had pretty well knocked your ship to pieces, you compelled them to make sail away from you, leaving you to your fate. If I recollect rightly, you bore up for Halifax with more than half your crew killed and wounded."

"You give me more credit than is my due, Sir Reginald," observed Captain Fancourt, "I was but a young lieutenant, though I did my duty. Captain Drury fought the ship, and we should all have lost our lives had not we fallen in with the *Hawk* brig, which rescued us just as the old *Hector* sank under our feet."

"Well, well, when our enemies find out that it is the fashion of English sailors to fight till their ship goes down, they will be chary of attacking them with much hopes of victory."

While the baronet was speaking, Harry had taken his seat next to a pretty dark-eyed young girl, giving her a kiss on the cheek and at the same time a pat on the back, a familiarity to which his sister Julia was well accustomed from her sailor brother, who entertained the greatest admiration and affection for her.

"You should not treat the demoiselle in that mode at table, Monsieur Harry," observed a lady who was sitting on his other side.

"I beg your pardon, Madame De La Motte, I ought, I confess, to have paid my respects to you first."

"Ah, you are mediant, incorrigible," said the lady, in broken English, laughing as she spoke.

"No, I am only very hungry, so you will excuse me if I swallow a few mouthfuls before we discuss that subject," said Harry, applying himself to the plate of chicken and ham which the footman had just placed before him.

"I'm afraid that you think I have forgotten my manners as well as the French you taught me before I went to sea. But I hope to prove to you that I retain a fair amount of both," and Harry began to address the lady in French. When he mispronounced a word and she corrected him he bowed his thanks, repeating it after her.

"Ah, you are *charmant*, Monsieur Harry, you have not forgotten your manners any more than the language of La Belle France, which I will continue to teach you whenever you will come and take a lesson with Mademoiselle Julia. When will you come?"

"Every day that I am at home till my country requires my services," answered Harry.

"I never learned French, but I should think it must be a very difficult language to acquire," observed a pale middle-aged lady of slight figure who sat opposite Harry, turning her eyes towards him, but those orbs were of a dull leaden hue, the eyelids almost closed. She was totally blind.

Her features were beautifully formed, and had a peculiarly sweet and gentle expression, though the pallor of her cheeks betokened ill-health.

"I will help you to begin, Miss Mary, while you are here, and then you can go on by yourself," said Madame De La Motte, in her usual sprightly way.

"I thank you, madame," answered Miss Mary Pemberton, "but I am dependent on others. Jane has no fancy for languages, and her time is much occupied in household matters and others of still higher importance."

"Yes, indeed, Mary speaks truly," observed Miss Pemberton, a lady of a somewhat taller and not quite so slight a figure as her sister, and who, though her features had a pleasant expression, could not, even in her youth, have possessed the same amount of beauty. She always took her seat next to Mary, that she might give her that attention which her deprivation of sight required. "While we have such boundless stores of works on all important subjects in our own language, we waste our time by spending it in acquiring another."

"Very right, my good cousin, very right," exclaimed Sir Reginald; "stick to our good English books, for at the present day, what with their republicanism, their infidelity, and their abominable notions, we can expect nothing but what is bad from French writers."

"Pardonnez moi, Sir Reginald," exclaimed Madame De La Motte, breaking off the conversation in which she was engaged with Harry, and looking up briskly. "Surely la pauvre France has produced some pure and religious writers, and many works on science worthy of perusal."

"I beg ten thousand pardons, madame, I forgot that a French lady was present. I was thinking more of the murderous red republicans who have cut off the heads of their lawful sovereign and his lovely queen, Marie Antoinette. I remember her in her youth and beauty at the court of her brother, the Emperor Leopold, when I paid a visit to Germany some years ago. When I think how she was treated by those ruffians with every possible indignity, and perished on a scaffold, my heart swells with indignation, and I am apt to forget that there are noble and honest Frenchmen still remaining who feel as I do."

"Ah, truly Sir Reginald, we loyal French feel even more bitterly, for we have shame added to our grief and indignation, that they are our compatriots who are guilty of such unspeakable atrocities as are now deluging our belle France with blood," said Madame De La Motte, putting her handkerchief to her face to hide the tears which the mention of the fate of the hapless queen seldom failed to draw from the eyes of French loyalists in those days.

"You will pardon me, madame, for my inadvertent remark," said Sir Reginald, bowing as he spoke towards the French lady.

"Certainly, Sir Reginald, and I am grateful for your sympathy in the sufferings of those I adore."

Just at that instant the butler entered the room bearing a salver covered with letters, which most of the party were soon engaged in reading. An exclamation from Captain Fancourt made every one look up.

"There is indeed news," he exclaimed. "Sir Roger Curtis has arrived with despatches from Earl Howe announcing a magnificent victory gained by him with twenty-five ships over the French fleet of twenty-six, on the 1st June, west of Ushant; seven of the French captured, two sunk, when the French admiral, after an hour's close action, crowded sail, followed by most of his ships able to carry their canvas, and made his escape, leaving the rest either crippled or totally dismasted behind him. Most of our ships were either so widely separated or so much disabled, that several of the enemy left behind succeeded in making their escape under spritsails. One went down in action, when all on board perished; another sank just as she was taken possession of, and before her crew could be removed, though many happily were saved. There had been several partial actions between them."

Exclamations of delight and satisfaction burst from the lips of all the party on hearing this announcement.

"I only wish that I had been there," exclaimed Harry, and Captain Fancourt looked as if he wished the same.

"You might have been among those who lost their lives," observed Miss Pemberton; "we would rather have you safe on shore."

"We must take our chance with others," said Harry. "I only hope, Uncle Fancourt, that you will soon be able to get me afloat again, though I am not tired of home yet."

"I shall be able to fulfil your wishes, for the Admiralty have appointed me to the command of the *Triton*, 38-gun frigate, ordered to be fitted out with all despatch at Portsmouth. Before many weeks are over she will, I hope, be ready for sea. I shall have to take my leave of you, Sir Reginald, sooner than I expected. I must go down at once to look after her. Harry need not join till I send for him."

"I congratulate you, Fancourt," said Sir Reginald, "though I am sorry that your visit should be cut short." The great battle was the subject of conversation for the remainder of the day, every one eagerly looking forward to the arrival of the newspapers the next morning for fuller particulars.

Chapter Seven
The Casteltons and Gouls

In those days, when coaches only ran on the great high roads, and postal arrangements were imperfect, even important news was conveyed at what would now be considered a very slow rate.

Adam knew no one in London to whom he could write about the little girl he had saved from the wreck, and many days passed before he could get to Morbury, the nearest town to Hurlston. It was a place of some importance, boasting of its mayor and corporation, its town-hall and gaol, its large parish church, and its broad high street.

Adam first sought out the mayor, to whom he narrated his story. That important dignitary promised to do all in his power through his correspondents in London to discover the little girl's friends, but warned him that, as during war time the difficulties of communication with foreign countries were so great, he must not entertain much hope of success. "However, you can in the meantime relieve yourself of the care of the child by sending her to the workhouse, or if you choose to take care of her, her friends, when they are found, will undoubtedly repay you, though I warn you they are very likely, after all, not to be discovered," he added.

"Send the little maiden to the workhouse!" he exclaimed, as, quitting Mr Barber's mansion, he pressed his hat down on his head; "no, no, no; and as to being repaid by her friends, if it was not for her sake, I only hope they may never be found."

The lawyer, Mr Shallard, on whom Adam next called, had the character of being an honest man, and having for many years been Sir Reginald Castelton's adviser, he was universally looked up to and trusted by all classes, except by these litigants who were conscious of the badness of their causes.

He was a tall, thin man, of middle age, with a pleasant expression of countenance. He listened with attention to Adam's account of his rescuing the little girl, but gave him no greater expectation of discovering her friends than had the mayor.

"You will, I suspect, run a great risk of losing your reward," he observed; "but if you are unwilling to bear the expense of her maintenance, bring her here, and I will see what can be done for her. Of course, legally, you are entitled to send the foundling to the workhouse."

"You wouldn't advise me to do that, I'm thinking," said Adam.

"No, my friend, but it is my duty to tell you what you have the right to do," answered the lawyer.

"Well, sir, I'd blush to call myself a man if I did," replied the fisherman, and without boasting of his intentions, he added that he and his dame were quite prepared to bring up the little girl like a daughter of their own.

When Adam offered the usual fee, the lawyer motioned him to put it into his pocket.

"Friend Halliburt, you are doing your duty to the little foundling, and I will do mine. If her friends can be found, I daresay I shall be repaid, and at all events, when you come to Morbury again you must call and let me know how she thrives."

Adam, greatly relieved at feeling that, having done what he could towards finding the child's friends, there was great probability that she would be left with him and his wife, returned home.

"Any chance of hearing of our little maiden's friends?" asked the dame, on Adam's return.

"None that I can see, mother," he answered, taking his usual seat in his arm-chair. "As it seems clear that they are in foreign lands, those I have spoken to say, now that war has broken out again, it will be a hard matter to get news of them."

"Well, well, you have done your duty, Adam, and you can do no more," answered his wife, looking much relieved. "If it is God's will that the little girl should remain with us, we will do our best to take care of her, that we will."

"What do you think, though?" he continued, after he had given an account of his first visit; "Mr Mayor advises us to send her to the workhouse. It made my heart swell up a bit when he said so, I can tell ye."

"Sure it would, Adam," exclaimed the dame; "little dear, to think on't."

"Mr Shallard said something of the same sort too, but he showed that he has a kind heart, for he told me to bring the child to him if we didn't want to have charge of her, and when I offered his fee he wouldn't even look at it."

"Good, good!" exclaimed the dame; "I've no doubt he'd act kindly by her, but I wouldn't wish to give her up to him if I could help it. It's not every one who would have refused to take his fee, and it's more, at all events, than old Lawyer Goul would have done, who used to live when I was a girl where Mr Shallard does now. There never was a man like him for scraping money together by fair means or foul. And yet it all went somehow or other, and there was not enough left when he died to bury him, and his poor heart-broken, crazy wife was left without house or home, and went away wandering through the country no one knew where. Some said she had cast herself into the sea and was drowned; but others, I mind, declared they had seen her after that as wild and witless as ever. Hers was a hard fate whatever it might have been, for her husband hadn't a friend in the world, no more had she; and when she went mad there was no one to look after her."

Then Dame Halliburt told a tale, interrupted by many questions by the good Adam, of which this is the substance.

Lawyer Goul had a son, and though he and his wife agreed in nothing else, they did in loving and in spoiling that unhappy lad. He caused the ruin of his father, who denied him nothing he wanted. Old Goul wouldn't put his hand in his pocket for a sixpence to buy a loaf of bread for a neighbour's family who might be starving, but he would give hundreds or thousands to supply young Martin's extravagance. He wanted to make a gentleman of his son, and thought money would do it. His son thought so too, and took good care to spend his father's ill-gotten gains. As he grew up he became as audacious and bold a young ruffian as could well be met with. He had always a fancy for the sea, and used often to be away for weeks and months together over to France or Holland in company with smugglers and other lawless fellows, so it was said, and it was suspected that he was mixed up with them, and had spent not a little of his father's money in smuggling ventures which brought no profit. Old Martin Goul had wished to give his son a good education, and had sent him to the very same school to which the sons of Dame Halliburt's master, Mr Herbert Castleton, went. There were two of them, Mr Ranald and Mr Ralph. Mr Herbert was Sir Reginald Castleton's younger brother. He was a proud man, as all the Castletons were, and hot-tempered, and not what one may call wise. He was sometimes over-indulgent to his children, and sometimes very harsh if they offended him. For some cause or other Mr Ranald, the eldest, was not a favourite of his, though many liked him the best. He was generous and open-hearted, but then, to be sure, he was as hot-tempered and obstinate as his father. While he was at college it was said he fell in love with a young girl who had no money, and was in point of family not a proper match for a Castleton.

Some one informed his father, who threatened to disown him if he married her. He could not keep him out of Texford, for he was Sir Reginald's heir after himself. This fact enraged him still more against his son, as he thus had not the full power he would have liked to exercise over him. When Mr Herbert married, his wife brought him a good fortune, which was settled on their children, and that he could not touch either. They had, besides their two sons, a daughter, Miss Ellen Castleton, a pretty dark-eyed young lady. She was good-tempered and kind to all about her, but not as sensible and discreet as she should have been.

When Mr Ranald and Mr Ralph left school young Martin Goul, whose character was not so well known then as it was afterwards, came to the house to pay them a visit. As they had been playmates for some years, and he dressed well and rode a fine horse, they seemed to forget that he was old Martin Goul's son, and treated him like one of themselves. To my mind, continued the dame, nothing belonging to old Goul was fit to associate with Mr Castleton's sons. Once having got a footing in the house, he used to come pretty often, sometimes even when the young gentlemen were away from home, and it soon became known to every one except Mr and Mrs Castleton that Lawyer Goul's son was making love to Miss Ellen. She, poor dear, knew nothing of the world, and thought if he was fit to be a companion of her brothers, it was no harm to give her heart to him. She could see none of his faults, and fancied him a brave, fine young fellow, and he could, besides, be as soft as butter when he chose, and was as great a hypocrite as his father. He knew it would not do to be seen too often at the house, or Mr and Mrs Castleton would have been suspecting something, and so he persuaded Miss Ellen to come out and meet him in the park, and she fancied that no one knew of it. This went on for some time till Mr Ranald and Mr Ralph came home from college. One evening, as Mr Ranald was returning from a ride on horseback, and had taken a short cut across the park, he found his sister and Martin Goul walking together in the wood. Now one might have supposed that if the account of his own love affair was true he would have had some fellow-feeling for his sister and old schoolmate, and not thought she was doing anything very wrong after all, but that wasn't his idea in the least. Without more ado he laid his whip on Martin's shoulders, and ordered him off the grounds, much as he would a poacher. Martin, the strongest of the two by far, would have knocked him down if Miss Ellen had not interfered and begged Martin to go away, declaring that if fault there was it was entirely hers. Martin did go, swearing that he would have the satisfaction one gentleman had a right to demand from another. Mr Ranald laughed at him scornfully, and, taking Miss Ellen's arm, led her back to the house.

Mr Ranald was not on the terms, as I have said, which he should have been with his father or even with his mother, so he said nothing to them, but taking the matter into his own hands, told his sister to go to her room and remain there. She, as I said, was a gentle-spirited girl, and did as she was bid, only sitting down and crying and wringing her hands at the thoughts of what might come of what she had done. Poor dear young lady, she told me all about it afterwards, and I thought her heart would break; and I was not far wrong, as it turned out at last.

Now, though Mr Ranald and Mr Ralph were not on affectionate terms as brothers should be, and were seldom together, they were quite at one in this matter. Mr Ralph was by far the more clever, and had gained all sorts of honours at college we heard; so that Mr Ranald looked up to him when there was anything of importance to be done, and took his opinion when he wouldn't have listened to any one else.

The brothers were closeted a long time together talking the matter over, as they thought very seriously of it, and considered that the honour of the family was at stake. They then got their sister to come to them, and tried to make her promise never to see young Martin Goul again; but notwithstanding all they could say, gentle as she was in most things, she would not say that. They warned her that the consequences would be serious to all concerned.

Martin Goul was as good as his word. He got another young fellow who passed for a gentleman, something like himself, to carry a challenge to Mr Ranald. The young fellow did not like to come into the house, so he waylaid Mr Ranald near the entrance of the park, and delivered a letter he had brought from Martin Goul. Mr Ranald, as soon as he found from whom it came, tore it up, and throwing it in the messenger's face, so belaboured him with his whip, that he drove him out of the park faster than he had come into it.

Mr Ralph had, however, in the manner he was accustomed to manage things, taken steps to get Martin Goul out of the way. The last war between England and France had just begun; the pressgang were busy along the coast obtaining men for the navy. Mr Ralph happened to know the officer in command of a gang who had the night before come to Morbury. He told him, what was the truth, that young Martin was a seafaring man, and mixed up with a band of smugglers, and he hinted to the officer that he would be doing good service to the place, and to honest people generally, if he could get hold of the young fellow and send him away to sea. Martin was seized the same night, and before he could send any message home to say what had happened, he was carried to a man-of-war's boat lying in the little harbour of Morbury, ready to receive any prisoners who might be taken. He was put on board a cutter with several others who had been captured in the place, and not giving him time to send even a letter on shore, she sailed away for the Thames, and he was at once sent on board a man-of-war on the point of sailing for a foreign station. Miss Ellen, when she heard what had happened, was more downcast and sad than before, and those who knew the secret of her sorrow saw that she was dying of a broken heart.

Poor Mrs Castleton had been long in delicate health, and soon after this she caught a chill, and in a short time died. Miss Ellen was left more than ever alone. From the day she last saw her worthless lover she never went into society, and seldom, indeed, except at church, was seen outside the park-gates.

Mr Castleton himself had become somewhat of an invalid, which made his temper even worse than before. He showed it especially whenever Mr Ranald was at home, and I am afraid that Mr Ralph often made matters worse instead of trying to mend them.

At last Mr Ranald left home altogether, for as he had come into a part of his mother's property, he was independent of his father. Some time afterwards a letter was received from him saying that he had sailed for the Indies. Whether or not he had married the young lady spoken of at college was not known to a certainty.

As may be supposed, old Martin Goul and his poor witless wife were in a sad taking when they found that their son had been carried off by a pressgang. Old Goul vowed vengeance against those who had managed to have his son spirited away. His own days, however, were coming to a close. He found out the ship on board which young Martin had sailed, and he tried every means to send after him to get him back. That was no easy matter, however; indeed, the money which he had scraped together and cheated out of many a lone widow and friendless orphan had come to an end. No one knew how it had gone, except, perhaps, his son. He himself even, it was said, could not tell, though he spent his days and nights poring over books and papers, trying to find out, till he became almost as crazy as his wife. No one went to consult him on law business, except, perhaps, some smuggler or other knave who could get no decent lawyer to undertake his case, and then old Goul was sure to lose it, so that even the rogues at last would not trust him.

He and his wife had had for long only one servant in the house. A poor friendless creature was old Nan. One day the tax-gatherer called when Martin Goul, who was seated in his dusty room which had not been cleaned out for years, told him that Nan had the money to pay, and that he would find her in the kitchen. He went downstairs and there, sure enough, was poor Nan stretched out on the floor. She had died of starvation, there was no doubt about that, for there was not a crust of bread in the kitchen, nor a bit of coal to light a fire. How Martin Goul had managed to live it was hard to say, except that his wife had been seen stealing out at dusk, and it was supposed that she had managed to pick up food for herself and her husband.

Meantime it was known that young Martin had been aboard the *Resistance* frigate, which had gone away out to the East Indies. At last news came home that the *Resistance* had been blown up far away from any help in the Indian seas, and that every soul on board had perished or been killed by savages when they got on shore.

Mr Ralph tried to keep what had happened from the ears of his sister, but she was always making inquiries about the ships on foreign stations. At last one day she heard what it would have been better she had never known. We found her in a dead faint. She was brought to, but the colour had left her cheeks and lips, and she never again lifted up her head. Mr Ralph came to see her.

"It was all your doing," she said to him in a reproachful tone. "He might have been wild, he might have been what you say he was, but he promised me that he would reform and be all I could wish."

"Of whom do you speak, Ellen," asked Mr Ralph.

"Of him who now lies dead beneath the waters of the Indian Ocean, of Martin Goul," she said, and uttered a cry which went to our hearts.

"That scoundrel's name is unfit to come out of your lips, Ellen," he answered with an oath. "He met a better fate than he deserved, for he died with honest men. Now put him away from your thoughts altogether, and never defile your lips by speaking of him."

Poor Miss Ellen made no reply. Nothing would induce her to leave her room. She grew weaker and weaker, and soon was laid beside her mother in the family vault.

A few months afterwards Mr Castleton died, and the place was sold. Mr Ralph, who had become a barrister, went away to live in London and married, and has been there ever since.

The death of his son was known to many others before Lawyer Goul heard of it, for it was no one's business to tell him, and few would have been willing to do so. At last, one day in an old newspaper which contained an account of the loss of the *Resistance*, his eye fell on the announcement. He let the paper drop, sank back in his chair, and never spoke again. His crazy wife took it up, and she, seeing what had happened to her son, not even stopping to learn whether her husband was dead or not, or trying to assist him, rushed away no one knew where. "Some say," said Dame Halliburt, as she finished her long story, "that she has long since been dead, and others that she is 'Mad Sal,' as the boys call her; but she does not look to me like old Goul's wife; and I cannot fancy that one brought up as a sort of lady, as she was, could live the life that poor mad woman does, all alone in a wretched hovel by herself among the cliffs, without a neighbour or a soul to help her."

"Well, it's a sad story, wife; I wonder you never told it me before."

"To say the truth, Adam, it's not a matter I ever liked talking about, and I don't know scarcely what made me tell it you now. It's not that I care about Lawyer Goul and his crazy wife and their son; but even now I cannot bear to think of poor Miss Ellen. It was a sad thing that a sweet innocent creature like her should have been cut off in her young days."

Chapter Eight
Gaffin, the Miller

Adam had just recounted to his wife his interviews with the mayor and lawyer of Morbury, and had listened to her history of Mr Herbert Castleton's family, and the unhappy fate of his daughter, when a knock was heard at the door. The dame opened it, but drew back on seeing their visitor.

"Good-day, neighbour," said the person who entered, a strongly-built man with a bushy black beard and a sunburnt countenance, the sinister expression of which was ill-calculated to win confidence, and whose semi-nautical costume made it doubtful whether he was a landsman or sailor.

"I have come to have a friendly chat with you, if you will give me leave?"

Without waiting for a reply, still keeping his hat on, he threw himself into a chair by the fire, glancing round the room as he did so.

"What have you got to talk about, Mr Gaffin?" asked Adam, disdaining to give the welcome he could not heartily offer, and instead of sitting down, standing with his hands in his pockets opposite his guest, while the dame continued the work in which she had been engaged.

"I hear you boarded a wreck the other morning and rescued a child from it," observed the visitor.

"I did so," answered Adam, curtly.

"What has become of the child, then?" asked Mr Gaffin, looking round the room as if in search of her. The visitor was Miles Gaffin, the miller of Hurlston, as he was generally called.

"She has gone out for a walk," said the dame, coming up near her husband on hearing the subject of the conversation.

"You will find the maintenance of a child in addition to your own somewhat burdensome in these hard times," observed the miller.

"We can judge better than our neighbours whether the burden is more than we can bear," answered the dame; "so you see, Mr Gaffin, that need not make any one uneasy on our account."

"Very likely, my good woman, and all very well at present; but the day will come when she will require schooling and clothing, and I suppose you had not time to bring much property belonging to her on shore, Adam Halliburt?" said Gaffin, in an inquiring tone.

"No, Miles Gaffin, I had less time to bring anything away than those who visited the wreck before me," he answered, fixing his eyes on the visitor, who met his glance unmoved.

"What! did any one else get on board the wreck, do you think?"

"I am sure of it; and whoever they were, they were heartless villains to leave a little child to perish when they might have saved her."

"Perhaps if people did visit the wreck they were not aware that any human being remained on board," said Gaffin. "Did you see any of the crew? No one has heard of them, I understand."

"It's my belief that they attempted to escape in the boats, which were swamped on crossing the sands," answered Adam. "They deserved their fate, too, if they recollected the poor child and her nurse who were left behind. Though the little dear was saved by their base conduct, as she would have been lost had they taken her, not the less shame to them. However, no one can tell how it happened."

"Of course they attempted to escape in their boats, there is no other way to account for their disappearance," answered Gaffin; "few craft except such as ours on this coast could live in the sea that was then running, for it was as bad as could well be, as I hear. I myself was away to London on business," he added, carelessly.

Adam kept his eyes on his guest while he was speaking, but the countenance of the latter maintained the same bold, defiant look which it generally wore.

As Gaffin made the last remark, Jacob, with his little charge, entered the cottage.

Maiden May, on seeing a stranger, kept tight hold of Jacob's hand, and drew away from the fireplace, where he was seated.

"Is that the child we have been speaking of?" asked Gaffin, looking towards her. "She is indeed a little beauty. Well, my friends, I conclude you don't intend to bring her up as a fisherman's daughter—pardon me, I don't mean to say anything disrespectful—even supposing you fail to discover to whom she belongs?"

"As to that, Mr Gaffin, God placed her under our charge, and we intend to do our duty by her," answered Adam, firmly.

"Your duty would be to obtain for her every opportunity of retaining the position in which she was born," said Gaffin. "That's no common person's child."

"Maybe she is not; but, as I said before, we will do our best. More than that we cannot do," answered Adam.

"Now, my friend, I have a proposal to make," said Gaffin, speaking in as frank a tone as he could assume. "She will be a heavy burden to you some time hence, if she is not so at present; my wife and I, as you know, have no daughter, although, like you, we have three sons. We are more independent of the world than you are, as my wife had money; you will understand, though, I do not eat the bread of idleness; and as she would very much like to have a little girl to bring up to be her companion when our boys are away, we are willing to take charge of that child and adopt her, should her friends not be discovered. To show you that I am in earnest, here are five guineas as payment to you for going off and bringing her on shore in the gallant way I understand you did. It's a trifling reward, I own, but if I have the power I will increase it should you accept my offer."

Adam stood with his hands in his pockets as he had been doing while his visitor was speaking.

"Keep your money, Mr Gaffin, for when it may be required," he answered, quietly. "My lads and I only did our duty, and what any one with the heart of a man would have tried to do. That little maiden has been placed in my charge, and until her rightful friends appear, my wife and I will take care of her without looking for payment or reward. You have our answer, I speak for myself and dame; there is no use wasting more time in talking about the matter."

"Well, well, neighbour, I cannot take your reply as conclusive," said Gaffin, trying to conceal his annoyance; "just think it over, and you will be doing a great pleasure to my wife and lay us under an obligation if you agree to my proposal."

Adam had given his reply, and was determined to say nothing more. He was anxious, too, to get rid of his guest.

Gaffin at length, finding that he could gain nothing by staying, rose to leave the cottage. The dame took up May and retired with her to the farther end of the room, while Adam stood as before with his hand firmly thrust down into his pocket, as if determined not to shake that of his departing guest, while Jacob opened the door as wide as he could. Gaffin, unabashed, nodded to the fisherman and his dame, and with a swagger in his walk to conceal the irritation he felt, left the cottage. Jacob watched him till he had got to some distance.

"He has gone," he exclaimed. "He shall not have our Maiden May if I can prevent him."

"No fear of that, Jacob. He, with his cursing and swearing, and his wild, lawless ways, and his poor heart-broken, down-spirited wife, bring up a little maid in the way she should go! She would be better off with us as long as we had a crust to give her; and take her from us he shall not, whatever reasons he may have for wishing it. So don't you fear, Jacob, that I will listen to him even if he comes with 50 in his hand, or 500 for that matter. As I said before, if we don't find fairer friends for her than he and his wife are like to prove, Maiden May shall be our child, bless her."

Chapter Nine
A Sail in the Nancy

Captain Fancourt took his departure from Portsmouth to commission the *Triton*, promising to send for Harry as soon as the frigate was sufficiently advanced to give a midshipman anything to do on board.

"I will ride by a single anchor, so as to be ready to slip at a moment's notice," answered Harry.

Harry recollected his engagement to take a cruise in Adam Halliburt's boat.

"Come, Algernon," he said to his elder brother, a tall, slight youth, three or four years his senior, with remarkably refined manners, "you would enjoy a trip to sea for a few hours in the *Nancy*. It would give you something to talk about when you go to college, and you have never been on salt water in your life."

"Thank you," said Algernon. "I do not wish to gain my first experience of sea life in a fishing boat."

"I want to see how these fishermen live, and I should have been glad of your company," answered Harry; "but perhaps you would find it rather too rough a life for your taste, so I will go alone, and to-morrow when I return I will ride with you wherever you like."

Harry, after luncheon, set off on his pony to Hurlston, while Algernon accompanied his mother and the two Miss Pembertons in the carriage to the same village, where they wished to look at a cottage which Sir Reginald had told them was to be let, and which they had proposed, should it suit them, to take. They were much pleased with its appearance. It stood on the higher ground above the village, surrounded by shrubberies, in an opening through which a view of the sea was obtained. On one side was a pretty flower-garden, and as Miss Pemberton led her sister through the rooms and about the grounds describing the place, they agreed that had it been built for them they could not have been more thoroughly satisfied. Mr Groocock therefore received directions to secure Downside Cottage, and they determined to occupy it as soon as it could be got ready for them.

Sir Reginald, on hearing of the decision of the Miss Pembertons, invited them to remain in the meantime at Texford, where he hoped, even after they were settled, they would become constant visitors.

"I am getting an old man now, and as I cannot hunt or attend to my magisterial duties, I am grateful to friends who will come and see me, and you have only to send over a note and my carriage will be at your disposal."

Miss Pemberton assured Sir Reginald that one of their chief inducements in taking the cottage was to be near a kinsman whom they so greatly esteemed.

Mrs Castleton the next morning had become anxious at the non-appearance of Harry. She had not heard of his intention of remaining out during the night till Algernon told her. He agreed to ride down to Hurlston to ascertain if the boat had returned, and as the Miss Pembertons wished to pay another visit to the cottage, the carriage was ordered and Mrs Castleton accompanied them.

The weather, as it frequently does in our variable English climate, had suddenly changed by the morning, and although it had been calm during the night, by the time the ladies reached Hurlston a strong east wind sent the surf rolling up on the beach in a way which to the ladies, unaccustomed to the sea-side, appeared very terrible. Algernon, who was on horseback, met them.

"The boat Harry went out in has not come back," he observed; "but as the fishing-boats generally return about this hour, she will probably soon be in."

Mrs Castleton, her anxiety increased by the appearance of the weather, begged her companions to wait.

"Is that the boat?" she asked, pointing to a sail approaching the shore.

"I think not—that seems a large vessel," answered Algernon, and he rode towards the pier, where a number of people were collected, while others were coming from various directions. There seemed some excitement among them. They were watching the ship observed by Mrs Castleton, which, in the distance, had to her appeared so small, though in reality a large brig.

"She brought up an hour ago in the roads, but only just now made sail again," was the answer to Algernon's question. "As she is standing for the mouth of the river she is probably leaky, and her crew are afraid of not keeping her afloat in the heavy sea now running."

Algernon watched the brig, which, under a press of canvas, came tearing along towards the mouth of the harbour; and as she drew nearer the jets of water issuing from her scuppers showed that his informant was correct in his opinion. She laboured heavily, and it seemed doubtful whether she could be kept afloat long enough to run up the harbour.

The larger fishing-boats were away, but two or three smaller ones were got ready to go out to her assistance, though with the sea then rolling in there would be considerable danger in doing so.

At length the brig drew near enough to allow the people on board to be easily distinguished. The master stood conning the vessel—the crew were at their stations. So narrow was the entrance that the greatest care and skill were required to hit it. Algernon heard great doubts expressed among the spectators as to the stranger being able to get in.

In a few seconds more, a sea bearing her on, she seemed about to rush into the harbour, when a crash was heard, the water washed over her deck, both the masts fell, and her hull, swinging round, blocked up the entrance. The men on shore rushed to their boats to render assistance to the unfortunate crew, but as the foaming seas washed them off the deck, the current which ran out of the river swept them away, and though so close to land, in sight of their fellow-creatures, not one of the hapless men was rescued.

Algernon could not repress a cry of horror.

"Oh, what will become of Harry?" exclaimed Mrs Castleton, when she saw what had occurred.

"I trust he is safe with an experienced fisherman like old Halliburt," answered Algernon. "I wish, mother, you would return home. I will bring you word as soon as he comes back."

Mrs Castleton, however, could not be persuaded to leave the shore.

At length several tiny sails were seen in the distance, and were pronounced by the people on the pier to be the returning fishing-boats. Some were seen standing away to the north to land apparently in that direction, while three steered for Hurlston.

In consequence of the mouth of the river being blocked up, Algernon found that the boats would have to run on the beach, all of them being built of a form to do this, although those belonging to Hurlston could usually take shelter in their harbour.

As the boats drew near, signals were made to warn them of what had occurred. The people in the leading boat, either not understanding the signal or fancying that there would be still room to get up the harbour, kept on, and only when close to it perceived what had occurred. On this the boat hauled her wind and attempted to stand off, so as to take the beach in the proper fashion, but a sea caught her and drove her bodily on the sands, rolling her over and sending the people struggling in the surf.

The men on shore rushed forward to help their friends.

Mrs Castleton shrieked out with terror, supposing that Harry was in the boat.

Algernon, who was not destitute of courage, rode his horse into the surf and succeeded in dragging out a man who was on the point of being carried off. Again he went in and saved another in the same way, looking anxiously round for Harry. He was nowhere to be seen, and to his relief he found that the *Nancy* was one of the sternmost boats. Two poor fellows in the boat were carried away, notwithstanding all the efforts made to secure them. Much of the boat's gear was lost, and she herself was greatly damaged.

"Which is the *Nancy*?" inquired Algernon, round whom several people were collected, eager to thank him for the courage he had just displayed.

She was pointed out to him. On she came under a close-reefed sail.

Adam, probably suspecting that something was wrong by having seen the boat haul up to get off the shore, was on the look-out for signals.

The second boat came on shore, narrowly escaping the fate of the first. Still the *Nancy* was to come. She was seen labouring on amid the foaming seas. Now she sank into the trough of a huge wave, which rose up astern and robed in with foam-covered crest, curling over as if about to overwhelm her. Another blast filled her sails, and just escaping the huge billow which came roaring astern, the next moment, surrounded by a mass of hissing waters, she was carried high up on the beach. Most of her active crew instantly leaped out, and joined by their friends on shore, began hauling her up the beach, when another sea rolling in nearly carried them off their legs. Harry, however, who had remained in the stern of the boat with Halliburt, leaped on shore at the moment the waters receded and escaped with a slight wetting.

As they made their way up the beach, a fair-haired, blue-eyed little girl ran out from among the crowd and threw herself, regardless of Adam's dripping garments, into his arms.

"Maidy May so glad you safe," she exclaimed, as the fisherman bestowed a kiss on her brow. "We afraid the cruel sea take you away."

"There was no great danger of that, my little maiden," answered Adam, putting her down. She then ran towards Jacob and bestowed the same affectionate greeting on him. Holding his hands, she tried to draw him away from the surf, as if afraid that, disappointed of its prey, it might still carry him off.

Harry remarked the reception the fisherman and his son met with from the interesting-looking child, and he never forgot those bright blue eyes and the animated expression of that lovely countenance.

Summoned by his brother, he now hastened to assure his mother of his safety.

"My dear boy, we have been very anxious about you," exclaimed Mrs Castleton, as he came up; "and I do hope that you will not go off again in one of those horrible little fishing-boats; you run dangers enough when on board ship in your professional duty without exposing yourself to unnecessary risk."

"I assure you I have been in no danger whatever, except, perhaps, when the boat was running in for the beach," answered Harry, laughing. "When we went off we did not expect to have to do that, and I am very sorry that you should have been anxious about me. However, I promise to remain quietly on shore till I am summoned to join my ship, and as I am somewhat damp, I will get my pony, which I left at the Castleton Arms in the village, and ride home with Algernon." The ladies accordingly, re-entering the carriage, drove towards Texford, and Harry and his brother followed soon afterwards.

Chapter Ten
May's New Friends

Harry refrained from making another trip in the *Nancy*, though he told Adam Halliburt that he had hoped to do so. He seldom, however, caught sight of the blue sea in his rides without wishing to be upon it.

One day he and Algernon, on a ride over the downs, passed near the old mill. Miles Gaffin was standing at the door, while behind him, tugging at a sack, was his man, whose countenance appeared to Harry, as he caught sight of it for a moment, one of the most surly and ill-favoured he had ever set eyes on. "No wonder the farmers prefer sending their corn to a distance to having it ground by such a couple," he thought. The miller took off his hat as he saw the lads. Algernon scarcely noticed the salute.

"I am sorry, young gentlemen, not to have had the pleasure of giving you a trip in my lugger," said the miller, in a frank, off-hand tone. "If, however, you and your brother are disposed to come, we will run down the coast to Harwich, or to any other place you would like to visit, and I will guarantee not to get you into such a mess as old Halliburt did, I understand, the other day."

"Thank you," said Harry, "my brother has no fancy for the salt water, and as I shall be off again to sea shortly, I cannot avail myself of your offer."

"Did any one advise you not to go on board my craft?" asked Gaffin, suddenly.

Harry hesitated.

"Adam Halliburt offered to take me a trip, and as Mr Groocock thought I should prefer the *Nancy* to any other craft, I arranged to go with him," he said at length.

"Ah, I guessed how it was. My neighbours are apt to say unpleasant things about me. Mr Groocock told you I was not a man to be trusted, didn't he?"

"My brother has said that he preferred the fisherman's boat," said Algernon, coming to Harry's assistance, "and I consider that you have no right to ask further why he declined your offer. Good-day to you, sir; come along, Harry," and Algernon rode on.

"Proud young cock, he crows as loudly as his father was wont to do," muttered the miller, casting an angry glance at the young gentlemen; "I shall have my revenge some day."

"I do not like the look of that fellow," observed Algernon, when they had got out of earshot of the mill. "I am glad you did not go on board his vessel."

"He seems rather free and easy in his manners, and his tone wasn't quite respectful, but I suppose his pride was hurt because I chose another man's boat instead of his," answered Harry.

"You did not observe the scowl on his countenance when he spoke," said Algernon.

Algernon evidently possessed the valuable gift of discernment of character which some can alone gain by long experience.

The family party were separating one morning after breakfast, when, the front door standing open on that warm summer day, Harry, as he passed through the hall, caught sight of Dame Halliburt approaching with her basket of fish, accompanied by the blue-eyed little girl he had seen when landing from the *Nancy*.

"Come here, Julia," he exclaimed. "Does not that sturdy fishwife with her little daughter trotting along by her side present a pretty picture? I wish an artist were here to take them as we see them now."

"Yes, Gainsborough would do them justice. He delights in rustic figures, though the child should have bare feet, and I see she has shoes and stockings on," answered Julia.

"The little girl would, at all events, make a sweet picture in her red cloak and hat," observed Miss Pemberton, who with her sister as they crossed the hall had heard Harry's exclamation, and had come to the door; and she described her to Miss Mary.

"I should like to speak to her. I can always best judge of people when I hear their voices," observed Miss Mary.

Harry proposed asking Dame Halliburt and the little girl to come up to the porch, but they had by this time passed on towards the back entrance.

"The dame is probably in a hurry to sell her fish and to go on her way," observed Miss Pemberton. "We will talk to her another time."

"Come, Harry, madame is ready to give you your French lesson," said Julia, and they went into the house.

Before luncheon Madame De La Motte proposed taking a walk.

"And we will talk French as we proceed. You shall learn as much as you will from your books," she said, inviting Harry to accompany her and her pupil. Harry gallantly expressed his pleasure, and they set out to take a ramble through the fields in the direction of Hurlston.

They had got to some distance, and were about to turn back, when they saw in the field beyond them the same little girl in the red cloak who had come with Dame Halliburt to the house.

Two paths branched off at the spot she had just reached. She stood uncertain apparently which to take, when, at that instant, a bull feeding in the field, irritated by the sight of her red cloak, began to paw the ground and lower his head as if about to make a rush at her. The child becoming alarmed uttered a cry, and ran in the direction of the gate near which they were standing. Harry leaped over the gate and hurried to her rescue. Seeing him coming she darted towards him.

"Throw off your cloak," he shouted.

She was too much frightened to follow his advice. The bull was close upon them when Harry reached her, and in an instant tearing off her cloak he threw it at the bull, and lifting her in his arms darted on one side, while the savage animal rushed over the spot where the moment before they had stood, and catching the cloak on its horns threw it over its head, and then stopping in its course looked round in search of the object at which it was aiming. Seeing Harry running off with the little girl, it again rushed at them. He had just time to lift her over the gate, and to spring after her, when the creature came full tilt against it.

The courage of Madame De La Motte and Julia had given way as they saw the bull coming, and believing that the gate would be broken down, they had run for safety to a high bank with a hedge above it a little on one side of the field.

"You are quite safe now, little girl," said Harry, trying to reassure the child. "See, though the bull knocked his horns against the gate, he could not throw it down, and is going off discomforted. Come, Julia, and help her," he shouted; "she has been dreadfully frightened, and not without cause."

Julia and her governess, feeling a little ashamed of themselves, descended from their safe position.

"I hope you are not hurt; but how came you to be in the field by yourself?" asked Julia, addressing the little girl.

"Mother told me to take the path across the fields while she went round by the road to call at some houses," she answered.

"To whom do you belong; and what is your name?" asked madame, looking admiringly at the child's delicate and pretty features.

"I belong to Adam Halliburt, and he calls me his Maiden May," answered the child.

"Maiden May! that is a very pretty name," observed Madame. "But you are very young to go so far alone."

"We must not let you go alone," said Harry; "I will take care of you till you meet your mother, but I will first get your cloak. I see the bull has left it on the grass, and I hope has not injured it."

"Take care, Harry," exclaimed Julia, "the bull might run at you if he sees you in the field."

"I do not mind running away from him, and I suspect I can run the fastest," answered Harry, laughing, as he leapt over the gate.

Julia and Madame De La Motte watched him anxiously, not more so, however, than did Maiden May.

"Oh, I hope he will not be hurt, I would much rather lose my cloak," she said, following him with her eyes.

The bull having gone to a distance, Harry was able to reach the little girl's cloak, and by keeping it in front of him the animal did not catch sight of it, and he soon returned with his prize.

"If you will come to the hall we will send one of the servants with you," said Julia.

"No, no," said Harry, "you go back, as you must be in at luncheon, and I will take care of the little girl."

"Thank you, thank you," repeated Maiden May, "but I am not afraid."

Harry, however, with true chivalry, though the object of his attention was but a little fisher-girl, insisted on escorting her, and at length induced his sister and her governess to return, promising to hurry back as soon as he had placed the child under Dame Halliburt's care.

They soon found the style which led into the path May should have followed. She took Harry's hand without hesitation, and as she ran along by his side, prattled with a freedom which perfect confidence could alone have given her. She talked of the time he had been off in the *Nancy*, and how anxious she had felt lest any harm should befall the boat.

"And you are very fond of the sea?" she said, looking up in his face.

"Yes; I am a sailor, and it is my duty to go to sea, and I love it for itself," said Harry; "I hope as you live close to it that you love it too."

"Oh no, no, no," answered May; "I do not love it, for it's so cruel, it drowns so many people. I can't love what is cruel."

"It could not be cruel to you, I am sure," said Harry. "Does your father ever take you in his boat?"

"Yes, I have been in the boat, I know, but it was a long, long time ago, and I have been on the sea far, far away."

She stopped as if she had too indistinct a recollection of the events that had occurred to describe them.

Harry was puzzled to understand to what she alluded, and naturally fancied that she spoke of some trip her father had taken her on board his boat, not doubting, of course, that she was the fisherman's daughter.

In a short time they caught sight of Dame Halliburt, when Harry, delivering Maiden May to her care, without waiting to receive her thanks hurried homewards as he had promised.

Chapter Eleven
Harry off to Sea

A letter from Captain Fancourt at length arrived, summoning Harry to join the *Triton*. He bade an affectionate farewell to his kind old uncle. His brother had remarked the failing health of Sir Reginald.

"I shall be very sorry when he goes, but probably when you next come to see us, you will find us here," observed Algernon, "unless our uncle should turn up and claim the title and property, and as he has not been heard of for a long time, I do not think that likely."

"I have no wish to be here except as Sir Reginald's guest," answered Harry, with more feeling than his brother had displayed. "I hope that our old uncle will live for many a year to come."

In those times of fierce and active warfare it was far more trying to the loving ones who remained at home when the moment of departure arrived, than to the brave and gallant soldiers and sailors who were going away to fight their country's battles. They could not help reflecting how many were likely to fall in the contest, and that, though victories should be gained, their aching eyes might some day see in the list of killed or wounded the names of those from whom they now parted so full of life and spirits.

"Do not be cast down, mother," exclaimed Harry, as Mrs Castleton pressed her gallant boy to her heart. "I shall come back safe and sound, depend on that; remember the verse of the song in Dibdin's new play:—

"'There's a sweet little cherub who sits up aloft
To take care of the life of poor Jack.'"

"Let us rather trust to Him by whom the hairs of our head are all numbered—without whose knowledge not a sparrow falls to the ground—instead of talking in that light way," murmured Miss Mary, who was sitting knitting near the window. "Let us pray to Him, my dear Harry, that you may be brought back in safety."

"I will, Cousin Mary," said Harry, "and I am sure mother will too. I spoke thoughtlessly. It is the way of speaking one is accustomed to hear."

"Too much, I am afraid," said Miss Mary. "We are all too apt to speak lightly on such matters." The carriage came to the door.

"You will continue to study French diligently, Master Harry," said Madame De La Motte, as she wished him good-bye. "Though my countrymen are your enemies, you will love the language for my sake, will you not?"

Harry promised that he would do as she advised; indeed, he was well aware that the knowledge he already possessed was likely to prove very useful to him on many occasions.

His sister Julia was the last of the family he embraced. "The next time I come home I must bring my old shipmate, Headland; I am glad to find that he has joined the *Triton*. He is one of the noblest and most gallant fellows alive," he said, as he wished her good-bye.

"Though we shall be happy to see your friend, I only want you to bring yourself back, Harry, safe and sound, with your proper complement of arms and legs," she answered, smiling through her tears.

"I would sacrifice one or the other to have my name in the *Gazette*, and to gain my promotion, so I can make no promises," he replied, springing into the carriage after Algernon, and waving his hat as it drove off.

A number of the surrounding tenantry had assembled near the park-gates to bid farewell to the young sailor who was going off to fight King George's enemies on the high seas. Harry stopped the post-boy that he might put his hand out of the carriage to wish Mr Groocock, who was among them, good-bye, and to thank them for their good wishes, promising at all events to do his best to prevent the French from setting foot on the shores of England, and disturbing them in their quiet homes. Their hearty cheers as he drove off restored his spirits.

"It pays one for going away when the people show such kind feeling, and I hope when I come back to be received with as hearty a welcome," he remarked to Algernon, who accompanied him as far as the next town, through which the coach passed.

There seemed a blank at Texford after Harry had gone.

The next day the Miss Pembertons moved into Downside Cottage. To some of the more worldly guests their departure was a relief, as they freely expressed opinions which were looked upon as savouring too strongly of what was called Methodism to be uttered in polite society.

Although she could not see the expression which her remarks called forth on the countenances of the company, Miss Mary was often aware by the tone of their voices that what she said was unpalatable. This, however, though it grieved her gentle spirit, did not anger her, and she spoke in so mild and loving a way that even those who were least disposed to adopt her principles could not help acknowledging that she was sincere and faithful in her belief.

The Miss Pembertons had not been long settled in their new abode before they began to visit their poorer neighbours. The blind lady and her sister were soon known in all parts of the village, and might be seen every day walking arm-in-arm, now stopping at one cottage to admire the flowers in the little plot of ground before it, or now at another to inquire after the health of one of the inmates. The sick and the afflicted received their first attentions; Miss Mary could quote large portions of the Scriptures, and explain them with a clearness and simplicity suited to the comprehension of the most ignorant of those she addressed.

The sisters had no carriage, for their income was limited; but those in distress found them liberal in their gifts, and the inhabitants of Hurlston averred that they might have kept not only a pony-chaise, but a carriage and pair, with the sums they annually distributed in the place. Their charities were, however, discerning and judicious, and although those who had brought themselves into poverty received assistance when there was a prospect of their amending, if they were known to be continuing in an evil course they might in vain look for help, and were pretty sure to meet with a somewhat strong rebuke from Miss Jane, as Miss Pemberton was generally called. In their inquiries about the people they were helped by a good dame, one of the oldest inhabitants, Granny Wilson, who lived in a nice tidy cottage, with an orphan grandchild. Though their charity was generally distributed by Miss Jane's hand, Miss Mary was the greatest favourite. The sweet expression of her sightless countenance, and her gentle voice, won all hearts. Though Miss Mary never ventured outside their gate without her sister, she was wont to wander about the grounds by herself. The flower-garden was under her especial care. She was said to know, indeed, every flower which grew in it, and to point not only to any rose-tree which was named, but to each particular rose growing on it, with as much certainty as if she could see it before her.

A year had passed since the two spinster ladies had taken possession of Downside.

One morning, while Miss Pemberton had gone over to Texford, her sister was engaged, scissors in hand, in clipping the dead flower-stalks in front of the cottage.

"Good morning, Miss Mary," said a voice. "Am I to leave any fish for you to-day?"

"Pray do, Mistress Halliburt; Susan knows what we require. And you have brought your little girl with you; I heard her light footstep as she tripped by your side. I should like to talk to her while you go in. Come here, my dear," she said, as the dame went round to the back entrance; "I have heard of you, though I forget your name; what is it?"

"My name is Maiden May, please, Miss Mary; and I have heard of you and how kind you are to the poor; and I love you very much," answered the little girl, looking up naïvely at the blind lady's face.

"Your name is a pretty one," said Miss Mary, a smile lighting up her countenance as she spoke, produced by the child's remark. "Why are you called Maiden May?"

"Father called me so when he found me a long time ago," answered May.

"When he found you, my child, what do you mean?" asked Miss Mary, with surprise.

"When I came in the big ship with my ayah, and was wrecked among the fierce waves," answered May.

"I do not clearly understand you. Is not Dame Halliburt your mother?"

"Oh, yes, and I love her and father and Jacob and the rest so much," said May. "I have no other mother."

"Is your mother's name Halliburt?"

"Yes."

"I cannot understand what you mean, my dear; I must ask Mistress Halliburt to explain to me," said Miss Mary.

"Ah, yes, do; she will tell you. But I remember that father found me on board the big ship, and brought me home in the boat, and mother took care of me, and Jacob used to walk with me every day till I was old enough to go out with mother."

"But who is Jacob?" asked Miss Mary.

"He is brother Jacob, and he is so kind, and he tries to teach me to read; but he does not know much about it himself, and I can now read as fast as he can."

"Does your mother not teach you?" asked Miss Mary.

"Not much, she has no time; but father on Sunday tells me stories from the Bible. He can read very well, though he sometimes stops to spell the words, just as I do. There is only the Bible and one book we have got at home."

"Would you like, my little girl, to come up here and learn to read? My sister will teach you, and I think I can help, though I cannot see what is printed in a book."

"Oh, yes, so much, if mother will let me," answered May. "I am sure I should remember all you tell me, and then I might teach Jacob to read better than he does now. Ah, here comes my mother."

"You can go round the garden and look at the flowers while I talk to her."

"Thank you, Miss Mary; I so love flowers. We have none near our cottage, for they would not grow on the sand," and May ran off, stopping like a gay butterfly, now before one flower, now before another, to admire its beauty and enjoy its fragrance.

"If you can spare a few moments, Mistress Halliburt, I should like to learn from you more than I can understand from the account your little girl has been giving me of herself," said Miss Mary, as the dame approached her. "She has been talking about a wreck and being brought on shore by your husband. Is she not really your child?"

"We love her as much as if she was, but she has been telling you the truth, Miss Mary," answered the dame. "We have been unable to gain any tidings of her friends, though we have done all we could to inquire for them, and though we are loth for her sake to bring her up as a fisherman's child, we would not part with her unless to those who could do better for her welfare."

The dame then described how May had been brought from the wreck, and how, from the dress the little girl had on, and the locket round her neck, and more especially from her appearance, there could be no doubt that she was the child of gentlefolks.

"From the tone of her voice and the account my sister gave of her, I feel sure that you are right, Mistress Halliburt," said Miss May. "If you can spare her to-day, I should like to keep her with me, and you can call or send for her when you have finished your rounds. I shall esteem it a favour if you will bring her up to-morrow morning, and let my sister see her, and if we can in the meantime think of anything to benefit the child, we will let you know."

The dame expressed her gratitude for the interest Miss Mary took in Maiden May, but she could not help feeling somewhat jealous lest the blind lady should rob her and Adam of some of the affection which the child had bestowed on them. Still she was too right-minded to allow the feeling to interfere with May's interest. She readily agreed to let her remain, and also to bring her up the next morning, that Miss Pemberton might see her and form her own opinion about the child.

Calling May, she told her that she was to stay with Miss Mary, "and if Miss Mary wants you to lead her about, you must be very careful where you go, and mind to tell her everything you see; but don't talk too much if it seems to weary her," added the dame in a whisper, as, kissing May, she wished her good-bye.

Chapter Twelve
May's Schooling

Maiden May, on finding herself alone with Miss Mary, at once went up, with a confidence she might not have felt with a person not deprived of sight as the kind lady was, and took her hand.

"Mother told me to ask whether you would like me to lead you about the garden. May I do so?"

"I should like you to lead me about very much, though I think I know my way pretty well. But you must stop whenever you come to a flower you admire, and I will tell you its name, and you must describe to me anything else you see—birds or butterflies or other insects. As my eyes are blind, you must use yours instead of them for my benefit."

"Oh, yes, Miss Mary; I will try and do what you say," exclaimed May, delighted to find that she could be of use to the blind lady. A new existence seemed suddenly opened out to her. The gentle and refined tone of voice of Miss Mary sounded pleasing to her ear, although she did not understand all that she said, her language was so different to that she had been accustomed to hear used in the fisherman's cottage.

Then she was delighted with the new and beautiful flowers, and her wonder was excited when she found that they all had names, and that Miss Mary, though blind, could tell their colours and describe them so perfectly. Miss Mary also told her the names of the birds whose notes they heard as they walked about the grounds, and May in return described with a minuteness which surprised her blind friend a number of objects both animate and inanimate which she thought would interest her, while she asked a variety of questions which, though exhibiting her ignorance, showed a large amount of intelligence and desire to obtain information. The child was evidently natural and thoroughly unaffected, without either timidity or rustic bashfulness. She had, indeed, been treated with uniform kindness, and with even a certain amount of respect, which the fisherman and his family could not help feeling for her. Though the dame had not failed in endeavouring to correct any faults she might have exhibited, yet she had done so with that gentleness and firmness which made the little girl sensible that her kind protectress did so for her benefit alone. The dame found the task a very easy one, for Maiden May rarely required a rebuke.

Still, though her voice was gentle, the child had caught the idiom and pronunciation of the fisherman's family; but even in that respect there was a natural refinement in the tone of her voice; and as Adam was a God-fearing man, and had brought up his sons to fear God also, no coarse language or objectionable expressions were ever heard in his cottage. Indeed, more true refinement is oftener found among the lower classes where religious principles exist than is generally supposed.

Miss Mary, after walking till she was tired, invited her young guest into the house. Luncheon was placed on the table; Susan attended her mistress and placed delicacies before May such as she had never before tasted. In spite, however, of Susan's pressing invitations to take more, she ate but sparingly, to the surprise of the kind woman, who thought that the little fisher-girl would have done more justice to the good things offered her.

"She has quite a young lady's appetite," she observed afterwards to Miss Mary.

"That is not surprising, for a young lady she is, depend on that. It will be a grievous pity if her relatives are not to be found," was the answer.

After luncheon, Miss Mary got out a book and placed it before May, and begged her to read from it. By the way May endeavoured to spell out the words Miss Mary discovered that she had made but very little progress in her education.

"Please, I think I could say my lessons better in the Bible if I could find the verses father teaches me," said May, with perfect honesty.

Miss Mary rang to obtain Susan's assistance, and May asked her to find the Sermon on the Mount. May read out nearly the whole of the first chapter, with a peculiar tone and pronunciation, which she had learned from honest Adam, following the words with her finger.

"I rather think, my little maid, that you know the verses by heart," observed Miss Mary.

"Oh, yes," answered May, naïvely, "I could not read them without; but I will try and learn more before I next come."

Miss Mary was, however, inclined to advise her not to make the attempt, as she would learn to pronounce the words with the accent which sounded so harsh to her ears.

"But, however pronounced, they are God's words," she thought to herself. "I should not prevent her learning even a verse from His book. She will soon gain the right pronunciation from educated people."

The time passed as pleasantly with Miss Mary as with May herself.

At length Susan appeared to say that a fisher-lad, one of Dame Halliburt's sons, had come to fetch the little girl.

"Who is it?" asked Miss Mary.

"Oh, it is sure to be brother Jacob, the rest have gone out with father," answered May.

Jacob was desired to walk in. He stood in the hall, hat in hand, watching the door of the drawing-room, through which Susan had intimated May would appear. As soon as she saw him she ran forward and took both of his hands, pleasure beaming on her countenance. He stooped down and kissed her.

"Are you ready to come with me, Maidy May?" he asked; "you don't want to stop away from us with the ladies here, do you?"

"Oh, no, no, Jacob!" answered May, holding him tightly by the hand; "I don't want to leave father or mother or you; I will go back with you as soon as you like."

Miss Mary overheard the latter part of the conversation as she followed May out of the drawing-room.

"I hear, my good lad, that you have been very kind to the little girl; and pray understand that we do not wish to rob you of her; and if we ask her to come up here, it will only be to help you in teaching her to read, as I understand you have been accustomed to do."

"Please, ma'am, I am a very poor scholar," answered Jacob; "but I do my best, and I shall be main glad if you will help me."

Hand-in-hand May and Jacob set off to return home.

That evening Jacob might have been seen with the Bible before him, and May seated by his side, while he tried to help her to read. As the lamp fell on their countenances, the contrast between the fair, delicate-looking child and the big, strongly-built fisher-boy, with his well-bronzed, broad and honest face, would not have failed to be remarked by a stranger entering the room.

Jacob spelt out the words one by one, pronouncing them with his broad accent as he gained their meaning, while May followed him, imitating exactly the intonation of his voice. Sometimes she not only caught him up, but got ahead, reading on several words by herself, greatly to her delight.

"Ah, May! I see how it is," said Jacob, with a sigh. "You will be quicker with your books than I ever shall be, and if the kind ladies at Downside wish to teach you, it's not for me to say them nay; but I would that I had more learning for your sake, and I shall be jealous of them, that I shall, when I find that you can read off out of any book you have got as smoothly as you do the verses you have learned by rote. Oh, you will be laughing at me then."

"No, no, Jacob! I will never laugh at you. You taught me all I know about reading, and I shall never forget that, even if I learn to read ever so well."

Next morning, when Adam came home from fishing, the dame told him the interest Miss Mary Pemberton seemed to take in Maiden May, and of her expectation that the Miss Pembertons would wish to have the little girl up to instruct her better than they could at home. Adam agreed that it would not be right to prevent their charge enjoying the benefit which such instruction would undoubtedly be to her.

"But they must not rob us of her altogether, dame. I could not bear to part with the little maiden, and what is more I won't, unless her own kindred come to claim her, and then it would go sore against the grain to give her up. But right is right, and we could not stand out against that."

"If the Miss Pembertons wish to take the little girl into their house and make a little lady of her it would not be right, I fear, Adam, to say 'No' to them."

"She is a little lady already," answered Adam, sturdily. "They could not make her more so than she is already."

"But I am afraid the way we live, and speak too, Adam, is not like that of gentlefolks; and though our Maiden May is a little lady, and better than many little ladies I have known in all her ways, she will become in time too much like one of us to please those to whom she belongs, I am afraid," observed the dame, who had from her experience as a domestic servant in Mr Castleton's family, a clearer perception of the difference between the habits of her own class and those of the upper orders of society than her husband. Still Adam was not to be convinced.

"We are bringing her up as a Christian child should be brought up, to be good and obedient," he observed, in a determined tone, "and that's more than many among the gentry are. You know, Betsy, you wouldn't like her to be like that Miss Castleton you told me off."

"No more I should," answered the dame; "But though the Pembertons are of her kindred, they are truly Christian ladies, and Maiden May could only learn good from them."

As is often the case in a matrimonial discussion, the wife had the best of the argument, but they were still uncertain whether the Miss Pembertons would even make the offer which the dame had suggested as possible. She, at all events, had promised to take Maiden May up to them, and Adam could not prohibit her doing so.

Chapter Thirteen
May an apt Scholar

On Miss Pemberton's return to Downside, while seated at their tea-table, Miss Mary gave her a description of her young visitor of the morning, and told her of the proposal she was anxious to make about her.

"I should just like to see the little girl," said Miss Pemberton. "If she is really as the dame supposes, of gentle birth, it would be undoubtedly right to try and give her some of the advantages of which she has been deprived. At the same time we should be cautious—perhaps the dame may have been mistaken, and it will be unnecessary, if not imprudent, to try and raise her above the position in which she was born, unless she possesses qualities calculated to make her happier and better in a higher station."

"Well, Jane, I could only form an opinion from her sweet voice and from what she said. Adam Halliburt and his wife are devotedly fond of her, and do you not think that we may help them by judicious training."

"Well, Mary, I see that you are determined to think highly of the child, and unless we find that you are mistaken, I shall be very glad to see her as often as her worthy protectors will allow her to come," said Miss Pemberton.

"I trust that it will be found that I am right in my opinion of the sweet little girl," said Miss Mary, nodding her head and smiling. "I can always judge best of people by their voices, and I detected in her's that true tone which can only proceed from a true heart."

"Well, well, we shall see, and I hope that my opinion will agree with your's, Mary," observed Miss Pemberton.

Next morning Mistress Halliburt arrived with Maiden May. The little girl was scrupulously clean and neatly dressed, though her garments were befitting a fisherman's daughter of plain and somewhat coarse materials, except that she wore the unusual addition of shoes and stockings.

"I have brought our little maiden to you, ladies, as you desired, and if you will please to tell me how long you wish to keep her, I will send my Jacob up to fetch her away at the proper time," said the dame as she entered the hall into which the Miss Pemberton's had come out to meet their young guest.

Miss Pemberton scanned her narrowly with her keen grey eyes before replying.

"Good morning, my dear," said Miss Mary, "come and shake hands."

May ran forward and placed her hand trustfully in that of the blind lady. "May I lead you about the garden as I did yesterday, Miss Mary," she asked, "and tell you of the birds, and butterflies, and flowers I see? I shall like it so much." Miss Mary smiled and nodded her consent to the proposal. "Thank you, thank you," exclaimed Maiden May. "You need not send for the child till the evening, Mrs Halliburt," said Miss Jane, who had been watching May. "We shall not grow tired of her I think, and she, I hope, will be happy here."

The dame went away in the hopes that Maiden May had made a favourable impression on the ladies. "The elder is a little stiff and won't win the child's heart like the blind lady; but she is kind and may be thinks more than her sister," she said to herself. "She won't spoil the child or set her up too much—that's a good thing, or maybe she might not like coming back to us and putting up with our ways, and that would vex Adam sorely."

The little girl spent a very happy day with the kind ladies. She led Miss Mary as she had proposed about the garden, and was as entertaining to the blind lady as on the previous day, while she gained a considerable amount of information tending to expand her young mind.

Miss Jane commenced giving her the course of instruction she had contemplated, and Maiden May proved herself a willing and apt pupil. When invited to come to dinner, Miss Jane was pleased to see her stand up with her hands before her, ready to repeat the grace which she herself uttered.

"Father always prays before and after meals though he does not say the same words; but I think God does not care about the words so much as what comes out of the heart. Oh, He is very very kind, I always thank Him for what He gives me. If He had not taken care of me, I should have been washed away in the sea with my poor ayah and all the people on board the ship."

"And you love God my little maiden," asked Miss Pemberton. "Oh, yes, how could I not when He has given us His dear Son, and with Him all things else which we can want to make us happy."

"The child has been well taught by the good fish wife," observed Miss Mary aside to her sister. "She has set us an example which we must be careful to follow."

"Yes, indeed," said Miss Jane, "we can better give her lady-like notions and habits than the good old woman could have done, but she has acted faithfully in imparting that knowledge which is above all price." It is true May did several things at table not in accordance with the customs of polite society, but Miss Jane refrained from saying anything for fear of intimidating the little girl.

"You will observe, May, how I behave at table, and you will try, I am sure, to do as I do," she said quietly.

May nodded, and after this so narrowly watched all her movements that Miss Jane began almost to wish that she had not made the remark. If Miss Jane helped herself to salt so did Maiden May, when she drank the little girl lifted her small tumbler to her lips, her knife and fork was held exactly in the same way she saw Miss Jane doing, or held daintily in her tiny hand while Susan took her plate for some more chicken.

"Our young friend will prove an apt scholar, I suspect," observed Miss Jane, to her sister. "I will tell you why I think so by and bye."

After dinner Miss Jane gave May her first writing lesson. She had never before held a pen in her hand, and her attempts to make pot-hooks and hangers, and even straight lines were not very successful.

"I think I could make some letters like those in a book, if you will let me, Miss Jane," she said, looking up after surveying her performance.

"I do not want you to make such as those at present; but I will write some which you can copy."

To her surprise the little girl imitated the letters, as she told Miss Mary, with a neatness and precision which was truly surprising.

"I like to do them much better than those ugly things," said Maiden May, and she was spared the task of copying the pot-hooks and hangers, and was allowed to learn writing more according to her own fancy.

She was so happy that she thought Jacob had arrived sooner than it was necessary to escort her home. She went, however, very willingly, tripping along by his side as she held his big hand, and describing with glee all she had seen and learned.

"You will soon be thinking little of our home I am afeared, May," said Jacob with a sigh.

May protested honestly she liked home best. Jacob felt that in a few years she would think differently. He scarcely dared to allow himself to contemplate the wide gap which would be placed between them.

Day after day May went up to Downside Cottage.

"We ought not to give you the trouble to come for your little girl, Mistress Halliburt," observed Miss Jane; "Susan can escort her if you do not think her old enough to go by herself."

"If she were my own daughter, or any other poor person's child, I would have let her go and come back by herself long ago, but there is one living not far off, who, for reasons of his own which I cannot fathom, would, I am afraid, like to spirit her off," said the dame mysteriously. "I have never lost sight of her except when she has been with you or my Jacob, besides that time when near Texford Mr Harry saved her from the wild bull, and I was so frightened then that I made up my mind never to let her go by herself again. If she had come to harm I should have almost died of it, and Adam would never have forgiven me."

"That was an accident not likely to occur again, and surely no one would injure the child," observed Miss Jane.

"It's no fancy of mine if I think there is," said the dame. "He came once and tried to get her from us by fair means, but we would not give her up for all his promises. But when he finds out as he is sure to do before long, that she is with you, and coming backwards and forwards, he will be on the watch for her. He is not often here now since the war began, and Adam thinks he is about no good. He does come back sometimes for a day or two, and Satan will be helping him if he thinks of mischief."

"No doubt about that, Mrs Halliburt," observed Miss Jane. "But there is one more powerful than Satan who will protect the innocent."

"True, marm, but He will protect them through the means of their friends, and it's our business, if we suspect evil to guard against it," said the dame.

"You are right. But who is the person of whom you speak who is likely to injure our little girl?"

"We must not speak ill of our neighbours, Miss Pemberton," answered the dame. "I know that; but if our neighbours do ill we may warn others against them. The man I mean is Miles Gaffin, the miller, as he calls himself. Now, I cannot say exactly what ill he does, except that I never heard of his doing any good or saying even a kind word, though he says many a bad one: but Adam, my husband, has a pretty strong notion of the sort of business he carries on, and that it's not by his mill he makes his money. There are few about here who don't stand in awe of him, and yet it would be hard for anyone to say exactly why. Only one thing is certain, that if he had a mind to do a thing he would do it, and set the law at defiance. To say the truth, I cannot tell you more against him than I have, but I am just afraid of him, and cannot help feeling as how he would work mischief to our Maiden May if he had the chance. But, Miss Pemberton, you will not repeat what I have said?"

"Certainly not, dame, certainly not," said Miss Mary, "but after all I cannot say that you have brought any serious accusation against the miller, nor can I understand why you should fancy he is likely to injure our Maiden May."

"That's just it, Miss Mary, no one about here can say exactly what he does, or why they don't like him. Still, no one does like him, and I feel a sort of tremble whenever I set my eyes on him, just as I should, begging your pardon, ladies, if I was to meet Satan himself, though I know well he cannot hurt me, for I trust in one who is able to keep evil at a distance."

"Though I still remain in the dark as to why we should be cautious of this man Gaffin, we will always keep a careful watch over Maiden May, and when you or your son cannot come for her we will send her home with some prudent person who will take care that neither he nor anyone else runs off with her," answered Miss Jane.

Chapter Fourteen
At Portsmouth

Portsmouth was a busy place in those stirring times of warfare, and as the coach, on the top of which Harry was seated, rattled and rumbled down the High Street, parties of sailors came rolling along, laughing and talking, several in their heedlessness almost running against the horses in spite of the shouts of the coachman, who had more than once to pull up to avoid driving over them. Now a pressgang passed along, dragging a number of unwilling captives to serve on board the fleet, some resigned to their fate, others with frowning brows resenting the treatment they had received, and some glancing round, hoping against hope for an opportunity to escape. Officers in cocked hats and glittering epaulets were walking quickly along, while post-chaises came driving in bringing Admiralty officials or Captains to join their ships. Groups were collected in front of the different inns, and Jews were looking out for customers, certain of obtaining a ready sale for their trumpery wares. Ballad singers, especially those who could troll forth one of Dibdin's new songs, were collecting a good harvest from eager listeners, and the apple-stall women were driving a thriving trade; as were the shopkeepers of high and low degree, judging by their smiling countenances, while the sound of revelry which came forth from the numerous inns showed that the landlords were rejoicing in the abundance of custom: in short, there was little chance of grass growing in Portsmouth streets in those days.

As Harry leaped down from his seat he found his hand grasped by another midshipman, a handsome looking youth, somewhat taller and older than himself, who had made his way through the crowd gathered round the coach.

"I have been on the look-out for you, Harry, with a message from the Captain," said the latter, as they cordially shook hands. "You are to come on board at once, for we are all ataunto and the frigate goes out of harbour this evening."

I have to order a few things at my tailor's, and shall be quite ready, answered Harry.

"Well, Headland," he added, taking his friend's arm after he had given his portmanteau into charge of a porter, "I was so glad to find that you had joined the Triton, and as the captain knows and esteems you, he is sure to give you a lift whenever he can. We shall see some more service together, and I hope that you, at all events, will mount a swab on your shoulder before the ship is paid off."

"Your uncle will get you promoted first, I should think," answered Headland, "though I hope some day my turn will come."

"You are my senior, and have done not a few things to merit it, and Captain Fancourt is the last man to favour a relation by passing over another with greater merits."

"Come, come, you have learned to flatter while you were studying French on shore. We shall both do our duty, I have no doubt about that."

Harry having called at his tailor's, he and Headland went down to the point now so crowded with men-of-war's boats, and wherries coming in and shoving off marines and sailors, watermen, and boat-women, and gaily dressed females and persons of all description, that they had no little difficulty in gaining one of the wherries. Reaching her, however, at last, they off to the frigate lying mid-channel, with her sails loose, ready to get under way.

Harry, having reported himself, had some old friends to greet, and a number of new acquaintances to make, and he soon found himself at home in a midshipman's berth.

As soon as the captain came on board, the frigate, slipping her moorings, glided out of harbour, and took up a berth near Lord Howe's fleet, which had a short time before arrived after the glorious victory of the 1st June.

Captain Fancourt having sent for Harry, gave him a kind welcome, and said:—

"You shall go on shore with me to-morrow to attend the king and queen, who are coming on board the fleet. It is the best opportunity you may have of seeing their majesties till you go to court on your promotion, which I hope, however, you will gain before many years are over."

Accordingly, the next morning the captain went on shore in his boat, taking Harry with him, and pulled to the dockyard.

Never had Portsmouth harbour presented a gayer scene. Every vessel afloat was dressed with as many flags as could be mustered, from the proud line of battle ship to the humble lighter, while banners waved from numberless flagstaff's on shore. The shores were everywhere lined with people on the watch for the flotilla of boats which were collecting before the Commissioner's house in the dockyard. The whole garrison was under arms, and the Lords of the Admiralty, whose flag was hoisted on board the Queen, and most of the Ministers of State were present.

Shouts rent the air as at length the king issued from the Commissioner's house, carrying in his own hand a magnificent diamond-hilted sword, accompanied by the queen, and followed by several of the princes and princesses. He thus proceeded down to his barge waiting at the steps, when, amid the shouts of the multitude, and the firing of guns, he embarked with his family and attendants. The barge, then urged by the strong arms of her crew, proceeded down the harbour, followed by a vast fleet of boats, and steered for the Queen Charlotte, the most conspicuous of the ships at Spithead.

As soon as the barge arrived alongside, the royal standard was hoisted, that of the venerable admiral being shifted to a frigate, and a royal salute thundered forth from all the ships, while hearty cheers rose from the throats of the gallant crews as they stood on the outstretched yards.

On the deck of the Queen Charlotte were collected the gallant admirals and captains, by whose courage and seamanship the first of that long series of victories which contributed so greatly to England's naval glory had been won.

The king would allow no one to take the sword from him, but as soon as he reached the deck, eagerly advanced towards Lord Howe. He presented it to him as a mark of his satisfaction and entire approbation of his conduct. Rich gold chains were then presented by the king to Sir Alexander Hood, to Admiral Gardener, and also to Lord Howe's first captain, Sir Roger Curtis.

"I am sorry that their wounds prevent Admiral Bower and Admiral Paisley from attending," said the king. "I must have the satisfaction of presenting them with gold chains; and as soon as medals can be cast to commemorate the victory, I will send them that they may be attached to the chains."

It was an interesting sight when, on that occasion, the flower of the English navy, with the gallant men who had fought that glorious action, were presented by the venerable admiral, for Lord Howe was then seventy years of age, to the good king on the quarter-deck of the flag ship. His Majesty exhibited much genuine feeling as the admirals captains and lieutenants in succession came up to him. He had a kind word for everyone, and one of sympathy for those who had so far recovered from their wounds as to be able to be presented.

"Who would not be ready to shed the last drop of his blood when we have our dear country to fight for, and so first-rate a king to reign over us," exclaimed Harry, enthusiastically to his friend Headland, for they both had accompanied their captain on board, and witnessed the spectacle from a distant part of the ship.

The levee being concluded, the king dined with the admiral on board, and then returned in his barge to the harbour, accompanied as before by a squadron of boats.

His Majesty was so eager to see the prizes captured by his fleet, that, before going on shore, he insisted on pulling up the harbour to have a look at them. There, at their moorings, lay the six huge line of battle ships which had lately belonged to the republican French, now the prize of English valour. The Northumberland, Achille, La Just, Impetueux, and America, the two latter the finest seventy-fours that had ever been seen in the British harbour, the Sans-Pareille, almost equalling in size the Queen Charlotte, and noted for her swift sailing. The Venguer would have been among them had she not sunk just after she struck her colours.

In the evening the town was brilliantly illuminated, and the next day the king attended the launch of a line of battle ship, the Prince of Wales. Directly afterwards, the indefatigable monarch, with the queen and princess, rowed out to Spithead, embarked on board the Aquilon frigate, royal salutes firing from all the ships while the crews manned yards and cheered, and the bands played their most lively music.

The Aquilon getting under way stood towards the Needles, when the king returned to Portsmouth to spend the Sunday.

On the following Monday he sailed in the Niger frigate for Southampton, whence the royal family proceeded in carriages for Windsor.

Such is a description of one of the many visits the king delighted to pay to the fleets of England, so that both the officers and men of the navy were well acquainted with his person, and very many could boast of having had the honour of conversing with him.

The Triton, however, was soon to be far away from such scenes, and to be engaged in the stern reality of warfare. Her destination was the Mediterranean, and her captain and crew being eager to distinguish themselves, the grass was not allowed to grow on her keel. Still, though a bright look-out was kept, and leagues of water had been ploughed by her, a couple of privateers, a few merchantmen, and Gunda costas, only had been captured, she having hitherto encountered no worthy antagonist.

Unhappily fever broke out on board, and going into Gibraltar she was compelled to leave thirty men at the hospital. Even after she sailed again, a considerable number remained on the sick list; indeed, she had almost an equal number with those left behind unable to do duty.

Though his crew were thus reduced in strength, Captain Fancourt continued his cruise in search of the enemy.

The Triton, approaching the neighbourhood of Carthagena, a number of large ships were seen hull down between her and the land. They were known to be the Spanish fleet. Their movements were watched, and they were observed standing back to port. The Triton kept them in sight, and then standing away, continued cruising on the ground they had before occupied. In vain, however, Captain Fancourt watched for their return, that he might carry information of their whereabouts to the admiral.

Day after day went by and not a sail was seen.

"This is vexatious work," exclaimed Harry, as he and Headland were walking the quarter-deck during the first watch, when the frigate lay becalmed about ten or a dozen miles off the coast.

"It's more than vexatious to me who have no friends to help me, and who, unless I get the opportunity of fighting my way up the ratlines, have but little hope of promotion," answered Headland. "You who have a father in Parliament are sure of yours as soon as you have served your time."

"That may be the case, but I would rather gain my promotion in hard service, than as a matter of favour. I am sure that you will make opportunities for yourself, and I hope to find them too, though they may not come as willingly as we may desire," said Harry. "But how is it, Headland, that you speak of having no friends? You know me well enough, to be sure, that I could not wish to pry into your affairs from idle curiosity; but the truth is, that being known to be your friend, I have several times been asked about you, and I have been compelled to confess that I know nothing of your history. That has made people fancy that there is something you would desire to conceal, though, as I know you, my dear fellow, to be the soul of honour, I am very sure there is nothing, as far as you are personally concerned, which you would desire to be kept secret."

"You do me no more than justice, Harry," answered Headland, in a tone which denoted honest pride—a very different feeling to vanity. "There is nothing in my history which I wish to conceal. On the contrary, I would rather have it as widely known as possible, though the fear of being considered egotistical has prevented me talking about myself. For this reason alone I have hitherto, even to you, never spoken about my early days, and now you put the question to me, I can scarcely otherwise account for my silence on the subject."

"You have spoken at times of a kind-hearted seaman who took care of you as a child, and of having served as a ship's boy before you were placed on the quarter-deck, and of other circumstances which have made me suspect that your early history was not a little romantic. From strangers being present, or from other causes, I have, however, always been prevented from questioning you more particularly on the subject, and even now, as I honour you for yourself, I would not ask you to tell me anything, but that I believe it would be for your advantage, and certainly, as I said before, not to satisfy my own curiosity."

"I am sure of that, my dear Harry," answered Headland, "and I will try to give you as much of my early history as I possess myself. To do so I must exert my memory, and help it out with the information I have obtained from my early protector and devoted friend, Jack Headland, whose name I bear, though I know from him that it is not my proper one. I have no reason, however, to be ashamed of the name, and therefore gladly retain it, hoping some day to make it known with honour. I confess, however, did I possess any means of being recognised, my earnest wish would have been to discover my parents and family, but as you will learn, from what I am going to tell you, all possible clue that would enable me to do so has been lost, and I have therefore made up my mind to be content with my position, and to gain a name for myself."

Chapter Fifteen
A Yarn at Sea

"If it gives you no painful recollections, my dear Headland, I shall much like to hear your history," said Harry. "On this calm night the thread of your narrative is not likely to be broken."

"I will try to go back, then, as far as my memory will help me," said Headland.

I have a dim recollection of living in a large Eastern style of house, with a number of black servants dressed in white, and a black woman who spoke in a language which has now become strange, though I think I then understood it. She attended especially on me. There was a tall gentleman of a slight figure, and a very fair lady, who was, I am sure, my mother. I have a faint recollection of her blue eyes and sweet smile as she took me in her arms, or looked down upon me as I played at her feet. Still, it is only now and then like the vision in a dream that her countenance rises to my memory. After that there comes a blank, and I found myself on board a ship—brought there by my black nurse, accompanied by the tall gentleman. I remember him clearly in the cabin, talking to a lady who then took charge of me, my nurse, I conclude, returning on shore, for she disappears from my recollection. While the gentleman was on deck, as I was afterwards told by Jack Headland, he suddenly, looking at the mate, asked him if he was not somebody he had known in England. The mate seemed for a moment taken aback, but, recovering himself, replied quite quietly that the gentleman was mistaken; that he had never heard of such a person, and that his name was Michael Golding, which, as Jack said, as far as he knew to the contrary, was the case, for that was the name he went by on board, though he was generally spoken of as the mate. The gentleman at last seemed satisfied, and returned on shore.

The ship sailed, and I remember seeing the blue water bubbling and hissing alongside as she clove her way through it, and playing with a ball on deck, which rolled out through one of the ports. The lady was very kind, and used to sing to me, and tell me stories, and, I fancied, tried to teach me my letters, though I was somewhat young to learn them. She was, however, very different to my mother, much older I suspect, and I did not love her half so much.

It came on to blow after a time, the sea got up and the ship tumbled about, and the poor lady was unable to watch over me.

There were other passengers, but they were all ill, and the stewardess was too busy to attend to me, but the mate came one day and told the lady that he would watch over me, or get some one else to do so when he was engaged.

From the first I did not like him, for he was a dark, black bearded man, with an unpleasant expression of countenance, so I cried out whenever he came near me. The captain must, I think, therefore, have given me in charge to Jack Headland, a young apprentice, whose looks I liked much better than the mate's. At all events, I was frequently with Jack, and no one could have taken better care of me.

There were not many English seamen, most of the crew being dark-skinned fellows—Malays, I suppose.

The vessel was, I know, not an Indiaman, but a country trader bound to Calcutta or Bombay.

I told Jack—so I learned from him—that I did not like the mate. He advised me not to say that to any one else, and promised that he would be my friend.

Most thoroughly he fulfilled his promise. Strange as it may seem, the mate intentionally left me near an open port several times, in the hopes that I might by chance slip through, so Jack thought, though he could not guess at his motive. Still it was clear that the mate had a bitter spite against me.

We had been some time at sea when we were caught in a fearful hurricane. The ship was dismasted, and I remember hearing a dreadful crash, when all was confusion on board. The sea broke over the ship, and a number of people were washed away. Even then Jack did not forget me. He found me in the cabin, and seizing me in his arms carried me to the fore part of the ship, which still hung to the rocks, while the after part, directly we had left it, broke up, and the poor lady who had had charge of me with many others was lost. The mate, who had made his way forward with half-a-dozen men, advised Jack to let me go, as it was impossible I should survive, and that he would probably lose his own life in attempting to save mine.

"No, no," answered Jack. "I promised to take care of the youngster, and I will as long as I have life in me."

The noble fellow held me the faster with one arm, while he clung to the wreck with the other. Scarcely had the mate spoken than he was washed away; but Jack saw him gain a piece of the wreck to which he was clinging, when he disappeared in the gloom at night.

When morning broke, the shore was seen. The hurricane was over, and the sea was becoming calmer. Jack securing me to the stump of the bowsprit with three or four of our surviving shipmates, contrived to form a raft. When this was launched he came for me, and fed me with some biscuit which he had in his pocket, I conclude. We then embarked, and partly by paddling with pieces of plank, and partly by sailing, we reached the shore.

We had not long landed when a number of natives came, and made the whole party prisoners. While they were consulting what to do with us, some others were seen along the shore dragging the mate in their midst. Three Malays had been saved on the raft, who, poor fellows, were quickly knocked on the head. The lives of the white men were spared. Jack kept me tightly in his arms, and entreated the natives not to take me from him. The mate, however, seemed to be able to make them understand him, and Jack said that he was certain from the way he looked at me, that he was endeavouring to persuade the natives to separate us. Though we had fallen among a tribe of murderous pirates, such as frequent the coasts of many of the Indian Islands, they had still some of the kinder feelings of human nature lingering in their breasts. Notwithstanding what the mate might have said Jack was allowed to keep possession of me, and our captors making signs to us to accompany them, we proceeded to their village, situated on the shores of a creek, on the bank of which several piratical proas lay moored.

By this time I was suffering dreadfully from thirst. Jack seeing this entreated the natives to give me some water. The houses were raised on platforms, with steps leading to them some height from the ground.

One of the natives, a headman, calling out a pleasant-looking young woman, brought down a calabash of water, which she gave me to drink. She smiled as she watched me. As soon as I had satisfied my thirst, I put it to Jack's mouth, and he swallowed the remainder. The young woman seemed to have taken a fancy to me, and saying something to the head man, who was her husband, the latter made signs to Jack that he was to give me to her. On this she seemed highly pleased, and Jack, thinking I should be safe in her keeping, made no resistance.

As soon as she got me, she carried me up into the house. Jack was going to follow, when some of the natives seized him and dragged him away. My new nurse brought me some dry native clothing, and while doing so discovered round my neck a gold chain to which an ornament was attached; but she did not attempt to take it off, and I have ever since carefully preserved it in the hopes that it might assist to identify me. She then gave me food, and placed me on a mat, where I soon fell asleep.

Day after day passed by, and though I frequently asked for Jack, he did not appear. The young woman who had no children of her own, treated me with great kindness, and dressed me up like a native. I do not remember having had my own clothes restored.

I remember once, if not twice, seeing the mate while I was playing in front of the house; but my protectress, fancying that he wanted to take me from her, ran out and carried me inside.

I was beginning to learn the language of the people with whom I was thrown, and could make my wants known, so that I must have been some time with them. I had not forgotten Jack, however, and continued hoping that he would come back for me; and whenever I went out I was on the watch for him. Once I fancied I saw him in the distance, but as I was dressed as a native child, he did not recognise me.

Many months went by. I afterwards found that the white men had been compelled to labour as slaves, though the mate had managed to gain the confidence of one of the chiefs, and had risen in his favour. The proas frequently went out of harbour, and were absent often for a considerable time. When they came back they brought all sorts of things, which were placed in their store houses, and were certainly not obtained by peaceable commerce.

AT THAT MOMENT A MAN LEAPED UP THE STEPS.

One day the young woman who had charge of me seemed very unhappy. I was now able to understand all she said, so I asked her the cause of her grief, and she told me that the chief whose slave the mate had become, wanted to persuade her husband to give me up to him, and that she could not bear the thoughts of parting from me. I entreated her to keep me, and promised that if I was taken away I would run back to her. I then asked her if she knew what had become of my friend Jack. She said he was not far off, but that his master would not let him come to see me. I begged her, at all events, not to let me be given up to the mate. She at last told me one day that I need have no fear of the mate, as he had disappeared, and was supposed to have made his way out to sea in a canoe to a vessel which had appeared off the coast.

The pirates lived tolerably easy lives on shore, apparently believing that though they must have made enemies in all directions, their village was so securely hidden, they were not likely to be molested.

Thus time went on, when one night I was awoke by hearing a fearful uproar, rapid reports of firearms, shouts and shrieks of men fighting desperately. Presently flames burst forth from different parts of the village. They were approaching the house where I was. The one next to it was on fire. My kind protectress did not forget me. At first, not knowing what to do, she had remained watching the progress of events, hoping probably that the enemy would be driven back. When, however, the fire surrounded her house, she saw that it was time to fly. Seizing me in her arms she was about to do so, when the crackling and hissing flames burst forth around us. At that moment a man leaped up the steps. Though so long a time had passed since we had parted, I at once recognised my friend Jack. Snatching me from the woman's arms, he sprang down to the ground, telling her to follow him. Bullets were whizzing through the air in all directions. He made his way as fast as his legs could carry him out of the range of fire, and then directed his course towards the river, where he sat down on the ground beneath some bushes, and I believe I fell asleep.

It was just daylight when I awoke, and Jack creeping with me down to the water's edge, we saw several boats full of men. Jack shouted to them, and one of them put in and took us on board. They were, he afterwards told me, the boats of two Dutch men-of-war, which had been sent up the river to destroy the nest of pirates. This they had done effectually, and were now on their way back to their ships. Jack was the only one of the shipwrecked crew who had escaped; what had become of the others he could not tell, but concluded that they had been murdered.

It was a long time, however, before I could speak to him or understand what he said, for I had been so long without hearing a word of English that I had almost forgotten it, while he knew but very little of the native language in which I had in the meantime learned to express my wants.

We were kindly received on board one of the Dutch frigates. Jack tried to tell the captain the little he knew about me, but as the Dutchman spoke no English, and Jack was ignorant of Dutch, he did not, I suspect, give him a very lucid account. Jack having been but a short time at the port from which we sailed, as he had joined the ship from a vessel which had arrived only the day before, had entirely forgotten its name, and being no navigator he had not the slightest notion from what direction we had come. He was not much happier in recollecting the name of the vessel, except that there were two of them both ending, as he said, in "jee."

Before long a Dutch seaman who spoke English was found on board, and through his interpretation Jack was able to give a rather more clear account of me than at first. The captain was at all events satisfied that I was the child of English parents of a good position in life, and taking compassion on my destitute condition, he desired Jack to leave me in the cabin, giving him permission, however, to come aft and attend to me. Jack would rather have kept me forward with himself, but believing that this arrangement was for my good, he submitted to it. I was soon rigged out like a young Dutchman by the ship's tailor, and Jack used to come into the cabin to look after me in the morning, and to attend to me at my meals, while he watched during the best part of the day as I ran about the deck.

The frigates were bound for Batavia. As soon as we arrived there the captain took me on shore, and he so interested a wealthy Dutch merchant and his wife in my favour that they offered to receive me into their house and adopt me should my parents not be discovered. I at once became a great favourite of the lady's, who had no children of her own, and for my sake they sent for Jack and asked if he would wish to remain on shore and enter their service. As he was very unwilling to part with me he accepted their offer, though, as he afterwards said, kind as they were, he did not like the thoughts of my being turned into a Dutchman. He was my constant companion when I was not with Mynheer Vanderveldt or his excellent Frau, and he did his best to teach me English. They, however, did not neglect either my education or my manners, but took great pains to bring me up as a young gentleman.

Three or four years more passed by, and I had become a biggish boy, and should, in spite of Jack's efforts, have been soon turned into a Dutchman, when my kind friends determined to return to Europe. I suspect that all this time, from their wish to keep me, they had taken no great pains to discover to whom I belonged; indeed, the only clue that Jack could give them was so slight that I feel that they really had a sufficient excuse for their negligence. My faithful friend Jack, still unwilling to part from me, accompanied my friends in the *Prinz Mauritz*, on board which we embarked. He and I were doomed, however, to be unfortunate in our voyages, though more fortunate than our companions.

We had been some weeks at sea when, during a dark and blowing night, a terrific crash was heard. I sprang out of my berth and dressed, and within a minute my faithful Jack was by my side.

"The ship is on shore and will go to pieces before daylight, but I will not desert you, my boy," he said. "As I came aft I made out a rock close aboard of us, and as the masts are sure to go over we may manage to gain it if we take the proper time. I wish I could help Mynheer and the Frau, but I must look after you first."

Scarcely had he said this when another and another crashing sound reached our ears.

"There go the masts!" he exclaimed. "Come along!" and seizing me by the arm he dragged me on deck.

As he had expected, the head of the mainmast rested on the rock, which could now be seen as a bright flash of lightning darted from the sky. We were the first on the spar, and making our way along it gained the rock. A few others seeing us followed. I entreated Jack to look after my friends, forgetting the danger to which he would be exposed in doing so. The people coming along the mast prevented him from going, and just then a heavy sea rolling in sent a sheet of spray over us, completely hiding the ship. When we looked again she was gone. The sea had lifted her, and falling off the rock she had sunk, dragging her fallen masts with those still clinging to them.

Six people, besides Jack and me, had alone escaped, all the other human beings on board, including my kind friends, had perished. We remained till daylight on the rock, and at daybreak managed to get to the island, partly by wading and partly by swimming. It was itself only a huge rock, about three miles long, rising in some places to the height of a couple of hundred feet above the sea.

We employed the whole day in collecting provisions and part of the cargo washed ashore. We went in search of water and found a spring, so that we had no fear of dying from hunger or thirst for some time to come. One of our first cares was to erect a flagstaff as a signal to any passing ship. I felt deeply grieved for the loss of my friends; but I did not think so much about the fact that I was reduced from affluence to perfect poverty. Jack told me that he knew Mynheer Vanderveldt intended to leave me all his property.

"He made his will before he left Batavia, and I am pretty sure he had it with him, so that if any of his chests are washed on shore, as I should know them, there may still be a chance of finding it. Though I am no scholar myself, you might make it out, and some day get what the good man intended to be yours."

So impressed was Jack with this idea that he employed a considerable portion of his time in hunting along the shore for my friend's chests.

Though we did not get them, we found several articles which were of more use to us just then, so that the time was not fruitlessly spent.

We lived in a hut built partly of stones and partly of the wreck, and thus suffered no great hardship. After we had spent three months on the rock we saw a sail in the distance. She approached—our signal was discovered. A boat came and took us off, when we found ourselves on board an English frigate, the *Nymph*, which had been driven by a gale out of her course. Had it not been for this circumstance we might have remained on the rock many months longer, or till we had all died of starvation.

Captain Biddell sent for me, and desired to know who I was.

"That's more than I can very well tell you, sir," I answered in the broken English I then spoke; "but my friend Jack Headland can tell you more about me than I can."

He accordingly sent for Jack, who told him all he knew. He seemed, by his remarks, to have some doubts of the truth of the story.

"Well, all I can do is to enter you both on the ship's books," he observed. "I shall see how the boy behaves himself and act accordingly."

Jack was asked by what name I should be entered.

"I'll give him mine," he answered. "I don't want him to be a Dutchman, and I don't know any other to call him by."

And so I was entered as young Jack Headland, and young Jack I was called ever afterwards, while he was known as old Jack, though he was not very old either, for he was still a fine active young fellow.

"You heard what the captain said," observed old Jack to me. "What you have got to look after is to behave yourself and to do your duty. Though he is somewhat cross-grained in his manner, he is all right at bottom, or the ship would not be in the good order she is, or the men so well contented. Though I have never served on board a man-of-war before I can judge of that."

I followed Jack's advice, and having shifted my shore-going clothes, which were pretty nearly worn out, for a seaman's suit, I was soon able to do my duty as well as any of the other boys in the ship.

Captain Fancourt was then first lieutenant of the frigate, and having heard Jack's account he spoke to me and found that at all events I was a young gentleman in manners and education.

"Do you wish to keep your present knowledge, my lad?" he asked one day, calling me to him. "It is a pity you should lose what you know."

I replied that I especially wished to do so, but that I had no books, and should find it a hard matter to read them for'ard, even if I had.

"Very well," he answered. "You shall come to my cabin every day, and I will assist you in your studies."

The other officers following his example, also took me in hand. The master gave me lessons in mathematics and navigation, and the purser taught me writing and arithmetic, so that though I was still berthed for'ard I had advantages which even the midshipmen did not possess. They, in a short time, finding I was a gentleman in manners, applied for leave to the captain, and I was admitted into their berth. I do not know that I gained much by the change in some respects, but I was glad to escape from the rough boys with whom I had at first to associate. I still did duty as a ship's boy, and by this means Jack was able to instruct me in knotting and splicing, and other minutiae of a seaman's education, which I found especially useful.

We had been in the Indian Seas about three years, chiefly engaged in protecting British merchantmen from the pirates which swarmed there. The boats had been sent away in chase of three or four of their craft, cut off from a piratical fleet which were endeavouring to make their escape along shore. My friend Jack belonged to the second cutter. Night came on, and the frigate stood after the boats, making signals for their return. Three of the boats at length got alongside, but the second cutter did not appear. The weather changed—a heavy gale sprang up, and we were compelled to stand out to sea. As soon as the weather moderated, we returned and cruised up and down the coast, the boats being sent on shore at various places; but nothing could be seen of the second cutter, and we had every reason to fear that the officer in charge of her and all hands, had either been killed or fallen into the power of the pirates. I was very much cut up at the loss of my kind friend, who had indeed acted like a father towards me. The captain sent for me into his cabin, and expressed his regret at the loss of my old protector.

"I wish to make all the amends I can to you, my lad," he said. "As your conduct has been thoroughly to my satisfaction since you came on board, and as there is now a vacancy by the death of Mr Watson (the midshipman lost in the boat), I will place you on the quarter-deck and give you the rating of a midshipman."

I thanked him very much; but I remember saying, "I would rather old Jack were alive though."

"I appreciate your feeling, my lad," he answered; "but even if he does return I won't disrate you, and I will see how we can best manage to get you an outfit."

Thus by the loss of my honest friend, whom I greatly lamented, I got my first step on the ratlines.

After a further search for the missing boat we left the coast, and soon afterwards going to Calcutta received our orders to return home.

Your uncle has been my friend ever since. He obtained his promotion on our arrival in England, and was at once appointed to the command of the *Ariel*, corvette, in which I accompanied him to the West Indies, where we were actively engaged, and I had there the opportunity I had so much wished for of performing two or three acts which gained me credit. I was still more anxious than ever to make a name for myself, as since the loss of my protector, Jack Headland, I had no possible clue by which to discover my parents with the exception of the gold chain, which I wore round my neck, and which I still preserved. A small bundle containing a child's clothes and shoes, and the figure of an Indian tumbler, which were found in Jack's kit, I felt sure had belonged to me. Whether or not they are sufficient to identify me I am very doubtful. Not wishing to throw a chance away I deposited them for safety with my agents in London.

Such was Headland's history, and Harry assured him at its close that he always knew he must be a gentleman by birth, as he was in every other possible way.

"I heartily wish," he said, "that you may some day find out to whom you belong. Whoever they are you may depend on it they will welcome you joyfully. Why there goes eight bells. Our watch has indeed passed quickly away."

The two midshipmen were relieved and went below. They had scarcely, as they supposed, closed their eyes, when the boatswain's rough voice and shrill pipe roused them up with a cry of "All hands on deck!" followed by the quick roll of the drum, the well known beat to quarters.

Chapter Sixteen
Home, with Promotion

As Harry and his friend reached the deck they caught sight of a strange frigate standing towards the *Triton*, which was, as has already been said, off the port of Carthagena, and as they looked towards the land they observed a small vessel under all sail running in for it. That the stranger was an enemy there was no doubt, and as she was evidently as heavy a frigate as the Triton, there appeared, even should she be captured, with the Spanish squadron close at hand, little prospect of her being brought off. There was indeed a great chance that the *Triton* herself would not escape should she be crippled.

"The odds are against us," observed the captain to his first lieutenant. "We must not, however, show our heels to a single frigate, and will do our best to take her before the enemy can come out to her rescue."

"Ay, ay, sir; take her we shall, and I hope get off with her too," was the answer.

The crew were at their quarters, stripped to the waist, waiting eagerly to begin the action. The second lieutenant being left on shore and the third being ill, Headland and Harry were doing duty in their places, though the third lieutenant came on deck when he heard of the pending action.

The stranger, which hoisted Spanish colours, and was seen to be of 34 guns, two more than the *Triton*, approaching within hail then hauled to the wind, on the *Triton's* weather beam.

"Give her a shot!" cried the captain, "to prove her."

Scarcely had the flash been seen than a whole broadside fired by the enemy came rattling on board the *Triton*. It was returned by the British crew. Broadside after broadside was given and received. In vain Captain Fancourt endeavoured to haul either ahead or astern of the enemy to rake her. She kept her advantageous position, and the Spaniards, whatever may sometimes be said of them, fought their ship gallantly. The action continued to be a regular broadside to broadside one. The boatswain was seen examining the masts with anxious looks. They and the bowsprit had been wounded pretty severely, while the rigging hung in festoons, and her sails were shot through and torn. Still the British seamen fought their guns as energetically as at first.

"Keep it up, my lads!" cried Headland, as he with Harry and other officers moved from gun to gun. "We have given her as much as we have received, and something more into the bargain."

As far as the canopy of smoke which hung round the ships could enable the British crew to distinguish the condition of their antagonist, they saw that every shroud had been cut away, and her boats and upper works knocked to pieces, while hitherto but very few of their own crew had been hit and not one killed. The action lasted an hour and twenty minutes, when the Spaniards' fire sensibly slackened.

The *Triton*, giving her antagonist another broadside, now forged ahead. The crew were ordered to leave their guns, and in an instant the greater number swarming aloft began knotting and splicing the damaged rigging, while fresh sails were got up and bent with a rapidity which looked like magic. Meantime the Spaniard was similarly engaged, and her helm being put up she endeavoured under such sail as she could set to make off. The sight still further stimulated the British crew to exertion, and in twenty minutes, with rigging refitted, she went about and with every gun reloaded stood down once more towards the enemy. Though the latter had hitherto fought with the greatest courage, yet no sooner did the *Triton* come within range than the proud flag of Spain was hauled down. A cheer, such as British sailors alone can give, burst from the victorious crew.

Headland and Harry were sent on board with the only boat that could swim, to take possession.

The brave Spanish captain delivered up his sword with a dignified bow, and Headland, complimenting him on his gallantry, requested him at once to go on board the *Triton*. That he had not yielded till the last moment was evident, for the booms having fallen down had disabled all the waist guns of the frigate, and fully thirty men lay on the decks, while an equal number were found wounded in the cockpit, many of them mortally.

Not a moment was to be lost, and as soon as two other boats could be patched up, more of the *Triton's* crew were sent on board to repair the damages the prize had received.

She proved to be the *Mahonesa*, and her brave captain, Don Tomas Ayaldi.

"Well, we have done something now at all events," said Harry to Headland, as the severed shrouds and running rigging of the prize having been repaired and sail made she and her captor were steering for Gibraltar.

The *Triton* remained sometime at Gibraltar to refit.

After another cruise up the Mediterranean, where she did good service, and fought an action not inferior to the first, when she captured her antagonist, she was ordered home. On her way she looked into Lisbon, and Headland, who received his commission as lieutenant, was put in charge of their first prize, with Harry as his second in command, and another midshipman and thirty men to carry her home.

They reached Plymouth in safety, and when the *Triton* was paid off, Captain Fancourt being soon afterwards appointed to a ship in commission in which there were no vacancies, Harry and his friend were separated. They were employed for nearly three years on different stations and saw much service, both obtaining their promotion, while Headland, by several gallant acts, gained the credit he so eagerly sought for.

During the time, being then lieutenants, Harry belonging to the *Naiad* frigate, and Headland to the *Alembic*, they had the good fortune to capture two Spanish frigates, the *Thetis* and *Santa Brigida*, laden with specie to the value of upwards of 300,000 pounds sterling. Though two other frigates joined in the chase, each of the lieutenants of the four ships obtained 5000 as their share of prize money, while the four captains received upwards of 40,000 pounds a-piece.

"If you ever have to establish your claims, you will now have the means of doing so," observed Harry to his friend when they arrived at Plymouth. "And remember my share shall be at your service."

"I am very sure you will help me to the last penny you possess if I should require money," answered Headland. "But I have long given up all hopes of success, and really now think very little about the matter. I am not ambitious of wealth, and when the piping times of peace come round, and I am sent on shore to shift for myself, I shall have saved enough to live on in comfort and respectability."

"What, with a wife!" asked Harry. "She may not be satisfied with what you consider a competency."

"I have not thought about marrying," answered Headland, laughing, "and I do not suppose any lady I should like would accept an unknown adventurer such as I should be considered," he added, and a shade came over his countenance showing that he felt his position more than he was willing to acknowledge.

"Adventurer! nonsense; no one has a right so to call a naval officer who has already made a name for himself, and will make a greater some day or other," answered Harry. "Don't let such an idea take possession of your mind. There are dozens of girls who would accept you gladly for yourself, and perhaps be better pleased to find that they had not married a whole tribe of relations, sisters and aunt, who might interfere with their domestic arrangements. Depend on it if every lieutenant and ward-room officer of our four fortunate frigates were to go on shore at once, we could each of us be married within a fortnight."

"Very likely," answered Headland. "But the ladies would take us for our prize money not for ourselves, and I should not wish to have a wife on those terms."

"Nor should I, indeed; when I was last on shore during the London season, and went out with my mother and sister, I saw enough of fashionable society to make me resolve whenever I might take it into my head to look out for a wife, not to seek for her in such an atmosphere. I saw numbers of pretty girls, I confess, and, I daresay, some of them possessed sterling qualities. If I particularly admired any one fair lady, on discovering that I was only a midshipman, she was sure to freeze me up the next time I met her."

"Had she found that you were a lieutenant with a share of the *Santa Brigida's* treasure, she might have looked more affectionately on you," said Headland, laughing.

"Exactly; but I should not, as you were remarking, have been flattered had I been aware of the motive which prompted her feelings."

"So it seems that we are perfectly agreed," said Headland, "and the less we think about the matter till the time comes the better. At all events I intend never to entertain any thoughts of marrying unless I find some one who, rising above ordinary prejudices, is ready to link her fate with mine, regardless of my unknown birth and name." See there are the waggons to carry off our treasure.

As he spoke, he pointed to a large number of artillery waggons which had driven into the dockyard, close to which the prizes had been hauled.

Two days were employed in landing the rich cargoes, which were escorted by horse and foot soldiers, and armed seamen and marines, and accompanied by bands of music and an immense concourse of people, to the Citadel of Plymouth, in the vaults of which the treasure remained till it was removed to London, and finally deposited in the Bank of England.

A similar scene occurred at different times when treasure ships were taken.

On one occasion an English captain sailed into port with huge silver candlesticks at his mastheads, and ordinary seamen found themselves possessed of two or three hundred guineas prize money, frequently squandered before many weeks were over; while the officers obtained a proportionate share of wealth. Few, perhaps, thought of the suffering and injustice endured by the owners when gold was captured which belonged to private individuals, and though in some instances when such was the case it was returned, yet in many others non-combatants lost their lives and their property at the same time.

Harry and Headland were among the fortunate officers who, having many opportunities of distinguishing themselves, gained wealth and honour together.

At length the great victory of the Nile, in which Headland took a part was won, Napoleon's armies had been defeated in Syria and Egypt, Copenhagen had been bombarded, and the treaty of Amiens, speedily again to be broken, had been signed.

The ships in which the two lieutenants served came to an anchor at Spithead, within a few days of each other.

Harry went on board the frigate in which Headland was serving as first lieutenant.

"You are sure of your promotion, Headland," he said after their greeting was over. "I have just got a letter from my uncle telling me your name is on the list. You deserve a spell on shore. We are to go into harbour to be paid off to-morrow, and as soon as I am free you must start with me for Texford, where my family are now residing. Captain Fancourt has already spoken to them of you, and you will receive a hearty welcome. No excuses, old fellow, you will be Captain Headland by that time, and that alone will be sufficient introduction to any family in the land."

Headland hesitated. He thought of making a tour round England, and perhaps going over to France, to have a look at the country from which Englishmen had so long been excluded, but Harry overcame all objections, and Headland agreed should he not be appointed to a command, which was not very likely, to accompany his friend to Texford.

Chapter Seventeen
Second Period of Maiden May's History

Time went on, and nothing occurred to interrupt the even tenor of the Miss Pembertons' well-spent lives. They never wearied in their efforts to benefit the bodies and souls of their poorer neighbours, and if some were ungrateful, many blessed them for the words they spoke, and the kind acts they performed. Their young pupil, in winter and summer, rain and sunshine, continued to come to them every day. She never wished for a holiday, and it would have been a trial to her to have had to keep away from Downside. Though she was as loving as ever to those at home, she was able to bestow an equal amount of affection on the ladies who devoted themselves to her instruction.

She was now no longer the little fisher maiden she had appeared in former years; but the charms of her mind and person having gradually been developed, though she herself was scarcely aware of the change, she had become a truly lovely girl already entering womanhood.

Adam had lost none of the affection he had from the first felt for the child, whose life he had saved. He could no longer, however, properly call her his little Maiden May, for she had become a full-grown damsel, full of life and spirits; and if, conscious that she was not his daughter, she did not bestow on him all of a daughter's affection, she yet treated him with respect, and so lovingly and kindly, that he had no cause to complain. Her tastes were refined, and her intellect expanding as she advanced in knowledge, she could not help seeing the space gradually widening between herself and her foster-parents and their sons. Yet, with tact and right feeling, she had contrived not to let the young men feel how fully alive she was to the difference between them. They, however, gradually became aware of it, and treated her with that deference which they considered to be her due, as superior to themselves. To the elder ones this was easy, but it caused Jacob no small exercise of self restraint not to behave towards Maiden May as he had been accustomed to do, when under his charge she was allowed to go blackberrying, or to wander along the shore picking up shells.

May's dress, though plain and simple in the extreme, was such as was suited for the companion of the well-born Miss Pemberton's, and she had entwined herself so completely round their hearts that they regarded her in the light of a beloved niece. She had now for sometime resided entirely with them. She, however, paid frequent visits to her kind foster father and mother, as she now called Adam and his wife.

It had been a hard struggle to Dame Halliburt and her husband to part with her, but they saw clearly that it would be for her benefit, and that their cottage was not a fit abode for a young girl destined to occupy a higher rank than their own. Even they felt that there was already a broad line between them, and the dame, not having forgotten her own training in a gentleman's family, could not help treating May with much more deference than she would have shown to her had she been really her daughter.

May herself, conscious of the change in the dame's manner, could scarcely tell why she had become so much more formal than she used to be, though she had too much confidence in the kind woman's love to suppose that it arose from any want of affection. Adam was, however, as hearty as ever, but then he had for long treated her with a certain amount of respect, moderating that exhibition of his affection his big warm heart would have inclined him to bestow. He still generally called her his Maiden May, but sometimes addressed her as Mistress May, and seldom offered to press the hearty kiss on her fair brow with which he had been accustomed to greet her after a day's absence.

Adam and the dame had undergone severe trials during the last years, though they bore up under them with christian fortitude and resignation. Their second son Sam had been crossed in love, and as a consequence went off to sea on board a man-of-war. He was a steady well-conducted young man. He had become a petty officer, and there was every prospect of his doing well.

A short time after Sam had gone to sea Ben, who was his father's mainstay, had on one occasion gone to Morbury, just at the time when press-gangs were hard at work along the coast, laying hands on every seafaring person, whether willing or unwilling, to man the fleet. Ben, not suspecting danger, was walking along the quay, when a party of seamen rushed out of a public-house and surrounded him. Though he endeavoured to make his escape, he was quickly overpowered, and being dragged into a boat, was carried on board a cutter outside the harbour. As many other brave fellows acted when he found his fate inevitable, he submitted with a good grace, and determined to do his duty.

He did not return, and for several days Adam could gain no tidings of his son, though he suspected what had occurred. At length he received a letter from Ben saying that he had been seized by a pressgang, and that he was on board a frigate destined for the East India station. Adam went to Mr Shallard with a message from the Miss Pemberton's saying they would be answerable for any sum required to obtain Ben's discharge, but the lawyer feared that so urgent was the need of men for the navy that success was improbable. He did his best, but before any effort could be made to obtain his discharge, the frigate sailed, carrying Ben as one of her crew.

Thus Adam was deprived of the services of his two elder sons. Still he hoped that they would some day return, and be again able to assist him on board the *Nancy*.

A still greater blow, however, was in store for him and his wife. News came that the ship on board which Sam was serving had been engaged in action, and as they anxiously read the account of the battle, their eyes fell on his name in the list of killed.

"God's will be done! Poor Sam," exclaimed Adam, with a deep groan.

The dame expressed her grief in a louder manner, but honest Adam's was the deepest.

May did her utmost to comfort her foster-parents, showing all the sympathy for their sorrow which her gentle heart prompted her to express. Day after day she came to see them, sometimes accompanied by Miss Jane, who, although she urged arguments innumerable to prove that excessive grief was wrong, failed to convince them of the truth of her assertions. Their perfect confidence in God's love and justice, however, brought resignation to their hearts, and they recovered in time their usual spirits. The dame became once more as active and loquacious as ever, and Adam went through his daily labours with his ordinary industry and perseverance.

Adam Halliburt, who had been out fishing all night, had just risen from his noonday rest, when the dame returned from her usual round.

"Sad news from the Hall, Adam," she said, putting aside her basket.

"Old Sir Reginald has gone at last. Poor dear gentleman, he will be missed by many around. I met Mr Groocock, who had been over to Morbury to arrange about the funeral with Mr Shallard, who was Sir Reginald's lawyer you know. He pulled up just to have a talk for a minute, though he was in a great hurry to get back. Sir Reginald had sent, when he found himself getting worse, for his nephew, Mr Ralph, his nearest of kin in England, whom he seemed to have a great desire to see again. Mr Ralph, however, could not set off at once, and when he arrived at Texford, his uncle was no more. It seems a question whether he is now Sir Ralph or not. Mr Ranald has not been heard of for eight or nine years or more, though his brother and old Sir Reginald have been making all the inquiries they could. Mr Groocock says that Mr Shallard always speaks to Mr Ralph as Sir Ralph, and says he has no doubt whatever that his brother is dead, and that he is the heir. He himself seems to think so, and as Mr Groocock said to me, for his part he is ready to serve whoever has possession as faithfully as he did his old master, and if Mr Ranald is dead, and has left no sons, his younger brother must be Sir Ralph. At all events, Sir Ralph considers himself, and as such has taken possession, and gives orders as if he were, without doubt, the owner of Texford. There will be a great change there shortly, for he has already let Mr Groocock understand that his lady, and daughter, and eldest son, will be coming down soon, and Mr Harry is expected home before long. If he is like what he was when he was here last, he will keep the house alive. I remember hearing that Mrs Castleton, or we must call her Lady Castleton now, was a very nice kind lady, and so, though many will be sorry that Sir Reginald has gone, there will be others who will think that the change is for the better. Mr Groocock, however, has his own opinion. I would not say anything against Sir Ralph for the world, but I remember that he was a somewhat proud and haughty young gentleman, and though he was quiet and grave enough in his manner, he was hot-tempered too, and could carry things with a high hand sometimes."

"Well, well," said Adam, "Sir Reginald had nigh reached four score years and ten, and that's a fair age. He was a kind, good man, and will be missed by many; but we will hope that Sir Ralph may be like him, and it's our duty to think as well of our betters as we can. I should like to see Master Harry again, for I mind the brave way he saved our Maiden May from the bull, and how he spoke to you so kindly and modest-like afterwards, as if he had just done nothing out of the way. I blessed him then, and I bless him now, and every time I hear his name, for what would have happened to her, young as she was then, without knowing how to save herself, it's more than I like to think of."

Sir Ralph, no one appearing to dispute his title, took possession of Texford.

Chapter Eighteen
A Visit

A longer time than usual had passed since Maiden May had paid a visit to the cottage of her foster-parents.

Adam and the dame were seated in their usual places by the fire, the dame, never idle, busily employed in mending one of her son's garments.

"You or I, mother, must go up this evening and inquire for our May," said Adam, knocking the ashes out of his pipe. "She would never stay away from us so long of her own free-will; and either one of the ladies must have been taken ill, and they cannot spare her, or she herself may be ailing."

"I pray heaven nothing has happened to her," replied the dame. "I will just finish off Jacob's coat and then go up myself. If she is ill I must ask the ladies' leave to stay with her. I would sleep on the bare floor by her side rather than not be with her, sweet dear."

"Yes, do," said Adam in an anxious tone. "The Miss Pembertons will be glad to have you, mother, for there is no one—not even they themselves— can know better how to tend her than you."

Just as Adam had finished speaking the latch was lifted, and a sweet-looking young girl entered the cottage. Her complexion was beautifully fair and glowing with health, her features delicately chiselled. A bright smile beamed from her blue eyes, while her figure was light and graceful, and though her dress was simple, there was that air of elegance and refinement about her rarely seen in so humble an abode.

The dame hurried across the room to fold her in her arms, while Adam put out both his hands to take hers, which she stretched forwards towards him. He bestowed a kiss, half reverential, half paternal, on her brow.

Her appearance, for it was Maiden May herself who entered, banished all their fears about her health.

"It does my heart good to see thee, my own Maiden May," he said, gazing at her affectionately, and placing a chair for her by the side of his own. "We almost thought that thee had forgotten us. And yet, no, no—we knew thee would'st not have done that; but what kept thee away, my dear?"

"Miss Mary has been unwell, and required constant attention," answered May; "and Miss Jane has been at Texford to see poor Sir Reginald. You probably have heard that he is dead."

"Yes, mother has just brought the news," said Adam. "He will be a great loss to many."

"Yes, indeed he will," said May, "especially to my kind friends. I fear that Sir Ralph will ill supply his place. Miss Jane, who waited to receive him, has come back much hurt at the way he behaved to her. He looks upon them as gloomy Methodists, and inclined to censure his worldliness, and he partly hinted that they must no longer come to Texford as they had been accustomed to do in Sir Reginald's time, unless with an especial invitation. I am truly sorry for it, as Miss Jane used to enjoy her visits there; and though, now Sir Reginald has gone, it will be very different, yet she thought she should like Lady Castleton and her daughter Miss Julia, and her sons, especially Mr Harry, who greatly took her fancy when he was there before. She tells me he is the young gentleman who saved me from being tossed by the bull when I was a little girl, and so kindly brought me back to you, mother. I remember the circumstance, though I have but a dim recollection of him, except that he was very good-natured and laughed, and told me I was a little heroine, though at the time I confess I did not know what he meant. I only remember that I was dreadfully frightened, and very grateful to him for saving me."

"Ah, yes, good reason too we had to be thankful to him, for it would have broken our hearts if any harm had come to our Maiden May," observed Adam, looking affectionately at the young girl. "But I am main sorry to hear what you say about Sir Ralph."

"Miss Mary thinks, however, that perhaps Miss Jane, who was in much grief at Sir Reginald's death, might have spoken more seriously to Sir Ralph than he liked. You know she does occasionally say things with which worldly people are not pleased, and perhaps that put him out of humour. She, however, asserts that she ought not to be ashamed of her principles, and that she merely reminded Sir Ralph that he was but a life tenant of Texford—that the time would come when he too would lie, as Sir Reginald does now, on the bed of death, and his body be carried to the family vault, while his soul has to stand before the Judge of all things, and give an account of his stewardship while here below. Miss Mary observed that, although what Miss Jane had said was very right and true, she might not possibly have taken the proper time for making her remarks, and that, perhaps, had they come from a clergyman, he would have received them in a different spirit.

"Miss Jane replied that she was sure, in the first place, that the clergyman would not make them, and felt that the time might pass when they could be made at all, if she did not, while, as she supposed, he was grieving for the death of his excellent uncle. Miss Jane, however, confessed that she had made a mistake in supposing that his heart was in any way touched with sorrow; but, on the contrary, she feared that he felt nothing but satisfaction at becoming the possessor of Texford, and was annoyed at being reminded of the uncertainty of human life.

"But I ought not, perhaps, to repeat, even to you, dear mother and father, what my kind friends say; only, in this instance, I am sure they would not object to my doing so."

"It's safer not to repeat what we hear, there is no doubt about that," observed the dame. "But, you know, what you say to us never goes to other ears. Now, to my mind, Miss Mary is right. Miss Jane can say strong things when she thinks it is her duty to say them, and people do not always take them in the same spirit they are spoken. I hope when my lady and Miss Julia come things will be put to rights, and that the Miss Pembertons will not be shut out of Texford more than they like."

"For their sakes I hope, at all events, they may be on friendly terms with their relatives," said May. "However, Miss Mary has no wish to leave home even for a day, and I always enjoy being in her company alone, and attending to her. I can never feel weary in trying to repay the kindness she has shown me. She has taught me much of what I know, even more than her sister has, and her memory is so retentive that she can talk over the books we have read together, and remind me often of portions which I have forgotten."

"Ah, she is a dear lady; it's a wonder she knows so much, and no eyes to see with," observed the dame. "She may not be so wonderful a woman as her sister is, who can talk every bit as cleverly, if not better, than Mr Simms, the apothecary, and it's my belief she could bleed as well if she thought fit, though she says she sees no reason to take honest blood out of people's bodies, but that a little sulphur and milk in the spring and the fall will answer the purpose as well."

The dame was enlarging still further on Miss Jane's medical knowledge, when May, turning her head, saw Jacob, who had entered, and was standing watching her at a distance, and unwilling, it seemed, to be observed. A blush rose to his cheeks when he found that he had been discovered.

"I promised not to be long away, and I ought to be on my road back again," she said. "So good-bye, mother; good-bye, father."

May put out her hand to Jacob, who pressed it in his own rough palm, casting a look at her, in which reverence was mingled with affection. Not noticing his glance she tripped lightly away.

He followed from the cottage, keeping, however, at some distance behind, till he had seen her enter the gate of Downside Cottage.

"What can have come over our Jacob," said the dame, after he had gone.

"He looks of late as if he was afraid of our Maiden May, instead of being friendly with her, as he used to be. I suppose, as she seems a fine young lady, that it would not become him, a poor fisher-lad, to be talking to her as he did when she was a little girl," observed Adam. "To be sure he does sometimes look curious, and often forgets things I tell him; however, he is as good a lad as ever, so I will say nothing agen him."

Neither his father or mother knew the true cause of poor Jacob's changed manner.

Chapter Nineteen
The New Squire

Mr Reginald's funeral took place, and was conducted with the pomp usual in those days when a county magnate was carried to his final resting-place. Sir Ralph and his eldest son attended as chief mourners, and the heads of all the county families, from far and near, either came in person or sent representatives to pay their last tokens of respect to one who had been held in honour among them. The tenantry of the Texford property followed on horseback or foot.

For many years so large a gathering had not been seen in that part of the country. Even the boatmen and fishermen from the neighbouring coast, among whom were Adam Halliburt and his sons, managed to get on shore in time to join the cortege, walking two and two, with the flags of their boats furled round the staff carried at the head of each party. There were several real mourners in the crowd. One of the most sincere probably was Mr Groocock. He had lost a kind and indulgent master, who had ever placed confidence in his honesty of purpose, and he had reason to doubt whether the new lord of Texford would treat him in the same way.

As the assembly gathered round the family tomb of the Castletons, Mr Groocock, happening to look up, observed among the crowd, standing directly opposite where the chief mourners were collected, a dark bearded man, whose eye was fixed on Sir Ralph, his countenance exhibiting a peculiarly evil expression.

"That man comes here for no good," thought the steward. "He had no love for Sir Reginald, and he is not one who would put himself out of his way for an object which could be of no advantage to him. Still he has not come without an object, of that I am very certain."

The minister had uttered the last solemn words, "earth to earth, dust to dust, ashes to ashes," and the burial service was concluded. Those who felt disposed to do so moved down into the vault to take a last look at Sir Reginald's coffin ere the tomb was closed till another occupant might claim admission. Mr Groocock had been among the first to descend, and remained unwilling to quit the spot. As he stood there he saw the man he had observed among the crowd enter the vault just as the last of the other visitors had left. He did not appear to cast a glance even at Sir Reginald's coffin, but he was seen to stop before three others on the opposite side, not aware apparently that anyone else remained in the vault. The steward could not see his features, but the working of his shoulders showed that he was agitated by some strong feeling. A groan escaped his bosom.

"I will have vengeance on your murderer," he muttered.

Suddenly turning round as if by a powerful effort, he hastened out of the vault.

"This is strange," thought the steward, "what can have made him say that."

He was alone.

"Good-bye, dear master," he said in a sobbing voice. "I shall not meet your like on earth, but I hope to see you in heaven when my time comes."

Before he left the vault he turned to examine the coffins at which the stranger had been gazing. Above one of them was the name of "Ellen Castleton, aged 18."

"I cannot make it out," muttered the worthy steward; "it's strange, passing strange," and his thoughts thus set to work, went back to years and events he had well-nigh forgotten.

The funeral guests were dispersing with the exception of those of higher position, who had been invited by the young baronet to partake of a breakfast provided at the hall.

As Adam and his party were making their way back to Hurlston, Miles Gaffin, mounted on the powerful horse he usually rode, galloped by apparently not observing the suspicious glances which were cast at him as he passed.

"The miller looks as if the foul fiend had got possession of him," observed one of the men. "They say he has had dealings with him for long past."

"Ay, ay, if it hadn't been for that he would have been in limbo before now for some of the things he has done in his time," observed another. "To my mind, mates, Satan lets them go on in their own way without ever showing himself to them; and as to helping them out of danger, depend on it he would leave them to perish soon enough if he had the power over them," observed Adam. "There is another more powerful than him who looks after human beings; and not one of us, good or bad, can leave this world without He thinks fit. Its only when He knows that the cup of their iniquities is full that He allows even the worst to perish."

Sir Ralph remained some time at Texford after his uncle's death, giving directions for certain repairs and alterations which he wished to have executed immediately.

Sir Ralph had summoned Mr Groocock to the library, a fine old wainscotted room, with bookcases against two of the walls, while over and on either side of the fireplace were hung family portraits. Sir Reginald was there, occupying the centre position, with those of his younger brother, Mr Herbert Castleton, with his wife and their two children, the long lost Ranald, and their daughter Ellen, hers executed when she had just reached her sixteenth summer, and Ranald when he was about nineteen. The features of Ellen fully bore out the description which Dame Halliburt had given of her beauty.

Sir Ralph was seated with his legs crossed and his arm resting on the table when the steward entered. Sir Reginald would have desired him to sit down and welcomed him with a kind smile, and enquired after his health. Sir Ralph allowed the old man to stand before him while he issued his directions.

The house was to be freshly painted, and the furniture for some of the best rooms sent down from London.

"I purpose making Texford my summer and winter residence when my political duties do not require my attendance in London," he observed to Mr Groocock.

Sir Ralph had sat in parliament for a close borough for the last three years, and he had let it be known that he intended to stand for the county at the next general election.

"Hurry on with the work, Mr Groocock, for Lady Castleton wishes to come down as soon as possible."

The steward promised to see that his master's orders were executed to the best of his ability.

"But you see, Sir Ralph," he observed, "workmen are often dilatory, and we cannot always depend upon their doing what they promise."

"They will do the work if you keep a watchful eye on them, Mr Groocock," answered the baronet. "I am not accustomed to have difficulties raised when I give orders. My late uncle has been somewhat over-indulgent, I suspect. You will get all the rent paid up and proceed against defaulters, according to the power the law affords you. I desire to have no injustice done to anyone, but I suspect that the rents of several of the tenants ought to be raised. You will give them notice that they must expect it."

"I will act as you desire, Sir Ralph, but I venture to observe that it may be a hardship to some of them if we act according to the strict letter of the law. The tenant may, from unforeseen circumstances, have got into difficulties, or he may have expended a considerable amount on his farm, and thus increased its value, or he may have a large family, and find it a hard matter to make the two ends meet, or he himself, or his wife or children, may have been suffering from sickness. In such cases Sir Reginald was wont to give me discretionary power, and was always more inclined to lower than raise the rent of a farm."

"I do not consider myself bound to be guided by what my uncle, an old bachelor without ambition or any other aim in life beyond enjoying existence, might have thought fit to do," answered Sir Ralph in an angry tone. "You will see that my directions are carried out."

Mr Groocock bowed, and tried to suppress the sigh which he found rising from his bosom.

"If Sir Ralph wishes to stand for the county he will find his object defeated by these proceedings. My dear old master would have grieved if he had known the changes likely to be made, but I must obey orders—I must obey orders," he thought to himself.

Having received his final directions, Mr Groocock bowed and retired from the room.

Sir Ralph went back to London. The steward felt relieved at his absence, though he had many unpleasant duties to perform.

He spoke in consequence of the directions he had received to the tenants, and naturally tried to exonerate himself from the suspicion that he had advised the proceedings he was compelled to carry out, yet he gained more ill-will than he had ever before experienced since he became steward of Texford. The miller of Hurlston, whose rent had been, however, very small, was among the most indignant at receiving notice that it was to be raised considerably should he wish to renew the lease as he had the option of doing. He rode over to Texford to expostulate.

"Very well, Mr Gaffin, you can give up the mill if you wish," observed the steward, who would have been glad to get rid of a person whose character he had reason to suspect was none of the best.

"That may not be convenient, and it is very hard to have the rent raised on me after I have been working for years to bring a trade to the mill," answered the miller. "I'll not give it up, however, and you can tell your master that I'll pay the rent he demands."

His eye kindled as he spoke, and a dark frown gathered on his brow, adding, in a low fierce mutter as he left the steward's room, "and with interest too, such as he does not expect." Mr Groocock, however, did not catch the words, and believing the matter settled was glad to get rid of his surly visitor.

The house was at length got ready. Lady Castleton and her daughter Julia, with Madame De La Motte, who had now become rather her companion than governess, arrived, and were shortly after joined by Algernon. He had sometime before left college, where he had taken high honours, and was looked upon as a young man likely to rise in the world. He was, however, very delicate, and hard study had contributed to make him somewhat of an invalid. As his mother observed his spare figure and the hectic flush on his pale cheeks, she could not help at times fearing that he would be but little able to go through the career for which his ambitious father destined him.

"He must get into parliament as soon as possible, and in a few years I hope we shall see him a Minister of State," Sir Ralph had observed to her as she was setting out from London.

He himself, however, had little wish to commence the career his father proposed.

"At present, at all events, let me enjoy Texford, and yours and Julia's society, mother, and when my father vacates his seat for Mumbleton it will be time enough for me to decide whether or not I wish to occupy it," he said to Lady Castleton when she spoke to him of his father's wish.

When Sir Ralph arrived he did not appear to remark how ill his son looked; he was so occupied with politics and his various projects that he troubled himself about little else. When his wife tried to draw his attention to Algernon his only reply was—

"Yes, he reminds me very much of myself when I was of the same age that he is. I was slight and tall, and I suspect that my cheeks were paler than his, although I was accustomed to more exercise than he indulges in, and was fonder of riding and field sports. If he would take to hunting and shooting he would soon get round, and be well able to go through a political campaign in London."

The time of mourning for the old baronet was over. Several guests had arrived, others had been invited, and whatever some of the tenants might have thought of the exactions, as they considered them, which the new baronet had imposed, there appeared every probability that Texford would become a far more lively and sociable mansion than it had been during the latter years of Sir Reginald's life.

Chapter Twenty
Young Miles Gaffin

Sir Ralph and his family had been for some time settled at Texford, when the dame brought the news, gained from her usual source of information, Mr Groocock, that Mr Harry with another officer were daily expected at the hall.

"Mr Groocock says that Mr Harry has done all sorts of brave things, and that he will be captain himself before long," observed the dame to her husband and May, who had just then come in from Downside to pay her a visit. "It seems but the other day that he was a young midshipman, and now to think that he is old enough to be captain of a big ship, though he cannot be *very* old either."

"I have known captains of nineteen," observed Adam; "and though they had not much experience, when it came to real work they did it as well as their elders and better than many. It's not so much what age a man is as what is in him, and that will show itself even though he has not got a hair on his lip."

"Mr Groocock says there are to be grand doings at the hall in honour of Mr Harry's return from sea," continued the dame. "All the tenantry are to be invited, and the labourers and tradesmen and workpeople from Morbury, and the fishermen too from Hurlston; and he made me promise to come and to bring my daughter, for he always calls you my daughter, May, and seems to forget what I once told him, for I am sure I did tell him all about you, though in truth you are my daughter, if a mother's love can make you one."

"I trust that I always shall enjoy that love," said May, taking the dame's hand. "I think I should like to go with you to Texford if the ladies do not object, for they certainly will not go. Miss Mary would not like the crowd, which I suppose there will be, and indeed it is possible that they may not quite approve of such proceedings; besides which, Sir Ralph and Lady Castleton have never asked them to the hall since they took possession, though her ladyship once called at Downside and left her card, but when Miss Jane returned the visit she was not admitted, and has not felt disposed to call again."

"But the ladies must remember Mr Harry, as they were staying with Sir Reginald when he was last there, and Mr Groocock says that he was as great a favourite with them as he was with everybody, so perhaps for the sake of seeing him, if they are asked, they may be persuaded to go," remarked the dame.

"Not if they consider it wrong to give such a fête," answered May. "I am uncertain of the opinion they will form. I cannot myself think it wrong to afford amusement to a number of people from whom they cannot expect to receive the slightest benefit in return."

"Well, if you don't go with the ladies, May, I hope you will come with me. I should have little pleasure by myself; if I was to see you liking it I should be pleased also. You need not go and dance in the crowd. I should not wish to see you do that, even if you were really my daughter; but as you are a young lady, and there is no doubt about that, it would not be proper for you to mix with any but young ladies, and that, perhaps as you would not know any of those present, you would not wish to do."

"No, indeed," answered May. "It is strange that I should never in my life have spoken to a young lady, and I have no notion, except from the descriptions given in Miss Burney's novels, of the way young ladies in general behave, or speak, or think. I should be terribly afraid of them if they are like some of the heroines whose histories I have met with in 'Evelina and Cecilia,' which I have read to Miss Mary, and in a new story she has lately had sent to her, called 'Camilla,' but I have not finished it yet."

"I don't know what sort of young ladies are put into books; but you need not be at all afraid of anyone, May, I am sure of that," observed the dame. "I have known several young ladies in my time. There was poor Miss Ellen Castleton, and three very nice girls who all married well at another house where I was in service, and they could not have held a candle to you, that they couldn't; but I must not say that for fear of making you vain, my dear. Just do you feel what is true, that you are equal to any of them and that will make you comfortable and at home. However, as Mr Harry has not come home and the day is not yet fixed, there will be time to talk about it; only if the ladies say anything just tell them that I should be so much obliged if they would let you go, and that I will take good care of you, and you shall come to no harm or do anything they won't like."

May gladly promised, for she felt curious to see Texford, since she had only a very faint recollection of the place.

As evening was approaching she wished her foster-parents good-bye. Just as she left the house Jacob came up from the boat. She greeted him in her usual unaffected way, but he seemed even less at his ease than he had been of late when he met her.

"Brother Jacob," said May, "I am so glad you are come. I wanted to ask you to collect me some shells, as many as you can find time to gather; not all winkles and cockles, remember, but as great a variety as possible. The ladies have a fancy for making a grotto in the garden, and I have undertaken to adorn the inside with shapes of all sorts of strange creatures to be formed with the shells. They will, I am sure, gladly pay you for your trouble, and I shall be much obliged to you if you can get them as soon as possible."

"If it's to please you, Miss May, I will do it with all my heart, and I want no payment," answered Jacob, his strong manly voice trembling more than he was aware of. Jacob was now a fine specimen of a stout young sailor.

"What has come over you, Jacob?" exclaimed May, with a look of surprise, yet laughing as she spoke. "I never heard you call me Miss May before. I hope you are not offended at my saying that the ladies would pay you; they would not think it fair to employ your time without some recompense."

"But if it's for you, I want no pay, and cannot take it," said Jacob, his voice softening as he spoke. "I will get the shells, that I will gladly, as many basketfuls as you may want; only tell me when I bring them if there are not enough, and I will get more."

"Thank you, Jacob, I am sure you will," said May, and without further noticing his peculiar manner she tripped lightly away on her homeward road.

Jacob stood gazing at her with his hand on the door till she was out of sight. He then, instead of entering the cottage as he had previously intended, made his way in the direction she had gone.

May continued her walk towards Downside. Having stopped at the cottage of an old woman (one of the many the Miss Pembertons were in the habit of visiting) to enquire whether she had got over her last attack of rheumatics, May, as she turned round, caught sight of Jacob in the distance. It was not the first time she had discovered him following her, but she knew him too well not to believe that he had some good motive for so doing.

"Mother has not got over her fear of that man Miles Gaffin, and sends Jacob to watch that he does not run off with me, as she used to fancy he would do when I was a little girl," she said to herself.

The old dame assured her that she was much better for the stuff Miss Jane had sent, when May, as she wished her good-bye, looked back once more, but Jacob had disappeared. She therefore continued her walk, taking little further thought of him. Once, however, as she happened to turn her head for a moment, she fancied that she saw him, but he again disappeared round a corner.

She was still some way from Downside when, on a part of the road where there were no cottages in sight, she observed a young man leaning against a gate at some little distance in front. He was dressed in the fashionable costume of the day—a green riding coat and top-boots, with a huge frill to his shirt, while his hat was set rakishly on one side. Though his features were not bad his countenance had a coarse unpleasant expression, and notwithstanding the dress he wore his appearance was not that of a gentleman.

On seeing May he started forward and advanced towards her. Making her a bow as he approached, he said—

"Highly pleased, Miss, to meet you. I have been on the look-out for the last two hours. I thought you were not coming."

May did not reply, but moved on.

The young buck, however, was not to be daunted.

"Saw you at church last Sunday, and thought you had seen me; but I suppose you were attending to the parson, or your eyes were on the prayer-book."

May, wondering who this intruder could be, and beginning to feel excessively annoyed at his impertinence, walked on as fast as she could.

As he spoke of having seen her at church, she recollected remarking in a pew at some distance a youth who appeared to be staring at her.

"I fancy you must be under some mistake in addressing me," she said at last. "I am residing with the Miss Pembertons, and wish to have no acquaintances unless introduced to me by them."

"No, Miss, I do assure you that I am under no mistake whatever," answered the youth, in a tone of assurance. "I have not the honour of being acquainted with the old ladies, but I have great respect for them on account of the care they take of you. They are not likely to be acquainted with a young buck like me, though they cannot object to your being so, and I would only ask you to give me the favour of seeing you safe home."

"Thank you, sir, I am very well acquainted with the road and require no one to accompany me," said Mary, assuming as composed and dignified an air as she could put on. She, however, unaccustomed to assume any manner besides her own natural one, did not succeed much to her satisfaction. Her annoyance was greatly increased when, notwithstanding her remarks, the youth persevered in walking by her side. She now began to regret that she had not invited Jacob to accompany her, for she was very sure that no one would have ventured to have spoken to her thus had he been her attendant. She instinctively looked round in the hopes that he might still be following, but she could not see him. She therefore went on, trusting that her silence would induce the impertinent stranger to allow her to proceed alone.

"Ah, Miss, though you don't seem to know me I have known you for all your life nearly. I am young Miles Gaffin, and I remember when you were a little girl living with old Halliburt and his wife, and I often saw you when I came home for the holidays, though I have been now long away from Hurlston studying the law, in which I hope to make a figure some day. A fine profession for making money, and the only way to make a figure in the world is to get that, in my opinion," and he laughed at his own intended wit.

Still May kept on her way in silence.

"Can this person be a son of that dreadful man Gaffin?" she thought. "If the stories about the miller are true it is the sort of conduct to be expected from a son of his."

She felt that her best course was not to speak to the youth whatever he might say.

He continued walking by her side, beating his boot with his riding whip. At length he began to grow impatient at her silence.

"You have got a voice I know, for I heard it sound very sweetly just now. Can't you use it just to say something? It's not pleasant when a person speaks to a young lady not to have a word in return."

Still May was firm in her determination not to speak. The youth, probably unaccustomed to such treatment from the young women he usually associated with, entirely lost patience.

"Come, come, Miss, let's be friends! Though you do live with the Miss Pembertons, there's no reason you should look down upon a young man who is in a respectable position, and would make you an independent lady if you would let him."

As he spoke he tried to seize her hand, and put his other arm round to draw her towards him. She started back to escape his touch, and as she did so, looking over her shoulder, she saw Jacob following in the distance. She turned and flew towards him faster than she had ever run in her life. Jacob hastened to meet her. She took his arm panting and scarcely able to speak as she told him the insult to which she had been subjected.

"I saw some one walking alongside you, and thought it wasn't by your wish, but couldn't tell, you see, though I ought to have known better. But the impudent fellow shall rue it, that he shall. I'll serve him as I would a conger!" exclaimed Jacob. "Let me be after him now—I'll catch him before he has got far, and I'll warrant he shall never speak to you again."

"Oh, no, no! pray do not, Jacob," said May, leaning on his arm to support herself. She was more agitated than she could have supposed. "Let him alone, whoever he is, though I suspect from what he said that he is a son of Miles Gaffin. It will be only necessary, I hope, to warn him not to behave again as he has done; and as I shall tell Miss Pemberton, she will probably speak to him, and that will be sufficient."

"If the audacious young scoundrel is Miles Gaffin's son, and he is like his father, he will care neither what Miss Pemberton nor any other lady says to him," exclaimed Jacob, doubling his fist, while his eye assumed a fierce expression it seldom wore. "He will care what this says to him though, and I'll make it speak in a way he won't like, that I will. But don't you be afraid, there is no harm will come of it. How he should have dared to speak to you is more than I can tell; but I will find out if he has a tongue to answer me, and it will be the last time he'll try it."

Had young Gaffin heard Jacob, and seen his brawny arm and huge fist, he would have had no inclination to fall in with him; but feeling that it would be wise not to encounter the sturdy protector to whom May had appealed, he had, after pursuing her a few steps, leaped over a gate and run into a wood, which concealed him from sight. It is possible that, from his place of concealment, he might have observed May leaning on Jacob's arm as they proceeded towards Downside.

"Thank you, Jacob, for your kindly succour," she said when they reached the door. "You will come in and see the ladies, for they will wish to thank you as I do."

"Oh, May, you don't fancy that there is any need of thanking me—no, not even if I had saved your life, for that would have made me happier than I can tell you," answered Jacob, with a half reproachful look. "As to that villain, I will find him out, and then I'll come and tell the ladies how I have served him."

"I must again entreat you not to use any violence," said May. "It will be quite sufficient if you can learn who he is, that I may be protected from his insults, but for no other reason do I even wish to ascertain his name."

While they were speaking, Miss Jane, who had heard their voices, came out, and May hurriedly told her what had occurred.

"May has spoken very properly to you, Jacob," she said. "Do no more than she has advised."

Jacob's countenance assumed a more dogged look than May had ever seen it wear, and, unwilling to receive more of Miss Jane's stem exhortations, or May's milder entreaties, he wished them good evening, and casting a look expressive of his devotion at May, hurried away.

As May was able to identify the youth who had spoken to her with the young man who had appeared at church on the previous Sunday, Miss Jane, with her usual sagacity, ascertained that he was staying at the Texford Arms, and that Miles Gaffin, the miller had met him on his arrival. It was supposed that he was the eldest son of that person.

"I fear there will be but little use complaining to the father," observed Miss Jane; "but it will be more prudent, my dear May, for you to confine your walks to the grounds till he has left the place, unless you accompany Mary or me. Jacob will undoubtedly let his parents know what has occurred, and we shall, probably have the dame up here to make enquiries. I will then tell her not to expect a visit from you till you are no longer likely to be subjected to the same annoyance."

May agreed to the wisdom of this proposal; indeed she would have been very unwilling to venture beyond the grounds by herself.

Chapter Twenty One
The Smuggler's Vault

The appearance of young Gaffin at Hurlston must be accounted for.

The old mill on the cliff, which belonged to Sir Reginald Castleton, was in a somewhat decayed condition, and had long been unoccupied, when a short time before the period at which our story commences, a stranger, calling himself Miles Gaffin, a miller by trade, called on Mr Groocock, and offered to take it. As he was ready to give a better rent than the steward expected to receive, he was glad to let it.

Miles Gaffin had occupied the mill for about a year, when, leaving it in charge of his man, he disappeared for a time and returned with a wife and three boys, whom he placed in a neat cottage at some little distance from the mill. His wife was a foreigner, of dark complexion, who spoke no English, a care-worn, spirit-broken woman, it was said.

She had little or no intercourse with her neighbours, who were unable to find out anything about her; indeed, either by her husband's order or her own wish, she never admitted any of them within her doors.

Some time after Miles Gaffin had been established at the mill, a lugger appeared off the coast, on board which he was seen to go. He had previously declared to Mr Groocock, notwithstanding his sunburnt countenance and undoubted sailor-like look, that he knew nothing of nautical affairs.

Mr Groocock began to suspect that he had been deceived in the matter on finding that Gaffin had sailed away in the lugger, and did not return for many weeks.

He confessed with a laugh when he next met the steward that he was really fond of the sea, and that whenever his business would allow him, he proposed taking a trip to indulge his fancy. He went so far even to invite Mr Groocock to accompany him, his offer, however, as may be supposed, being declined.

On one side of the mill the ground sloped rapidly down for twenty feet or more, and here a house was erected, the roof of which reached scarcely higher than the basement of the mill itself, so that the arms on which the sails were stretched could pass freely over it. This building had been in even a more dilapidated condition than the mill itself. The lower portion was used as a stable, where the miller kept his horse, the upper contained two rooms. Miles Gaffin had partially repaired the house, and had had the two rooms fitted up as sleeping apartments, that he might, as he said, put up any guest whom he could not accommodate in his own house. From the time he had taken possession of it he had, however, admitted none of his neighbours, though it was rumoured that strange men who had landed from the suspicious lugger had been observed entering the house, and sometimes leaving it, either on foot or on horseback, and making their way inland; lights also had been seen at all hours of the night when certainly the mill itself was not at work. It was remarked, too, by several of the fishermen in the neighbourhood, that the stranger had been carrying on some work or other either inside the house or below the mill, as they had observed a large quantity of earth which had been thrown down over the cliff, and though part of it had been washed away by the spring tides, it still went on increasing. When one of them made an observation to him on the subject, he replied promptly that he had heard a noise one night, and had no doubt that part of the cliff had given way. However, considering the risk there was, should such have been the case, of his mill being carried down bodily to the beach, he took the matter very coolly.

From time to time a still larger quantity of earth was observed, and it was whispered by one or two of his more sagacious neighbours that Miles Gaffin must be excavating a vault beneath his mill, possibly for the purpose of forming a granary in which to store corn purchased by him when prices were low. Why, however, he had not employed any of the labourers in the neighbourhood, or why he should have the work carried on in secret, no one could determine. Still the idea prevailed that a vault of some sort had been formed; but after a time the matter was forgotten. No one, indeed, had much fancy for asking the miller inquisitive questions, as he generally gave such replies as to make people wish that they had not put them. He was, indeed, looked upon as a morose, haughty man, who, considering himself superior to the other inhabitants of the village, was not inclined to allow any familiarity. He had never been known to seek for custom. He had brought a man with him to work the mill who was even more surly and morose than his master. Poor Dusty Dick, as he was called, was deaf and dumb, so that he could only express his feelings by his looks, and they were unprepossessing in the extreme. When corn was brought he ground it and returned the proper quantity of flour on receiving payment, though he would never give it up without that.

The miller wished it to be understood that he ground his neighbour's corn as a favour, and that his chief profits arose from turning into flour the wheat which came by sea on board the lugger. This statement was borne out by the large number of sacks which her crew were frequently seen landing. Waggons from a distance also frequently arrived, and being loaded with flour, were sent off again to the places from whence they came. The miller's business, however, it was evident, was not a steady one; sometimes for weeks together the long arms of the mill were only seen working for a few hours now and then, and at others the miller and his companions were as busy as bees, while the sails went spinning round at a great rate, as if trying to make amends for lost time.

Miles Gaffin continued to make frequent voyages in the lugger, of which he was generally supposed to be the owner. Sometimes he was several months together absent. When he came back he was so busy at the mill that he was seldom seen at the cottage where his family resided.

As soon as his boys were old enough he sent them away to school. When they came back for their holidays they were noted chiefly for being the most noisy, wild, and worst mannered lads in the place, especially held in dread by Miss Pemberton, who had frequently rebuked them when she saw them playing games on a Sunday in the village, and had received rude answers in return. The youngest was, notwithstanding, a fine, manly looking boy, and the only one ever seen in his father's company.

On one occasion Gaffin had taken him on board the lugger, but the lad had not returned, and it was said that he had been knocked overboard in a gale of wind, and drowned.

On Gaffin's return after this event, his wife, as it was supposed, on his suddenly communicating the boy's death, became ill. A doctor was sent for, but the stroke had gone too far home for human cure, and in a short time the hapless woman breathed her last.

On this Miles sent back his sons to school, and from that time, greatly to the relief of Miss Pemberton, they did not make their appearance in the village. He gave up his cottage, and after that took up his abode, when at Hurlston, entirely at the mill-house.

A short time before the reappearance of his son at Hurlston, as just mentioned, he had himself, after a considerable absence, returned. He had been of late unsuccessful in his undertakings, whatever they were, and even Dusty Dick, as he observed his master's countenance, thought it prudent, as much as possible, to keep out of his way.

Several strangers had come with him on board the lugger, and had taken possession of one of the rooms in the mill-house, while he occupied the other. They were personages unaccustomed apparently to soft beds or luxuries of any sort, so that they were perfectly at home in the roughly furnished room; and when they wished to sleep they found, when wrapped in their cloaks, all the comfort they desired.

Besides a couple of tressel beds, a long deal table, with benches on either side, were the chief articles of furniture.

The miller and his guests were seated round the table, on which stood the remnants of their supper. Their conversation related chiefly to an adventure in which they had lately been engaged, while political subjects were also discussed.

"Now, mates," said Gaffin, rising, "I have got business to attend to before I turn in, but I will leave you to put on your night-caps whenever you have a fancy."

"This is the only night-cap I ever put on," answered one of the men, pouring out half a tumbler of brandy. "It serves for night-cap and blanket too, and keeps a fellow from dreaming, an occupation I have no fancy for."

"You are not going to leave us yet, captain, are you? We have not reached the small hours of the night," said a second. "Another stoup of liquor, man; we are on firm ground, and no king's cruisers are in chase of us; you need not fear if it sends you to sleep, or makes you see double for once in a way."

Gaffin still, however, refused to sit down again, even though other urgent appeals were made to him, couched in much coarser language, interlarded with not a few strange oaths, which need not be repeated.

"I have told you, mates, that I have business to attend to. Amuse yourselves as you list, only don't get to brawling, or burn the house down in your revels; if you do, remember you will chance to burn with it before your time comes."

The smuggler captain, for such he appeared to be considered by his ruffianly companions, without again speaking left the room.

He repaired at once to his own chamber, and sitting down at a table, on which a lamp burned, he opened a desk, took a huge pocket-book from his coat, and began to examine several documents which it contained.

"I must raise the wind by fair means or foul to satisfy my fellows, as well as to make another venture before I cry die. Unless that is as unsuccessful as the last, I shall soon redeem my fortunes."

He sat for some time ruminating, now and then turning to his papers, and casting up accounts. Suddenly a thought occurred to him.

"How came I so long to forget the chest I got only off the wreck from which old Halliburt saved the little girl?" he muttered. "Though I took out not a few valuables, there were all sorts of things at the bottom of the chest, which, now I think of it, I never turned over. I will have a look at them this very night. Even a few gold pieces would be welcome, and it was evidently the treasure chest of some Indian nabob or other, his ill-gotten gains from the wretched natives he had fleeced and cheated."

He went to a chest of drawers in which he found a key.

"This must be it," he said, "by its foreign make."

Taking the lamp he left the chamber, and descended the stairs. The sound of boisterous revelry proceeded from the room where his guests were assembled.

"The drunken brutes are not likely to disturb me," he growled out, "and Dick is fast asleep in his loft."

Going across the stable, on removing a heap of straw he found a low door, which opened with a key he produced from his pocket. Going through it, he closed it carefully behind him.

He now stood in a low vaulted cavern, the earth supported by upright pieces of stout timber, with flat boards above them, which prevented the sandy soil in which it was cut from falling in. This was the excavation which he, with a few trusty companions, had formed many years ago.

Various sorts of goods were piled up in it—casks of spirits, bales of tobacco, silk, and several other articles. In a recess at the further end was a large chest.

After several attempts, for the lock from disuse was rusted, he opened it, and placing the lamp, resting on a piece of board, at one corner of the chest, he sat down on a cask by its side. On first glancing into it there appeared to be little or nothing within; but, on examining it further, he found that there was a large tray at the bottom, which apparently, on some former hurried examination, had escaped his notice. On lifting this a number of articles were revealed closely packed; they were mostly cases of various sizes. There was a jewelled-handled sword, a curious dagger, and a brace of richly ornamented pistols, two or three silver bowls and cups, and other articles which had probably been presented by native princes or other wealthy men to the owner of the chest. Several of the cases contained jewels evidently of great value, which, as they glittered in the light, the smuggler gazed at with intense satisfaction.

"And I have had all this wealth at my command and never knew of it," he muttered. "I guessed the girl must have had wealthy friends, and as this chest must have belonged to them, it would have been worth my while to get hold of her. As, however, they have never appeared, I have been saved the trouble and expense she would have been to me, and now this store comes just in the nick of time when I want it most. The only difficulty will be to dispose of all these things without raising suspicion as to how I came by them. Still, at the worst, I can but tell the truth should questions be asked, and prove that I got them from a wreck. At all events, there are Jews enough in London who will give me cash for them, though it may cost me not a little trouble to wring their proper value out of the close-fisted hypocrites."

Such were the thoughts which occupied the smuggler's mind as he examined in succession the articles which have been mentioned.

At last he came to another case or writing-desk, which was locked.

"I may as well overhaul the whole at once," he thought. "I must get this opened somehow."

A sailor's strong knife was the only implement at hand. He broke off a portion of the blade in making the attempt. At length he succeeded, though he injured the case in the operation. Placing the desk on his knees, he examined the contents, which consisted of a number of papers, title-deeds, official documents in oriental characters, and other papers apparently of value, together with several bills of exchange for a large amount, and rolls of gold coin.

"Ah, ah! these will save me from going to the Jews as yet," he exclaimed. "I will keep the jewels and other things till any future necessity compels me to part with them."

Having examined the coin to assure himself that he was not mistaken, he was glancing carelessly over the papers, when his eye fell on a name which attracted his attention. He eagerly read through the paper, and then looked for another and another. A deep frown settled on his brow, while a look of satisfaction kindled in his eye.

"If Satan himself had been asked to do my command, he could not please me better than this," he exclaimed. "I can now more amply than I had expected accomplish the design I have for years waited for. And while I enrich myself, I shall without risk humble those I have good reason to hate."

He was now lost in thought, now again glancing over the papers.

"They and the other things will be safer here, where they have lain so long, than in the house which may get burned down through some drunken spree by the fellows I have to harbour. But the coin may as well go into my pockets at once," he said to himself, as he put back the desk with its contents in the chest.

Having replaced the tray, he brought some straw from another part of the vault, and threw in a sufficient quantity to conceal it should by any chance the chest be opened by any one else.

"This will make it be supposed that there is nothing below," he said to himself, as he closed the lid and locked it.

At length leaving the vault, he returned to his chamber. His companions' revels had ceased, and now loud snores only came from the room where they were sleeping. He threw himself on his bed, but his busy brain was too hard at work to allow him to sleep.

Chapter Twenty Two
Miles Gaffin, Junior

Miles Gaffin lay on his bed turning over in his thoughts the information he had obtained, and considering how he could gain the most advantage from it. Returning to the table, he sat down to write. He was a man of decision. With him to propose was to act. "My son Myles," he wrote, for it was not his wont to use terms of endearment, "you are to come here at once. Tell Mr Crotch so from me; you need not say more to him. I want you to make your fortune by a way to which you will not object marrying a young and pretty wife. When you come you shall know more about the matter. Get a good rig out, so as to appear to advantage. Wait at the Texford Arms, where I will meet you, but don't come to the mill. From your father, Miles Gaffin."

The letter was speedily sealed and directed, and sent off the next morning to the post by one of his companions, who, by that time, was sufficiently sober to undertake the errand.

Gaffin's lugger, the *Lively*, lay at anchor off the mill. She had no contraband goods on board, so that a visit from the revenue officers need not be feared. He had previously intended going away in her, but he now was anxious to see his son before he sailed. His difficulty, in the meantime, was to dispose of his guests. They, however, as long as his supply of liquor and provisions lasted, would be content to remain where they were. He had no wish to bring his son among them, for bad as he himself was, he had, since the loss of his youngest boy, kept his other two children ignorant of his mode of life, though it was possible that the eldest might have suspected it from circumstances which he must have remembered in his younger days.

Gaffin waited with more patience than he generally exercised, till he calculated that a sufficient time had elapsed to allow of his son's arrival. He then walked down to the little inn in the village.

Just as he readied it, a post-chaise drove up to the door, out of which stepped a young man, whom he recognised as Miles, though he had not seen him for the last three or four years.

"You are my son, Miles, I conclude," said Gaffin.

"You are my father, I suppose," answered the young man in the same tone.

"You are right," said Gaffin. "Pay the post-boy, and let him bring your portmanteau into the house. I will order a room, and we will talk over the matter in hand."

The landlady having shown Gaffin into a room, young Miles did as he was directed, and followed him.

"Well, I want to know more about this business you sent for me about," said the young man, throwing himself into a chair. "I have done as you told me, and I hope you think I have got a good chance."

Gaffin surveyed his son for a moment.

"Yes, you will do, as far as that goes," he answered. "Now listen to me; I don't want to be asked questions, but do you trust to me and go ahead. There is a young girl whom you remember when you were a boy. She was found on board a wreck by Adam Halliburt, the fisherman, and brought up by him and his wife. Two old ladies here took a fancy to her, and have given her an education which has made her fit to be the wife of any gentleman in the land. She is pretty, too, and everything a young fellow could wish for. I happen to know to a certainty that she is a prize worth winning. When you have seen her, I am much mistaken if you would not give your eyes to have her, without asking any questions, and I am not going to answer them, if you do. I have your interests at heart, and wish to serve you in the matter."

"I have no doubt you have, but I should like to have a look at the girl before I decide," answered young Miles.

"That you can do to-morrow at church where she is sure to be, and when you have seen her don't let there be any shilly shallying; make up to her at once, most girls like to be won in an off-hand manner, and just do you go and tell her how you have seen her and fallen in love with her, and all that sort of thing. I daresay you have had some experience already."

"Pretty well in a sort of way," answered the young man in a conceited tone. "If I have got your word that she is worth winning, you will find I am not backward, and I hope, before long, to give a good report of progress."

Gaffin, satisfied that his son would do all he desired, charged him to keep himself quiet and not get into any scrapes while at Hurlston.

"People here will know you are my son, so just get a good name for yourself, and whatever they may think, they cannot say you are not a fit match for the old fisherman's foster-daughter," and Gaffin gave way to a laugh such as he rarely indulged in. "I will come down here again and have a talk with you after you have seen the girl. Now there is one thing more I have got to say, though I do not know to a cute fellow like you whether the caution is necessary; don't go and be blabbing to others of what you are about."

"I have been too long with Mr Crotch not to know how to keep a secret," answered the young man; "and I fancy I can manage this affair as I have done several others for my employer. I do not mean love affairs though, but matters of business in which I have given him perfect satisfaction, he tells me."

The conference over, Gaffin again charged his son to behave himself, and with no more show of affection than he had exhibited on the young man's arrival, took his departure and returned to the mill.

He kept within doors endeavouring to maintain order among his lawless associates. He wished not to be seen in company with his son, or to let it be supposed that he was instigating him in his siege on Maiden May's heart. From the accounts he had received from Mr Crotch of that young gentleman's talents, he believed that he could allow the matter to rest securely in his hands. If impudence was to carry the day young Miles would come off victorious, as he was known to possess no inconsiderable amount of that quality.

Gaffin had an excuse for remaining at the mill, as a larger quantity of grist than usual had been brought, and, for a wonder, its long arms with the sails stretched out went merrily round and round, giving Dusty Dick ample employment. The smuggler's crew grumbled at not having their dinner cooked in time. Dusty Dick had to take charge of the kitchen in addition to his other duties, and the mill required his attention. Gaffin had accordingly to serve out an additional supply of liquor to keep his guests quiet. He succeeded so effectually that, seasoned as they were, one and all were soon unable to quit the house, leaving him at liberty to attend to his own affairs.

"The beasts," he said, as he looked in upon the drunken ruffians, some sleeping with their heads on the table, others fallen under it, and others stretched their length on the beds, or at the side of the room. "They will stay there quiet enough till I want them, and no one is likely to come prying this way to disturb their slumbers."

Securely bolting the door of the house he passed by a back way into the mill, where, after giving some directions to Dusty Dick, he descended to the beach. A small boat lay there which he was able to launch by himself, and pulling off in her he went on board the lugger. He had left the most trusted part of his crew in her, including his mate, Tom Fidget, on whom he could always rely, not that Tom objected to get drunk "at proper times and seasons," as he observed, but duty first and pleasure afterwards was his maxim. His notions of duty were, to be sure, somewhat lax, according to the strict rules of morality, and his only idea of pleasure was a drunken spree on shore when he could leave the craft without risk of her suffering damage either from wind and weather, or the officers of the law. He was a bullet-headed fellow, with a figure almost as wide as long, small keen eyes, and a turned up nose scarcely perceptible beyond his puffed out copper-coloured cheeks.

Pipe in mouth he was taking his usual fisherman's walk, when the captain stepped on board.

"The craft shall not be kept here longer than can be helped, Tom, and you must be ready to start at a moment's notice," he observed. "I have some business to attend to first, however, so it won't be for a day or two, though that does not matter, as the weather promises to hold fine. Only keep the fellows sober, for I have as many drunken men on shore as I can manage, and it won't do to have all the hands in the same state. The next time it will be your turn to go on shore, and you may then drink as much liquor as you can hold, and enjoy yourself to your heart's content."

Gaffin having given these directions, returned on shore again. Several days passed and Gaffin again went in the evening to the Texford Arms to meet his hopeful son. The young gentleman was in, the landlady answered, in the room upstairs.

"Well, what progress have you made?" asked Gaffin, as he entered and found young Miles lounging lazily alone, a pipe in his mouth and a glass of brandy and water by his side.

"I thought I knew something about girls," was the answer, "and that I could come round her much as I have done with others, who wouldn't think themselves much beneath her, in our town, and I was not going to be stopped by any nonsense."

"I don't want to hear what you thought, but what you did," said his father.

"Well, you shall, if that's your wish," answered Miles. "I went to church on Sunday and had a good look at her, and thought she saw me with my eyes fixed on her from one end of the service to the other, but she hurried home among a lot of people, and I hadn't a chance of getting alongside to put in a word. For three whole days she never showed outside the gates, and I thought at last of going and calling on the old ladies with a story I had got up, but when I came to learn what sort of people they are, I found that would not do. Then I thought of another plan."

"I tell you I don't want your thought's," growled Gaffin. "What were your acts?"

"That's what I was coming to," answered Miles. "As ill-luck would have it I was off watch when she slipped out, and I discovered had gone down to old Halliburt's. You may be sure I kept a look-out for her on her return. I saw her coming along, and thought I had got the game in my own hands, but by—" and he swore a fearful oath, "the girl was altogether different to those I have had to do with. Beautiful, I believe you, she is, but as haughty as if she was a born princess; and just as I was going to show her what sort of a fellow I was, she slipped away and ran off towards a young chap and took his arm, just as if she had been accustomed to keep company with him. I watched them as they went by, and he seemed to be looking for me in no very friendly mood, for I saw him double his fists, and he was not the sort of fellow I wished to come to close quarters with, or I would have gone up to him and asked what he meant by carrying off the girl I was talking to."

"The long and short of it," said Gaffin, as soon as he could master his anger, "is that you frightened the young lady, and got a rebuff which you might have expected. But as for the young fellow, I know who he is, and he won't interfere with you. Just do you go on and persevere, and if you do not succeed we must try other means. Marry the girl I am determined you shall, whether she likes it or not, and I can depend upon you. Remember I am not one to have my plans thwarted, least of all by my own son."

"I will not thwart them, you may trust me for that," answered Miles. "The girl is about as pretty as I ever set eyes on, and I am obliged to you for putting me up to the matter. But, I say, I should like to know more about her. You led me to suppose that there is some secret you had got hold of—what is it?"

"That's nothing to you at present. Your business is to win the girl, whether she is a fisherman's or a lord's daughter. She was brought up as the Halliburt's child, though I suppose she knows that she is not, yet she has no reason to think much of herself, except on account of her good looks, and those, from what I have heard of the old ladies she lives with, they would have taught her not to pride herself on."

Gaffin's last directions to his son were to keep himself quiet for a time, and to wait his opportunity for again meeting May under more favourable circumstances.

"I will write to Crotch and tell him that a matter of importance keeps you from returning just yet, and if good luck attends us you may not see his face again. I will not say that though, eh?" and Gaffin indulged in a chuckle, the nearest approach he ever made to a laugh.

Chapter Twenty Three
Caught in a Thunderstorm

Harry's ship had been paid off, and Headland having received his promotion, the two friends started in a post-chaise and four for London. It would have been unbecoming for two naval officers, with their pockets full of prize money, to travel in a less dignified way. The last time Harry had come that road it had been on the top of a coach.

Captain Headland had been very little on shore in England, and everything was new to him and full of interest. The country girls at the cottage doors struck him especially.

"I had no idea English women were so pretty," he observed.

Harry laughed.

"I thought your philosophy would soon be capsized. If you think them attractive, I suspect that you will find the girls of higher rank enchanting."

They remained in town to attend a levee, when Captain Headland was presented on his promotion, and Harry on his return from foreign service. Headland was in no hurry to leave London, for never having before been in the big city, he found so much to interest him; but Harry was anxious to be at home. Julia had written him word that they hoped to have a number of visitors, and intended to give a fête in honour of his return.

They posted to Texford, agreeing that a pair of horses would take them there as fast as four, which their dignity no longer required.

Headland received a warm welcome from Sir Ralph and Lady Castleton as their son's friend, and Julia extended her hand as if she had known him all her life. He thought her a very charming girl, and wondered that Harry had never spoken to him of her beauty. Her frankness soon set him at his ease. He had mixed but little in ladies' society, and at first felt awkward. Algernon was kind and polite, but was somewhat cold and stiff in his manner, like his father, and Headland suspected that he should never be very intimate with him.

Next morning Julia volunteered to show several of the guests who had lately arrived, including Captain Headland, over the grounds. Algernon had in the meantime asked Harry to ride with him, and invited their guest to join them.

"Miss Castleton has engaged me to be one of the walking party, and as I am no great horseman you will, I hope, excuse me."

Harry begged that he would do as he had promised. He wished to ride with Algernon to enjoy some private conversation. He had been struck by his brother's changed appearance. He had a short teasing cough, of which, however, he made light, observing that it generally disappeared with the warm weather, though it annoyed him a little longer that year.

The brothers had much to talk about after their long separation. Harry enquired if any authentic account of their uncle's death had been received. Algernon replied that though their father and Mr Shallard had made every possible enquiry, the only fact they had learned was that the ship he had sailed in had never been heard of, and that there was no doubt she had gone down in a hurricane which had occurred during the time she must have been at sea.

"It would be a trying state of things if our uncle were after all to make his appearance and claim the title and property," observed Algernon. "I suspect that our father would be very unwilling to give them up, and possession is nine-tenths of the law."

"Surely he would not hesitate if convinced of our uncle's identity," said Harry, "and would be thankful to welcome his brother back to life."

"He is so firmly convinced of his death that it would be difficult to persuade him to the contrary," replied Algernon. "For my own part I am not ambitious of becoming a baronet, and as far as I am individually concerned I should be ready to welcome with sincerity our long lost uncle."

"So should I," cried Harry warmly, "and surely our father with his political interest can, if he chooses, obtain a baronetcy for himself."

"He would prefer exerting that influence in gaining a higher rank," observed Algernon with a sigh. "He wished me to be in parliament, but he only a few days ago, greatly to my relief, acknowledged that he was afraid my health for the present would not enable me to stand the wear and tear I should have to undergo in the 'house.' I am afraid that it has greatly disappointed him. He probably will wish you to take the place he intended for me."

Harry laughed heartily.

"I in parliament," he exclaimed, "I should indeed feel like a fish out of water. I wish to stick to the service, and hope to get my flag some day."

"But there are naval men in parliament, and you may do that notwithstanding," said Algernon.

"I do not wish to disobey him, but the very thoughts of the life I should have to lead, talking and debating, or worse, listening to long debates in the close atmosphere of the House of Commons, would make me miserable. So, pray, if he suggests such a thing to you, tell him you are sure that I should not like it, and beg him to let me off."

Algernon promised to do as his brother wished.

They had taken the way to the downs to the south of Hurlston.

Harry enquired for their cousins, the Miss Pembertons. On hearing that they were still living there he proposed paying them a visit.

"To tell you the truth, I have not called since we came to Texford," answered Algernon. "You know that they have peculiar notions. Our father, looking upon them as puritanical dissenters, has no wish to have them at the house. I have not seen the old ladies for some years. I remember that they did not make a very favourable impression on me when I met them last."

"I suppose I may call on them," said Harry. "They were kind to me when I was a boy, and I liked cousin Mary, as we called her."

"Yes, there can be no objection to your going," answered Algernon. "They will not consider it necessary to return your visit, and will look upon it as a kindness."

The young men had been riding on further than they had intended, and being engaged in conversation while passing along lanes with high hedges on either side, they had not observed a storm gathering in the sky. Emerging from the lanes Harry invited his brother to take a gallop across the wide extended downs spread out before them, and thus they did not observe till they turned the thunder clouds sweeping up rapidly towards them.

"We shall get wet jackets, I suspect, before we reach home," observed Harry.

"I hope not," answered his brother, "for I have been especially charged to avoid the damp and cold, and I feel somewhat heated. I wish there was some place where we could get shelter."

"I am very sorry that I led you on, for I see no shed or cottage anywhere," said Harry, gazing round; "and I am afraid we shall have the rain down upon us before many minutes. Our shortest way to the nearest house at Hurlston will, I suspect, be across the downs. Come along, there is no time to spare."

They put their horses into a gallop. The downs though at a distance appearing to be level, were intercepted by several deep ravines, and the young men had not gone far before they were compelled to turn inland by coming to one of the most rugged and wild of these ravines, the side of which was too steep to allow them to ride down it.

A little further Harry observed a place which he thought they could descend without difficulty, and thus save some distance. As he reached the bottom, followed by Algernon, he saw nestling under a rock on one side a hut built party of rough stones, and partly of the planks of some wreck cast on shore. At the same moment a bright flash of lightning darted from the clouds, followed by a crashing peal of thunder, when immediately down came the rain.

"We may, at all events, find shelter in yonder hut," said Harry, "though it seems scarcely large enough to admit our horses, but I will hold them while you go inside."

They made their way down the ravine, when Algernon dismounting pushed open the door and ran in, while Harry leading the horses followed him.

At the further end of the hut a woman was seated on a stool before the wood fire blazing on the hearth, over which she bent, apparently engaged in watching the contents of an iron pot boiling on it.

"Who dares intrude unbidden into my mansion," she shrieked out in a wild unearthly tone, which made Algernon start back.

Her long grey hair hung down on either side of her colourless face, from which beamed forth a pair of wild eyes, glowing with the fire of madness. Her dress being of the same sombre hue as was everything in the hut, had as Algernon entered prevented him from observing her till she turned her face full upon him.

"SEE, THE HEAVENS FIGHT ON MY SIDE."

"SEE, THE HEAVENS FIGHT ON MY SIDE."

She rose as she spoke, confronting the two young men. "Who are you?" she repeated; "speak, or begone, and trouble me not."

"I beg your pardon for entering without leave," said Algernon; "but the rain is coming down so heavily that we should have been wet through in another minute, and there is no other shelter at hand."

"That's no answer to my question," she exclaimed. "What care I for rain or storm; let the lightning flash and the thunder roar, and do its worst. Go your way, I say, and leave me to my solitude."

"My brother would suffer should he get wet," said Harry, stepping in. "And I must beg you, my good lady, not to be annoyed if we remain till the storm is over; it will probably pass away in half an hour, and we beg not to interrupt you in what you are about."

"You are fair spoken, young sir, but you have not answered my question. Who are you, I ask again?"

"We are the sons of Sir Ralph Castleton, and we discovered your hut by chance, while looking for a place to obtain shelter from the rain."

"Spawn of the viper, how dare ye come hither to seek for shelter beneath my roof?" exclaimed the woman in a voice which made the young men start, so shrill and fierce did it sound, high above the roar of the thunder, the howling of the wind, and the pattering of the rain.

"A fit time ye have chosen to come and mock at me; but I have powers at my command to overwhelm you in a moment. See, the heavens fight on my side."

As she spoke a bright flash of lightning darted down the glen, which, with the crashing peal of thunder that followed, made the horses snort and plunge so violently, that Harry had no little difficulty in holding them, and was drawn out from the doorway in which he had been standing.

"And you deem yourself the heir of Texford," she continued in the same tone, gazing with her wild eyes intently fixed on Algernon. "Though you rejoice in youth and wealth, I see death stamped on your brow; and before many months have passed away, instead of dwelling in your proud and lordly hall, you will have become a tenant of the silent tomb. I can command the elements, and can read the future. It was I who summoned this storm to drive you hither that you might hear your fate, that fate which the stars last night revealed to me. Ah! ah! ah! you now wish that you had passed by instead of seeking shelter beneath my roof; but your destiny drove you hither, and against that you fight in vain."

Algernon feeling that it would be wiser not to reply to the wild ravings of the strange creature looked anxiously out of the hut, strongly inclined, in spite of the rain, to make his escape. Harry, who, having been engaged with the horses, had not heard what she first said, now brought them back again, and stood once more beneath the roof of the hut.

"At all events now we are here, my good woman, I hope you will not object to our remaining till the storm is over," he said, hoping that by speaking in a quiet tone he might calm her temper.

"I invited you not to come, I welcomed you not when you did come, and my curses will follow you when you go," she shrieked out.

"We really had better not stay," said Algernon to Harry. "I cannot understand what has irritated the poor woman, and I fear nothing we can say will have the effect of soothing her."

"I cannot consent to your going out and getting wet through," said Harry; "so notwithstanding what she says we must stay till the rain has ceased."

"My good woman, I really think you are mistaken with regard to us," said Harry, turning to the mad woman. "When we saw your cottage we were not aware that it was inhabited, and as we have taken up your time in interrupting you in what you were about, we shall be glad if you will accept a present as a recompense;" and Harry, giving the reins to Algernon to hold, took out half-a-guinea, and offered it to their hostess.

"You cannot bribe me to reverse the orders of fate," she shrieked out, snatching the coin from his hand and throwing it into the fire, and uttering a piercing shriek she frantically waved about her arms, now high above her head, now pointing at them with threatening gestures, till Algernon declared that he could stand it no longer. In vain Harry entreated him to remain till the rain had altogether ceased.

The old woman shouted and shrieked louder and louder, encouraged possibly by observing the effect her behaviour had produced on the eldest of the brothers. At last the rain moderating, Algernon rushed out of the hut.

"This is not to be endured," he exclaimed, as he mounted his horse.

Harry followed his example, and they rode up the glen as fast as the rugged nature of the road would allow them, the wild shrieks and cries of Mad Sal, as she watched them from the door of her hut, sounding in their ears till they gained the open downs.

"I am glad we are out of hearing of that dreadful old creature," said Algernon, as they galloped along. "I hope she will not prove a true prophetess."

"I don't believe in wizards or witches," answered Harry, "although sometimes by chance their predictions may appear to be fulfilled; and we should be foolish if we allowed the nonsense she talked to weigh on our spirits. I am very sure that the thread of our lives will not be cut shorter from anything she can do, and she certainly will not make me the less willing to go afloat, and fight as readily as I should have done had we not fallen in with her. She has evidently some dislike to the name of Castleton, and hearing us mention it, vented her feelings by trying to frighten us."

"Poor woman, she is perfectly mad. I am curious to learn who she is," observed Algernon. "Perhaps Groocock or some of the Hurlston people may know."

Although the rain had moderated, the young men were nearly wet through before they had made their way across the down; and instead of stopping at Hurlston, as they had intended, they rode on to Texford.

In spite of the exercise he had taken, Algernon complained of the cold, and Harry observed that he shivered several times. As he, however, hurried to his room immediately on his arrival, and changed his wet things, his brother hoped he would not suffer.

Chapter Twenty Four
Julia Castleton

The party whom Miss Castleton had offered to escort round the — grounds consisted of several ladies and gentlemen, most of them young, with the exception of an old military officer, General Sampson, who, however, was as active and gallant as the youngest, and a matronly dame, Mrs Appleton, who went with the idea that a chaperone would be required on the occasion.

As is not unfrequently the case under similar circumstances, the party before long separated. The general and Mrs Appleton had sat down to rest in a summer-house, while the rest of the party went on. The chaperone, on discovering that they had got out of sight, started up, and was hurrying forward to overtake them, when her bonnet, adorned with huge bows, caught in a low hanging bough, and, to her horror, before she could stop her progress, not only was it dragged off, but so was her cap, and the wig she wore beneath. The general doing his utmost to maintain his gravity hastened up to her assistance. At the same moment three of the young ladies, with two of the gentlemen who had accompanied them, having turned back appeared in sight, and hearing her cries hastened towards her. The general, who was short of stature, though of no small width, had, in the meantime, been in vain attempting to unhook the bows from the branch.

"Let me, general, let me," exclaimed poor Mrs Appleton, who was tall and thin; and she made an effort to extricate her bonnet.

While she was thus employed, leaving her bare head exposed, her companions reached the spot, trying in vain to stifle their laughter.

By the exertions of a tall gentleman of the party, her bonnet was at length set free, and with the assistance of the young ladies was, with the wig and cap, replaced on her head.

"Well, my dears, the same accident might have happened to any one of you," she remarked, with a comical expression, which showed that she was less put out than most people would have been by the occurrence, "though to be sure, as you have only your natural hair beneath your bonnets, that,

I conclude, would have stuck faster to your head than mine did, which, as you have discovered, is for convenience sake removable at pleasure."

Captain Headland, on leaving the house, wishing to be polite to all, had addressed himself to three or four of the young ladies in succession, but either finding the conversation uninteresting, or that he could not keep it up, had walked on by the side of Julia. He soon found that his tongue before tied, became perfectly free. She had so many questions to ask about Harry, and the various adventures they had gone through together, that he soon found he had plenty to say. He was led on to speak of himself, of the battles in which they both had taken a part. While he gave her rapid and brilliant accounts of them, he found her often looking up with her bright eyes fixed on his countenance. So interested did she become, that she forgot that she had undertaken to act as guide to the rest of the party. Not till they had walked on a considerable distance, and had reached the opposite side of the lake, did she and the young officer discover that they were not followed.

"Our friends cannot be far behind us," she said. "We ought to go back, and we shall soon meet them. I promised to guide them through the labyrinth which leads to Fair Rosamond's Bower, as the summer-house on the top of the mound overlooking the lake is called, and no one will otherwise be able to find it."

"I was scarcely observing where we were going. What a beautiful view of the lake we have from hence," remarked Headland, as they turned.

"Yes, this is one of the most beautiful; but there are several other lovely points on the shores, especially at the further end," said Julia. "I intended to have conducted our friends to them. This lake was, I believe, in our great grandfather's time but little more than a wild-fowl decoy, with almost bare shores. He had trees planted on the banks, and the lagoon deepened and considerably enlarged, while, with the earth and gravel thrown out, mounds were raised which give the picturesque variety you observe to the banks. We have two boats on the lake; but do you not think the model of a man-of-war floating on the surface would add to the picture?"

Captain Headland naturally thought so, and said he should be happy to assist Harry in getting one built and rigged.

"Oh, I am sure mamma would like it," said Julia, "and papa, though he might not take much interest in the matter, would not object. Till Harry went to sea, we had no naval men in the family, and neither Sir Reginald nor his predecessor, our great grandfather, took any interest in nautical affairs, as they were fox-hunters and sportsmen."

Captain Headland said he would talk to Harry on the subject, and see what they could do.

They continued walking on, but none of their friends appeared, they having, as it happened, turned away from the lake in a totally opposite direction. Julia thought that they might have gone round to the side she had proposed visiting. She therefore led her companion in that direction.

Their conversation continued as animated as before. Headland, who had a real taste for the beauties of nature, admired the views which the lake exhibited; the wooded islands, the green points, the drooping trees and weeping willows hanging over the waters, their forms reflected on its surface; stately swans with arched necks which glided by leading their troops of cygnets. The only sounds heard were the splash of the fish as they leaped out of their watery home, the various notes of birds, and the subdued hum of insects flitting in the sunshine, where here and there an opening in the foliage allowed it to penetrate into the otherwise shady walk.

They at length reached the end of the lake; it was the furthest point almost in the grounds from the house.

Just then the storm which had overtaken Algernon and Harry burst above Texford. It had come on so suddenly that not till a loud peal of thunder crashed almost above their heads were they aware of its approach.

"I fear the rain will come down before we can reach the house, Miss Castleton," observed Captain Headland. "If there is a boat near at hand I might row you across the lake, which would both shorten the distance and save you the fatigue of walking."

"One of the boats is generally kept a little further on, and if you think we can go faster by water, I shall be much obliged to you."

Before the boat was reached heavy drops of rain began to fall.

"There is a summer-house close at hand overlooking the lake," said Julia, and led her companion to it.

They had scarcely got under shelter when the rain descended in torrents.

Julia and Captain Headland naturally renewed the interesting conversation in which they had before been engaged, not aware how time went by. Every minute the young officer was in Julia's society, forgetting his previous resolutions, he admired her more and more.

It was so evident that she had unintentionally separated from their companions that he did not for one moment think her forward or designing. With her delicate and refined beauty he had been struck from the first, and was now still more pleased with her animated and intelligent conversation.

"I wonder Harry did not speak more to me about her," he thought, "though perhaps he might have fancied had he praised her I might have supposed he wished to offer her as an attraction to me to visit Texford. However, I am convinced that such a thought never entered his mind."

Although the rain at length ceased, the walks were so wet that Julia confessed she should prefer crossing the lake to returning home by land.

At the other end of the lake an artificial stream of sufficient depth for the boat, known as the Serpentine, meandered through the grounds and reached almost to the house. There were several rustic bridges which crossed it here and there, but they were of sufficient height to allow the boat to pass under them. Julia having told Headland where he could find the boat while she remained in the summer-house, he went to fetch it. As it was kept under a shed it was perfectly dry. He handed her into it, and pushing off from the bank they commenced their voyage.

The sun again shone forth brightly, and the air felt fresh and pure after the storm. For some distance he rowed close to the shore where a number of water-lilies floated on the surface. He had seldom seen such beautiful flowers. He described, however, the marine gardens in the Eastern seas visible through the clear water for an immense depth below the surface.

"Have you been much in the East?" asked Julia.

"I believe I was born there," he answered, forgetting his intention of not speaking of himself. "Indeed my early days were at all events passed in that part of the world. I have been at sea the greater portion of my life, and have comparatively but little knowledge of the shore or the dwellers on it. I had no notion that there were such beautiful places as this appears to me in England. I conclude there are not many such."

"Oh, yes," said Julia. "There are many far more magnificent and extensive, though I might not admire them more than this, and certainly should not love them so much. Though we have not been here very long, I spent months when I was a girl with our uncle Sir Reginald, and became greatly attached to the place. We did not know at the time that we should ever come to live here, as papa's elder brother was then alive. Though he has not since been heard of he is supposed to be dead, and papa consequently came into possession of the title and estates."

Julia said this not feeling that there was any necessity for keeping the matter a secret from their guest indeed she would not have been surprised had he replied that her brother had told him of the circumstances.

Headland rowed slowly over the calm water. He was in no hurry to finish the voyage, and the young lady seemed to enjoy the scenery. Now and then he stopped and let the boat float quietly on, that they might admire some fresh point of view.

"Do you sketch, Captain Headland?" asked Julia.

He replied that he had had no opportunity of taking lessons in his younger days, except now and then from a mess-mate who had enjoyed the advantage on shore, though he was accustomed to draw ships and to sketch the outlines of the coasts that he might recognise them on subsequent visits, but that now, with the probability of remaining on shore, he should be glad to study the art.

"I should like to come out on the lake and make some sketches," said Julia. "I have hitherto had no one to row the boat, and Algernon can seldom be tempted on the water; indeed, he is not much of an oarsman."

Captain Headland expressed the pleasure it would give him to be of service in that capacity, and Julia said she should be glad to take advantage of his offer.

At length they reached the end of the lake and entered the Serpentine. There was just room to row the boat along between the grassy banks. Here and there the trees overhung the channel, and sometimes they had to bend down to avoid the branches.

They had nearly reached the end where there were some stone steps with a gravel walk above them, leading directly to the house, and a rustic bridge spanning the stream.

The old general who had taken post on the bridge, and had been for some time watching their approach, hailed them.

"Hilloa! gallant son of Neptune, I congratulate you on discovering our missing Ariadne who was to have been our guide through the labyrinthine walks of Texford. Fortunately we missed our way, and found ourselves close to the house just as the storm came on."

"I must apologise, General Sampson, for leaving you and our other friends; but we had got to some distance before we discovered that you were not following," said Julia, somewhat annoyed at the general's remarks.

"The truth is, my dear young lady, it is we who have to apologise to you for not keeping pace with your fairy-like movements, and fearing that Sir Ralph and Lady Castleton might justly blame me as the senior of the party for deserting you, I hurried out as soon as the rain ceased in the hopes of finding you before you reached the house, to entreat you to offer some excuse for my conduct. But I suspect the captain is chiefly to blame, and if you will enter into a compact with me we will sacrifice him."

Won from the Waves | 143

"I am ready to be the victim should Miss Castleton consider any excuse necessary," said Captain Headland, as he handed Julia out of the boat, while the old general stood on the top of the steps.

They walked together to the house, the latter talking in the same style as before. Julia ran in, glad to escape him.

"You will be a lucky dog, captain, if you succeed in securing so fair a prize," whispered the general, giving the young officer a not very gentle dig in the ribs. "I have entertained some thoughts in that direction myself, but I see that a soldier has no chance with a naval man as his rival."

"Really, general, you allow your imagination to go too fast. I am a comparative stranger to Miss Castleton, and have no merit which could justify me in hoping—"

"Of course, of course, my young friend we must all feel our personal want of merit when a lady is concerned. Nevertheless she may possibly regard you in a more favourable light than you suppose, from the reports we have heard of your gallant deeds."

Chapter Twenty Five
May's Guardians

Dame Halliburt made her appearance at Downside early the next morning to enquire after May. Miss Pemberton, who had expected the good woman, begged her to step into her dispensary, as she called the small room in which she received her poorer visitors, that they might talk over the matter.

The dame said that she should have come up the previous evening, but that Jacob had not returned till late at night, when he told her what had happened. He had been on the look-out for young Gaffin to bring him to account for his conduct, but had been unable to find him.

"I am sorry for that," said Miss Jane. "I charged him to use no violence towards the young man."

"Lord bless you, marm," answered the dame, "our Jacob is as gentle as a lamb. I don't think he could use violence towards any man, though to be sure if he had fallen in with that impudent young chap he would have given him a pretty sound drubbing."

"I fear that your son's style of drubbing would be a pretty strong act of violence," observed Miss Jane. "Judging from the appearance of his arm, it possesses sufficient strength to fell an ox, and one blow from it might injure the youth for life."

"I don't doubt but that our Jacob could hit pretty hard if his spirit was up," observed the dame with a smile of maternal pride. "I cannot say, however, but what I am glad he didn't find young Gaffin."

"One thing is certain, we must not let our May run the chance of being spoken to again by this young fellow. If he is stopping at the inn he probably will not remain long in the place, and she will soon be able to go to and fro from your house as usual. Indeed, I hope from the proper way she treated him that he will not again make the attempt to speak to her."

"Fellows of his sort are not so easily put down as you may suppose, Miss Jane, and if he is the miller's son, he may be as audacious as he is impudent," observed the dame.

"Whatever he is, we will take good care that he has no opportunity of exhibiting his audacity," said Miss Pemberton; "and I beg that you will charge your son to take no further notice of the affair. If your husband could see the young man and warn him of the consequences of his conduct, he might induce him to behave properly in future. Now you will like to see May."

Miss Jane went out, and sent May into the room.

The dame received her with a warm embrace, but as the subject of young Gaffin was a disagreeable one, she did not speak much about it.

"Have you told the ladies about the grand doings to take place at Texford?" asked the dame.

May confessed that she had forgotten all about it.

"Then while I am here I will just put in a word. A little change will do you good, and if I tell them I'll keep you by my side all the time, I don't think they will object."

"We will think about it," was Miss Jane's answer, when the dame told her. "I am not an admirer of fêtes and fantastic worldly doings such as I conclude will take place at Texford. I fear there is more harm done than pleasure obtained."

"The scene may amuse her, as she has seen nothing of the sort," observed Miss Mary. "Far be it from me to countenance even indirectly the follies of worldly people, but as this fête is intended to afford amusement to the tenantry and labourers, it must be kindly meant, and if May herself desires to accompany Dame Halliburt, I think that we ought not to deny her the amusement."

"Thank you," said May, simply. "I should like to go, very much."

The dame returned home satisfied that May was not likely to receive any further annoyance from young Gaffin, and well pleased that there would be no difficulty about her attending the fête.

Jacob arrived in the evening at Downside with a basket of shells. May could not help asking him whether he had seen young Gaffin, and again entreated him not to interfere.

"I have not seen him, but I know where he is," answered Jacob; "and I don't think he will show his nose outside the house without having me at his heels."

Every day before going off for the night's fishing in the *Nancy*, Jacob managed to find time to get up to Downside.

He would have been a bold man who would have ventured to encounter the young fisherman with any intention of annoying Maiden May. Honest love, when the object loved is to be benefited, wonderfully sharpens the wits. Jacob, who would never have thought of such a thing under other circumstances, had set a boy to watch the inn, and bring him word of Miles's movements. When he was away, the lad was to inform his mother.

Miles, either in obedience to his father's directions, or because he had found out that he was watched, kept himself a prisoner, and did not venture beyond the precincts of the garden at the back of the house, where he spent most of the day sauntering up and down, smoking his pipe, and forming plans for winning the young lady in spite of the obstacles in his way. Though unable to appreciate any higher qualities, he had been really struck by her beauty, and was as much in love as it was in his nature to be. He was thus perfectly ready to enter into any scheme which his father might propose for gaining her, either by fair means or foul.

"I would not hurt her feelings if I could help it," he said to himself; "but I am pretty sure I have a rival in that young fellow Halliburt. I guessed that when she took his arm and ran off from me. She knows well enough that he is not her brother, though they have been brought up together, and girls are generally apt to admire those big, sturdy-looking chaps who have done them a service, more than well-dressed, gentlemanly young men like myself," and Miles glanced approvingly on his new and fashionable costume. "If she still turns a cold eye upon me that worthy dad of mine must manage to get the young fisherman out of the way—it won't do to have him interfering—and with a clear stage I shall not have insuperable difficulties to overcome, I flatter myself."

Still Miles had to remain inactive some days longer. At last he received a note from his father telling him to go, if he pleased, to the fête at Texford, and simply state, if asked, that he was the son of a tenant, saying that he was spending a few days at Hurlston, and had come instead of his father, who was unable to attend. "I find that Dame Halliburt is going, and I have no doubt she will take her daughter, as she calls her, with her," he added. "You will thus have an opportunity of meeting the girl under more favourable circumstances than before, and if you mind your P's and Q's it will be your own fault if you do not work yourself into her good graces."

Miles received this communication with intense satisfaction. Having a thoroughly good opinion of himself, he had now little doubt that he should succeed in his enterprise.

Chapter Twenty Six
The Fête at Texford

No summer's day could be more bright and lovely than that on which the fête at Texford took place. Visitors of high and low degree—for it was to be a meeting of all classes—were seen at an early hour moving along the roads from every direction towards the park, some in carriages, some on horseback, others in light tilted waggons and carts, and no inconsiderable number on foot.

The distance between Hurlston and Texford was upwards of two miles by the road, but the inhabitants of the village could enjoy a pleasanter and much shorter path across the fields.

The dame arrived at Downside in good time to escort May. She to the last felt some hesitation, however, about going, as it was evident that Miss Jane was doubtful as to the propriety of the proceeding, but Miss Mary, with whom she had discussed the subject over and over again, always concluded with the remark that though it might be dangerous to trust a gay and a giddy girl in such a scene, their steady and sensible May was not likely in consequence to gain a taste for the frivolities of the world, and that, as she had never seen anything of the sort, she could not fail to be amused, while, from her unremitting attention to them, she certainly deserved a holiday. May, not to appear out of place while in company with the good fishwife, had dressed herself in a costume as much as possible like that which a well-to-do fisherman's daughter would wear; and although she had not intended to produce any such effect, her neat straw hat and cloak set her beauty off to even greater advantage.

Adam, who had with the dame's earnest persuasion consented to accompany her, waited outside. Jacob, strange to say, had declined accompanying his mother and May. He had work to attend to on board the *Nancy*, and had no fancy for jigging about with the girls of the village, while May did not intend to join in the revels. Jacob, indeed, felt that he should be out of place. He knew that it would not do to be seen standing near his mother and May all fête time, and he should take no pleasure in wandering about away from them.

May was perhaps relieved when she heard that Jacob was not coming. Although she regarded him with esteem for his honesty and bravery, and his devotion to her, she felt instinctively that the less he was in her society, the better for him.

"You will come home early," said Miss Jane, as she wished her good-bye; "and you will keep to your resolution in not mixing with the throng more than you can help."

"You must tell me all that takes place when you come back," said Miss Mary. "If you see Miss Castleton and her brothers, and you will scarcely fail to do so, I shall like to hear all about them. Julia must have grown into a tall young lady, and Harry and Algernon into full-grown men. I shall be interested in hearing what Harry is like especially; he was a great favourite of mine when a boy. He has now become a fine gallant officer. I wish I could let him know how much I should like to see him; for although Sir Ralph and Lady Castleton have been so inattentive, we should not, therefore, feel the less regard for their son, and I am sure he would not hesitate to come, if he remembered that we are here."

This was said in the presence of the dame.

"If I have a chance of speaking to Mr Harry, I will tell him," she said. "I will remind him how he saved our Maiden May from the bull, and maybe he will remember Adam and me, and come up and speak to us, as he won't have forgotten his trip in the *Nancy*, though he is not likely to wish to take another."

"Tell him, then, that we hope to see him," said Miss Mary.

The dame promised to deliver the message.

When the dame and her companions arrived at Texford, she remarked that the appearance of the place was totally changed. There stood the house, certainly, as usual, but the park looked like a huge fair. There were numerous booths and tents in all directions, and swings and roundabouts, targets for archery, courses marked off for running races, arrangements for the old game of quintain, for Sir Ralph was somewhat of an antiquarian, and wished to re-introduce it. There were three bands of music, the best stationed near the house, and the others at, a sufficient distance not to interfere with it. A band of Morris dancers had been arranged by Sir Ralph's desire, and there were a couple of jugglers who went about performing feats which greatly astonished the rustics. As May and her friends passed along the lake, they saw a number of boats which had been brought there from Morbury, that races and other aquatic sports might be indulged in. Indeed, everything had been prepared which could possibly be thought of for affording amusement to the assemblage.

The sports on the lake were to be, as the dame suspected, under the charge of Mr Harry and his naval friend, Captain Headland, who were, however, both too energetic not to take a part in everything that was going forward.

The guests of higher degree were already assembling on the broad steps or the gravel walk in front of the house, when the dame and May found themselves among the crowd of tenants and others on the lawn, who felt that it would be disrespectful until invited to approach the neighbourhood of their betters.

Mr Groocock was going about attending to the multifarious duties imposed on him. Though he was as active as ever, his task appeared to give him more trouble than pleasure.

"Glad to see you, dame, and Miss May and friend Adam," he said, as he once passed close to where they were standing.

"Thank you, Mr Groocock. It's a beautiful sight," observed the dame, in reply.

"Well enough," answered the steward, "but the work it imposes is more suited to young limbs, than to mine," and he passed on to give some directions.

The signal for the sports to begin was now given, and a large portion of the people collected were soon engaged according to their tastes—some dancing, some running races, others amusing themselves with the various games, and others witnessing the feats of the jugglers, or looking on at the pantomimic performances of the Morris dancers.

It required some exertion, however, of the directors of the fête to set the guests in motion, or to keep them entertained in the variety of ways which had been prepared for their amusement. Among the most active who were thus engaged were Harry Castleton and his friend Headland, it being more in accordance with Algernon's taste to devote himself to the guests of higher degree.

"I must go and get yonder crowd of rustics under weigh again," Harry observed to Headland, on seeing a number of people standing idle near one of the spots devoted to dancing.

Dame Halliburt and her companions had taken up a position not far off it, on a grassy mound under the shade of a tree, where, a little removed from the crowd, they could observe all that was going forward. Harry was passing by when he saw the dame, who had recognised him, following him with her eyes. It is possible that at the same time he may have caught sight of May's sweet countenance; at all events he stopped, and going up to the dame, said—

"I think I ought to know you."

"Yes, please you, Mr Harry; and maybe you remember the trip you took in the *Nancy* with my good man here."

"Ah, how fares it with you, my friend?" he said, shaking Adam by the hand. "I remember the trip right well."

"You have pretty nigh grown out of remembrance, but I am right glad to see you, Mr Harry," answered Adam.

"Maybe you recollect, sir, saving our Maiden May from a wild bull?" said the dame, looking towards May, who blushed as she spoke, for Harry glanced up, and her eyes met his fixed on her lovely countenance with an unmistakable expression of admiration.

"I was very glad, I know, to have been of service, though I suspect I ran very little personal risk in performing the exploit," said Harry, still looking at May, and wondering at the delicate beauty and refined manner of the fisherman's daughter.

"I suspect that I was too young to have thanked you for the service you rendered me as I ought to have done," she said, "for my mother has since told me that had it not been for you I might have been killed by the fierce creature."

"All I did I remember was to throw your red cloak at the animal, and that required no great exertion of courage or strength," answered Harry, smiling. "I then ran off with you, and lifted you over the gate. I can only feel thankful, now you bring the circumstance to my recollection, that I came up at the moment to save you," answered Harry. "But are you not going to join the dancers?"

"I promised some kind friends with whom I live to avoid mixing with the crowd," answered May; "and they would especially object to my dancing. Indeed, I confess that I have never danced in my life."

"Very strange," said Harry. "Who are they, may I ask?"

"The Miss Pembertons," answered May. "You surely, Mr Castleton, remember them, and they desired mother and me to express their great wish to see you again."

"Oh, yes, my good cousins, of course I do. Pray tell them that I will call upon them to-morrow, or the first day I possibly can. I am not surprised that they do not quite approve of dancing; but have they actually prohibited you? We shall form some fresh sets shortly nearer the house, which my sister and other ladies will join, and can you not be tempted to come too? You would have no difficulty, as the figures are not intricate, and you need only move through them as you see others do."

May smiled, but shook her head.

"No," she said, "the Miss Pembertons made no exception with respect to those with whom I might dance, and I fear that they would object as much to my dancing in a quiet set as they would to my joining those who are rushing up and down so energetically out there;" and May looked towards the spot where a country dance of rustics was going on, the swains dragging their partners along at no small risk of pulling off their arms, though sometimes the case was reversed, and the damsels were engaged in hauling on their more awkward partners. "I must say that I have no reason to regret not being among them," she added, with her eyes full of laughter as she watched the vehement movements of the dancers to which she had called Harry's attention.

"Oh, but we shall move much more quietly in the dance I ask you to join, and I am sure it will suit your taste better," he said.

Still May declined firmly, though gently. Harry was convinced that she was not to be persuaded. Had he consulted his own inclination he would have stopped and talked to her as long as she remained, but he remembered that he had numerous duties to perform.

"Are you likely to be walking about the grounds, or do you intend to remain where you are?" he asked.

May turned to the dame for the answer.

"While this sort of fun goes on I do not think we can be better off than where we are," answered the dame.

"I will see you again," said Harry, who admired the manner in which she obeyed her friends' wishes, and hesitated to repeat his request. "Perhaps my sister would like to send a message to our cousins. Pray tell them that she regards them with the same feeling she has always done."

"I will gladly carry the message to the Miss Pembertons," said May.

"Thank you," said Harry. "I will try to get my sister to give it you herself," and he tore himself away.

"What a lovely creature that little girl with the blue eyes has grown into," Harry thought to himself. "I remember she was a sweet child, and now she is as near perfection as I can fancy any human being. I wonder if I should think so if I saw her dressed as a young lady in a ball room. Yes, I am sure of it—any dress would become her. I must get Julia to see her. And yet I do not know, she might possibly say something I should not like. Maiden May, what a pretty name. She spoke, too, of living with our cousins. Can she be their servant? Yet she does not speak or look like one. Her manner and tone of voice is perfectly that of a young lady. But I must not think too much about her, or I shall forget what I have to do."

Harry hurried on, trying to collect his thoughts, which the vision of Maiden May had scattered.

He had now to set a troop of boys running races, now to arrange another rustic dance.

It was some time before he made his way back to the house, where his friend Headland had got before him, and was now engaged with Julia and other friends in arranging the sets to be formed by ladies and gentlemen, and in which some of the daughters of the upper class of tenantry and shopkeepers would take their place.

Harry excused himself from leading out a partner on the plea that he had so many duties to perform, and before long he again found himself approaching the spot where Adam and his wife were standing. As he did so he saw a man come up to them and make a low bow, beginning to speak to May, at which she turned away with a look of annoyance, not unmingled with scorn, while she put her arm into that of the dame.

So Harry interpreted the expression of her countenance. Had it not been for this Harry would have hesitated to approach.

"I am sure, Miss, I do not wish to offend you, and I have a thousand pardons to ask," he heard the stranger say. "It's all a mistake to suppose that I intended to be otherwise than polite and respectful."

The dame, as she drew May nearer to her, looked up at her husband, and was going to speak. Adam made a step or two towards the young man, and looking him firmly in the face, said—

"This is not the place where I can treat you as you deserve; but there is only one thing I have to say, that is to take yourself off, and don't come near our Maiden May if you wish to keep a whole skin on your back."

Young Miles, for it was he, knowing that he was perfectly safe from personal violence in Texford Park, putting on a swaggering look, was about to reply, when he saw Harry coming up, and observed an angry frown on the young officer's brow.

"I'll make you pay dearly for this, old fellow," he muttered between his teeth, and turning round, slunk away towards the nearest group of persons, among whom he soon concealed himself.

"Who was that young man?" asked Harry, glancing in the direction Miles had gone. "He seems to have caused you some annoyance," and he looked at May, who however did not reply.

The dame spoke for her.

"He is an audacious young fellow, who came to Hurlston a few days ago, and has had the impertinence to speak to our Maiden May when she was alone out walking; and if it had not been for our Jacob, I don't know what she would have done. He is the son of the miller at Hurlston, and we have reason to think he would speak to her again if he had the chance, so she has had to keep inside the grounds at Downside ever since, till she came out with my husband and me, and we little thought he would have been here; but it only shows what he is capable of."

"What, did that fellow dare to speak to you against your wish?" exclaimed Harry, indignantly. "I must take measures to prevent his doing so again. If the miller cannot keep him in order, I must beg Mr Groocock to desire him to send the fellow away again. You say he only came here lately," he added, turning to the dame.

"Yes, Mr Harry, he only came to Hurlston lately, though he was born and bred in the place. He was sent away after his mother's death some four years ago, and has not been back that I know of till lately."

"Depend on it he shall not cause you any further annoyance," said Harry, again addressing May, "and pray do not let the matter trouble you further. I scarcely dare ask whether you are still resolved not to dance?"

"Quite as resolved as at first," answered May. "Even if I greatly wished to do so, I could not break my promise to my kind friends."

Harry took notice of her reply.

"Surely she would not speak of them as her kind friends if she was in their service," he thought, and he longed to ascertain the position she held in his cousins' family. Her costume gave him no clue, but her manner, her tone of voice, and her mode of expressing herself, showed him that she was a person of education. He was greatly puzzled. He longed to ask her more questions, but was afraid of appearing inquisitive.

"When the people begin to get tired of their present amusements, we are going to have some boat racing on the lake, and as soon as it grows dark there are to be fireworks, which will have a pretty effect on the water. I hope that you will remain to see them," he said.

"I regret that we cannot do so," answered May. "Neither of the ladies are well, and I never like to be absent, especially from Miss Mary, long at a time, as Miss Jane having a cold there is no one else to read to her."

"Are you fond of reading?" asked Harry.

"Yes. Indeed, it is the chief source of amusement I have," answered May. "I have read, I believe, every book the Miss Pembertons possess, and with their usual kindness they have procured a good many fresh ones for me. Though Miss Jane is not an admirer of the French, she allowed me to study their language, so that I can read it with ease, though I fear that I should find myself greatly at a loss were I to attempt to speak it."

"When you have the opportunity of hearing it spoken, I am sure you will soon get over that difficulty," observed Harry.

"I hope to do so if I am ever able to mix with French people, or to obtain a French master."

"I am considered to speak it well, and perhaps you will allow me when I call to give you a lesson," said Harry, now thoroughly convinced that, at all events, the fisherman's daughter was not in a menial capacity in his cousins' family.

He felt relieved. There would be nothing derogatory in his attempting to become better acquainted with the fair young creature with whom he had been so greatly struck. Though very unwilling at present to leave her, he was conscious that he ought not, with so many eyes likely to be turned in that direction, to remain longer in her society.

"I must attend to my duties," he said, nodding to Adam and his wife. Unconsciously he lifted his hat to May with the same respect he would have shown to any high born young lady in the land.

May watched him till he was lost in the crowd. If he by chance approached young Miles, that worthy kept out of his way. Harry had undertaken to start the rowers on the lake with the assistance of Headland. It was remarked that he made two or three mistakes, which were, however, remedied by his friend. His eyes continually wandered among the crowd on the banks as if in search of some one. Headland rallied him when they were alone for a few minutes.

"Why, Harry, you look quite bewildered! Has anything happened?" he asked.

"Yes, indeed," laughed Harry, who had no secrets with Headland. "I have made a discovery. I have seen such a lovely girl. I wanted to point her out to you and Julia, but I could not find you. I went a second time myself to be satisfied that I had not gazed at her with rose-coloured spectacles, but I found that she was even superior, if possible, to what she at first appeared. I am romantic, you know, but I tell you she is perfectly charming."

"Who is she?" asked Headland.

"Only a fisherman's daughter, but she is living with my cousins, and, from what I understand, has been educated by them, though they certainly could not have given her the graceful manner and sweet tone of voice so remarkable in her had she not possessed them naturally."

"My dear Harry, charming as she may be do not lose your heart to her, or attempt to win hers in return, if she is of the parentage you tell me, for although I have no right to lay any stress on the point of birth, yet I am very sure that others will, and you may be entangled in a way which will produce much suffering, and may be painful to her as well as to you."

"I have been thinking of that," answered Harry, "and if she were only an ordinarily pretty girl I would at once put up my helm and run away from her; but she is so perfectly lovely that I feel capable of overcoming every possible objection, could I win her."

"Perhaps when you see her again you may discover some slight defects which were not discernible at your first interview," observed Headland, smiling. "Did I not think this very possible I would advise you not to call at your cousins as you propose. Otherwise I should certainly say, keep out of her way. I know you too well not to feel sure that you would not wish to win her love without feeling sure that you could make her your wife."

"I should be a wretch indeed if I wished otherwise," said Harry. "If you saw her perhaps you would agree with me that she is the essence of all that is pure and modest, and I could not approach her with any other thought in my mind."

"For that very reason, Harry, I would advise you simply to pay your cousins the visit you propose, and then keep away from Downside till you are about to join another ship."

"At all events I will go there to-morrow," said Harry. "If I find that I am mistaken there can be no harm done; but I am not blind, and I am too well accustomed to ladies' society not to be able to distinguish between what is refined, and graceful, and lady-like, and their opposites," exclaimed Harry.

"Well, be cautious what you say, and how you look and act," answered Headland, knowing Harry's impetuous character.

The friends again parted. The aquatic sports were concluded, the fireworks over, and the fête in the park came to an end.

The more select guests, however, had been invited to remain for a dance in the house.

Some of the young ladies thought Lieutenant Castleton was much less entertaining than they had expected to find him, for though he danced indefatigably, he had very little to say for himself.

Headland made himself as agreeable as usual, though it was remarked that his eye brightened and a smile lighted up his countenance whenever Julia Castleton passed near him, or he had an opportunity of speaking to her.

Chapter Twenty Seven
Harry's Visit to Downside

"And what do you think of my friend Headland? I have not overpraised him, have I?" asked Harry, when he happened to find himself alone with Julia in the garden the morning after the fête.

"You certainly have not overpraised him," answered Julia, examining some flowers amid which they were walking. "I do not remember that you ever said very much in his favour."

"Oh, yes, I did, I am sure, for I admire him more than any other fellow I know, and I am sure when I was last at home I constantly told you of the gallant things he had done."

"That was before I saw him, and I suppose I forgot all about it."

"Well, I am glad you like him, indeed, I am sure everybody must. But, by-the-bye, Julia, do not fall in love with him, however gallant a fellow he is, or I shall be sorry that I brought him here, though I should never suppose you likely to be guilty of such a weakness. Perhaps I ought to have told you at once that I know, to a certainty, he is not a marrying man. He and I have frequently talked the subject over, and he has assured me that he should never think of taking a wife unless, in the first place, she was charming and lovely, and refined and highly educated, and perfect in every way, indeed, next door to an angel, and would love him entirely for himself. Perhaps also I ought to have told you before that he is a man of no family, or rather he does not know to what family he belongs, as he was separated from them when an infant, and has lost all means by which he can discover who his parents were."

Harry did not observe the colour which his remarks brought to his sister's cheeks while they walked on, for she turned her head as if looking at the flowers at her side.

"I have not liked to mention this circumstance to any one, not thinking it fair to my friend, as it would set people talking about him. But you well know how very tenacious our father is on the subject of birth, and so I fancy is our mother, and they would blame me excessively if you were to captivate

Headland and be captivated by him; and Algernon, who, I confess, put me up to speak to you on the subject, says he is certain that they would never give their consent to your marrying my friend, though, to confess the truth, there is nothing I should like so much. In fact, Julia, whether or not he thinks you come up to his standard of perfection, I cannot help fancying that he admires you excessively, and so, as Algernon insisted on it, I felt that I must warn you in time."

"In time!" murmured Julia. "You should have said this before."

"I never should have thought of saying it at all, my dear sister, if it had not been for Algernon," answered Harry. "You know, intimate as I am with Headland, I could not say anything of the sort to him, or warn him not to make love to you. And Algernon agrees with me on that point, as to a man of his delicate honour and sensitive feeling, it would be equivalent to telling him he must leave Texford, or it would appear as if I wanted to put the notion into his head."

"Oh, pray do not on any account say a word to him!" exclaimed Julia. "You would not be justified in saying anything which might make your friend suppose he is not welcome at Texford."

"Oh, no, depend on my discretion," said Harry, now for the first time observing Julia's countenance, which in spite of her efforts betrayed the agitation of her feelings. "My dear Julia, I almost wish that I had not spoken. I am afraid that what I have said has in some way annoyed you. Believe me, that nothing would give me greater pleasure in life than to see you become Headland's wife; in fact, it used to be one of my boyish dreams of happiness. But, as I said, I felt that I must do as Algernon wished, and warn you, should he pay you any particular attention, not to encourage him, as also not to allow the admiration you naturally have for him to ripen into a warmer feeling. There, I have done my duty, and I will not say another word on the subject, and I would not have said it now if I had not been persuaded that I ought to do so for your happiness," and honest Harry stopped at last, greatly to his sister's relief.

She pressed her brother's hand, showing that she believed his sincerity, and then hurried to her room. She would rather have remained in the fresh air, but she was afraid of meeting any one, and she felt that she could not just then enter into conversation; least of all would she wish to meet Captain Headland.

Her brother's words had suddenly revealed to her the state of her own heart. She had heard Captain Headland praised and spoken of as one of the most gallant among the gallant officers of the day, and he had himself recounted to her in modest language some of the daring deeds he had performed; and yet this brave officer when speaking to her was so gentle and deferential, that he seemed to feel as if he was addressing a being infinitely his superior. He evidently preferred her society to that of any other lady in the house, as he always, when an opportunity occurred, singled her out from the rest; and several times, when he fancied she was not watching him, she had observed his eyes fixed on her, while, whenever he addressed her, his features brightened up in a way which she had not observed when he was speaking to any one else. She could not be mistaken with regard to his manner towards her, for she was confident, noble and honourable as he was, he would not trifle with her feelings.

"Harry ought, indeed, to have told me this before," she said with a sigh. "It is now too late. If Headland really loves me, and I am sure he does, I cannot be mistaken. If he proposes to me I must not leave him to suppose that I am indifferent to his love."

During the morning Miss Castleton did not appear, and many enquiries were made. General Sampson especially was very anxious to know what had become of her, and having his suspicions, was not satisfied that they might not possibly be correct till Captain Headland came in alone, and, when asked, assured him that he had not seen Miss Castleton since the morning.

"Ah! I thought, captain, that she might have put your nautical experience into requisition, and employed you in rowing the boat on the lake."

"No," said Headland, "I hope to have the pleasure of being employed in that way in the afternoon, and I shall be glad if any other lady will trust herself to my pilotage."

Harry, in the meantime, recollecting that he had promised to pay the Miss Pembertons a visit, ordered his horse, and took the road to Hurlston.

As he approached the village, having never been at Downside, he thought he would first call at Adam Halliburt's cottage and enquire the way. The cottage, from its remarkable structure, he remembered well.

Calling to a boy to take care of his horse, he dismounted and knocked at the door. The dame opened it.

"This is an honour, Mr Harry," she said, begging him to enter, with a look of pleased surprise on her countenance. "To think that now you are a grand officer you have come to see poor folks like us," she continued, dusting a chair, while Adam in his frank, hearty way held out his hand to welcome his guest. He would probably have done the same had the king come to his cottage.

"To tell you the truth, I am on my way to Downside, and thought I would call here first to enquire the road," said Harry. "I hope you and your daughter were not tired by walking about so much yesterday at the fête."

"Thank you, Mr Harry, not a bit; besides, as our May didn't dance she hadn't so much cause to be tired as most of the young people had."

"She looks somewhat delicate, and ill able to go through what many girls would think nothing of," observed Harry, for he wished to get the dame to talk about her daughter.

"Bless you, she is strong and hearty as she ever was, and some time ago when both the ladies were ill, she sat up night after night watching them, and was none the worse for it, and fine weather or foul she goes about the village for that matter all the year round, visiting the poor and sick when the Miss Pembertons cannot go to them," and the good dame ran on expatiating on her favourite theme—the praises of May.

Harry was somewhat surprised to hear her speak in such unmeasured terms of her daughter's good qualities.

"The worthy woman naturally appreciates her daughter, and in her honest pride feels that she can never speak too highly of her," he thought.

While she was speaking the door opened, and May entered, looking bright and blooming as usual, and Harry thought her even more lovely than the day before. She started, and the colour rose slightly to her cheeks, as she saw him. She evidently did not expect to find a visitor.

Harry naturally enquired if she had enjoyed the fête.

"Yes. She had been amused at all events," she answered with a smile. "And it was a pleasure to be able afterwards to describe it to the Miss Pembertons. I mentioned meeting you, sir," she added, "and they look forward to seeing you before long."

Harry of course said he was on his way to pay his respects to his cousins, but being uncertain as to their house, had called at her father's to enquire which it was.

"Our May will be able to show it to you, Mr Harry," said the dame. "She seldom likes to be long away from the ladies, and I suppose will soon be going back there."

May hesitated. She did not look upon Mr Castleton as a stranger, but she naturally felt a degree of timidity at the thoughts of walking with him alone. When, however, she looked up into his frank open countenance, after he had sat talking for some time, the feeling vanished.

He told Adam how well he recollected his trip in the *Nancy*, and declared that even now he should like to take another. Then he remembered the little blue-eyed girl he had seen rush into Adam's arms, utterly regardless of his wet clothes.

Maiden May smiled.

"I remember that I was dreadfully frightened at seeing the boat coming in, thinking you would all be lost."

She was about to make another remark, which would possibly have greatly puzzled Harry, when looking up at the clock, she exclaimed —

"I had no idea it had been so late. I got leave to run down and see you for a few minutes, mother, and ought to have been back again by this time."

Harry instantly rose.

"I hope that I have not detained you; but if you will kindly, as your mother proposes, show me the Miss Pembertons' house, I shall be grateful to you."

May replied that she should be happy to do so, and Harry wishing the fisherman and his wife good-bye, went to look for the boy who had charge of his horse. May, stopping to say a few words to the dame, came out by the time he had returned to the door of the cottage.

Harry, instead of mounting, taking the rein in his hand, walked by her side.

The subject of their conversation might seem commonplace, though perhaps it was interesting to themselves. Harry was at length led to speak of some of his adventures at sea, from a question May had asked him, and on mentioning one of the battles in which he was engaged, he was surprised to find that his companion was thoroughly well acquainted with the details as well as with all the events which had lately taken place. During the walk Harry could not accuse himself of having said anything which could have been construed into making love to the fisherman's fair daughter.

On reaching Downside May went into the house to send for the gardener to hold his horse, and to announce his visit. The two ladies came to the door to welcome him.

"I should have known you by your voice," said Miss Mary, taking his hand, "though you have grown from a boy into a man since we met you last. But there is something I discern in a voice which never alters: yours is the tone I like to hear."

"We must not flatter Harry, and I do not do it," observed Miss Jane. "I see the same expression in his countenance which won my regard when he was a midshipman. You recollect him, May, do you not?"

"I recognised Mr Castleton at once yesterday," said May without hesitation. "I should have been ungrateful had I not," and May turned her blue eyes towards the young officer.

His met them, and, strange to say, May speedily withdrew hers, while a slight blush rose on her cheeks.

"I am indebted to Miss Halliburt for finding my way here so easily," observed Harry, "for I have never been in this part of Hurlston before, and did not know where your cottage was situated. What a beautiful spot it is. If I ever settle on shore, it is the sort of place I should like, with just that peep through the trees to remind me of the ocean which I have been wont to live on. Perhaps if peace lasts I shall be compelled to take up my abode on shore."

"Grant that it may," said Miss Jane. "I should think the nations of Europe must be sick of the fearful strife which has raged so long, and will be very unwilling to recommence it."

"Things do not look much like it," answered Harry. "The First Consul has shown no great love for peace; and as I wish to obtain my promotion, I confess that I should like to have a little more fighting before long."

"I suppose that is but a natural wish for you to entertain," observed Miss Jane with a sigh. "Yet I would that you saw the case in a different light, and might thus be led to reflect how contrary is the love of fighting to the religion of mercy and peace which we profess. And even though I acknowledge that fighting may be necessary for the defence of one's country, we should mourn the stern necessity which compels men to engage in it."

Harry had no wish to dispute the point with his cousins, although perhaps he did not quite enter into their views on the subject.

He gladly accepted their invitation to remain to luncheon. As he watched May attending to Miss Mary, he could not help remarking how lady-like and graceful was every movement she made; he could scarcely believe that she had been born and bred in a fisherman's cottage, for honest and worthy as Adam and his wife appeared, they were plain and blunt in their manners, though the dame was in some respects certainly above her class.

"We must show you the grounds," said Miss Jane, when luncheon was over, "if you are not in a hurry to return home."

Harry was sure he should not be missed at Texford, and would very much like to see their garden.

The ladies got their bonnets and shawls and went out, May leading Miss Mary.

"Our dear May has quite spoilt me," observed the blind lady. "Instead of letting me learn to grope my way about, she always insists on my taking her arm, so that I can step out without fear of falling over anything in the path."

May looked affectionately at Miss Mary, as if she felt the duty was one in which she delighted.

They had just left the house when a girl came running up, saying that her mother was ill, and would be grateful if Miss Jane would come down and visit her.

"I must go at once, Mary," she said, "and leave you and May to do the honours to Harry. I daresay I shall be back before you go," she added, turning to him, "as the cottage is not far off."

Harry begged her not to hurry.

The grounds, though not extensive, were very pretty, for the Miss Pembertons had done much to improve them since their arrival. There was a lawn on the garden side of the house, with a number of flower beds and shrubberies and walks, and here and there seats, with a rustic arbour covered with creepers. At the further end of the grounds, where a spring of water bubbling up formed a pool surrounded by rocks, over which moisture-loving plants had been taught to creep, was a grotto, artificially constructed of masses of rock. Miss Mary called Harry's attention to it, as she and her sister were very proud of the work, it having been formed under their directions, and she begged him especially to admire some figures formed with shells, a few only of which were finished, though they intended that the whole of the interior should be ornamented in the same style.

"This is just the sort of thing I should like to work at," exclaimed Harry. "It should be a thoroughly marine grotto. I see that there is a covey of flying fish already finished. You might have Neptune and his car and attendant tritons at the further end, dolphins and swordfish and other inhabitants of the sea on either side. I must compliment the artist who executed those flying fish. They are most natural."

"Here she is, then, to hear your praises," said Miss Mary. "But we shall be very glad if you will come and assist, as you take an interest in the sort of thing, as I am afraid that otherwise it will be a long time before it is completed."

"I shall be very glad to be of use and to serve under Miss Halliburt, for she has made so admirable a beginning that she must remain director of the works. Will you accept my services?" he asked, looking at May.

"I cannot refuse them when they are so frankly offered," she said, looking up somewhat timidly as she spoke; "though I must leave the Miss Pembertons to decide who is to be director."

As some baskets of shells and cement for sticking them on were in the grotto, Harry, with May's assistance, tried his skill and produced a very creditable flying fish in addition to the covey she had commenced.

"I am very certain I could not have produced the result had I not had your model to copy from," said Harry.

Miss Mary seemed as much interested as if she could have seen the designs, and May and Harry worked on till Miss Jane returned, apologising to him for her long delay. He thought she had been absent only a few minutes, and was quite surprised to find that an hour or more had passed away.

They had still some portion of the grounds to visit, and on their return to the house he was surprised to find, on looking at a clock in the hall, that he had barely time to gallop back to Texford and to dress for dinner.

Chapter Twenty Eight
Miles Gaffin's Proposal

Jacob had been at work on board the *Nancy* when he found that it was time to return home for dinner. He caught sight, as he approached the cottage, of May, as she and Harry Castleton were setting off on their way to Downside.

"Who can that be?" he thought, a strange feeling oppressing his heart. "It is not that scoundrel young Gaffin. No, no, she would not walk so quietly alongside him; but I don't like it, that I don't, though, as far as she is concerned, it's all right; she would not do what is wrong, I am sure of that, and mother must know all about it."

Jacob watched May and Harry as long as they were in sight, and then something like a groan broke from his bosom. After some time he entered the cottage. The information he gained from his mother did not make him much happier, for he could not believe that a young man such as his mother described Mr Harry could see May without falling in love with her; and if so! Poor Jacob groaned as he thought of what might be the consequence. He mechanically hurried over his dinner without appetite, and then, taking a basket, went off to the beach to collect some more shells, and to fetch some which he had deputed some fisher-boys living at a considerable distance along the coast to obtain for him. He felt more downcast than he had ever been in his life as he now began to realise the wide distance which existed between himself and May.

"Of course she is just like an angel of light to a poor rough chap like me; yet I love the very ground she treads on," he murmured to himself, as he went on. "There's not anything I would not do if she was to ask me, yet if I was to tell her so, I don't know what she would say; it would not make her angry, it would frighten her though, I am afraid, and maybe she would be very sorry, and tell me I must not think of such a thing. Of course she would. I wish I had never been born," and Jacob felt as if he could have thrown himself down on the sand and cried his big, honest heart out. Though the struggle was a rough one, he overcame his feelings for the moment, and trudged on.

"I said I would get some shells for her and the ladies, and I will; and if I do but have a sight of her but for a moment it is recompense enough."

Jacob went on collecting shells on the way, till he reached the furthest point to which he intended to go, where he met the lads who had collected a good supply. He was returning pretty heavily laden under the cliffs when, weary with his walk, he sat down on a bank of sand thrown up by the tide, placing his basket by his side. Thoughts such as seldom troubled him were passing through his mind when he saw a man approaching him from the direction of Hurlston. As the stranger drew near he recognised Miles Gaffin.

The miller coming up to him slapped him on the shoulder and sat down close to him, and in the frank hearty tone he often assumed, said—

"How fares it with you, Jacob? Why, lad, you look somewhat out of sorts."

"Do I, Mr Gaffin? It's more than I wish to do then," answered Jacob, who had no desire to enter into conversation with the miller.

"Perhaps I know the reason why you are not as happy as you would wish to be," said Gaffin, fixing his eyes on the young man's face. "There is a pretty girl in the case whom you thought you would like to make your wife."

"Every man's thoughts are his own, Mr Gaffin," answered Jacob, "and I do not see how you can know mine more than I can know yours."

Miles Gaffin laughed, not pleasantly.

"The old can read the thoughts of the young better than you may think. Now, lad, I tell you that you are following a will-o'-the-wisp if you ever think to make the girl your father saved from the wreck your wife. She would laugh you to scorn if you breathed such a notion in her ear, and tell you to go and drown yourself, or be off to foreign lands so that she might never set eyes on you again. Don't I say what is true, lad?"

In spite of his resolution a groan escaped Jacob's breast.

"I thought so," continued his tormentor. "Now, Jacob, I have known you from a boy, and I will be frank with you. You fancy that I want my son to succeed where you are certain to fail, but I have no such notion in my head, though there is a difference, you will allow, between him and you. I don't, however, guide the young man's proceedings, or pretend to dictate to him, he is old enough and clever enough to act for himself; and I want it to be understood that I have nothing to do with his movements. You will mention that if you have the opportunity. And now, my honest Jacob, if you are disposed for a trip to sea just let me know, and I will give you a chance which will suit your taste, I have a notion, and fill your pockets with gold. I know I can trust you, so I can say to you what I would not to others. Are you inclined for a trip on board the *Lively*? There is a berth for you if you are. Whatever way you may think she is employed, I can tell you that she carries a commission as good as any of the king's cruisers, though I do not pretend to say that in peace time she does not engage in a little free trade occasionally, yet that is not the business which I am employed on."

Miles had laid his hand on Jacob's arm so as to prevent him rising, which he showed an intention of doing.

"Do you wish to be convinced, lad? Look here, I know you can read," and Gaffin drew from his pocket a paper signed by Mr Pitt desiring any naval officers or others, who might fall in with Miles Gaffin, the bearer, not to interfere with him, he being engaged in the secret service of His Majesty's Government.

Jacob read the paper, and though he did not very clearly comprehend its meaning, it made him feel a greater fear, if not respect, for the bearer than he had before entertained.

Gaffin might possibly have shown one from the First Consul of France, of the same description, had he been disposed, but that was kept for use on the other side of the Channel. He was not the only person so employed at that time by the rival powers, to whom it was of the greatest importance to obtain information of each others preparations.

"You see, my friend, that I invite you to engage in the service of your country. We want a few fresh steady hands, and if you know any lads who would like to accompany you, your recommendation will be in their favour."

At no time could Gaffin have made such a proposition with a better prospect of success. Still the honest fellow was far from trusting his tempter. He knew well enough that whatever Gaffin might say to the contrary, the *Lively* was engaged in smuggling, though she certainly had escaped capture in a wonderful way, which was perhaps now partly accounted for. His father had always set his face against contraband traders, and had warned his sons never to have anything to do with them. But there was another motive influencing him still more; May was in danger of being insulted by the son of the very man who was trying to persuade him to leave home. She might scorn him, but he would stop near her to watch over her safety. He would never leave his father and mother either without their sanction.

Gaffin, not aware of the thoughts which were passing through his mind, watched him for some minutes without speaking.

"Well, my lad, what do you say to my offer?" he at length asked. "That I am not going to leave my old father and mother whatever you or any other man may say to me, Mr Gaffin," answered Jacob, putting his arm through the handle of his basket and rising. "Good evening to you." He walked on.

Gaffin after sitting for a moment, somewhat taken aback, followed him. "Come, think of my offer, lad, I wish you well. I have no reason to do otherwise," he said in his most insinuating tone.

"It's no use your wasting words on me, Mr Gaffin; if you are going to the south'ard you had better go—I am homeward-bound."

"That was not a civil remark, my lad; but I will overlook it, and perhaps you will think better of the matter."

"I can't think better of a bad matter, Mr Gaffin," answered Jacob, firmly, hurrying on.

The smuggler folded his arms and stood watching the young man as he trudged sturdily over the sands. "I will win him over yet, though his father may be too obstinate to move," he muttered to himself as he made his way up the cliff to the mill.

Jacob carried his basket of shells to Downside and deposited them with Susan, for the ladies were at tea, and they did not hear of his coming. She spoke of the visit Mr Harry Castleton had just paid.

"Such a nice gentleman," she observed. "The ladies kept him here all the afternoon helping Miss May to work at the grotto. And I have a notion that he was very well pleased to be so employed. I should not be surprised but what he will be back here again before long," she added.

Jacob did not stop to hear more, but, emptying his basket of shells, hurried home. What he had heard did not contribute to raise his spirits. He at once told his father of his meeting with Miles Gaffin.

"If you care for me or for your own happiness, don't have anything to say to him," said Adam, earnestly. "He bears none of us any love, and depend on't he means mischief."

Chapter Twenty Nine
Making the Grotto

Harry had paid several visits to Downside. The old ladies welcomed him cordially, and were much pleased at the interest he took in their grotto.

"It got on rapidly," they observed, with the assistance he so kindly gave May. She received him as a relative of the ladies without supposing that had she not been his fellow-labourer he might not have taken so great an interest in the work. Frequently Miss Jane and Miss Mary were present, but sometimes they sent May and Harry by themselves, and only followed when at leisure. Those moments were very delightful to the young people. They did not perhaps hurry on with the grotto as fast as they might otherwise have done, and when the ladies arrived they had not always made much progress. Yet Harry believed that he said nothing to May which he would not have been willing for his cousins to hear, and probably had he been accused of making love to the fisherman's daughter, he would indignantly have denied that he was doing so. She did not stop to enquire why she felt unusually dull when he did not come, or why her ear was so eagerly on the watch for the sound of his horse's hoofs at the hour he generally arrived.

Every day Harry fancied that he had discovered new graces in her mind, and the slight degree of rusticity which he might have first detected when he compared her with his sister Julia, had entirely worn off. In person he thought her faultless.

Harry was anxious that his mother and sister should see May without knowing who she was—he was sure that the Miss Pembertons would be pleased at receiving a visit from them, and he was in hopes that he might be able to induce them to call without showing his anxiety that they would do so. He made no secret at home of his visits to Downside, observing that the Miss Pembertons had employed him to ornament a shell grotto for them, and as he hated to be idle, he was very glad to find employment suited to his taste, and at the same time to do anything to please the kind old ladies.

Sir Ralph had been called to London on political business, and was likely to remain some time away. Most of the visitors had left Texford. Those who remained were able to amuse themselves, and did not require the attention of their host and hostess. Captain Headland, being looked upon as Harry's guest, was quite independent. Lady Castleton was therefore more at liberty than she had been for some time.

"By-the-bye, mother, you should drive over some day and call on our cousins, and see the grotto. They will be much pleased, I am sure, with the visit, and will be delighted to show you over the garden, which is a perfect gem in its way."

"I confess that we have somewhat neglected our cousins, but your father was annoyed with the way Jane spoke to him, and was afraid that she might come here oftener than would be agreeable, so that he begged me not to encourage her," said Lady Castleton. "However, as she has shown no inclination to do that, he will not object to my calling again, and Julia and I will drive over there to-morrow."

"I am sure they will be pleased to see you, and I will go on ahead, and let them know that you are coming, lest by any chance they may have thought of going out," said Harry, well pleased that his suggestion had been taken.

"You appear to be very fond of the old ladies, Harry," observed his mother.

"They are kind good creatures, and are so pleased to see me that I cannot help liking them," and Harry turned away, lest further observations might be made.

Although he was unwilling to mention May to his mother and sister, and still more so to his brother, he did not hesitate to speak of her to Headland.

"But, my dear Harry, have you well considered what will be the consequence of your frequent interviews with this beautiful young creature?" asked his friend. "You appear already to have lost your heart, and what will be the effect of your attentions on her?"

Harry was what he would have called taken aback at the question.

"You are right in supposing that I have lost my heart, but if I know what love is, I believe that I love her as sincerely and devotedly as a man can love a girl. Had she been uneducated and living with her father and mother, I would not have attempted to see her again. When I found her as lady-like and refined as the best born in the land can be, I could not resist my cousin's invitation, and, I own, yielded to her attractions without considering the consequences. Still, whatever may be my feelings, I have done my utmost not to exhibit them, and she receives me so calmly and modestly, simply as a visitor to the Miss Pembertons, while she appears so unconscious of her own beauty, that I am not vain enough to suppose her feelings are in any way interested in me."

"I am a person of little experience with regard to women's hearts," said Headland; "but it strikes me that a country girl wholly unaccustomed to the society of gentlemen is very likely, in spite of all your caution, to be more interested in you than you may in your modesty suppose. Whatever your cousins, who, from your account, must be unusually simple-minded, unworldly ladies, may think, their young protégé may suspect that you would not come over every day for the sole purpose of working at their grotto, and may have a suspicion that she herself is the attraction."

"Indeed, I believe I like them so much, that had they asked me to come and make a grotto for them, I would have done so even if Miss Halliburt had not been with them!" exclaimed Harry. "Though I confess that the pleasure is enhanced by working with her."

"It may be so, Harry," said Headland. "But if Miss Halliburt is there, and you admire her so warmly, can you sufficiently conceal your admiration as to convince her that she is not the attraction, and if you did so, might she not be unconsciously piqued by wishing to bring you to her feet."

"She is too pure and simple-minded to do anything of the sort!" exclaimed Harry in an indignant tone. "If I find I have gained her affections, I will offer her my hand, and stand the consequences. I shall feel that I am in honour bound to do so; indeed I should be utterly miserable if, conscious that I possessed her love, I was compelled to give her up."

"My dear Harry, it is not for a man of unknown birth like myself to warn you against the consequences of a misalliance; but you tell me that the Castletons are a proud race, and that your father and brother are like the rest of the family. You cannot for a moment suppose that they would be otherwise than indignant were you to propose to marry this girl, charming and beautiful as she may be. And I am afraid that your mother and sister, though they might be pleased with her, would strongly oppose your wishes."

"I should have hopes of winning them over. Algernon has no right to interfere, and I do not think he would; and my father, proud as he is, has so great an admiration for female beauty, that I believe were he to see May, he would be compelled to acknowledge I had ample excuse for wishing her to become my wife."

"I trust it may be so, Harry," said Headland. "I have spoken to you as I felt bound to do as one of your oldest friends, and as I know you to be thoroughly honourable and right-minded you would not be the cause of pain and disappointment to any woman, especially to the young and innocent creature you admire so much."

"I am grateful to you, Headland, indeed I am," exclaimed Harry, taking his friend's hand. "I should have been wiser had I not spoken a second time to Miss Halliburt, but I am sure that I should have been less than human had I not done so. The fact is, my dear fellow, I am in for it. But I will remember your warning, and, for her sake rather than my own, not make love to her, and then, at all events, I shall have to suffer alone, should insuperable difficulties to our marrying arise."

Though Headland had spoken thus frankly and faithfully to Harry, Harry, from delicacy, could not bring himself to speak in the same way to his friend. He felt very sure that Headland admired Julia, and from what she had said, he fully suspected the secret of her heart. Would not his father, however, object as much to Julia marrying Headland as he would to his marrying the fisher-girl. The cases were, however, very different. Headland, though of unknown birth, had gained a position for himself, and Captain Fancourt had written in the highest terms of him, and would, he thought, support his suite if he proposed. Still he was too well acquainted with his father's proud unyielding temper not to fear that in either case there would be difficulties to contend with.

Headland had already made a considerable sum in prize money, so that the only objection which could possibly be raised against him was his ignorance of his family.

Harry trusted that as he himself was a younger son, his father might not object so much as he would have done, had Algernon been in his place. This gave him some slight hopes that the difficulties which he knew must arise would finally be overcome. At all events, as long as the Miss Pembertons wished him to come to their house, he arrived at the conclusion that he was perfectly justified in going there.

Chapter Thirty
May's Introduction to the Castletons

Miss Mary, led by May, was taking a stroll after breakfast, when Harry arrived.

"We shall be truly glad to see your mother as she so seldom visits us," said Miss Mary, mildly; "and as I hope she and Julia will stop to take luncheon, I will go in and order preparations, for Jane is out visiting at some cottages in the neighbourhood and may not be back just yet. As I suppose you do not wish to be idle, pray, if you feel disposed, go on in the meantime with the grotto, and May will, I daresay, be glad to assist you."

Harry, after his conversation with Headland, had been more observant than usual of May's behaviour. A blush suffused her cheeks as Miss Mary said this, and as her eyes met Harry's he was convinced that she had no disinclination to do what Miss Mary proposed.

Accordingly, after they had attended Miss Mary to the house, they went together, Harry carrying a fresh basket of shells brought up by Jacob on the previous evening. May was more silent than usual, though she answered when Harry spoke to her in that soft tone he so much delighted to hear, which she had learned from Miss Mary rather than from her elder sister.

Harry at length made a remark which caused her to reply.

"I am thinking of the visit we are to receive from Lady Castleton and your sister, and I confess that I feel somewhat nervous."

"Why so?" asked Harry.

May looked up in his face but did not answer.

"Do you fancy they can do otherwise than admire you, and think you all that is sweet, and charming, and excellent, and loveable as I do, May," and he took her hand which she did not withdraw, though her eyes were cast down, and the blush deepened on her cheeks. "Oh, May, I did not intend to say so much, but I had resolved to tear myself from you unless I could hope that you were not indifferent to me."

"Harry," said May, trying to calm her agitation; she had always before called him Mr Harry, "I was thinking of your mother's proposed visit, and afraid lest she should believe that I was the cause of your frequent visits to Downside. Knowing, as I do, the pride of your family, I feared that you might be induced to give up your visits here; and oh, Harry, that we might be parted."

"No, no, May," exclaimed Harry, letting all his sober resolutions fly to the wind, and pressing more lovingly her hand. "My parents, even should they wish to do so, have no right to insist on my giving up one against whom they cannot allege a single fault. The circumstance of your birth ought not to be an impediment, and believe me, May, with all the desire I possess to be an obedient son, I could not be influenced by such a reason. I do not invite you to share poverty with me, for I have already an ample income to support a wife, and as I need not ask my father for a single shilling, I do not think he will have any just reason to oppose my wishes."

"Harry," said May, "I own I love you, but I must not run any risk of creating dissension between you and your parents. That and that alone can prevent me from giving you my hand as you already have my heart. I have been told of a sad history of a member of your own family, your father's brother, who, against his parent's wishes, married a young lady to whom they objected on account of her birth, and he was banished from his home ever afterwards, living an exile in foreign lands. I should fear that your father and mother would look upon me as an unfit match for you, and discard you, should you persist in marrying me."

"You speak of my uncle Ronald," exclaimed Harry, "who married, I am told, a very lovely girl, and simply because she could not trace her pedigree to the same stock as the Castletons, my grandfather refused to receive her as his daughter-in-law, and my uncle, rather than subject her to the annoyance to which she might have been exposed at home, took her abroad. Surely my father, after he has seen the consequence of the harsh treatment his brother received, would not behave in the same way to me; besides, you know, he is my father's eldest brother, and it is not at all certain that he is dead, so that he may some day return and claim the baronetcy and Texford, and if so, I shall be but a younger brother's youngest son, and no one need trouble their heads who I marry. But, my dear May, if I wore a ducal coronet, you would be the richest prize I could wish for to grace it; though do not suppose, though I would rather, for the sake of avoiding difficulties, be of the humblest birth, that I consider you unworthy of filling the highest rank in the realm."

May had never told Harry that she was not Dame Halliburt's daughter. Why she had not done so she might even have found it difficult to say. At first, a feeling of modest reserve had prevented her from speaking about herself. The Miss Pembertons, in their simplicity, had not thought it likely that Harry would fall in love with her, merely by coming a few times to the house, if he supposed her to be Adam Halliburt's daughter; but they had sufficient worldly wisdom to know that should they excite his interest by telling him her romantic history, he, in all probability, would be moved by it. May herself, however, now felt she ought not longer to conceal the fact from him. It could not fail to be a satisfaction to him, as both the ladies and her foster-parents were fully convinced that she was of gentle birth. She was on the point of telling him when Susan hurried up with the information that Lady Castleton's carriage had just driven to the door.

The young people had not marked how rapidly the time had gone by.

May suddenly felt even more agitated than before. Harry's declaration, though delightful, was not calculated to prepare her for receiving his mother and sister with the self-possession and calmness she would have wished to exhibit.

"Do, Harry, go in first, and I will come into the drawing-room as soon as I can compose myself. You have made me very happy, but I must be alone for a few minutes before I can meet any one."

They returned to the house together. Susan had gone on before.

Lady Castleton and Julia had been for some time seated in the drawing-room when Harry entered.

"I am glad to find Harry makes himself so useful to you," observed Lady Castleton to Miss Jane, as he took his seat near Julia, who was talking to Miss Mary.

"Yes, indeed, we are much obliged to him, and hope to have the pleasure of showing his handiwork to you after luncheon," answered Miss Jane. "He and the young friend residing with us have done nearly the whole of the ornamental part of the work, and have exhibited a great deal of skill and taste."

Harry overheard the remark, and feared that his mother would inquire who the young friend was; but she observed instead—

"It is a great thing when naval officers are on shore if they can find employment. So few care for field sports, and as my brother, Captain Fancourt, observes, they too generally fall in love with some fair face and marry, and then have speedily to go off, and leave their young wives to pine in solitude, often for long years."

Harry dreaded what next might be said.

"Ah, they are greatly to be pitied," observed Miss Jane.

"My mother will be sure to suspect me the moment she enters," thought Harry. "I almost wish that I had not persuaded her to come here; and yet she cannot but be satisfied with my choice; she and Julia must love May the moment they see her."

Harry tried to join in the conversation which Miss Mary and Julia were carrying on. Julia had always liked their blind cousin, and now exerted herself to amuse her, mentioning only such subjects as she thought would do so. Harry found, however, that his remarks were not very relevant. Miss Mary was more surprised than Julia. At last he got up and went to the window, whence he could watch the door.

At length it opened, and Lady Castleton and Julia turned their heads as May glided into the room. Both instinctively rose from their seats as Miss Jane introduced her as "a friend who is living with us."

They bowed, and, taking their seats, continued their conversation, while May took a chair a little on one side between where Harry was standing and his mother and sister.

They both looked at her several times, and Harry observed that their countenances exhibited surprise, and he believed at the same time no small amount of admiration.

At last Julia, drawing her chair a little back, addressed May, and asked if she had been long at Hurlston.

"Yes, ever since I was a child," was the answer.

"May has resided with us several years, and a great blessing and comfort she has proved to me especially," observed Miss Mary.

Julia looked more puzzled than ever. More than once she glanced up at Harry, who now came forward and took a seat near May.

"I was not aware that you had any guest in your house," said Julia; "but I hope we shall now have the pleasure of frequently meeting each other," and she looked towards May with a slight bow.

"It will give me very great pleasure to see you, Miss Castleton," said May, who, in spite of her efforts, found herself blushing whenever she spoke, conscious as she was, too, that Lady Castleton was watching her from the other side of the room.

Though she would have liked to talk to Julia, she wished that Miss Mary would again engage her in conversation. Julia, on her part, was somewhat puzzled what to say without appearing rudely inquisitive, and yet she was eager to know who the beautiful young creature could be who had been so long living with her cousins; possibly she was some orphan whom they had protected.

At this juncture luncheon was announced. Miss Jane conducted Lady Castleton into the dining-room, telling Harry to take care of his sister, while May, as usual led Miss Mary.

"What a beautiful creature; who is she?" whispered Julia, looking up in her brother's face.

"I knew you would admire her," he answered, evasively, meeting her glance, without as he hoped betraying himself. "Our cousins consider her as excellent in every way as she is lovely."

"But what do you think of her?" asked his sister.

"My eyes are not more penetrating than yours: you shall form your own opinion before I reply."

They entered the dining-room before Julia could make any further remark.

May attended to Miss Mary with all the calmness she could command, though she felt that Julia's and Lady Castleton's eyes were fixed on her all the time.

Harry exerted himself with considerable success to entertain his cousins and their guests. He could not help wishing, however, that his mother and sister would take their departure as soon as they had seen the garden, for he longed to be again alone with May, and he dreaded lest they might ask their cousins who the beautiful young stranger was. He wished them to admire her first, and he was sure she could not fail to win their admiration, and that they would then be less unwilling than might otherwise be the case to receive her as his promised wife. He would not, indeed, allow himself to see the difficulties which would certainly arise directly they learned who she was; nor could he bring himself to believe that, however great might be their admiration, it would vanish immediately the truth was known.

Though May spoke but little, her voice was sweet and musical, and what she said showed her sense and judgment.

After luncheon, Miss Jane invited Lady Castleton and Julia to walk through the grounds, and to see their grotto.

"And is this all your doing, Harry?" asked his mother, after they had admired the grotto and its surrounding rock-work, with the clear pool of water shaded by lofty wide-spreading trees.

"Only partly; I did not originate the designs, to that young lady is due all the credit which they deserve," he answered, looking at May. "I had merely acted as a workman under her superintendence."

"I must not allow the merit they possess to be given to me; Mr Castleton suggested and executed many of the designs," said May, heartily wishing that the ladies had not brought their guests to see the grotto at all.

Lady Castleton was evidently more than ever puzzled. Knowing the world she was now very certain that this fair stranger was her son's chief attraction to Downside, and determined to cross-question him on the first opportunity.

They returned to the house where, after sitting a few minutes, Lady Castleton begged that her carriage might be ordered. As Harry handed his mother into it, she said quietly—"I am not surprised that you take so much interest in grotto building. You will follow us soon, I hope."

"Oh yes," answered Harry, telling the coachman to drive on. "We shall have time for a little more work," he said, entering the hall where Miss Jane stood watching her departing guests. May resumed her hat and accompanied him to the grotto.

"I feel as if I was acting the hypocrite to my kind friends. I ought to tell them, Harry, and not allow you to come here under false pretences."

"They cannot object to my coming even though you are the attraction. We will tell them at once."

May and Harry, as may be supposed, did very little work; they would probably have been less successful than usual had they attempted it.

At length his watch told him that it was nearly time to return to Texford. They went into the house and found the ladies in the drawing-room. May sat down next to Miss Mary and took her hand.

"I ought to lose no time in telling you what has occurred," she said, trying to maintain her calmness. "Mr Castleton has asked me to marry him."

"My dear!" exclaimed the two Miss Pembertons, in different keys, Miss Jane fixing her eyes on Harry.

"What have you said in reply?" asked Miss Mary.

"Do you suppose that I could refuse him."

"I see, my dear, that you have not," observed Miss Jane, "judging from his countenance. We love you both, and I am sure no two young people could be better suited to each other. But when we invited Harry here we did not dream of such a result. Have you both considered well the consequences."

Yes, Harry declared that he had thought them over seriously.

"At all events, cousin Jane," he exclaimed, jumping up and taking her hand, "you and cousin Mary will not object to my continuing to come here."

"You know we ought to do so should your father and mother not approve of your intentions."

Harry replied that now his mother and sister had seen May, they could not fail to love her.

"Of that I have no doubt," whispered Miss Mary, pressing May's hand.

Miss Jane was less sanguine. Still they would be happy to see Harry until Sir Ralph prohibited his coming.

Harry continuing to refuse to see any clouds in the horizon, rode home rejoicing that he had won Maiden May.

Chapter Thirty One
Young Miles Gaffin again

May had been anxiously looking forward to another visit from Harry on the morning after he had openly declared his love, and she had more than once gone to the front door to watch for his coming. She endeavoured, however, to fix her thoughts as she read, as usual, to Miss Mary from the book of books, and to listen to Miss Jane's comments, though she might have been puzzled to give any very clear account of the remarks she heard.

"Our May does not seem quite herself," observed Miss Mary, when the two sisters sat together the next morning. "Poor girl, it must have been very trying when she felt that Lady Castleton's and Julia's eyes were fixed on her during their visit, especially if they suspected that Harry admires her."

"We ought to have foreseen the consequences of encouraging him to come here," said Miss Jane, "though my conscience acquits me of having designedly thrown the young people together."

"I love May for her gentleness and sweet manner, and her kindness to me," observed Miss Mary. "It never occurred to me that she possessed the beauty which would attract a young and gallant officer like our cousin."

"I shall blame myself if the peaceful happiness May has hitherto enjoyed is interrupted from our want of discretion, dear girl," said Miss Jane. "Though nothing we can do can effectually restore it, we can make her all the amends in our power; and I have long been thinking of placing her in as independent a position as is possible should we be removed from the world. I have determined to make my will and to leave her all my property."

"The very thought which has occurred to me," said Miss Mary, "and I should wish to do the same."

"I am glad to find that you agree with me, and the sooner we do so he better," observed Miss Jane. "I will write to Mr Shallard and beg him to come over here the first day he is at leisure. Sir Ralph ought to be able to well provide for his children, and they cannot miss our small fortune, nor has he any reason to expect that we might have left it to them."

Scarcely had the two sisters come to this understanding than May entered the room. Her countenance, usually so bright and cheerful, looked sad.

"What is the matter, my dear May?" asked Miss Jane.

"Mrs Brown's daughter, Peggy, has just come up to say that my kind mother is very ill—the doctor has been sent for, but that she seems anxious to see me," answered May. "With your leave I will go to her at once, and I hope to be back before Harry leaves you, should he come to-day."

"Had she not unwisely sent for the doctor I would have tried to accompany you, though I feel scarcely able to leave the house," said Miss Jane. "But I must not interfere with him."

"I am sure that you would be welcome, as you are everywhere. But if you will allow me I will run down to mother at once and ascertain what is the matter with her."

"Do so, my dear, and send Peggy back if you find that you must remain with Mistress Halliburt."

May, though greatly disappointed at thus missing Harry, hurried down to the cottage with Peggy Brown, often looking in the direction of Texford in the hopes of seeing him coming along the road. Still the duty and affection she owed her kind foster-mother prompted her to hasten on.

She found the dame in bed. Seldom having been ill, the good woman was greatly alarmed about herself. She had caught a chill and was feverish and weak. Adam, and Jacob were away in the *Nancy*, and there was no one except Peggy to attend to her, as Mrs Brown had only waited for May's coming to go back to her own cottage. May regretted that Miss Jane had not accompanied her, as the dame, she thought, would probably have been benefited by her skill.

At length the doctor arrived.

"Cheer up, Mistress Halliburt, we will soon bring you round; with your fine constitution you have nothing to be afraid of. I can leave you safely under charge of this young lady," said the doctor in a cheerful tone, bowing to May. "I will look in by-and-bye, and if I find you better, as I am sure I shall, she can return home. Send Peggy up and she will bring you back the medicine I wish you to take immediately."

May felt greatly relieved at hearing this, though the dame shook her head, apparently not believing him. In spite, however, of her fears the dame got better by the time Adam came back, and the doctor soon afterwards looking in assured May that she might leave her mother without the slightest anxiety, for as it was Saturday Adam was not going to sea in the evening.

May, leaving a message for Jacob who was still on board the *Nancy*, thanking him for the last shells he had brought, and saying that more would be acceptable, set off on her walk home.

Jacob had ascertained, so the dame told her, that young Gaffin and his father had been seen to leave the inn some days before on horseback, with valises behind them, and that she thus need not fear being again annoyed by him. She hurried on, her heart beating quicker than usual at the thought of meeting Harry. She was sure he would have remained at Downside till her return; indeed she had fancied that he might have come down to the cottage, but perhaps the wish not to attract the attention of the inhabitants of the village induced him not to do so. She had nearly reached the gate of Downside when she saw standing before her not ten paces off, the very youth who had before given her so much annoyance.

"He will not surely dare to speak to me now," she thought. "If he does I can run home without replying. If I turn back it would show that I am afraid of him, and he would overtake me before I could reach any cottage."

She had but little time, however, for consideration, so she walked steadily on, simply crossing over to the other side of the road and keeping her eyes directly before her.

Miles, however, had no intention of letting her escape so easily. Advancing a few steps he took off his hat with an air which he intended to be full of respect, saying as he did so in a humble tone—

"I came, Miss Halliburt, to beg your pardon and to express a hope that you will forgive me for what occurred. I have been miserable ever since."

May took no notice of this speech, but only walked somewhat faster than she had hitherto been doing towards the gate.

Won from the Waves | 183

"Won't you deign even a reply to my humble address?" said Miles, in a half whining tone, which scarcely concealed the irritation he felt.

Still May remained silent, hoping that in another minute she should be safe within her friends' grounds.

Miles went on speaking in the same strain, but the tone of his voice showed that he was losing patience. Suddenly he changed his tone.

"Just listen to me," he exclaimed. "I have the means of making your fortune, and my own too. I know who you are, and if you will marry me I will enable you to gain your rights, and make you as wealthy as any lady in the land need wish to be."

May, believing that what he said was a falsehood, merely uttered to gain her attention, hurried on as before.

"I say I am not going to stand this a second time," exclaimed the young ruffian, seizing her by the wrist. "If you won't come to terms by fair means, you must expect me to use a little force when it is for your own good. Don't be screaming out; I will tell you what I want you to know, and what you yourself would give anything to learn, though I can only tell you if you will promise to marry me, and keep it a secret till then."

"Let go my hand!" were the first words May uttered, still not attending to what he said, her alarm prevented her from understanding the meaning of his words, as it did also from crying out for help; indeed, so few people passed that way, that unless her voice was heard at Downside, it was not probable that any help could be obtained.

"Listen," he exclaimed, trying to force her back from Downside. "I tell you I have got something particular to say to you, and I won't say it unless you will listen quietly."

"Let me go," repeated May again. "I do not wish to listen to you, all I require is to be allowed to go home. If you really have anything to say you can communicate it in a letter to the Miss Pembertons."

"That won't suit me," answered Miles. "I have told you before, if gentle means won't succeed I must use force, though I am sorry for it," and he again began to drag her forward.

HE WAS LAID PROSTRATE ON THE GROUND.

May, though now more alarmed than ever, recovered her voice, and made use of it by uttering a loud shriek. It might have been heard at Downside, and Miles seemed to think that it was, for he turned his head anxiously in that direction, expecting apparently to see some one issue from the gate.

May, struggling to get free, looked also the same way. Again she uttered a cry for help. At the same moment a man bounded round the corner of the road, and before Miles was aware of his approach, he was laid prostrate on the ground by a blow from Jacob Halliburt's powerful fist. "Run, Miss May, run," he exclaimed, "there are other men coming, but I will settle this one before they are here."

May instinctively ran to the gate. No sooner had she gained it than she turned round intending to beckon Jacob to follow her to the house, and to leave the wretched man without inflicting further punishment on him. As she did so she saw Jacob lifting Miles on his feet. Scarcely was he up than Jacob, telling him to defend himself, again knocked him down.

Jacob, as soon as he had done so, seeing that she had not reached the house, again entreated her to hurry there.

"If you will go I will follow you in a moment," he shouted, "you won't be safe till then."

As Jacob spoke she saw four armed men on horseback galloping along the road. Believing that Jacob was following close behind her she rushed into the house. He sprang toward the gate intending to defend it should the horsemen, as he thought they would, attempt to enter. Had he possessed any weapon he might have held his post, but in another instant one of the horsemen dealt him a blow with the butt end of a pistol, which laid him senseless on the ground.

By this time Miles had began to recover his courage, and one of the men leaping from his horse helped him up. A gleam of satisfaction lighted up his eyes as he saw what had occurred to Jacob.

"If it hadn't been for that fellow I should have kept the girl till you came up," he exclaimed. "Let us make sure of him at all events, and I will manage to get hold of her another time when there will be no one to interfere."

Scarcely a word was spoken, the men seeming ready enough to agree to what Miles proposed. A couple of leathern thongs were produced, and some pieces of rope, and before Jacob recovered his senses he was bound hand and foot, and lifted up in front of one of the men on horseback.

"We can do no more now, and the sooner we are away from this the better," said Miles, "or some one will be down upon us, and we shall be suspected of making off with the fisherman's son. I must be away over the fields, and shall be down at the beach almost as soon as you are."

Chapter Thirty Two.
Lady Castleton

Whatever resolutions Captain Headland might have made when he first went to Texford, he had not been there long before he felt a strong inclination to break them. Once or twice he had almost determined to go away, but on hinting at the possibility of his having to do so, Julia had given him a look which made him immediately alter his mind, and every day he remained he found a greater difficulty in tearing himself away.

The party were assembled in the evening in the drawing-room after Lady Castleton's visit to Downside. Julia had had no opportunity of taking the sketches on the lake she proposed.

"You promised to act as my boatman, Captain Headland."

He had not forgotten it, and they agreed to go the following morning.

Without being vain, Headland could not help discovering that Julia seemed happy in his society. As she sang that evening he looked over her music, and asked her to sing a ballad, which described the grief of a maiden whose sailor lover had fallen in the hour of victory. Julia hesitated, and tears sprung to her eyes as she turned them towards the young officer, while he placed the music before her. She quickly recovered herself, but he would have been blind had he not observed that there was a tenderness in her manner towards him, though she apparently was unaware of it.

After the ladies had retired, Harry invited Headland to take a stroll through the grounds to enjoy the moonlight. Harry did not speak till they had got to some distance from the house.

"You remember, Headland, the advice you gave me yesterday," he said at length. "I would have followed it, much as it might have cost me, had I found May indifferent to my affection, but she has confessed that she loves me, and nothing shall prevent me from making her my wife. If you saw her, you would agree that she is well worthy of the most devoted love a man can give, and I will do my utmost to make her happy. There may be opposition, but that I am resolved to overcome, unless she herself changes her sentiments, and that, I think, is impossible. You, I know, will stand my friend, whatever may occur."

"Of course I will, Harry, though I fear I can give you but little assistance," said Headland. "I am very unwilling to run the risk of hurting your feelings, but, my dear fellow, are you certain that the mutual affection which you tell me exists is as deep on both sides as you say? You were struck by the girl's beauty, and she is flattered by your attentions. Perhaps if you were to be separated for a time, and mixed in society, you would find them more evanescent than you are at present disposed to believe possible."

"I am very certain that I love her as much as a man can love a woman, and that I should be miserable if I were to be doomed to lose her," answered Harry, firmly. "I can only judge by what she says and how she looks, and by my knowledge of her character, which is perfect in every respect, and, I am sure, one of the most valuable of qualities, constancy is not wanting in it. My cousins, who have known her from her childhood, highly esteem her, and bestow on her the love as to the nearest relative. What more can I say? I must get you to come and be introduced to her. Will you ride over with me to-morrow? and if you do not agree with me, never trust my opinion again."

"I promised to row your sister on the lake to-morrow—she wishes to sketch," said Headland, "or I should be glad to accept your invitation."

"I won't ask you to break such an engagement," said Harry, smiling archly; "but if you and Julia will ride over in the afternoon, I will come back and meet you, for I want my sister to become better acquainted with May."

"I shall be at Miss Castleton's service, and will gladly accompany her," said Headland.

The two friends continued pacing up and down the moonlight walk. Harry, knowing Julia's secret, would liked to have ascertained his friend's feelings towards her. He was certain that he admired her, but aware how diffident he was in consequence of his position, he was very doubtful whether he would venture to tell her so. Harry's respect for his sister prevented him from even suggesting the probability that he would not be refused should he make her an offer. From everything Headland said, however, Harry felt convinced that he only required encouragement to do so.

The following morning Julia appeared with her sketch-book.

"I have not forgotten my promise," said Headland, and his countenance brightened as he looked at her. "I shall be happy to accompany you on the lake."

They set out, and Harry went to order his horse to ride to Downside.

Just as he was starting, the servant brought a message from Lady Castleton, who wished to speak to him. Though disliking the delay, he went immediately, guessing why she had sent for him.

"Sit down, Harry," she said in her gentle tone. "I was very much struck yesterday with the beauty of the young lady we met at our cousins. Knowing how you must naturally admire her, I am very sure that she is the attraction which draws you daily to Downside."

"Yes, mother, I do not deny it," answered Harry; "and I am delighted that you and Julia admire her so much."

"We could not fail to do that. But let me ask you, Harry, do you know her history? are you acquainted with her family? She is, I suspect, a dependant on the Miss Pemberton's bounty. And have you not reflected that you may have won her heart as you may possibly have lost your own?"

"Mother," said Harry, rising and taking Lady Castleton's hand, "I love her for herself and herself alone; she has given me her love in return, and you would not wish your son to marry for mercenary or any other motives except such as influence me."

"I wish to see your happiness secured, my dear Harry, but I fear that your father will not view matters in the light you do. He will certainly not approve of your marrying any one beneath you in rank."

Harry argued as most young men would have done under similar circumstances.

"You might persuade me, my dear boy, but I fear that you will find it impossible to overcome your father's strong notions on the subject. I must write and inform him of the state of affairs; and depend upon it, I will do my utmost to give him a favourable impression of the young lady."

"But why trouble my father now about the matter?" urged Harry. "It will be time enough when he returns home to let him know my wishes, and he can then express his opinion. Pray do not object in the meantime to my visiting Downside. Our cousins invited me there in the first instance, without the slightest idea of the consequences; and I surely have a right to visit them as long as they give me permission. Remember I persuaded you to call there, a proof that I had no desire for concealment. However, as only you and Julia even suspect the state of the case, do let me ask you to keep the matter a secret at present, for I do not wish even Algernon to know it, as I am doubtful how he might act; he entertains the same opinion as Sir Ralph on most points, and might think fit to expostulate in a way I should not approve of."

In spite of her previous resolutions, Lady Castleton was so far gained over by Harry, that she promised to wait and see how things were likely to go.

"Thank you, mother," exclaimed Harry, kissing her brow; "all will go right. We must get Sir Ralph to see May without knowing who she is, and depend on it he will be enchanted with her, perhaps insist that I shall forthwith go and make her an offer of marriage."

Lady Castleton smiled at her son's enthusiasm, but directly afterwards sighed, for she knew her husband far better than did her son.

Harry was eager to set off for Downside, and hurrying downstairs mounted his horse, which the groom had been leading up and down waiting for him.

Just as he was starting, a dark, black-whiskered man, on a strong looking horse, rode up. Harry fancied that he recollected his features.

"Good morning, Mr Castleton," said the stranger, lifting his hat. "I remember you, though a good many years have passed since you were at Texford."

"You have the advantage of me, knowing my name. Have you business with any one here?"

"Yes; I wish to see Mr Groocock, the steward. I am the miller at Hurlston, and have to say a word or two about the rent of the mill," answered Gaffin. "I remember you as a young midshipman, when I had the pleasure of offering to give you a cruise in my lugger, though for some reason or other you objected to accompany me."

"I probably had good reasons for doing so," answered Harry, recollecting what he had heard of Gaffin's character, and that he was the father of the young man who had insulted May. "If you have business with the steward, you will find him in his room; good morning, sir," and Harry was riding on.

"Pardon me, Mr Castleton, if I detain you for a minute," backing his horse across the road. "You are perhaps not aware that though I have held the mill at Hurlston for a number of years, and have expended considerable sums in repairing it, Mr Groocock has given me notice that the rent is to be raised, and I wish to appeal to Sir Ralph against the injustice of the proceedings."

"I cannot interfere in the matter, as Mr Groocock has my father's perfect confidence, and he probably considers the rent you have hitherto paid as too low."

"Where there is a will there is a way; if you wished to serve me, Mr Castleton, you could do so," exclaimed Gaffin in an angry tone, as if his aim was to pick a quarrel with the young officer.

"I have no wish to interfere, and have no intention of doing so," answered Harry. "I must again say good morning, sir."

"You are willing to see an act of injustice done without any desire to prevent it," said Gaffin.

"I do not believe that Mr Groocock would commit an act of injustice, and I consider it impertinent in you to infer that Sir Ralph Castleton acts unjustly."

"I infer nothing; facts are stubborn things, Mr Castleton. I see how it is, your father wishes to drive me from the mill; but he is mistaken if he expects to succeed. If I am compelled, I will pay the additional rent, and remain, though I am not likely to be grateful to those who have ill-treated me. A few words from you would probably have favoured my cause."

"I have already given you my answer, I cannot be longer delayed in discussing the subject," and Harry, putting spurs to his horse, rode on.

Gaffin gave an angry glance towards the young officer, and then turning round, made his way towards the wing of the mansion in which Mr Groocock's office was situated.

Chapter Thirty Three
The Bird Flown

Great was Harry's disappointment on reaching Downside to find that May was not there. His cousins also, he fancied, received him with less cordiality than usual. Had he understood their feelings better, he would have had no cause to complain.

"Sit down, Harry," said Miss Jane, in a somewhat formal tone, Harry thought. "May has told us of your offer. You must be aware that we have no legal control over her, but we feel it our duty not to encourage your visits here until we know that you have the permission of Sir Ralph and Lady Castleton, and that, we have our fears, will not be very readily given. As far as we have the power, we purpose making the dear girl independent, and have sent for Mr Shallard to make our wills accordingly."

"Bless you for the thought," exclaimed Harry, starting up. "I wish you would get Mr Shallard to make mine, and then, if I have to go to sea, and am killed before I marry, it will be a consolation that she is provided for."

"Nothing but generosity would have prompted you to say that," observed Miss Mary. "We only act, my dear Harry, according to the dictates of duty; we must not encourage a son to disobey his parents."

"Then you need not object to my coming here," answered Harry, brightening up. "I have told my mother, and I believe that I have won her over. She and Julia were delighted with May, as, of course, they must have been."

Harry hoped that he had satisfied the consciences of the two good ladies. He begged them to let him know when Mr Shallard was coming over.

"It is very sad, Harry, to think that such a will as you propose making should ever come into effect, for it would make May very unhappy to hear of it."

"Then don't tell her on any account. And depend upon it, I do not intend to be killed if I can help it; only when shot are flying about, one may take me off as well as another man. Ships, too, sometimes founder with all hands, or blow up, or cast on shore, or a sea washes over the deck, and sweeps all before it, or the masts are carried away, and crush those beneath them."

"Oh, pray do not talk of all the fearful things which happen to sailors," exclaimed Miss Mary. "I am sure I wish that you could get Sir Ralph's leave to marry, and come and settle quietly at Downside, instead of roaming about over the ocean; it would be a happier life, I think."

Harry, as he pictured May as his wife, thought so too at that moment, but could he abandon the profession he loved, and the prospects of promotion and honour? For May he could abandon all; but would it be wise? That was not a subject he could just then think very clearly about.

He waited and waited, but May did not return. At last he thought of going to work at the grotto. The ladies said they should be much obliged if he would do so.

At length he recollected that he had promised to escort Headland and Julia. He would ride back to Texford, and by the time he had returned with them he hoped to find May at Downside.

Chapter Thirty Four
Mad Sal

We must now go back to Jacob. On recovering his senses and finding his limbs tightly lashed, he in vain attempted to free himself. He was unable to shout out for assistance, for a gag had been thrust into his mouth, while an handkerchief tightly bound over his eyes prevented him from seeing.

What his captors were going to do with him he could not tell. "They will not dare to murder me," he thought; "if they do, no matter; I have saved May, and father and mother and the ladies will see that they must keep a careful watch over her lest these villains do what I suspect they intended doing, and try to carry her off."

As far as Jacob could tell by the feeling of the wind on his cheeks, the horsemen were taking their way to the Downs. That road was little frequented, and he knew his captors would not venture to carry him thus openly where they were likely to meet any one who would recognise him.

"I was sure it was the villain Gaffin who has played me this trick," thought Jacob, as he found the direction in which he was going. "He has missed his aim if it was to get hold of our May, that's one comfort."

At last the men stopped. Jacob found himself lifted from the horse and dragged into a house. He had little doubt that it was the mill-house. He had often heard of the desperate characters who frequented it, and they were not likely to have any scruple as to how they might treat him. He was left for some time on the ground, though he heard people speaking in low voices some way from him. Their voices grew louder and louder. At last he heard one say—

"We must not keep him here; the sooner he is aboard the better."

Shortly afterwards he was again lifted and placed on his legs. Several strong arms dragged him along, and he felt the prick of a cutlass in his back driving him forward when he attempted to resist. He was dragged down a steep path.

"I know all about it now," he thought. "That was the mill where they kept me, and now they are going to take me aboard the lugger, and maybe heave me overboard when they get into deep water. Poor father and mother, I care for them more than any one else; May will think little about me, I fear, and if it was not for my parents I should not care what becomes of me."

All doubt of the matter was at an end when Jacob felt his feet pressing the sand.

"If I once get on board I shall have no chance," he thought, and again he made a desperate effort to free himself. In doing so the bandage was torn off his head. He had sufficient time to see Gaffin, and he at once recognised the men who had captured him, while young Miles was standing by, though he kept at a respectful distance from his elbows.

At this juncture he heard a voice exclaiming—

"Are you still at your old work, ye hard-hearted ruffians, dragging off the young and helpless to be drowned in the salt, salt sea. Aren't ye emissaries of Satan; let him go free, or my curses rest on you." And Jacob saw the tall figure of Mad Sal descending the cliffs by a pathway few would have ventured to tread. Now and then she stopped and waved the long staff she carried in her hand.

"Who is that old woman?" asked Miles. "Make her hold her tongue, some of you, will you?"

"It's more than you or any other man can do," said one of the ruffians. "Try it yourself, master."

Miles however showed no disposition to confront personally the mad woman.

"Get this young fellow aboard as you were ordered, and never mind her."

This remark drew the attention of the mad woman, especially on Miles himself.

"Who are you?" she asked. "Are you a being of the earth, or a spirit from the nether world?" she shrieked out. "Speak, I command you, speak!"

"Be off, and don't interfere with us, old woman!" answered Miles, plucking up his courage.

"I thought my senses deceived me," shrieked out the mad woman, and she turned towards the men with whom Jacob was struggling as they endeavoured to drag him into the boat.

"Stay, I charge you, men, carry not off that poor lad on to the cruel salt sea if he is unwilling to go; the salt, salt sea, the cruel salt sea," and she burst out in her usual refrain.

The men paid no attention to her, and continued their efforts in dragging Jacob to the boat.

Seeing this she again shrieked out—

"Stay, I charge you, or my curses go with you and all who abet you in the cruel act. May a speedy and sudden death overtake you; cursed be the craft which bears you across the salt sea; cursed be the sails which drive you onwards; cursed be those who bear you company; may the raging waves, the howling tempest, the flashing lightning, and roaring thunder overwhelm you; may you all sink down into the salt sea, salt sea; it's a hungry, deep, and cruel sea. The sea, the sea, the salt, salt sea," and she whirled her staff around her head, and shrieked louder and louder as she saw that the men had succeeded in hauling Jacob into the boat.

Miles apparently had no intention of going off, but one of the men, seizing him by the arm, exclaimed—

"Come along, and see your business carried out, young master; as you set us to the task, we are not going without you. If you turn fainthearted we will land the fellow, and let him settle the matter with you as he lists."

Miles in vain expostulated. Mad Sal drowned his words with her wild shrieks, while she continued to wave her staff as if in the performance of an incantation. What with his unwillingness to face the mad woman should he be left on the beach, and the threats of the men, he was induced to go on board.

No sooner was he in the boat than the smugglers shoving off pulled towards the lugger, which lay in her usual berth about half-a-mile from the shore.

Mad Sal watched the proceeding, making her shrieks and wild shouts heard till the boat had got far off from the beach: she then suddenly stopped, and a gleam of sense appeared to pass through her mind.

"Instead of beseeching the villains to have mercy on the youth, I might have sent those to his aid who have the power to help him," she muttered to herself, and turning round she began to ascend the cliff.

Chapter Thirty Five
In Chase of the Lugger

Harry galloped back to Texford, and found the groom, with Julia's horse and Captain Headland's, waiting in front of the house.

Julia came downstairs in her habit as he arrived.

"We were afraid you were not coming," she observed. "I long to see our cousin's young friend again."

"I am ready to return at once," answered Harry. "Here comes Headland."

At that moment old General Sampson came out.

"What, my young friends, are you going to ride? I should have had the pleasure of accompanying you had I known it."

Harry devoutedly hoped that the general would not ask them to stop till his horse was got ready.

"We are merely going to call on some relations who live at a village in the neighbourhood," said Julia, who had as little wish for the general's company as did Harry.

"Then let me have the honour of mounting you, Miss Julia," said the old officer, shuffling down the steps.

At the same moment Mrs Appleton, who was passing across the hall, came to the door with most of the remaining guests.

Headland had been prepared to assist Julia in mounting, but the old general so perseveringly offered his services that she could not refuse them.

She placed her foot in his hand as he bent down, and sprang lightly into her saddle, but at the same moment the horse moving on, the general's head came in contact with the body of her habit, when his wig catching in one of the buttons, off it came, leaving him bald-headed. He bore the misfortune, however, with much less equanimity, especially as Julia, in spite of the effort she made, gave expression to her amusement in a hearty laugh which was echoed by the bystanders, even the grooms being unable to restrain their merriment.

"I beg your pardon, general," said Julia. "I had no intention to return your courtesy in so cruel a manner; here is your wig, do put it on, and forgive me."

"Of course, young lady, of course; though I do not see that the occurrence should produce so much merriment among our friends."

"My dear general," cried Mrs Appleton from the steps above, "pray do not take the matter to heart. Come into the drawing-room and look at yourself in the mirror, and you may arrange your peruke in a more becoming way than it is at present."

In fact, the general had in his hurry put on his wig hind part before, a mode which did not improve the appearance of his countenance, reddened with anger and annoyance.

Harry, eager to be off, called to Julia, who, again apologising to the angry general, followed her brother, and Headland soon overtook them.

Harry explained the cause of his being late, but he felt little inclined for conversation. Julia and Captain Headland were, however, perfectly ready to monopolise it, while Harry road on a little way ahead.

At length Julia called to him, and as he slackened his speed she came up to his side.

"Harry," she said, "you warned me some days ago not to allow myself to give my heart to your friend; but as he has assured me that I have his in spite of what you said, I could do nothing less than give him mine in return."

"You don't mean to say so," cried Harry. "What, has he proposed?"

"Yes, and I have accepted him, though he has told me his whole history. You won't be angry with me, will you? He has asked me to intercede for him."

"No, indeed, I will not," exclaimed Harry. "I am heartily glad for his sake and yours. I congratulate both you and him."

"Headland, my dear fellow, she has told me," and Harry grasped his friend's hand. "You offered to stand my friend, and I will stand yours, though really I consider your merits are sufficient to overcome all opposition. Still we may possibly have a hard battle to fight with Sir Ralph."

"Julia and I are prepared for it," said Headland, "though I cannot tempt her to be disobedient. I am sure that perseverance will overcome all difficulties."

"Spoken like yourself, Jack," said Harry. "In your case, I am sure it will. For myself, I am not quite so certain; even my good cousins began to lecture me," and Harry described how the Miss Pembertons had spoken to him in the morning. "I do not think that May will quite agree with them, however," he added. "No one will forbid her acting as she thinks right."

"Then are you actually engaged to that beautiful girl?" asked Julia.

"Yes; and I told our mother, and she acknowledges that it would have been surprising had I not fallen in love with her; and I am sure you will think the same."

Harry felt in much better spirits as they rode on. He had determined, however, to say nothing of May's parentage till his sister had become better acquainted with her.

As they were approaching Downside, and had reached a part of the road between their cousins' and the Halliburts' cottage, the tall figure of Mad Sal was seen approaching them, waving her staff and talking wildly to herself. As she drew near she stopped, and, gazing at them, exclaimed—

"Who gave the command to bear the poor lad away over the salt sea, salt sea? Stay! answer me, I charge you!"

"What do you mean, my good dame?" asked Harry, as he at once recognised the occupant of the hut in which he and his brother had taken refuge from the storm.

"Good dame, forsooth; you call me so now, for ye have learned to respect me. I ask, was it by your orders yon lad was forced away against his will over the wide, salt sea?

"'The lot fell on the youngest,
    The youngest of the three,
That he should go a-sailing
    All on the salt sea, salt sea -
That he should go a-sailing
    All on the salt sea.'"

"I know of no lad having been forced to go to sea against his will," said Harry, quietly. "Of whom do you speak? Tell me his name."

She passed her hand over her brow, as if to collect her thoughts. She then answered in a calmer tone than before—

"He is the son of old Halliburt, the fisherman. Two of his sons have been borne away already to feed the insatiate maws of the cruel salt sea; 'tis hard that the old man should lose a third."

"I will do all I can to save the lad, and punish those who have attempted to treat him as you say," answered Harry, much interested. "If you can tell me where he has been carried to, I will do my utmost to get him set at liberty."

"I stay for no one when on my destined course," she answered, moving forward. "Your help will avail him nothing, as he will soon be far away from the shore," and Mad Sal, flourishing her staff, as she generally did when walking, took the way towards Adam's cottage.

Harry and his companions rode on to Downside. He intended, should May not have returned, to leave Julia there, and go in search of the mad woman. An undefined fear seized him that something might have happened to May. On reaching the house, Harry threw himself from his horse. Miss Jane, in a state of great agitation, was at the front door directing Susan to summon the gardener, that he might set off and ascertain what had become of Jacob. Harry fancied that she was speaking of May, and the dread seized him that she had been carried off.

At that moment he caught sight of her as she came out of the drawing-room, and forgetting everything else, he sprang forward and pressed her to his heart, as he exclaimed—

"Thank heaven you are safe, May! what has happened?"

"Jacob was attacked while defending me from some men on horseback, and I fear they have carried him off, as they failed to capture me," she answered, making no very great effort to release herself, though she saw that Julia's eyes were fixed on her.

Harry, however, recollecting that others were present released her, and having learned more particulars, had no doubt, coupling them with what he heard from Mad Sal, that Jacob had really been carried on board some vessel off the coast.

"We must do our best to recover him."

"Oh yes, do," exclaimed May. "Had it not been for him, I should probably have been carried away."

"Headland, will you accompany me?" asked Harry. "We will go to Adam Halliburt, who has a craft, in which we can pursue the vessel his son has been carried on board. When we get to the beach we shall probably ascertain what craft she is, as she cannot have got far."

Headland at once agreed to do as Harry proposed, and leaving Julia with the Miss Pembertons, they rode down to the fisherman's cottage.

They found Adam at the door, Mad Sal having just before left him; but the information she had given had been in such incoherent language, that not till Harry and his friend arrived did he comprehend what had happened.

"It must be the doing of that scoundrel Miles Gaffin," he exclaimed, "as his lugger is the only vessel lying off the mill. Ah, there she stands under all sail away from the coast," looking through his glass. "I saw a boat go off to her just now, but I little thought my Jacob was aboard. The villains cannot have the heart to hurt him, yet it's hard to say what they won't do. Oh Jacob, my boy, my boy," and Adam lifted up his eyes to heaven, as if for protection for his son.

Directly Harry spoke of the possibility of recovering him by going in pursuit, he exclaimed—

"Yes, to be sure, sir; the *Nancy* is as fast a craft as any, and there will be plenty of lads to go off with us."

Headland, meantime, was looking seaward.

"What is that craft out there?" he asked, "she looks to me like a cutter."

Adam lifted his glass.

"Yes, sir; she is the *Scout*, revenue cutter. But they will not trouble themselves with the lugger, for they know she has no cargo on board."

"But if we can get on board her," said Headland, "and send her in chase, she will have a better chance of overtaking the lugger than the fishing boat would have."

"Thank you, sir," exclaimed Adam. "I will let my crew know they are wanted, and when I have spoken a few words of comfort to my poor missus, who is ill in bed, I'll be with you on board the *Nancy*."

Adam, sending off a lad to summon his men, directed him at the same time to beg that Mrs Brown would come down and stay with his missus, while the two officers rode to the Texford Arms to leave their horses. They then hurried to the quay, where Adam and most of his crew were collected. As soon as the remainder arrived they went on board the *Nancy*. She was quickly under weigh, and the wind being off-shore ran out of the harbour.

"Is your boat a fast one?" asked Captain Headland of Adam.

"Yes, sir; not a faster out of the Tex, but I am afraid she has little chance of overhauling the lugger."

"But if the wind falls light we may pull after her, and shall then have the advantage," observed Captain Headland.

"She has got long sweeps too, sir. But we will try it, and my lads will give way with a will. I can trust them for that."

"Ay, ay, no fear," answered the men, looking towards the smuggler as if they were eager to be alongside her and to rescue Jacob.

"I believe that our best course would be to get on board the cutter, and for her to go in chase of the lugger," said Harry; "though I do not think the smugglers would dare to oppose us if we could get up with them."

"Whether or not, we will try to get back our Jacob, and the lads would make good play with the boat's stretchers in spite of the cutlasses and pistols the villains have to fight with."

"They would scarcely venture to use them when they see two king's officers in the boat," observed Headland.

"I am not so sure of that," said Adam. "But they have a bad cause and we have a good one to fight for. We will get the oars out, lads," he added, addressing his crew.

The Nancy thus assisted made good way, for the wind being light and off-shore, as has been said, the water was perfectly smooth, and the oars helped her along. Still it became evident to Captain Headland that she was not likely to overhaul the lugger. He therefore agreed with Harry that it would be best to get on board the cutter if they could.

The cutter was, however, sailing away from them, apparently watching the movements of the lugger. Their hope was that the *Nancy* might be seen, and that she might stand back to speak her.

The day was now drawing on, and Harry began to think of returning to Downside. Still they were unwilling to abandon all hopes of rescuing Jacob. They had no means of making a signal to draw the attention of the cutter, and if they could not get on board before dark, there was little prospect of their doing so at all.

The old fisherman sat in the stern-sheets, calm and apparently unmoved, though more eager than any one to overtake the craft on board which his only remaining son had been so barbarously carried off. Often he said to himself with the patriarch of old, "If I am bereaved of my children I am bereaved;" for he could not help seeing the little prospect there was of recovering his boy.

Already the sun had set behind the land, and the gloom of evening was stealing over the leaden ocean when the cutter was seen to haul her wind. Presently she came about and stood to the northward.

"We may still have a chance of overhauling her, sir," exclaimed Adam, his hopes reviving.

Headland and Harry thought so too, although both were unwilling to remain out longer than they could help.

"Julia will probably ride back to Texford by herself when she finds that we have not returned; or will remain at our cousins and send over to say that we have been detained," observed Harry, divining his friend's thoughts.

"I fear that we shall cause the ladies much anxiety, as they will not know what has become of us," observed Headland.

"I am afraid so," said Harry; "but still I cannot bear that the young fisherman should be ill-treated without attempting to save him."

"God bless you, Mr Harry, for saying that," exclaimed Adam. "I pray we may get back our Jacob, for I know the tricks of those villains; and the *Lively* has a fast pair of heels; there are few cutters can come up with her, and the *Scout* is not one of those that can. Still something may happen to help us, though it will not be man's doing. I can't deceive myself, and I don't want to deceive you."

Headland feared that the old man was right. At the same time, as long as Harry had any hopes of overtaking the lugger he determined to accompany him.

The cutter was now about a mile distant to the south-east, but it was a question whether the *Nancy* could cut her off before she had run past to the north and darkness had come on.

The *Nancy's* flag was run up to the mast-head and hauled down again several times in the hopes of attracting her attention.

As they approached, even though it was dark, their voices might be heard on board the cutter, and her commander would probably heave to to ascertain what they wanted.

Some more anxious minutes went by. At length Adam thought they had got near enough to make themselves heard; for though the gloom of night had come on, the cutter's phantom-like form could now be seen as she glided onwards over the smooth sea.

"Now, lads, I will give the word and we will shout together," cried Adam; and he and his crew, with Headland and Harry joining their voices, sent a loud shout across the ocean.

Directly afterwards the cutter was seen to haul up towards them.

Won from the Waves | 203

"They have heard us! they have heard us!" he exclaimed. "Wait a bit, lads, we will give them another."

After the second shout the cutter was hove to, and the *Nancy* was soon alongside.

"What is it you want, my men?" asked the commander, looking down into the boat.

Harry explained what had happened.

"I shall be glad to lay hands on the lugger, you may depend on that, for she has given me more trouble than any other craft on this coast," he answered. "We have two of our boats away, and are short handed, though we would tackle the fellow as we are. It would be better if some of your men would come on board, and if we can overtake the lugger, they will be able to identify the lad you are in search of."

"I will willingly accompany you," said Harry, who, knowing how anxious May was about Jacob, wished to do what he thought she would desire.

"If the captain will take charge of the *Nancy*, I will go also with two of my lads," said Adam. "I would take more, but must not leave the craft with fewer hands on board."

Headland was well pleased with the arrangement, and undertook to escort Julia back to Texford, if she had not already gone, when he arrived at Downside.

There was no time to consider the matter further, as not a moment was to be lost, or there would be no prospect of overtaking the lugger.

"I hope that you will be back to-morrow, Harry, and I will ride over to Hurlston to meet you," said Headland, as he stepped into the boat.

The cutter immediately kept away in the direction the lugger had last been seen, while the *Nancy*, hauling her wind, prepared to beat back to the shore.

Chapter Thirty Six
Sir Ralph's Arrival

The *Nancy*, close-hauled, stood for the shore.

"Two or three tacks will do it, sir, I hope," said Ned Brown, who, since Adam had been deprived of Ben's services, had acted as his mate. "The *Nancy* knows her way into the harbour."

"The oars will help her along though, I think," observed Headland.

The men got them out, and the *Nancy* glided swiftly through the water.

"I am hoping, sir, the cutter will catch Miles Gaffin's craft. There is not a bigger villain to be found than he is in these parts."

"What has he done to gain such a character?" asked Headland.

"That's just what no one can say exactly," answered Ned, "still it's pretty well known that there is nothing he would not dare to do if he chose to do it. He says he is one thing, and we know he is another. When he first came to Hurlston, he used to call himself a miller, and there is not a bolder seaman to be found anywhere. He does not now, however, pretend that he isn't. Many is the cargo of smuggled goods he has run on this coast, and yet he always manages to keep out of the clutches of the revenue officers. There are not a few decent lads he has got to go aboard his craft, and they have either lost their lives, or turned out such ruffians that they have been a sorrow and disgrace to their families. He is more than suspected of having been a pirate, or something of that sort, in foreign parts. And they say when he first came to Hurlston, he seemed to know this coast as well as if he had been born and bred here, though he told people that chance brought him to the place, and that he had never set eyes on it before."

"At all events, if common report speaks true, Hurlston will be well rid of him, if he does not venture back. I hope that the law will, at all events, be able to lay hands on the villain should it be proved that he kidnapped your friend Jacob," observed Headland.

"If the cutter catches his craft, Jacob may be saved. I am more than afraid that Gaffin will knock him on the head, and heave him overboard with a shot to his feet, if he finds that he is hard-pressed, and then he will deny ever having had the poor fellow on board."

"I trust, bad as he is, that he will not be guilty of such an act," said Headland, though, at the same time, he feared, from what he had heard of Gaffin, that he would not scruple to commit that or any other dark deed to serve his purpose.

Headland was thankful when at length the boat glided into the Tex, and ran alongside the quay.

Several people were standing there. The news of what had occurred had spread about the village. Headland, anxious to lose no time, asked if any boy would be willing to run on to the Texford Arms to order his horse.

"Say Captain Headland's horse, the gentleman who accompanied Mr Harry Castleton," he said.

"Captain Headland!" said a person standing near, stepping up to him. "May I venture to ask where you come from?"

"I shall be happy to reply when I know to whom I speak," said Headland, not quite liking the man's tone of voice.

"I am Miles Gaffin, the miller of Hurlston. My good neighbours here have been making pretty free with my name, and accusing me of carrying off one of their number on board a lugger, which I understand you have been chasing, sir, when I have had nothing to do with the matter, having been miles away at the time the occurrence is said to have taken place."

"I cannot say that I am unacquainted with your name, for I have just heard it mentioned, and I shall be glad to hear that you can give me the assurance that the young man has not been carried away," said Headland.

"I know nothing about the matter," answered Gaffin, "so I cannot tell whether the story I have heard is true or not. You, at all events, see, sir, that I am not on board the lugger, which I hear left the coast some hours ago. But I must again beg your pardon, and ask you to answer the question I put when I first had the honour of addressing you."

"I am a commander in his Majesty's service, and you must rest satisfied with that answer, sir," said Headland, not feeling disposed to be more communicative to his suspicious questioner.

"Were you ever in the Indian seas in your younger days, sir? You will believe me that it is not idle curiosity that makes me put the question," said Gaffin, in the blandest tone he could assume.

"You are right in your supposition," said Headland, his own curiosity somewhat excited by the question.

"And you were known as Jack Headland when a boy."

"I was."

"And you took that name from another to whom it properly belonged."

"I did. Can you tell me anything of him?" said Headland, eagerly.

"I wish to ask that question of you, sir," replied Gaffin. "He was an old shipmate of mine, and being struck by hearing your name, I thought there might be some connection. I have long lost sight of him, and should have been glad to hear that he was alive and well."

"He lost his life, I have too much reason to believe, in the Indian seas many years ago," said Headland.

"Ah, poor fellow, I am sorry to hear that. Good evening to you, Captain Headland," and Miles Gaffin, turning away, was soon lost to sight in the darkness.

Captain Headland, accompanied by one of the *Nancy's* crew, hastened on till he met his horse, and mounting rode back to Downside. He found the ladies somewhat anxious at his and his friend's long absence. Julia had sent a messenger on foot home to say that they were delayed, and hoped to return in the evening. Julia and the ladies made many inquiries for Harry, while May stood by, showing, by her looks, even still greater anxiety about him. Headland assured them that he would run no risk, though he probably would not be back till the following day.

Headland, for Julia's sake, wished to set off at once for Texford, but Miss Jane had supper prepared, and insisted on his taking some before starting. Whether or not they suspected that he would become their relation, they treated him as if he were one already, and completely won his heart.

"What dear, amiable ladies your cousins are!" he observed, as he rode on with Julia. "I have never had the happiness of meeting any one like them."

"Indeed they are," said Julia; "I wish they were more appreciated at home. I have till lately been prejudiced against them. It has been an advantage for that sweet girl to have been brought up by them. Though she would have been equally lovely otherwise, yet she might not have had the charms of mind which she possesses. I am not surprised that Harry should have fallen in love with her, though I fear he will have a severe trial to go through when our father hears of his engagement. Though I do not forget that we are bound to obey our parents, yet I could not counsel him to give her up."

"If she is all Harry believes her to be, I hope he may surmount that difficulty," said Headland. "Though I have no parents to obey, I feel that he would be wrong to marry against his parents' wishes."

"Then, how ought I to act should Sir Ralph refuse to allow us to marry," asked Julia in a voice which showed her agitation.

"I dare not advise you to disobey your father," answered Headland. "But believe me, dearest Julia, whatever opposition he may make, and whatever may be his conduct towards me, I will remain faithful."

"Should he forbid me to marry, to no one else will I give my hand," said Julia, sorrowfully.

Neither Julia nor Headland uttered a vow or protestation; such they both felt was not required, so perfect was the confidence they had in each other's love.

"I spoke this," said Julia, "because Harry warned me to expect opposition; and yet I trust, when our father knows you as I do, and that my happiness depends on becoming your wife, he will not withhold his consent."

"I wish that I could feel as little anxiety about Harry as I do about myself, and yet if our father can be induced to see May, I think she will do more to soften his heart than all Harry or I can plead in her favour. During the few hours I spent in her company, she completely won mine."

As they rode up to the house, two servants, who had evidently been on the watch for them, hastened down the steps to take their horses. Headland helped Julia to dismount, and led her into the hall.

Lady Castleton hurried out of the drawing-room to meet them.

"Sir Ralph arrived this afternoon. We have been very anxious about you; we could not understand your message. Where is Harry? What has happened, Captain Headland?"

Headland explained that a young Hurlston fisherman had been kidnapped by a band of smugglers, that he and Harry, indignant at the outrage, had set off in the hopes of recovering him, and that while he had returned on shore, Harry had continued the chase on board the cutter.

"Harry was scarcely called upon to go through so much risk and inconvenience for the sake of a stranger," observed Lady Castleton. "His father was much disappointed at not seeing him on his arrival."

Julia pleaded that Harry had done what he thought to be right, and then went in to see her father, who was reclining on the sofa, with his fingers between the pages of a book closed in his hand. He received her even more coldly than usual; he never exhibited much warmth of feeling even to her. She had again to recount what had happened, and he expressed the utmost surprise at Harry's acting in so extraordinary a manner. He did not allude to her ride home with Captain Headland, though she every moment thought he would speak of it. She excused herself for leaving him as soon as possible on the plea that she must change her riding-habit.

When Headland at last entered the drawing-room, the baronet received him with marked coldness, and made no allusion to his having been absent. The young captain could not help feeling that Sir Ralph did not regard him with a favourable eye.

Julia came down only for a few minutes before the usual hour for retiring for the night had arrived, and Headland had no opportunity of speaking to her.

Chapter Thirty Seven
No News of the Cutter

When Sir Ralph entered the breakfast-room next morning, Headland could not help remarking the formal politeness with which he greeted him.

"Has nothing been seen of my son Harry?" he asked. "Perhaps, Captain Headland, you would favour me by riding over to Hurlston to ascertain whether the cutter in which he embarked has returned."

Headland said that he should be very happy to do as Sir Ralph wished. He looked towards Julia, doubting whether he might venture to ask her to ride in the same direction.

Sir Ralph seemed to divine his thoughts, for he immediately said—

"Julia, I wish to have some conversation with you during the morning; we will afterwards, if you please, take a canter round the park."

The hint was too broad Headland saw to be misunderstood.

Julia looked annoyed, but quickly recovering herself, replied—

"I will come to you, papa, whenever you wish."

Algernon soon after came in, looking pale and ill. His father seemed struck by his appearance, and asked with more concern than usual if he had not slept well.

"Not particularly so; my cough somewhat troubled me, but with the advantage of a few warm days, I daresay I shall be soon to rights again."

The baronet's thoughts seemed to be diverted from their former channel by his anxiety for his son.

General Sampson and Mrs Appleton did their best to make the conversation more lively than it might otherwise have become, for Lady Castleton had evidently some anxiety on her mind, and was less able than usual to act the part of the hostess.

The old gentleman had discovered that Julia and Headland were in love before they were aware of the fact themselves, and he had a shrewd suspicion also that Master Harry had some greater attraction at Downside than his old maiden cousins could personally offer. He was now certain that some hitch had occurred. He had already paid a longer visit than usual, but a better motive than mere curiosity prompted him to stay to see the upshot. He had a sincere regard for Harry and Julia, and was much pleased with Headland, who took his jokes in most excellent part. "I may lend the young people a helping hand, and give my friend Sir Ralph, a stroke the right way," he thought.

Soon after breakfast, Headland's horse was brought to the door. He saw Julia only for a moment in the hall.

"Although I have had no opportunity of speaking to my mother, she, I suspect, guesses the truth, and has thought it best at once to speak to Sir Ralph, for she dare not conceal anything from him. I would rather you had been the first to inform him of our engagement, but he evidently wished to prevent you doing so, by begging you to go to Hurlston."

"I wish I could have spoken myself, but, pray, assure your father that I would have done so had he given me the opportunity. But as we have nothing for which to blame ourselves, we must trust that his prejudices will be overcome, and that he will not withhold you from me."

The old general entering the hall at that moment, prevented Headland from saying more.

Mounting his horse, the captain road on to Hurlston. He met several of the *Nancy's* crew. The cutter had not returned, and Ned Brown again expressed his conviction that if the lugger was to be caught, it would not be till after a long chase. Knowing that the ladies of Downside would be anxious to hear any news he could give, he proceeded thither. The Miss Pembertons welcomed him cordially. May was on the point of setting out to visit Dame Halliburt. She had from early dawn kept a look-out over the ocean, and was aware that the cutter had not returned. He was more than ever struck by her beauty and unaffected manners, though her anxiety on Harry's and Jacob's account made her paler and graver than usual. She expressed her regret at being compelled to set off at once, and Headland therefore did not mention Sir Ralph's arrival till she had gone.

"I am sorry to hear of it," said Miss Jane, "for I fear that it will terminate Harry's and May's present happiness, and that the troubles and trials which I foresee are in store for them will at once begin, though I trust that they may overcome them in the end."

Captain Headland felt the remark applied equally to his own case, though he did not say so. He had omitted on the previous evening mentioning his meeting with Gaffin. He now did so, remarking—

"I understood that he was the leader of the party carrying off the young fisherman, but he assured me that he knew nothing of the matter, and was several miles distant when it occurred."

"I almost wish that he had been of the party if such is the case, for if he remains here, I fear that our May will be exposed to danger," said Miss Jane.

"Surely no one would venture to injure a young lady living with you," observed Headland.

Miss Jane then told him of the annoyance to which May had been subjected from Gaffin's son.

Headland naturally felt indignant.

"Strong measures must be taken to get this man Gaffin and his son out of the way," he remarked. "As soon as Harry returns we will see what can be done. In the meantime I will ride down to the cottage and ascertain that your young friend has reached it in safety, and will wait to escort her back."

He soon caught sight of her at about half-way to Adam's cottage. At the same moment a person resembling the man who had spoken to him on the previous night appeared and seemed about to address May, who quickened her pace, when catching sight of Headland he apparently thought better of it and advanced to meet him.

"Good-day, Captain Headland," said the man, looking up at him with cool assurance. "Your friend, Mr Harry Castleton, will have a long chase after the lugger, a wild goose chase I suspect it will prove. I have been enquiring into the truth of the story you heard, and I find that it was spread by a wretched old mad woman whom the people about here take to be a witch. The sooner she is ducked in the sea, and proved to be an ordinary mortal who has lost her senses, the better. It is disagreeable for a man in my position to have his character belied in this way."

"We certainly heard a story from a mad woman, but she spoke in a way which led us to suppose she described an actual occurrence," said Headland. "From what you say I conclude you are Mr Gaffin who addressed me last night."

"The same at your service, Captain Headland. I have no further questions to ask, however, since you can give me no account of my old shipmate; I am sorry to hear of his death; good-day to you, sir," and Gaffin moved on, taking the direction of the mill.

This last interview left a still more unfavourable impression on Headland's mind of Mr Miles Gaffin. He did not like the expression of the man's countenance or the impudent swagger of his manner; while it was evident by the way he talked that he was a person of some education. Headland tried to recollect whether he had before seen him, or whether his old protector had ever mentioned his name.

As he rode on slowly, keeping May in sight, he suddenly recollected the description Jack Headland had given him of the mate of the ship on board which he had been placed by his supposed father, when a child. "Can that man in any way be connected with my history?" he thought. "He certainly must have known poor Jack Headland; he had some motive, possibly, in speaking of him."

The more he thought the more puzzled he became. The only conclusion he arrived at was that Gaffin and the mate of the vessel in which he had been wrecked might possibly be one and the same person, and if so, from Jack's account, he was undoubtedly a villain, capable of any crime.

Having seen May enter Halliburt's cottage, he rode to the Texford Arms and put up his horse, resolving to wait in the neighbourhood till she should again come out. He would then have time to get back and mount his horse — which he told the hostler to keep saddled — and follow her.

He in the meantime took a few turns on the pier, and got into conversation with two or three of the old seafaring men who were standing about; the younger were at sea in their boats, or had gone home after the night's fishing. He made enquiries about the man he had just met. They all repeated the same story; their opinion was that he had been a pirate or something of that sort on the Spanish main, or in other distant seas, and having for a wonder escaped, he had returned home to follow a more peaceful and less dangerous calling, though still in reality unreformed and quite ready to break the laws of his country. From the description they gave of his wife, Headland thought that she must have been an Oriental, and this strengthened his idea that he was the man of whom Jack had spoken. Had he enquired about the Halliburts he might have learned the particulars of May's early history, but he still remained under the impression that she was a ward of the Miss Pembertons, and had merely come down to visit the dame as she would any other of the villagers suffering from sickness or sorrow.

Notwithstanding Gaffin's assertion that he knew nothing about Jacob being carried off, the men were certain that though he might not have been present, it had been done at his instigation, as his crew were known to be ready to engage in any daring undertaking he might suggest. They, however, feared that there was very little prospect of the lugger being captured.

"That mate of his would sooner run her under water or blow her up than let a king's officer come on board, and it will be better for poor Jacob if the cutter does not come up with her," observed one of them.

Headland borrowed a glass and swept the horizon several times, but no craft like the cutter appeared. At length he went back to the spot whence he could watch Adam's door for May's appearance. She came out at last, and he hurried to the inn to get his horse. He soon again caught sight of her and followed her at a distance till she reached Downside.

If Gaffin was, as he supposed it possible, watching her, that person took good care to keep out of his sight.

After waiting for a few minutes, Headland rode up to the cottage. He thought it would be prudent to let Miss Jane know of his having again seen Gaffin, and he took an opportunity, while May was out of the room, to tell her. She thanked him warmly.

"We must keep a careful watch over the safety of our young friend," she observed, "and while that dreadful man remains at the mill, must not allow her to go out alone. I hear that Sir Ralph's steward has given him warning to quit it at the end of his present lease. He will be unable to find another place of similar character suitable to his purposes."

When May came in Headland had the opportunity of conversing with her, and no longer felt surprised that she should so completely have won Harry's affections. Though he thought her inferior in some respects to Julia, he acknowledged to himself that she was one of the most charming girls he had seen, and was as much struck with her modesty and simplicity as with her sprightliness and beauty.

"It is a pity Sir Ralph could not be induced to see her," he thought; and he resolved to advise Julia to try and get her father to call at Downside, if possible, before he was aware of Harry's attachment, so that he might be perfectly unprejudiced.

Headland naturally wished to be back at Texford, though unwilling to go without being able to take any news of Harry.

At last as evening was approaching he rode once more to a point in the village where he could obtain an uninterrupted view of the sea, but the cutter was still not in sight. Accordingly, wishing the Miss Pembertons and May farewell, he set off on his way to the park.

He could conscientiously assure Lady Castleton that she need not be at all anxious about her son, as there was nothing surprising in the cutter not having returned. Sir Ralph seemed vexed at not seeing him, but made no other remark.

Captain Headland felt conscious that though Julia was anxious to be with him, her mother took every means in her power to prevent their meeting alone without showing too clearly that she was doing so. Julia found an opportunity, and told him her father was aware of their love, but had said that he would reserve any expression of his intentions till he had seen Harry. With this Headland was compelled to be content.

The baronet was perfectly polite, if not cordial, to him during the evening, and next morning he asked him if he would again ride over to Hurlston.

Algernon apologised for not accompanying him on the plea of illness.

Headland could not help suspecting that he was sent to be kept out of Julia's way; and but for her sake and Harry's, he would at once have left Texford.

He spent the day by first going to the village, and then calling at Downside, after which he took a long ride over the Downs to the south, whence he could see the cutter should she return.

Again, however, he was doomed to disappointment.

On his way back he met Mr Groocock, and begging the steward to accompany him, mentioned what he had heard about Gaffin.

"The man is a mystery to me, Captain Headland. I believe him to be all you have heard. But he has possession of the mill, and until his lease is up the law will not allow us to turn him out. The law, you see, captain, assists rogues as well as honest men, provided they keep within it, and there is no evidence we can bring to prove that he is what people say he is. If smuggled goods were found in his mill they would be seized, or if his vessel was taken with contraband aboard she would be captured, and there would be an end of her, and if it is true that his people have carried off the fisherman's son, they will be punished, but the law cannot touch him or his vessel for that, and so, you see, he will laugh at us, as he has done for these years past. But the master he serves will play him a scurvy trick in the end, as he does all his willing slaves, I have no manner of doubt. But, in the meantime, if he keeps his wits awake, as he has hitherto done, he may do all sorts of things with impunity."

To the truth of these remarks Headland agreed.

As they rode on Mr Groocock kept frequently looking up at him.

"If it's not an impertinent question, Captain Headland, may I ask if you have been in this part of the country before?"

"No," answered Headland. "I have been very little in England at all. I was born abroad, and have been at sea the greater part of my life."

"Of course—of course; I ought to have thought of that," said Mr Groocock to himself; then he added, "I beg your pardon, captain, but you remind me of some one I knew in former years—that made me ask the question without thinking; you are much younger than he would have been by this time."

Headland would willingly have enquired of whom the steward spoke, but the old man at once abruptly changed the conversation, and they shortly afterwards reached the gates of Texford.

The evening passed by much as the previous one had done, though Lady Castleton and Julia had become still more anxious at not seeing Harry.

Julia thought of poor May, who would, she knew, feel still more anxious, and she resolved, if possible, to go over to Downside the next day to see her, and show her sympathy.

Chapter Thirty Eight
Alarms

The family had retired to rest. Headland, however, was sitting up, feeling no inclination to sleep, and having numerous subjects to occupy his mind. He looked at his watch. It was one o'clock.

"After all, the only course which honour dictates lies straight before me. I would not persuade Julia to marry me without her father's consent; and if he withholds it I shall remain pledged to her, and go to sea till he withdraws his opposition."

At that moment the hall door bell rang a loud peal. Taking his lamp Headland went downstairs, hoping to find that Harry had returned. As no servant had appeared, he commenced withdrawing the bolts. Not being accustomed to the operation, he was some time about it.

"Bear a hand, let me in as fast as you can," said a voice. It was Harry's. He spoke in a hurried and excited tone.

Headland succeeded at last, and Harry staggered in, looking very pale. There was blood on his coat-sleeve and down his side.

"My dear fellow, what has happened?" exclaimed Headland.

"I have been attacked by highwaymen or ruffians of some sort, and though I beat them off, one of them sent a bullet through my side, and another gave me an ugly slash with a hanger. Thanks to my good steed, and a stout stick I carried instead of my whip, I kept them at bay till I got clear away."

"Come to your room at once then, and have your hurts looked to; you seem weak from loss of blood."

"I am somewhat faint, and shall be glad of some refreshment if we can rouse up the butler; but I do not wish to alarm my mother and Julia by making any disturbance in the house."

Headland having helped Harry to his room, received his directions where to find the servants, and went in search of them without waiting to hear more of his adventures.

"Thieves and robbers in the house! I'll be after them anon," exclaimed Boodle, the old butler, from within, giving sundry grunts and groans while trying to arouse himself.

Directly afterwards he made his appearance with night-cap on head, his breeches just slipped on supported by a single brace, and his feet in slippers, while in one hand was a blunderbuss and the other held a candle.

"You will find no thieves to fight with," said Headland, smiling at his appearance. "We only want you to bring a bottle of wine as a cordial, and afterwards to obtain some bandages from the housekeeper. Call some one to take Mr Harry's horse, and come as soon as you can."

Headland hurried back to Harry's room.

"I believe I have only received flesh wounds of no great consequence, and shall soon be all to rights," said Harry.

"Had we not better send off for a surgeon," asked Headland, "though I will do my best in the meantime."

"He or the messenger might be shot at on his way," answered Harry. "Your doctoring will be quite sufficient for the present, and we shall see how I feel in the morning."

Boodle soon appeared with the wine. He almost let the bottle drop as he saw the blood on Harry's dress.

"Dear, dear! what has happened, Mr Harry?" he asked with a look of horror.

"Nothing of consequence," answered Harry.

"Shall I call up her ladyship and Sir Ralph and Mrs Trimmings?"

"Pray, my good Boodle, do nothing of the sort; just get what Captain Headland requires, and then turn in and go to sleep again. We sailors, you know, are accustomed to this sort of thing."

Boodle having become more composed, hastened away to get the bandages and some hot water, while Headland, who had at different times assisted the surgeon on board ship, prepared to dress his friend's hurts.

In due course Harry greatly revived, and was able to tell his story. "You will be anxious," he said, "to hear about our chase. We thought at first that we should overhaul the lugger, as we had the breeze while she was becalmed. Still she managed to slip through the water. We kept her in sight all night, and the next morning the wind coming ahead I was in great hopes that we should get up to her—indeed we actually got within half-a-mile. Another slant of wind favouring her, she went away with her sheets eased off to the eastward, and shortly afterwards we lost sight of her in a thick mist which swept over the German Ocean. We stood on for some hours in the hopes of sighting her again, but when the fog cleared she was nowhere to be seen. The commander of the cutter declared that he had done all he could, and that we might as well look for a needle in a bundle of hay as search longer for the lugger, so we stood back for Hurlston."

TWO FELLOWS STARTED UP IN FRONT.

TWO FELLOWS STARTED UP IN FRONT.

It was some time after nightfall when we landed, and having seen poor Adam safe in his cottage, I, of course, went up to Downside to let the ladies know of our return. I was not aware how quickly the time passed. At length, finding how late it was, I mounted my horse and rode towards Texford.

I had just got out of the village when two fellows started up in front of my horse and tried to seize the bridle, when they treated me as I told you. With two blows of my stick I made them let go, when the animal springing forward I got clear of them, and, as you may suppose, did not draw rein till I reached this. They may have been highwaymen, but I suspect that they belonged to the smugglers' gang, and waylaid me in revenge for my interference with regard to young Halliburt.

Headland, recollecting the character he had heard of Gaffin, suggested that he possibly, with one of his companions, had attacked Harry.

"We must see about it to-morrow," he added, "and I must now insist on your going to bed, Harry, and trying to go to sleep, or your hurts will probably bring on fever. You must let me take up my berth in this arm-chair, that I may watch over you during the night."

Though Harry objected, Headland insisted on remaining, and the night passed away, Harry having given him very little trouble.

Headland was fortunate enough to meet Julia before the rest of the family had made their appearance. He thus was able to give her the first account of what had occurred, and to assure her that though Harry might be kept in the house a few days, he was in no danger.

She at once hurried to his room. He made light of his hurts, and declared that he should come down to breakfast as usual. She persuaded him, however, to remain in bed. He consented to do so on condition that she would send over to May, and account for his non-appearance at Downside that day.

Sir Ralph was very indignant at hearing of the outrage, and determined at once to take steps to discover the perpetrators. He had wished to speak to his son, and was annoyed at being unable to do so, as Lady Castleton persuaded him that any agitation would be injurious to Harry.

A surgeon had been sent for and gave a favourable report, complimenting Captain Headland on the way he had treated his patient.

Julia and Headland met constantly in Harry's room, both being anxious to assist in nursing him.

In a couple of days he was able to dress and come downstairs. Perhaps he would have remained up longer had he known the ordeal he was about to go through.

Harry was sitting in the drawing-room when he received a message from Sir Ralph, requesting him to come into the study.

"My father is going to question me about May," he thought. "I had hoped to escape this for some time to come; but I must be firm and not allow his prejudices to cause her unhappiness."

He walked slowly in. Sir Ralph closed the door and placed him in an arm-chair, and took his usual seat at his writing-table.

"Harry," he said, "I had sufficient confidence in you to suppose that, when you brought your friend Captain Headland to the house, you knew that he was a man of family and good connections, so that should he fall in love with your sister no objections were likely to be raised. Am I right in giving you credit for this amount of wisdom?"

Harry felt greatly relieved on finding that he was not to be questioned about May.

"My friend Headland, sir," he said, "is a first-rate officer and an excellent fellow, and is sure to gain credit for himself and to rise high in the service."

"That may be," observed Sir Ralph. "But I wish to know if he is a man of family and a fit match for your sister, for I understand that he has of late paid her great attention."

"I think so highly of him that I am sure any girl would be fortunate in winning his affections," answered Harry.

"That's not the question I wish to have answered. I wish to know whether he is of good family, and has a sufficient fortune to support a wife, as Julia ought to be supported."

"On the first point I cannot enlighten you," answered Harry; "for I confess that I do not know of what family he is, but he has been very fortunate in making prize money, and I am sure he has quite enough to live in a way to satisfy Julia."

"I was afraid it might be so from never having heard him speak of his family," said Sir Ralph. "You have acted very imprudently, Harry, in bringing a man of his description here. Though I do not wish to act with discourtesy, I desire you will give him to understand that he is no longer welcome at Texford."

"That is impossible, father," exclaimed Harry. "He is devotedly attached to Julia, and I am sure she is to him. If he is told to go, I must go also. I have said that, though I do not know his family, for the simple reason that he does not know it himself. He is everything that is noble, and good, and excellent, and I would rather see Julia marry him than any other person in existence."

"I know the world better than you do, Harry, and such a marriage as you wish me to sanction for your sister is not calculated to promote her welfare, and that is the point I, as her father, have to consider."

"If she is not allowed to marry Headland she will be miserable," exclaimed Harry.

"I had considered the point maturely before I sent for you," said Sir Ralph, "and I wish to save your friend the annoyance of being spoken to by me. If you refuse to tell him my determination, I shall have to do so. And now, Harry, I have another matter to speak to you about."

Harry grew nervous.

"I understand during my absence you have paid frequent visits to Downside."

"Yes, sir," said Harry, "Our cousins kindly invited me there."

"I know they did, and placed a young lady, I hear, of some personal attractions in your way, and, like a sailor, you directly tumbled over head and ears in love with her. I strip the matter of the romance with which you may be inclined to surround it. Do I not speak the truth?"

"I confess, sir," said Harry, determined to speak boldly, "I have met at the Miss Pembertons a young lady to whom I have declared my love."

"You have declared your fiddlestick," exclaimed the baronet, with less than his usual dignity. "You could make no promise without my sanction, and that I cannot give you. You can let the girl know this in any way you like."

"My affections were engaged before I was aware of it, and as I am of age, and the young lady is in every way calculated to insure my happiness, and I have the means of supporting her without taxing you, I felt that I had a right to propose to her."

"In other words, you were entrapped before you saw the meshes spread to catch you, and discarding every other consideration, are ready to disobey me, and give up your profession, and all your prospects of advancement in life, for the sake of a pretty face," observed the baronet, sarcastically. "Though *you* are ready to make a fool of yourself, I must exert my paternal authority and save you from ruin."

"But I do not contemplate giving up my profession, and the prize money I have already made, with what I may hope to obtain, will give me ample means to support a wife," answered Harry.

"Have you calculated, may I ask, to what this princely fortune you speak of amounts?"

"Three or four hundred a year, sir, not including my pay; and the young lady herself is not penniless, for our cousins have resolved to leave her their property."

"Our cousins leave a stranger their property!" exclaimed Sir Ralph. "It should be Julia's or yours; it came through the Castletons, and should return to them."

"So it will, sir," said Harry, having, as he hoped, caught his father in a trap, "when May marries me."

"I see how it is," observed the baronet, not noticing Harry's last remark. "Our sanctimonious cousins wish to get a husband for this girl they have picked up, and as they are not likely to meet any other young gentleman in the secluded way they live, they have entrapped you."

"I assure you, sir, you do them great wrong," observed Harry, warmly. "I went to the house of my own accord, and I am sure it did not enter their heads that I should fall in love with their friend. I wish, sir, that you could see them and the lady you condemn. Possessing as you do so exquisite a taste in female beauty and refinement, I am sure you will admire her."

"I may possibly call at the Miss Pembertons, because I wish to express my opinion of their conduct in the matter," said the baronet, wishing not to appear influenced by his son's remarks. "I may then see this girl who has caught you. I tell you that if she were as beautiful as Venus, nothing would alter my determination. May I ask, do you know who she is? Your mother has only spoken to me of her as the Miss Pembertons protégé."

Harry, feeling perfectly sure that should he answer the question his father would be still more adverse to his marriage, and would possibly express himself forcibly on the subject, replied—

"I wish, sir, that you would see her before I answer the last question. I wish you to judge her on her own merits, independent of all other considerations."

Harry had maintained the conversation with a good deal of spirit, though he felt somewhat exhausted, when his father, turning to the table, began to write without apparently noticing him. While thus seated, his eye fell on the picture of his long lost uncle which hung next to Sir Reginald's. Though he had been often in the room, he had never particularly noticed it, for it was in a bad light, and the features were not distinct. A gleam of sunlight now coming into the room fell directly on it, and suddenly, as he gazed, a strange idea came into his mind. He thought, and thought. "Yes, the features and expression remind me much of what he was at the same age, and yet it must be fancy."

Sir Ralph suddenly interrupted his reveries.

"Harry," he said, "I do not wish to quarrel with your friend, that is not my way, but you will take an early opportunity of advising him to spend the remainder of his time on shore elsewhere."

"But has Headland proposed to you for Julia?" asked Harry.

"No, and I wish to prevent him from doing so," said Sir Ralph. "We shall part on much better terms than would be the case had I to refuse his offer, and I dislike such a scene as is likely to follow. If he goes away without being engaged she will soon forget him, and he, employed in active service, will forget her; the matter will thus be settled, and much inconvenience saved."

Chapter Thirty Nine
Sir Ralph at Downside

Harry had returned to his room when the surgeon, Mr Curtis, arrived.

"Pulse is not as satisfactory as I should have wished," he observed. "We must keep you quiet, Mr Harry, and I must request you to remain in your room till I see you again."

"What!" exclaimed Harry. "I thought of taking a ride to-morrow. I am very anxious to go over to Downside."

"Totally out of the question, Mr Harry. You would very likely bring on a fever, and I could not answer for the consequences."

"Have you seen the Miss Pembertons lately?" asked Harry.

"Yes. Miss Jane, though she generally considers her skill superior to mine, sent for me to attend the young lady who lives with them, and I suspect, Mr Harry, that you had something to do with her illness, though I am happy to say there is nothing serious. She heard somewhat abruptly of your having been attacked by the robbers, and it was said that you had only just time to reach the hall and fall down in a dead faint. When I assured her that you were in no danger at all, and would soon recover if you followed my advice, she quickly got better, and I hope to find her quite well when I next call."

"Though I may not ride, could I not drive there?" asked Harry. "I must see her, or she may still be fancying that I am worse than is the case."

"Not with my leave, certainly," said the doctor. "I will take care to let her know how you are getting on, and if, as I suspect, you are not indifferent to the young beauty, I shall be happy to bring you any message she may send you."

"I will write to her," exclaimed Harry. "I will not detain you long."

"No, no, my friend, I am happy to convey any verbal message, but must decline being the carrier of written despatches. I might possibly hand them to the wrong persons, and instead of a prescription which I had intended to leave, some demure middle-aged maiden might find herself in possession of a love letter. I know well enough all you have to say, and trust me for making the young lady understand you."

"By-the-bye, have you seen Dame Halliburt? I wish to know how she and her husband bear the loss of their son."

"She is about again, and both keep up their spirits in the hopes that the lad will manage to make his escape from the smugglers, and return to them before long. It is a sore trial for them though, as he was their only remaining child."

"The doctor forgets May," thought Harry; and very naturally did not mention her, by which he lost the opportunity of learning a fact which might have been of considerable consequence to him.

The doctor as he went down saw Lady Castleton and Julia, and charged them on no account to let Harry go out.

"I cannot be answerable for his life if he does," he observed, more, perhaps, for the sake of inducing them to be firm on the subject than because he had any apprehension of Harry's safety.

Sir Ralph kept to his resolution of going over to Downside. He set out followed by his groom, both of them carrying pistols in their holsters, while the baronet in addition wore a sword by his side, in case any of the gang of ruffians who had attacked his son might set upon him.

The Miss Pembertons had in the meantime kept to their purpose of making a will in favour of Maiden May. Mr Shallard arrived unexpectedly one morning. They explained their views, and as there was nothing intricate, he was able to draw it up at once, and Adam Halliburt and their gardener, who had been sent for, acted as witnesses. Adam's satisfaction at seeing his Maiden May thus amply provided for was very great.

"God bless you, ladies," he exclaimed; "if there is anything that could make me feel happy it is this."

"I remember your mentioning the little girl to me some years ago," observed Mr Shallard to Adam; "and I am afraid we have been remiss in not making more efforts to ascertain to what family she can belong, although the difficulties have increased by the length of time which has elapsed. The expense, however, will, I fear, be considerable, though really for the sake of so interesting a young lady I should be happy to bear it."

"If it would prove to May's interest to discover her parents I would also assist, and so would my sister Mary," said Miss Jane.

"We will see what can be done," said Mr Shallard, at length preparing to take his departure. Just as he reached the hall door, Sir Ralph rode up. "Good-day, Mr Shallard. What, have my good cousins been requiring your services?"

"Had I called professionally I should have been bound not to reveal the business even to you, my most respected client," answered the lawyer evasively. "I trust you can give me a favourable account of Lieutenant Castleton. We must hunt up the scoundrels who attacked him, but as yet the myrmidons of justice have made no progress I fear."

"They have not, and the country is indeed in an unsatisfactory condition when such outrages as have lately occurred can be perpetrated with impunity," observed Sir Ralph.

Mr Shallard, however, not wishing to have any longer conversation with the baronet, wished him "good morning," and rode off.

May had just been summoned to the drawing-room after the lawyer's departure. She was seated by Miss Mary's side, engaged with her needle, the light which streamed through the bay window falling on her fair countenance, and showing the golden hue in her hair. Had she intentionally placed herself in a position for appearing to the best advantage, she could not have been more successful. Miss Jane was seated nearer the door, when the baronet entered.

"Though your visits are rare we are glad to see you whenever you do come, Sir Ralph," she said, rising and putting out her hand, which the baronet lifted to his lips with his usual courtly politeness. "Here is Sir Ralph, Mary," added Miss Jane.

Miss Mary rose as did May in a graceful way, standing with one hand on the chair, as she felt an unusual trepidation seize her.

The baronet advanced, fixing his eyes on her, and then having pressed Miss Mary's hand, he made her one of his most courtly bows.

"Let me introduce our young friend to you," said Miss Jane, who had observed Sir Ralph's glance of admiration.

He was of too unbending a nature, however, to allow May's beauty to alter his determination. He entered into conversation, however, with the freedom of a man of the world, making the ladies believe that his visit was only one of courtesy. His critical taste could not help being satisfied with May's manners and the remarks she made, as much as it had been by her beauty, and she began to feel that regard for him which she naturally wished to have for the father of her intended husband.

The baronet, rising, said in a more formal tone than he had hitherto used—

"I must beg of you, Miss Pemberton, a few minutes private conversation before I bid you farewell."

"If you wish it we will go to the dining-room, or Mary and May will leave us alone."

"Not on any account would I have them quit the drawing-room," answered Sir Ralph, and stepping up to Miss Mary he lifted her hand to his lips, bowing at the same time to May, with that courtesy which he considered her beauty demanded, though his cold look gave her an unsatisfactory feeling.

"I am obliged to you for allowing me an interview in private," he said, as soon as he and Miss Jane were seated in the dining-room. "I wish to make enquiries with regard to the young person residing with you, and with whom, it appears, my son Harry has fallen in love. With all respect to you you must be aware that I cannot consider a person in her situation in any way a suitable wife for a son of mine, and though I do not wish to throw blame upon you, I cannot help feeling that you have been guilty of indiscretion, to use no stronger term, in allowing the young people to meet in the way it appears they have done. I should have expected, under the circumstances, that you would not have invited him to the house, and had he called of his own accord would have kept the young lady out of his way. I must therefore hold you responsible for the consequences."

The tone of this address—so unlike that in which Sir Ralph had been speaking in the drawing-room—took Miss Jane considerably aback; but she was not to be easily brow-beaten even by her cousin.

"I am not conscious, Sir Ralph, of having acted in any way in which I can blame myself," she answered, with as much dignity as she could command. "We had no design when we expressed our pleasure at seeing Harry at Downside, nor did we think of his falling in love with our young friend."

"May I ask whether she is a relation, or to what family she belongs?" asked Sir Ralph, abruptly.

"She is no relation, though we love her as one," said Miss Jane. "Has not your son told you her history?"

"Not a word; he declined doing so," said the baronet.

"It is a very romantic one," answered Miss Jane, and she described the way May had been rescued.

"Judging from her appearance, she may be of gentle birth," observed Sir Ralph, "but the fact that her family have not been discovered tends to prove the contrary, and nothing you have said alters my determination not to sanction my son's marriage to a girl depending on charity for her support."

"That alone interests us, and makes us more than ever ready to care for her," said Miss Jane. "We have this very day left her all the property we possess, or which may ever come to us, and she is therefore no longer helpless and dependent, as you suppose."

"I should have concluded you would have wished to leave to the Castleton family what originally came from them," remarked the baronet, with some heat in his tone.

"That is not a matter I am disposed to discuss," said Miss Jane. "Your daughter is, I conclude, well provided for, and we have not acted contrary to the wishes of your son Harry, who is the only other person we should have thought of making our heir."

"As you think fit—as you think fit," said the baronet. "I have only now to request that you will inform your protégé if she marries my son Harry she will not be received by his mother or me as a daughter, and will certainly justly compel us to discard him for his disobedience."

"Do you insist on my giving such a message to the poor girl?" asked Miss Jane, feeling very indignant, but, at the same time, still hoping to soften her cousin's heart.

"If you do not give it, I must myself. To tell you the truth, I came here for that purpose. It is always better to settle matters of this sort summarily."

"Oh!" said Miss Jane.

"Concluding that you will do as I request, I must wish you good morning," said the baronet. "I have further to beg that you will not admit my son into your house."

"I can make no promises," said Miss Jane. "I will, however, give your harsh message to our young friend, though I cannot undertake to advise her how to act. I regret, Sir Ralph, that the only visit with which you have honoured us while at Texford has not terminated in a more satisfactory manner to you and to ourselves."

Miss Jane did not even put out her hand, she felt too indignant with her cousin at what she considered his harsh and cruel conduct. He turned towards the door which she stepped forward and opened, accompanying him through the hall. He, not forgetting his usual courteous manner, turned and lifted his hat before descending the steps, at the bottom of which his groom stood holding his horse.

No further words were exchanged between the cousins, and Sir Ralph rode back to Texford satisfied at having exhibited his resentment to the only person on whom he could fix it, and, as he hoped, put an end to any further intercourse between his son and Maiden May.

Chapter Forty
Sir Ralph's Decision

Harry had heard from Julia that his father had gone over to Downside, and was looking forward with no little anxiety to the result of his interview with May. He had not yet brought himself to tell Headland all his father had said, for, knowing his friend, he was sure that he would, in spite of the grief it would cause him, at once leave Texford, and he wished to allow him and Julia to enjoy that happiness which he foresaw must so soon be cruelly terminated.

Headland was not a man to exhibit his feelings in the presence of others, and the baronet, who watched him narrowly, observed only that though he appeared to treat Julia with that attention which the young lady of the house had a right to expect, there was nothing peculiarly marked in his manner.

Julia ought undoubtedly to have told Sir Ralph of the offer she had received, and she would have done so had there been that confidence between the father and daughter which should have existed. But Sir Ralph had failed to secure the confidence and affection of his children.

Julia, not wishing that her father should discover her secret, took care not to invite Headland to walk with her in the grounds when Sir Ralph was likely to meet them, and as he seldom went far from the house on foot there was little probability of his doing so.

As Mr Curtis told Sir Ralph that Harry must be kept quiet for a few days, he did not allude to his visit, and Harry was therefore left in doubt as to the result.

The next time the surgeon came, Harry asked whether he had been again at Downside.

"I tell you there is nothing seriously the matter with the young lady, though she does not recover as rapidly as I had expected; her nervous system seems slightly affected. However, there is no fear, and in a few days she will be round."

If the doctor knew more of the true state of the case, he did not think fit to communicate it to Harry.

Such was the state of things when the post brought two official letters from the Lords Commissioners of the Admiralty, appointing Commander Headland to the *Thisbe* sloop-of-war, and Lieutenant Castleton to the *Aurora* frigate, with orders to join their respective ships at once. It was the first day Harry had come down.

"I congratulate you, gentlemen," said Sir Ralph in a tone Harry did not like. "You will both soon see active service, for, depend upon it, Napoleon will not let us remain long at peace."

Poor Julia, turning pale, nearly betrayed herself.

"I am obliged to their lordships; I scarcely expected to get a ship so soon," replied Headland, who did not exhibit that enthusiastic pleasure which might have been expected on being appointed to his first command.

"I should have been more obliged to them if they had appointed me to the same ship," said Harry. "You, I daresay, can manage to do it," he added, turning to his father. "Possibly the lieutenants may not as yet have been selected."

"I have not much interest at the Admiralty, and what I have I must keep for your promotion," said Sir Ralph. "We shall lose you, Captain Headland, sooner than was expected, for I presume that you will have to start to-morrow at latest."

Headland could not help feeling that this was a strong hint to him to hasten his departure.

"I will lose no time, Sir Ralph, in joining my ship, though I shall leave Texford with regret."

He glanced for a moment on Julia, but for her sake directly withdrew his eyes, judging truly from his own feelings what hers were.

"I am glad to see that both ships are fitting at Portsmouth," observed Harry, "and if we cannot travel together, and I suppose the doctor won't let me go for a few days, I will join you there."

Harry talked away, trying to keep up his own spirits as well as those of his friend. He felt that a crisis was at hand, and that Headland must openly declare his love for Julia, whether or not Sir Ralph was likely to give his sanction to their engagement.

Headland saw matters in the same light. He wished, however, first to consult Julia as to whether he should tell her father of their engagement, or leave her to do so.

Fortunately, Sir Ralph was engaged in writing letters and other business for some time after breakfast, and Headland, finding Julia alone, invited her to go into the grounds where they could talk without fear of interruption.

"Your going seems so sudden that I can scarcely realise it," she exclaimed. "I fancied that weeks and months would pass before you were ordered away to sea, and now Sir Ralph says you must set off to-morrow. Can it be necessary to go so soon?"

"It is so," said Headland, "but I go confiding in you, and hoping that the time may come when I shall return to claim you. Your father must be informed of our engagement, or he may justly accuse me of acting a dishonourable part. Either you or I must tell him as soon as possible. I am perfectly ready to do so, unless you think you can influence him more than I can expect to do."

"Oh, do you speak to him," exclaimed Julia. "You can plead the perfect right you had to win my affections; your position in the navy, and your prospects of rising; the ample means you already possess; and the gallant deeds you have performed. He cannot possibly blame you. And tell him that my heart and hand are pledged to you, and that though I will not disobey him by marrying against his will, I will never marry any one else."

Headland undertook to act as Julia advised.

They might enjoy an hour now in each other's society before Sir Ralph was likely to be disengaged, and how rapidly those moments flew by; but both felt that the time was come for a frank statement of their case.

They returned to the house confident in each other's love, and supported with the hopes that whatever clouds might now arise they would in time be dissipated.

Sir Ralph was alone in his study. Captain Headland knocked at the door, and was requested to enter.

"I must apologise for intruding on you, Sir Ralph, but before I leave Texford there is a matter of consequence on which I wish to speak to you," he said.

The baronet motioned him to take a chair nearly opposite where he himself sat.

"Pray, Captain Headland, what is it?" he asked, in a calm tone.

"I earnestly wish to make your daughter my wife, and I have her permission to request that you will give your sanction to our marriage when I next return on shore."

"A very clear if not a very modest request," exclaimed the baronet, with a well-feigned look of surprise. "Do I understand that Miss Castleton has pledged her hand to you without my sanction?"

"My express object in now speaking to you is to obtain that sanction," answered Headland, with all the calmness he could command.

"I am not at all disposed to give it unless to a man her equal in birth and family, and before I can reply, I must beg that you will inform me to what family you belong, and what means you possess."

Headland briefly described his position.

"I have, however, every prospect of rising in the service, and of adding to the credit which, with honest pride, I may venture to say, I have already gained. I have your daughter's authority for telling you that she will marry no one else till I return to ask her hand."

The baronet listened to him calmly without speaking till he had finished.

"I will make no remark on your conduct, Captain Headland, whatever I may think of it," he said, at length, after nearly a minute's silence. "But you will understand that I do not allow my daughter to pledge herself as you tell me she has done. You will understand that though I do not wish to treat you with discourtesy, I do not expect that you will honour me with another visit when you return on shore. I regret having to say this while you are still my guest, but you have forced me to express myself clearly on the subject. And now I think you will agree with me that to prolong this interview will not lead to any satisfactory result. You have clearly explained your position, and I have as clearly expressed my opinion. I will speak to Miss Castleton, and it may be a satisfaction to you if, as I expect she will, she states her readiness at my desire to set you free. I must beg, however, that what I have said may not induce you to leave Texford sooner than you had intended. I may say that I have that confidence in you that you will not in the meantime try to induce my daughter to take any step of which I should disapprove."

The baronet rose as he spoke, and Headland, not considering an answer to the last remark necessary, did so likewise, and with a formal bow, which Sir Ralph returned, left the room.

His heart swelling with indignation and sorrow, he repaired to his own chamber. He felt indignant at the way Sir Ralph had treated him: his sorrow was for Julia, for he knew too well the sufferings she would be called on to endure on his account. He threw himself into a chair to consider what steps he should take; could he remain longer as the guest of Sir Ralph? and then he thought, "he is Julia's father, and for her sake I must bear what I would not from any other man."

Harry, suspecting what had taken place, soon followed Headland to his room.

"My dear fellow," he exclaimed, "I am sure my father has spoken in a way you feel hard to bear; let me entreat you not to take notice of it. I do not ask you what he said, but I am right, am I not?"

"You are, and I was contemplating leaving the house."

"That is just what you must not do," exclaimed Harry. "You came as my guest, and I cannot allow it. Our father does not know what Julia is made of; when he comes to speak to her, he will find that she can be as firm as he is. I am very certain she will not discard you, and he may find that after all he has to give in, and allow you to go away awaiting for a time when you can return and claim her, which he may possibly hope will never arrive."

Headland was at length persuaded to do as Harry advised; indeed his own heart prompted him to remain, for even had Sir Ralph spoken to him in a still more offensive tone, he would not have left.

"You know me, Harry; and assure her that whatever your father may say, and however she may be compelled to act towards me, I shall remain pledged to her as long as there is a possibility of her becoming mine."

"In other words," said Harry, "unless she is compelled to marry some one else."

"I could not bear the thoughts of her doing so," exclaimed Headland. "Even then I should remain her devoted and faithful friend."

"I am sure you would," answered Harry. "I will tell her all you say, though I hope you will be able to tell her yourself. And, my dear fellow, I know my little sister well enough to be very sure that no power on earth will induce her to marry any one else."

Headland felt somewhat relieved by his conversation with his friend. Harry knew that he had his own trials in store, and could sympathise with him thoroughly.

He had become very impatient at not being able to ride out. The doctor had brought him better accounts from Downside; that was his chief consolation. He determined to go directly Headland left Texford; he would propose a ride with Julia, and she would not refuse to accompany him thus far.

Directly Headland quitted the study, Sir Ralph summoned Julia. She well knew what was coming, and bracing herself up for the interview, appeared before her father with as calm a countenance as she could assume.

"I understand, young lady, that your brother's friend and shipmate, Captain Headland, has proposed to you, and that without knowing who he is, or what are my wishes on the subject, you have ventured to accept him."

"Yes, papa, I have done so," said Julia.

"You have acted very improperly," remarked Sir Ralph.

"I saw nothing in Captain Headland that would make you object to him, on the contrary, everything to admire," answered Julia, in a firm tone.

"No girl can take such a step without her parent's permission."

"I had no reason to suppose that permission would not be given," said Julia.

"As you are mistaken you are absolved from your promise, and I desire you to tell Captain Headland that you set him free."

"Father," exclaimed Julia, rising, "if you can point out one single blemish in Captain Headland's character, if you can produce one sufficient reason, I would obey you so far as to set him free; but, at the same time, I must tell you I could never marry another. You, however, can allege no just reason why I should not marry him, and I will not utter a falsehood, and lead him to suppose that I do not love him with the most devoted affection."

The baronet listened to his daughter with a scornful curl on his thin lips, and a flush on his brow. Seldom did he exhibit more violent signs of anger.

"I am to understand, then, that you positively refuse to discard this unknown adventurer?" said the baronet, speaking very deliberately. "I regret that I did not use stronger language when speaking to him, but I expected to have your assistance, and wished to save a scene which might be disagreeable. I must send for him again, and explain myself more clearly."

"Father, I entreat you not to do so," exclaimed Julia, putting her hand on Sir Ralph's arm. "I will speak to Captain Headland, but you cannot, you must not, insult a gallant officer, your son's friend, a guest in your house; you would not gain your end, and you would only add bitterness to my grief at having to part from him."

"If, as I understand, he proposes to take his departure to-morrow, I will allow matters to remain as they are, you promising me that you will speak to him in the way I desire."

"I promise that I will tell Captain Headland of your objections, and I will not act in any way that will bring discredit on the name of Castleton, of which I am as proud as any member of the family."

Julia, with woman's tact, made the last remark, knowing that it would influence her father more than any vehement protestation she could utter.

Headland had been for some time writing in his room after Harry had left him, when the latter returned, and told him he would find Julia in the grounds. Headland eagerly hurried out, and joined her at the spot where Harry had told him she was waiting. They walked on till they reached a summer-house near the lake.

"You have had an interview with my father, and he has since talked to me, and desired me to speak to you, and I promised to obey him, but I do so under compulsion. He said that he would never sanction my becoming your wife, and that I must tell you so. I replied, that as you had my heart, to no one else would I give my hand."

Headland had every reason to be satisfied with all Julia said, though he felt that long years might pass before she could become his, while she could not hide from herself the numberless dangers he might have to encounter before he could return to claim her; and even then would her father have relented, and might not still difficulties be thrown in the way of their marriage? Hope, however, buoyed her up. Her great wish, in the meantime, would be to remain at Texford, and endeavour to benefit the tenantry and surrounding cottagers. London with its gaieties she felt would have no attractions for her, though she had reason to fear that her father would insist on her going there, and mixing in society, in the hopes of inducing her to form a match such as he would consider suitable for her.

Headland, more than ever convinced of Julia's attachment, was thankful that he had not taken offence at the language her father had used, and at once left the house.

That last meeting, as they sat together looking out on the placid lake, mirrored with the foliage of the overhanging trees, with swans gliding calmly across its surface, the only sound the sweet songs of the bird, or the occasional splash of the fish as they rose to seize the careless flies fleeting above them, could never be forgotten: it brought a sense of peace, and consolation, and hope to their hearts.

The time flew by. Both were unwilling to return to the house. It was the last opportunity they would have of meeting alone.

General Sampson's voice addressing Mrs Appleton in loud tones aroused them.

"I tell you, my dear madam, I shall win my bet notwithstanding," he exclaimed. "My friend, the captain, is not a man who is likely to strike his flag as long as he has a stick standing; he will renew the fight as soon as he has repaired damages."

"I tell you, general, I have known Sir Ralph longer than you have—a more determined, or rather obstinate gentleman does not exist, and unless this captain is a man of family, and that he is not, or I am very sure we should have heard about it, our friend will never give his sanction."

"Then, by Jove, the young people will run off and do without it, ah! ah! ah!" roared the general.

"Fie, fie, General Sampson, you would not approve of such a proceeding, I hope."

"I am not sure of that, Mrs Appleton," was the answer; and just then the couple came in sight of Headland and Julia, and must have been aware that their remarks had been overheard.

The young people were still more annoyed at being discovered. They both rose, and at the same moment the gong sounded from the house to summon the guests to dress for dinner.

"Pleasant sound that, captain, for those who have appetites," observed the general. "We must all obey it whether or not, and move homewards." Though Julia and Headland would willingly have lingered longer, they were compelled to follow the old general and Mrs Appleton to the house. How quickly that evening went by. Sir Ralph was as courteous as usual, and though formal in the extreme in his manner to Captain Headland, no one would have suspected what had occurred in the morning. Julia did her best to maintain her composure. Though Sir Ralph begged to have music, her mother interfered and saved her from the trial.

Next day arrived at length. Captain Headland was really gone. Julia felt bewildered and desolate; it seemed as if she had received some heavy blow from which it was impossible to recover. Sir Ralph spoke to her in a more kind way than usual, and tried to joke with her, while he amused his guests with the numerous anecdotes which he knew well how to tell.

The doctor, who came early, allowed Harry to take a ride. "It must be short though, and you must not gallop at headlong speed, as you naval officers are apt to do."

"I will get my sister to accompany me to keep me in order." Julia gladly agreed to bear him company.

"Thank you, dear Julia," said Harry, as soon as they were in the saddle. "We must go to Downside; I cannot exist another day without seeing May."

Julia nodded her consent.

"I thought she would have written to me, but I have my fears that either our good cousins have forbidden her to write or that her letters may have been stopped," he continued. "Did you write to her?" asked Julia.

"No, but I sent messages, and as the only person I could trust to take a letter declined doing so, I could not order a groom to take one, as I had my suspicions that it might be stopped or opened; besides, I have that confidence in May's love that I felt sure she would be content to wait till we could again meet, hearing in the meantime that I was rapidly recovering."

"You acted wisely," said Julia, "for it is impossible to say how our cousins may think it their duty to behave towards you in future."

She then told Harry of their father's visit to Downside, of the result of which she herself was ignorant.

"I am sorely tempted to set my father at defiance, and, if he refuses his consent, to marry without it."

"No, no, Harry—patience! May would never consent to such a course."

"Why, Julia, what do you intend to do?" asked Harry, wrongly feeling for the moment that even she had turned against him.

"To obey our father and not to act against his commands; but I will not obey him in doing a sinful act by marrying any one else whom I do not love. I can, therefore, with a clear conscience urge you not to persuade May to marry you until our father gives his consent, though I do not for a moment advise you to give her up."

"You are a clever casuist, Julia," exclaimed Harry.

Chapter Forty One
A Ride with General Sampson

On reaching Downside, Harry and Julia were told that Miss Jane was in the house, and that Miss Mary and May were in the garden.

"Go in and see cousin Jane," said Harry to his sister, as he assisted her to dismount. "I will go into the garden."

Without giving Julia the option of accompanying him, he hurried off in search of his blind cousin and her companion. He saw them seated on a bench under the shade of some overhanging trees. May was reading with her eyes bent down on the book. She was so absorbed in the subject that she did not hear Harry's approach.

Miss Mary's quick ear, however, soon detected the sound of his footsteps.

"Who is coming?" she asked abruptly.

May looked up, and uttering Harry's name in a tone of joy, sprang forward to meet him.

"Why, Harry, I had not expected to see you so soon," she exclaimed, gazing up into his face.

Holding her hand, he advanced to Miss Mary, who smiled kindly as she greeted him. He told them that it was the first day the doctor had allowed him to ride out.

"Did Sir Ralph know that you were coming here?" asked Miss Mary.

"No; I conclude he did not suppose I was able to ride so far."

"Then you have not acted against his orders."

"Certainly not," answered Harry; "he has not prohibited me from coming here."

"I am truly glad of that," observed Miss Mary, with marked emphasis. "I will leave you young people here, and go in and have a talk with Julia. I daresay you will have something to say to each other."

Harry and May offered to accompany the kind lady to the house.

"No, no," she answered; "I can find my way perfectly well alone, and shall not meet with an accident if there are no wheelbarrows or rakes in the way," and rising, she proceeded at a slow pace towards the house.

May told Harry how anxious she had been on hearing of his being wounded by highwaymen—how grateful she felt to him for having endeavoured to recover Jacob. Then Harry told her how, day by day, he had heard of her from the doctor, and how the knowledge that she was getting better did more to restore him than anything else. He refrained from telling her, as long as he could, what he knew would give her pain—that he was appointed to a ship which he must soon join. At length, however, he had to communicate the information.

"But May," he added, "if you will consent at once to be mine, we would marry before I go, and then no human power can separate us."

"Harry," she exclaimed, gazing at him fixedly as they sat on the bench together, "I had not thought that the time for parting would be so soon. You know my regard; but I must not tempt you to act contrary to what I fear are your father's wishes, and by so doing run the risk of injuring your prospects in life, and your advancement in your profession. Your father has been here, and has expressed his opinions strongly to Miss Jane, and she has told me all he said. I shall be as truly yours as if we were married, and you will thus avoid offending him, whose wishes you are bound to respect. My thoughts will be ever with you, my prayers hourly offered up for your safety, and I shall live in hopes that the obstacles which now exist to our union will be removed when you return. Your father may relent when he finds that you are constant, and I know you will be;" and she smiled as she gazed at his countenance, and felt the impossibility of his changing.

"But I know him so well that even then I am sure he will refuse his consent on the same grounds that he does now. Will you still believe that you ought not to marry me?" exclaimed her lover.

"Oh, Harry, do not press me for an answer," answered May. "I wish to do what is right, and your cousins tell me, and my conscience assures me that they are right, that I must not become yours while your parents object to your marrying me. I must not encourage you to do what is wrong, and expose you to your father's anger. And, Harry, though I am not proud, I could not consent to enter a family who would treat me with contempt, and consider that you had lowered yourself by marrying me."

"Oh, May, I did not expect to have this reply from you," he exclaimed at last, in a tone of bitter disappointment.

"I have spoken as I believe to be right, and therefore it must be for the best," said May, trying to calm her agitation. "How I might have acted without wise counsellors, I cannot say. Do not urge me further; I dare not, I cannot give a different reply."

In vain Harry endeavoured to induce May to alter her determination, although he reasoned as an ardent lover who was not willing to be convinced. May was not surprised that Harry should argue the point, perhaps she was pleased at his doing so; but, being satisfied that she was right, the very fact that her feelings prompted her to act differently assisted her to hold to her resolution. Harry was inclined to be angry, not with her, that seemed impossible, but with his cousins for advising her as they had done. He considered his father tyrannical and unjust in the matter, and he was even less disposed than ever to obey him. May endeavoured to soothe him. She succeeded at last. She spoke of the future when there might be no impediment to their happiness. They were both still very young, and when Harry had become a commander, or obtained his post rank, they might realise their wish of living in just such a cottage as Downside, and enjoy all the happiness their mutual love could afford.

They were interrupted by the appearance of Miss Jane and Julia. The latter had taken more note of time than had Harry, and considered that they ought to be on their return to Texford.

Julia led May to a distance.

"Your sister will tell you our wishes, Harry," said Miss Jane. "You know how May is situated, and you know how affectionately we regard you. Though we do not consider that your father is right in withholding his consent, we feel bound to obey his commands, and as he has insisted on our not encouraging you to come to the house, and as we understand you are to join a ship as soon as possible, we must beg you to bid May farewell. I say this with regret, but I am sure it will be the best for both of you."

"What! do you forbid me from coming here again?" exclaimed Harry. "Would you deny me the only happiness I prize on earth?"

"You must, I understand, in a few days join your ship, and though we would rather for your sake in the meantime that you did not come, we cannot turn you from our doors," answered Miss Jane, somewhat relenting. "Only you must promise not to try to induce May to waver in her resolution. You will then part with the consciousness that you have acted rightly, and may hope for your reward when you return from sea."

Though Harry would have lingered, Julia wisely considered that they ought to return homewards without delay.

May did not refuse to allow him to press her to his heart, and his cousins wished him an affectionate farewell, and he and Julia mounting their horses commenced their ride back to Texford.

Julia did her best to raise his spirits. Never could brother and sister more completely sympathise with each other.

The next morning Harry received a note from his cousin Jane, saying that she and Mary had resolved to pay a visit to some friends residing about forty miles away to the north of Hurlston, and that as, of course, May would accompany them, though they were grieved at his disappointment he must consider his visit of the previous day a farewell one. They hoped, however, that nothing would prevent them seeing him on his return from sea. A note was enclosed from May, giving him every assurance of her unalterable affection which he could desire, and expressing her grief at not seeing him again, though she endeavoured to persuade herself with his cousins that it was for the best.

This was indeed an unexpected and bitter disappointment. Harry, however, with right manly spirit, felt that it must be endured.

He was as eager now to set off from home as he had before been anxious to remain. He had, however, one duty to perform. As he had missed meeting the lawyer at Downside, he must ride over to Morbury to him.

The general heard him order his horse.

"In which direction are you going?" he asked.

Harry told him.

"If you will accept me as a companion, I shall be happy to ride with you," said the general. "You, I suspect, must not put your horse to greater speed than I have been accustomed of late years to jog along the road?"

Harry's politeness compelled him to say that he was happy to have his company.

General Sampson could make himself agreeable to old and young alike. He had seen a great deal of the world, knew all that was going forward, and seasoned his conversation with numerous anecdotes. Harry could not help being amused.

Harry had not ridden over to Downside day after day without the general suspecting the object of his visits, and he had managed to obtain pretty accurate information of the state of the case. He really liked Harry more than he did any other young man, and his present object was to draw him out of himself. He would have been glad to gain Harry's confidence, and to hear from him how matters stood, though he very well knew he should fail if he asked the question point-blank. He therefore beat about the bush for some time, talking of his own love affairs when he was a young man, and of those of several of his friends.

"You see, my dear Harry, we must all be prepared for trials in this rugged world, but then, according to my experience, we are the better for them in the end. If the lady is obdurate or coy, or if her friends throw obstacles in the way, or if want of means exist, we must try to win her by greater attention, or sometimes by pretended indifference, or we must set to work to overcome the obstacles, or to gain the means which are wanting, and we shall enjoy double satisfaction when we triumph. I sometimes wish that I were young again to take advantage of the experience I possess, but as that is an impossibility, I have great satisfaction in enabling others to benefit by it. You understand me, Harry, *nil desperandum* is the motto I advise you to adopt."

"Thank you, general," said Harry. "You seem to suppose that I am in a position to require your advice."

"Of course I do," said the general. "I know something about your love affair. Though my friend Sir Ralph and Lady Castleton may not see with your eyes, and may have other views for you, I can sympathise with you, and as far as my respect to them will allow me, I shall be glad to give you all the assistance in my power."

Harry thanked the general for his kind feelings, and supposing that he knew from Sir Ralph and his mother exactly how things stood enlightened him yet further on the subject.

"You should not be surprised at their objecting on the score of the lady's want of birth, charming as I doubt not she is," observed the general. "I regret, as she has gone away, that I shall not have the pleasure of being introduced to her, and by pouring her praises into Sir Ralph's ear, perhaps assist in softening his heart. However, as I said before, don't despair, but keep up your spirits, and you will soon be too busy in your professional duties to allow your thoughts time to dwell on the subject."

Harry again thanked him, and promised to follow his advice.

They reached Morbury. Harry proposed putting up their horses, and begged the general to take a few turns on the esplanade, as he had business which would occupy him some little time.

Harry was absent longer than he expected, and the general, after looking at his watch two or three times, began to wonder what he could be about.

"Can the fair lady have come to the place," he thought. "Perhaps the young fellow has been making a cat's-paw of me all the time, and has gone to church and got married, ha! ha! ha! that would be a joke; but by-the-bye it's out of canonical hours; he cannot have done that then."

He took another turn or two, exchanged a few words with the boatmen on the beach, looked about in the hopes of meeting an acquaintance, and resumed his seat on a bench facing the sea.

At last Harry made his appearance.

"What have you been about?" exclaimed the general. "I began to fear that you had given me the slip altogether, and that I should hear of you next at Gretna Green, or find that you had had a licence in your pocket all the time, and had been laughing in your sleeve while I was bestowing my sage advice on you."

"No, indeed," answered Harry, who did not like the general's joke. "To confess the truth, I have been making my will. I thought it was a matter which would occupy five or ten minutes at the utmost, but found that there were all sorts of complications, of which I had not dreamed."

"Make your will, my dear boy! What could induce you to do that?" exclaimed the general.

"When a man is going to run the risk of being shot or drowned, or cut down by fever, or finished in some other way, he naturally wishes to make such arrangements that his property may benefit those in whom he is most interested. I should have asked you to be a witness, but the lawyer found those who would answer as well, and I therefore did not think it necessary to trouble you."

"Well, we will talk about it as we ride homewards," observed the general. "It is time that we should be in the saddle, or we may be late for dinner."

The general, as they rode along, pumped Harry, curious to know how he had disposed of his property. He suspected from poor Algernon's condition that the younger brother would himself soon become heir of Texford, and would thus, should Sir Ralph die, have no inconsiderable amount of property to leave.

He succeeded in satisfying himself that should Harry Castleton be killed, Miss Pemberton's protégé would succeed to all the property he could leave.

"I hope, my young friend, you will be able to endow her with it in a different way," he observed, "and though I do not know what some may say to your intentions, for my part I think it is a very right thing to do. Supposing Algernon were to die, and you be killed, and I heartily hope that won't happen, your sister Julia will inherit Texford, and I shall be very much mistaken if your friend Headland does not some day become its master. Mrs Appleton and I agree that the young people are admirably matched. By the way, Harry, I want you and Headland to come and pay me a visit at a little box I have got near Portsmouth, if you can manage to get away from your ships before they sail, or when you come into port. I had thought of going to take a few weeks' shooting with my friend, Sir Pierce Berrington, but I have made up my mind to go home direct, and if you will give me your company we will travel together. You will find posting pleasanter than the coach, and we shall give a good account of any highwaymen who may think fit to cry, 'Halt; your money or your lives.'"

Harry gladly accepted the general's last offer, and promised to deliver his message to Headland. He was glad to secure so amusing a companion for his journey. He hoped also to pay the general a visit, for unless May and his cousins returned to Downside, he should have no wish to go home.

Chapter Forty Two
The Lugger again

A Post-Chaise which had conveyed Harry and the general to Portsmouth drove up to the "George," just as Captain Headland, who was living there, returned from a visit to his ship.

The old general, thinking that Harry would benefit by his society, had insisted on accompanying him, declaring that he had promised Lady Castleton to see him safe on board his frigate.

Sir Ralph, suspecting perhaps that Harry might take it into his head to run off with May, had encouraged the general in doing as he had offered, little aware that there was no risk of such an occurrence happening, while the general took good care to show that he had not come as a spy on his actions. Harry, indeed, was too generous to suspect him of such a proceeding.

The general having shaken hands with Headland, went into the hotel, as he said, to order rooms, leaving the two friends alone. He guessed that the captain would have enquiries to make about Julia. They joined him before long in the sitting-room he had engaged, and Headland thanked him heartily for the invitation which Harry had just delivered.

The general had ordered dinner, and insisted on the two young officers being his guests for the day.

"You shall give me a return dinner on board the *Thisbe*," he observed.

The dinner was the best the hotel could supply, and the wines were good, the general keeping his guests well amused.

"By-the-bye, I daresay you two young men would rather sail together than cruise in different ships, and as I have a modicum of interest in high quarters, though I do not boast of much, if you wish, Captain Headland, to apply for Harry, it is possible that I may induce the Lords Commissioners to grant your request, unless Harry would prefer remaining as he is."

Both Headland and Harry begged the general would do as he proposed.

"Well, do you write the official letter, and I will support it," said the general, "and if necessary I will run up to town and see my official friends.

Harry will get a longer spell on shore to recover from the hurts he received from those rascally highwaymen. I cannot compliment the police of your county for not catching them though. I always felt when riding about, the unpleasant possibility of having a bullet sent through my head."

Harry said the search for them was not over, however, and that Mr Groocock especially was taking every means in his power to discover them, though, for his part, as they had failed in their attempt, unless to prevent their attacking anyone else, he had no wish to have them brought to justice, as it might compel him to remain on shore as a witness.

Little was the general aware when he made this offer that Sir Ralph had expressly got the young men appointed to different ships, and had taken care that Headland's should be destined for a foreign station. How far, had he known this, he would have ventured to counteract the baronet's arrangements it is difficult to say.

The next morning Harry joined the *Aurora*. The same day he paid Headland a visit on board the *Thisbe*, which had just come out of dock and been brought alongside the hulk. She was a remarkably fine corvette of eighteen guns, just such a craft as a young officer would be proud to command, and, from her build, both he and Headland thought she would prove very fast.

Within a week Harry found himself superseded, and appointed first lieutenant of the *Thisbe*.

Orders came down the next day to hurry on with her equipment, and Portsmouth was again alive with preparations for war.

Lord Whitworth's final interview with Napoleon had taken place. The First Consul had stormed, and threatened, and insulted the English ambassador. All doubts as to his intentions vanished. The whole of England was aroused, for her shores were threatened with invasion. The militia were called out, and volunteers rapidly enrolled. A few months later, the great minister of England, his tall, gaunt figure dressed in regimental scarlet, might have been seen in his character of Lord Warden of the Cinque Ports, at the head of 3000 volunteers, drilling them as he best could. Not only he, however, but every Lord-lieutenant of England and Scotland was endeavouring to prepare his countrymen to drive the invaders from their sacred shores back into the Channel should they audaciously venture to cross it. In a short time, nearly 400,000 men, providing their own clothing, receiving no pay, and enjoying no privileges, sprang up at a word—a noble congregation of citizens, united as one individual soul, ready to fight to the death as long as a Frenchman remained in arms on their native soil.

As soon as war was declared, the general bade his naval friends farewell. "Though laid on the shelf so far as foreign service was concerned," he observed, "it would be found, he hoped, that there was still some life left in him for duty at home."

The *Thisbe* was rapidly got ready for sea. Though any men who had sailed with Captain Headland were willing to join her, there was great difficulty in procuring hands, and he knew too well the importance of having an efficient crew, to take any but the best men.

The *Thisbe* at length sailed with sealed orders, though still short handed. Unless she could obtain the remainder of her crew by taking them out of any homeward-bound vessels or fishing-boats, she was to put into Plymouth to make up her complement. She was to avoid, however, touching anywhere, and to proceed, if possible, with all despatch on her voyage southward. She lost sight of the Needles just as the sun sank into the ocean. A light breeze to the northward filling her sails, she made some progress during the night, but as morning approached, a thick fog came on, and she lay almost becalmed on the glass like sea. It was Harry's morning watch. Look-outs were stationed aloft to catch the first glimpse of any sail which might be near, though their hulls and lower rigging would be hidden by the mist. It was a time when vigilance was doubly necessary, for it was possible that an enemy's cruiser might have ventured thus far towards the English coast in the hopes of capturing any homeward-bound merchantmen in ignorance of the war.

At length dawn broke, and the mist assumed that silvery hue which showed that the sun was about once more to rise above the horizon. All hands were on deck, employed in the morning duties of a man-of-war's crew.

The sails which had hitherto hung down against the masts gave several loud flaps, then gradually bulged out, and the ship obtaining steerage way, once more glided slowly onwards.

Harry sent a midshipman forward to see that the look-outs had their eyes open.

Suddenly the fog lifted.

"A sail on the lee-bow," shouted the midshipman. "A lugger close-hauled standing across our course, sir."

At that moment the captain came on deck.

Won from the Waves | 249

"She shows no colours," again shouted the midshipman.

"We will speak her whatever she is," observed the captain.

The order was given to trim sails, and the corvette was steered so as to cut off the lugger should she continue on her present course.

Those on board the stranger only just then discovered the ship of war, and instead of continuing on close-hauled as before, she stood away with her sheets eased off to the southward.

"That looks suspicious," observed Headland. "If she were honest, she would not try to avoid us."

It was soon evident that the lugger was a fast craft. Every sail the *Thisbe* could carry was set, while the lugger, spreading out her broad canvas, did her best to escape.

"Perhaps the fellows think we may press some of them, and are simply anxious to escape being overhauled," observed Harry.

Though the lugger made good way, the loftier sails of the *Thisbe* carried her quickly through the water, and her commander and Harry hoped that she would deserve the character they first formed of her.

At length they got near enough to the lugger to send a shot from a bow-chaser as a signal to heave to. She, however, took no notice of it, and stood on. Other shots were fired in the hopes of knocking away some of her spars, and compelling her to obey. At length a shot had the desired effect, and her main-halyards being shot away, her huge mainsail came down on deck. To avoid the risk of the broadside which might follow, the lugger came up into the wind.

A boat, under the second lieutenant De Vere, was lowered to ascertain the character of the vessel. Some thought that she would prove to be a smuggler, with possibly a cargo on board. She was so completely under the lee of the corvette that everything going on on deck was seen.

"We may, at all events, get some of those fellows. Give them the option of volunteering whatever they are, but if they refuse, pick out half-a-dozen of the best hands, Mr De Vere," said the captain.

"Ay, ay, sir," was the answer, and the lieutenant proceeded on board.

He was seen to dive down below, and in a short time to return and muster the men on deck. They seemed by their movements inclined to refuse submission to his orders, but he pointed to the guns of the corvette as his authority, and one after the other having gone below to get their bags, they descended the side into the boat.

Six men had already been secured, whether they had volunteered or not it was difficult to say, when a struggle was seen to be taking place forward between some of the lugger's crew and a man who had made his way up the fore hatch. He dashed those who tried to stop him aside, and sprang aft to the lieutenant. A short discussion took place between De Vere and the master of the lugger. While it was going forward, the man took the opportunity of leaping over the side into the boat.

The second lieutenant, apparently considering that the lugger still had more hands than she required, now selected four additional men, who, evidently in a very sulky humour, obeyed his summons.

With the eleven men thus obtained he returned to the ship.

The breeze freshening, Headland was unwilling to delay longer, and therefore hailing the lugger, gave her permission to continue on her course, when the corvette's sails being filled, she once more stood down channel.

The newly pressed men were summoned aft.

"I cannot say that they were volunteers except this man," said De Vere, pointing to the one who had been seen to leap into the boat, a fine strong young fellow, though he looked somewhat pale and ill, while his jacket had been torn, and his head cut in the struggle. "He was willing enough to join, though the others tried to prevent him."

The men gave in their names. They were hardy-looking, but of a somewhat ruffianly appearance. They were not the less likely to prove useful seamen, only it would be necessary to keep a sharp look-out on them while the corvette was in Plymouth Sound.

When Harry asked the name of the man of whom De Vere had been speaking, he replied —

"Jacob Halliburt."

Harry looked at him, wondering whether he could be old Adam's son, and, as he supposed, May's brother.

He did not wish just then to ask the question in public. He had no doubts, however, when the young man stated that he had been carried off some time before from his home by the lugger's crew, and kept a prisoner on board ever since, being compelled to do duty when at sea, but being shut down in the hold whenever she was in port or might have an opportunity of making his escape.

"This was my only chance, sir, so I made a dash for it, and knocked down the fellows who tried to stop me, as I had a hundred times rather serve aboard a man-of-war than remain with such rascally lawless fellows."

"You did very right," said De Vere, "and you will find it to your advantage."

Before the day was over three large ships had been boarded, one of which had picked up a ship's crew of twenty men at sea. It seemed hard for the poor fellows after the dangers they had gone through not to return to their friends on shore; but necessity has no law. The greater number were sent on board the corvette, which, with several of the ship's crew, fully made up her complement.

As Headland was eager to get to sea, he was glad thus to avoid the necessity of having to touch at Plymouth, where it would have required great vigilance to prevent some of the lately pressed men from escaping.

Chapter Forty Three
Better than a Tonic

The *Thisbe* had doubled the Cape.

On opening his sealed orders, Captain Headland found that he was to proceed to the Eastern Seas, and to give notice of the commencement of hostilities to any ships-of-war or merchantmen he could fall in with.

The *Thisbe* had touched at Rio to obtain water and provisions, and had since made the best of her way eastward.

Little did Sir Ralph suppose when he had got Headland appointed to a ship destined for this service, that he was going to a part of the world in which he was so much interested.

Headland, as soon as he had opened the orders, determined, as far as was compatible with his duty, to visit every English settlement, and to make inquiries which might tend to elucidate the mystery of his birth. Although upwards of twenty years had passed since he had been put on board the merchantman by his supposed father, the circumstance, he thought, might still be recollected by some of the inhabitants, and if so, he might be able to trace his parents. His heart beat high with hope; Harry was sanguine of success.

"I am sure if you can find your parents you will have no more cause to be ashamed of them than they will have of you," he said, "and find them you will, I am very certain. I cannot help feeling that we were providentially sent out to these seas for that very object."

"At all events, we may make use of the opportunity to obtain it," said Headland, smiling.

Harry had taken the first opportunity of speaking to the young fisherman who had volunteered from the lugger, and, ascertaining that he was no other than Jacob Halliburt, had treated him with all the kindness which, in their relative positions, he was able to show.

"Do your duty, Halliburt," he said, "and I can answer for it that Captain Headland will endeavour to promote your interests, and give you a higher rating as soon as possible. I will write by the first chance, to give your friends notice of your safety, and you can do the same, and let them know what I have said."

"I am much obliged to you for your kindness," answered Jacob. "I knew, sir, when I saw you, that you must be Lieutenant Castleton who was at Texford, and I was thankful to think that I had to serve under you. If it had not been for that, I should have been heart-sick to return home to help poor father, for he must be sorely missing me." Harry was able to assure Jacob that his father's spirits were wonderfully kept up, and that he hoped Ned Brown would stick by him, and help him during his absence.

"And mother, sir, does she bear up as well as father?" asked Jacob. Harry, who had seen the dame just before he left home, was able to give a good account of her.

Jacob longed to ask after May, but he felt tongue-tied, and could not bring himself to pronounce her name. Harry was surprised at his silence. Jacob merely remarked that he hoped the family at Downside were also well.

"The ladies were sorry when they heard of your being carried off."

"Thank you, Mr Castleton, thank you," said Jacob. "I will try and do as you tell me, and though I could not have brought myself to leave father of my own accord, it may be my coming aboard here won't be so bad for me after all."

Harry was still under the belief that Jacob was May's brother, and Jacob had said nothing to undeceive him. Jacob at the same time had not the slightest suspicion that his lieutenant was engaged to marry the being on whom his own honest affections were so hopelessly set.

It was observed by his messmates that Jacob Halliburt was a great favourite with the captain and first lieutenant, but as he was a well-behaved man, and did his duty thoroughly, this was easily accounted for, as no particular favour was shown him of which others could be jealous.

Harry would often gladly have talked with Jacob about Hurlston and his family, but the etiquette of a man of war prevented him from doing so. He thus remained in ignorance of a circumstance which would have greatly raised his hopes of overcoming his father's objection to his marriage with May, for all the time he had supposed that Sir Ralph believed May to be, as he did, Dame Halliburt's daughter, and had been surprised that he had not spoken more strongly on the subject. His only other supposition was that Sir Ralph had made no enquiries as to May's parentage, and took it for granted that she was the orphan child of some friends of his cousins, whom they had charitably adopted.

The *Thisbe* continued her course day after day over the world of waters. Though a constant look-out had been kept, no prizes had been made, and no enemy's cruisers encountered. Both the captain and officers hoped before long to find some work either to bring them credit or prize money.

Light and baffling winds had of late detained the *Thisbe*, when, having got somewhat out of her course, Saint Ann, one of the Seychelle Islands, was sighted. Captain Headland stood in for the Mahé Roads, in the hopes that some of the enemy's privateers or merchantmen might be anchored there, and might be cut out without detaining him long.

The opportunity must not be lost. The wind favoured them, for, instead of blowing off-shore as it generally does, the sea-breeze carried them swiftly towards the harbour.

Eager eyes were on the look-out. A large ship was discovered at anchor without her foremast. From her appearance she would evidently be a prize worth taking; but whether or not she was too strongly armed to allow the *Thisbe* to make the attempt was the question. As she could not move, Captain Headland stood in close enough to ascertain this, and determined, should her size give him a fair hope of conquest, to attack her.

The cables were ranged with springs ready for anchoring, and the ship cleared for action. All on board eagerly hoped that they might have work to do, and every telescope was turned towards the stranger.

The *Thisbe* had hoisted French colours, that her expected antagonist might not take the alarm, and run on shore to avoid her.

It was at length ascertained that the stranger was a flush deck ship, and ten guns were counted on the only side visible. Though she was apparently larger than the *Thisbe*, and more heavily armed, Captain Headland no longer hesitated, while the master volunteered to take the ship in among the numerous shoals which guarded the entrance of the harbour. Taking his station on the fore-yardarm, guided by the colour of the water, he gave directions to the helmsman how to steer.

The stranger remained quietly at anchor, apparently not suspecting the character of her visitor.

Harry was amused, as he went from gun to gun, to hear the remarks of some of the men who saw the French flag flying at the peak of the corvette.

"I thought our craft was an English ship, and we British tars, and now I see we be turned into mounseers," said one, cocking his eye at the tricoloured flag.

"If we be, my boy, we will show yonder ship that the mounseers can fight their guns as well as British tars for once in a way," remarked another who stood near him.

"Never you fear, mate, that gay-coloured flag will come down fast enough before we open fire."

The last speaker was right—the moment to which all were looking forward was approaching. Every man was at his station. Not a word was now spoken except by the master as he issued his orders from the yardarm.

The stranger gave no signs that she was aware of the approach of an enemy.

"We will run alongside and carry her by boarding; it will save our anchoring, and we shall not injure her spars—an important object, as I hope we may have to carry her off to sea," observed the captain to his first lieutenant.

The *Thisbe* was now within 200 yards of the stranger's bows, when the master gave notice that there was a shoal ahead extending on either hand, while on shore a battery was seen commanding the passage, and several smaller vessels at anchor under it.

Headland instantly gave the order to anchor. The crew swarmed aloft to hand sails, the French colours was hauled down, and the English run up at the peak. At the same moment the stranger opened a hot fire from the whole of her broadside.

"Fire," cried Captain Headland, and the *Thisbe* returned the warm salute she had received.

The battery on shore and the small vessels at the same time began peppering away at her.

Broadsides were exchanged with great rapidity between the combatants. The firing calming the light wind which had been blowing, the two ships were soon shrouded in a canopy of smoke. The English crew redoubled their efforts. Several had been struck, yet two only lay dead on her deck.

The Frenchman's fire, however, at length began to slacken, and in little more than a quarter of an hour down came the tricoloured flag, loud cheers bursting from the throats of the *Thisbe's* crew. A boat was instantly sent under the command of the second lieutenant to take possession of the prize, but as he was pulling alongside the Frenchmen were seen lowering their boats, in which a considerable number made their escape to the shore.

The battery continued firing, and Captain Headland directed Harry to land with a boat's crew and silence it. Jacob accompanied him. The smaller vessels meantime cut their cables, some running on shore, and others endeavouring to make their escape through the intricate passages, where the English ship could not follow them.

Harry, ordering his men to give way, pulled rapidly for the beach, exposed to a hot fire of musketry in addition to that from the heavy guns in the battery. Forming his men, he led the way up the steep bank.

The battery had been rapidly thrown up, and offered no insuperable impediment. Sword in hand he leaped over the parapet, followed closely by Jacob and the rest of his men.

At the same moment a bullet struck him on the shoulder, and a tall French officer, supported by a party of his men, was on the point of cutting him down as he fell forward, when Jacob, with uplifted cutlass, saved him from the blow, returning it with such interest that his assailant fell back wounded among his men.

At this juncture a number of the French who had landed from the ship entered the fort to assist its defenders, and attacked the small party of English who had accompanied Harry. Jacob threw himself across the body of his lieutenant, and defended him bravely from the attacks of the French, who attempted to bayonet him as he lay on the ground. The remainder of the boat's crew springing over the entrenchments now came to Jacob's support. The garrison fought bravely, and disputed every inch of ground. Jacob's great object, however, was to protect Harry, and as soon as the Frenchmen had given way, springing back, he lifted Harry on his shoulders, and leaping over the entrenchments, carried him down to the boat.

In the meantime, Headland suspecting that the fort was stronger than he had at first supposed, despatched another boat to Harry's assistance. The men sent in her landed just as a party of Frenchmen had come round the hill, and were on the point of intercepting Jacob, who was hurrying down with his burden, regardless of the shot whistling by him.

The Frenchmen on seeing this took to flight, while the last party of English climbing the hill threw themselves into the fort, and quickly cleared it of its defenders. The French flag was hauled down by the young midshipman who had led the second party, and that of England hoisted in its stead.

No further opposition was made, the French seeking shelter in the neighbouring woods, where they were not likely to be followed. A few had been cut down while defending the fort, while others, unable to make their escape, were taken prisoners.

The fort was found to contain six guns landed from the ship, as also a furnace for heating shot.

As soon as the Frenchmen had disappeared, one of the boats was sent back with the wounded lieutenant, and two of the men who had also been hurt.

Jacob carried Harry up the side, evidently considering that it was his duty to attend on him till he had placed him in the surgeon's hands.

No time was lost in getting the captured vessel ready for sea, while the guns belonging to her, which had been in the fort, were brought on board. A new mast was found on the beach, ready to be towed off. It was soon got on board and stepped, and in a couple of days the *Concord*, a fine new sloop of 22 guns, was following the *Thisbe* out of the roads.

The command had of necessity been given to Lieutenant De Vere, as Harry was unable to assume it.

The surgeon looked grave when he spoke to the captain about him.

"We must keep a careful watch over him, for he has a good deal of fever, and in these warm latitudes it is somewhat a serious matter."

Harry had expressed a wish to have Jacob Halliburt to attend on him, and as it was necessary that some one should be constantly at his side, Jacob was appointed to that duty.

It would have been impossible to have found a more tender nurse, and no one could have attended more carefully to the directions given by the surgeon.

The fever the surgeon dreaded, however, came on, and for several days Harry was delirious. Often the name of "May" was on his lips, and Jacob, as he listened, discovered that his lieutenant loved her.

Several days went by, and Harry appeared to get worse. On his return to consciousness he felt how completely his strength had deserted him, and though the doctor tried to keep up his spirits by telling him that he would get better in time, so great was his weakness that he felt himself to be dying. He was anxious not to alarm his friend Headland; but as Jacob stood by his bedside, he told him what he believed would be the case.

"And I hope, my good fellow, that you will be able to return to your home, and if you do, I wish you to bear a message to your father and mother, and to your sister. I know that she no longer lives with them, and has become fit to occupy a different station in life; but you, I doubt not, love her notwithstanding as much as ever. Tell your parents how much I esteem them, and say to your sister that my love is unchangeable, that my dying thoughts were of her, my last prayers for her welfare. I have done what I could to secure it, and have left her all the property I possess. Mr Shallard, the lawyer at Morbury, will enable her to obtain possession of it."

"Miss May my sister!" exclaimed Jacob in a tone which aroused Harry's attention. "I will tell her what you say, sir, if my eyes are ever blessed by seeing her again, but she is not father and mother's child. Father found her on board a wreck when she was a little child, and though she is now a grown young lady, she does not mind still calling them as she did when she lived with us, and that's made you fancy she is their daughter."

This answer of Jacob's had a wonderful effect on Harry. He asked question after question, entirely forgetting the weakness of which he had been complaining. Jacob gave him a full account of the way May had been preserved, how she had been brought up by his parents, and how the Miss Pembertons had invited her to come and live with them.

At length the doctor coming into the cabin put an end to the conversation.

From that moment Harry began to recover. It seemed to him at once that the great difficulty which he had dreaded was removed, and, ready as he had been to marry May although she was a fisherman's daughter, he was not the less gratified to hear that she was in all probability of gentle birth although her parents were unknown. How he had not learned this before surprised him. He could only, as was really the case, fancy that the Miss Pembertons and May herself supposed him to be aware of the truth, and had therefore not alluded to it. He thought over all his conversations with May; he recollected that they had generally spoken of the future rather than of the past, by which alone he could account for her silence on the subject.

"How remarkable it is," he thought, "that my beloved May and Headland should be placed in precisely similar situations, both ignorant of their parents, and yet enjoying the position in life in which they were evidently born."

Headland was as much surprised as his friend when he heard the account Harry gave him.

"It must indeed be satisfactory news to you, Harry, and I am grateful to young Halliburt for giving it you, as it is the physic you wanted, and has done more than all the doctor's tonics in bringing you round."

Harry, indeed, after this rapidly got well, and before the ship with her prize arrived in Calcutta, he was able to return to his duty.

Chapter Forty Four
A Chase

The active little *Thisbe* had been for some time at sea, and had already performed her duty of giving notice of the recommencement of hostilities at the different stations, and to the men-of-war and merchantmen she met with.

Her captain, aided by Harry, had made all the enquiries he could relating to the circumstance in which he was so deeply interested, but without any satisfactory result.

Harry had heard in Calcutta of his uncle, Mr Ranald Castleton, who had gone to Penang soon after its establishment as the seat of government of the British possessions in the Straits of Malacca. He had, however, sailed for England some years before, during the previous war, and the ship had, it was supposed, either been lost or captured by the enemy, as she had not afterwards been heard of. Those who had known him were either dead or had returned home, and Harry could obtain no certain information, except the fact that he had had a wife and children, but that they were supposed to have perished with him.

Still neither Harry nor Headland gave up hopes of gaining the information they wished for.

Harry had, as he promised, kept his eye on Jacob, who, greatly to his satisfaction, had been made a petty officer. As he was becoming a thorough seaman, and read and wrote better than most of the men in the ship, the captain promised, should a vacancy occur, to give him an acting warrant as boatswain or gunner.

The *Thisbe* had been more than a year on the station. Harry had received no letters from home. How he longed to hear from May and Julia. He thought that both would certainly have written. His mother, too, ought not to have forgotten him; but in those days, when no regular post was established, letters were frequently a long time on their way. He had written several times to Julia, and not less often, as may be supposed, to May. He had enclosed his letters to her to the Miss Pembertons. He suspected she would wish him to do so, and also that they would have a better prospect of reaching her. He told her the satisfaction he felt at discovering that she was not, as he had supposed, Adam Halliburt's daughter, but in all probability his equal in birth, and that thus the great obstacle in obtaining his father's sanction to his marriage no longer existed.

He sent messages to Adam and the dame, assuring them that he would look after Jacob's interests, and he enclosed at different times letters from Jacob himself to his father and mother. Jacob's letters chiefly contained praises of Lieutenant Castleton and his captain. Though for his father's sake he regretted having been forced from his home, he was well content with his life, and spoke with enthusiasm of the strange countries and people he had visited, and of his prospects of advancement in the service.

The *Thisbe* had once more got free of the Straits of Malacca.

Having run down the coast of Sumatra, and touched at Bencoolen, was standing across the Indian Ocean, when towards sunset a large ship was descried from the mast-head, to the south-west. At the distance she was away it was impossible to say whether she was an enemy or friend, whether ship-of-war or merchantman. At all events the captain determined to overhaul her, and made all sail in chase. The great point was to get near enough to keep her in sight during the night, so as to follow her should she alter her course. When the sun went down she was still standing as at first seen, and had not apparently discovered that she was chased.

The night was clear, the sea smooth, and the graceful corvette, with all sail set below and aloft, made good way through the water, and was fast coming up with the chase. The captain's intention, however, was not to approach too near till daylight, for should she prove an enemy's man-of-war of much superior force, the *Thisbe* would have to trust to her heels to keep out of her way, though should she be of a size which he might without undue rashness attack, the captain's intention was to bring her to action, well knowing that he would be ably supported by his officers and crew.

But few of the watch below turned in, every spyglass on board being turned towards the chase. There were various opinions as to her character, some believing her to be a man-of-war, others a French or Dutch merchantman, and from the course she was steering it was believed she had come through the Straits of Sunda. The dawn of day which might settle the question was anxiously looked for.

At length a ruddy glow appeared in the eastern horizon, gradually extending over the sky, and suffusing a wide expanse of the calm ocean with a bright pink hue, and tinging the loftier sails of the stranger, while to the west the surface of the water still remained of a dark purple tint.

"She has hoisted English colours," exclaimed Harry, who had his glass fixed on the chase.

A general exclamation of disappointment escaped those who heard him.

"That is no proof that she is English," observed the captain. "The cut of her sails is English, and though she is a large ship, she is no man-of-war, of that I am certain. We will speak her at all events, and settle the point."

The stranger was seen to be making all sail; royals were set, and studding sails rigged out, but in a slow way, which confirmed Headland's opinion of her being a merchantman. This showed that her commander had no inclination to await the coming up of the corvette, of whose nationality, however, he might have had doubts.

Although the chase had now every sail set she could carry, the corvette still gained on her.

"Those heavy tea-chests require a strong breeze to drive them through the water," observed the master to Harry. "I rather think, too, we shall have one before long. I don't quite like the look of the sky, and we are not far off the hurricane season."

The crew were piped for breakfast, and the officers who could be spared from the deck went below. De Vere had been attacked by fever at Bencoolen, and was in his cabin. The master remained in charge of the deck.

Breakfast was hurried over.

When Harry and the captain returned on deck a marked change had taken place in the weather. Dark clouds were gathering in the northern horizon, and fitful gusts of wind came sweeping over the ocean, stirring up its hitherto calm surface, and sending the spoon-drift flying rapidly over it. Still the chase kept her canvas set, having altered her course more to the southward.

"They hope that we shall get the wind first, and be compelled to shorten sail, and that she will thus have a better chance of again getting ahead of us," observed the master.

Still the corvette carried on. The captain had his eye to windward, however, prepared to give the order to shorten sail. She had come up fast with the chase, which she at length got within range of her guns. A bow-chaser was run out, and a shot fired. The stranger paid no attention to it. A few more minutes were allowed to elapse, when another shot was fired with the same result as at first. On this Headland ordered the English flag to be hauled down, and that of France substituted. No sooner was this done than the stranger, hauling down the red ensign, hoisted the tricoloured flag.

"I thought so," exclaimed Headland, "shorten sail."

The studding sails were rigged in, the royals handed. Again the British flag was hoisted instead of that of France, and a shot fired. On this the stranger took in her studding sails and loftier canvas, and, as the *Thisbe* ranged up alongside, fired a broadside.

The *Thisbe's* crew returned it with interest, and before the enemy could again fire they delivered a second broadside, which cut away some of her standing and running rigging, and caused other damage. The stranger again fired, but after receiving a few more broadsides, evidently finding that she had no hope of escaping from her active antagonist, she hauled down her colours.

The wind had during the action been increasing, and the sea getting up, it was necessary to take possession of her without delay, as unless her canvas was speedily reduced, in all probability her masts would be carried over the side.

Harry volunteered to go on board, and a boat being lowered, accompanied by Jacob and seven other men, he pulled alongside.

He had just gained her deck, and was receiving the sword of the officer in command, when the gale which had long been threatening struck the two ships. The *Thisbe's* crew having secured their guns were swarming aloft to take in her canvas.

The deck of the prize presented a scene of the greatest confusion. Several of her men lay dead, some were endeavouring to secure the guns, a few had gone aloft to take in sail, but the greater number were running about not knowing what to do. Harry ordered his men to let go everything. The topgallant-sails, which were still set, were in an instant torn into ribbons, the foretopsail was blown out of the bolt ropes, and the mizzen-mast, which had been wounded, was carried over the side, and the prize lay a helpless wreck amid the raging seas which threatened every instant her destruction.

Chapter Forty Five
A Reverse

We must return to Texford. Julia had kept to her resolution of not going up to London.

She had soon a reason for remaining in the country, which even her father could not oppose. Algernon had joined a volunteer regiment formed in the country, and the exposure to which he was subjected rapidly tended to increase the pulmonary complaint from which he had long suffered. He was soon confined almost entirely to the house, except when the weather allowed him to be drawn about the grounds in a wheel-chair.

Julia watched over him with the most affectionate solicitude, and all that medical skill could accomplish was done to arrest the fatal malady, but in vain.

Lady Castleton came back from London to assist in watching over him, and she was soon, with a breaking heart, compelled to write to Sir Ralph to tell him that she feared that their eldest son's days were rapidly drawing to a close. He thought that she was over anxious, and he, absorbed as usual in politics, delayed his journey.

Algernon still retained the pride of the family which had always animated him, and though aware of the fatal character of the complaint from which he was suffering, he was as anxious as ever to prevent his sister from contracting a marriage with a man of unknown birth like Headland.

He had desired to be wheeled out to a sunny spot where he could enjoy a view of the lake. Having sent the servant away to the other side to gather water-lilies, he broached the subject to Julia. He could not, however, have chosen a more inappropriate locality, for it was here that Headland had first declared his love, and she had accepted him.

"My dear sister," he began, "I may or may not recover from this complaint, but, at all events, it would be a great satisfaction to me to know that you had given up all ideas of marrying Captain Headland. It was a most unfortunate thought of Harry's to invite him here. Though he may be a very fine fellow, our brother ought to have known that a man of his birth could not be welcome at Texford, and I must say it would have been wiser in you had you inquired who he was before you allowed your fancy to be captivated by him."

A fit of coughing prevented Algernon from continuing his remarks.

Julia felt deeply grieved. She was afraid of irritating him by replying as her feelings prompted.

"My dear brother," she answered, "we will not discuss the subject, but believe me I will endeavour to seek for guidance, and trust that I shall be led aright in the matter."

"But what you think right our father and I may consider very wrong," exclaimed Algernon, petulantly. "You ought to promise to discard the fellow at once when you know how we object to your marrying him."

"I have promised our father not to marry Captain Headland without his sanction, and let me entreat you to rest satisfied with that," answered Julia, looking out anxiously for the return of the servant.

"But I want to be satisfied that you never will marry him," exclaimed Algernon. "It is still more important, as Harry has taken it into his head to fall in love with this pretty little protégé of our cousins, and he is such a determined fellow that I should not be surprised if he marries her notwithstanding all opposition."

"I am not surprised that Harry should have fallen in love with her, for she is a lovely girl, and every time I have seen her I have admired her more and more: her love and devotion to our poor cousins is most admirable; but still even she would not consent to marry Harry without our father's permission, and would not, I think, act in direct opposition to our parents."

"Whether he does or does not, that will not alter your position with regard to Headland," said Algernon, returning to the subject from which Julia had hoped to escape. "Harry would raise his wife to his own station; you will be lowered by marrying a man like Headland."

"That is impossible," exclaimed Julia, indignantly. "I should be raised to the station which he has gained by his courage and gallantry; no lady in the land could be degraded by marrying him. I did not wish to say this to you, Algernon," she added, seeing the flush of anger rising on his pale brow.

"I see how it will be," he said, after he had recovered from another fit of coughing, "you will prove as obstinate as Harry."

Fortunately the servant returned with the flowers, which the poor invalid let drop by his side after looking at them for a moment. Julia signed to the man to wheel her brother home, for she felt very anxious at the change she had observed since they left the house. He with difficulty reached his room, but never again left it.

Julia, who, since Harry went away, had frequently ridden over to Downside, wrote to Miss Jane, sending the carriage, and asking her to come to Texford. Notwithstanding the neglect with which she and her sister had been treated, sympathising with Julia and Lady Castleton in their grief, she immediately complied. She did her utmost to comfort her cousins, while she faithfully delivered the Gospel message to poor Algernon, wondering that he should be so utterly ignorant of its tenor and object.

Lady Castleton again wrote to Sir Ralph, but when he arrived Algernon had ceased to breathe.

Miss Jane had returned to Downside in the morning. Brave as she was, she did not wish to encounter Sir Ralph. Sir Ralph exhibited no overwhelming grief at the loss of his eldest son; his thoughts seemed immediately to centre on Harry.

"We must write and have him home at once," he said to Lady Castleton. "I will get him into parliament, and with his nautical experience, he will be able to make a figure on all naval matters, and if he follows my advice, he must inevitably become a leading man. I hope he will have got over his foolish fancy for that pretty girl at our cousins. He must be kept out of her way, and we must take care that he does not come to Texford. You and Julia must do your best to amuse him in London as soon as he arrives. I have written to Fancourt, and he will arrange about his coming home at the Admiralty."

Julia was still able to remain at Texford after Algernon's death, as neither she nor her mother could mix in London society. Feeling sure that Harry would prove restive, and not willingly enter into his father's plans, she did not look forward to his arrival with the satisfaction she might otherwise have done. In her heart she could not wish him to give up May, whom she herself already loved with the affection of a sister.

She had one day ridden over to Downside soon after Algernon's death, when, the post arriving, a letter was put into Miss Jane's hands. As she read it, the expression of her countenance changed; it first appeared as if she was about to give way to tears, and then assumed a firm and determined look.

"I must not conceal the contents of this letter from you, Julia, nor can I from Mary and May."

May, turning pale, gazed anxiously at Miss Jane; the thought that the letter had reference to Harry crossed her mind. She gasped for breath.

"What is it, Jane?" asked Miss Mary, in a calm tone. "From whom is the letter?"

"From Mr Shallard; he writes that the M— bank, in which most of our property is invested, has failed, and he fears that but a small portion will be saved."

"Oh, how terrible," exclaimed Julia.

"Not terrible, dear Julia," said Miss Mary, "though trying. I grieve for others more than for ourselves," and she turned her sightless orbs towards May. "It will be very sad to have to give up Downside; and oh, dear May, it is sadder still to think that you will be so ill provided for."

"Oh, do not grieve for me, dear ladies," exclaimed May, going to Miss Mary's side, and taking her hand. "Perhaps you will not be compelled to leave Downside. I will work for you with heart and hand; if you have to dismiss your servants, I will serve you instead. I can attend to the house, and to the garden too; surely you will then be able to live on here."

"My dear, dear child," exclaimed Miss Mary, "I am sure you will do all you can, but you would soon overtax your strength. We must take time to consider what may be necessary to do."

"I am sure our dear May will not fail us. As you say, Mary, we must take time to consider, and, at all events, we must be resigned to God's will," said Miss Jane.

"Oh, how I wish that I could help you," exclaimed Julia. "Surely papa will be ready to assist you, his nearest relatives, and I am confident that mamma will gladly do so."

"We feel grateful to you, Julia, for your sympathy, but we must not expect assistance from others. Mr Shallard says that our property is not entirely gone. As I am thankful to say that we have lived within our income, we may have enough to support us in our old age, without relying on charity," answered Miss Jane, with a slight tinge of pride in the tone of her voice.

Julia was at length compelled to return to Texford. She was struck with the appearance of cheerfulness which May maintained, while she did everything she could think of to cheer the spirits of her friends.

On her return home, Julia told her mother what had occurred.

"I fear that Sir Ralph will not even offer to assist our cousins; however I will write to him, and suggest the propriety of his doing so."

Her mother's answer did not give Julia any strong hopes that she would be successful.

Lady Castleton herself drove over to condole with her cousins. They received her in their usual manner, and not till she introduced the subject did they speak of their loss.

"We are much obliged to you for your sympathy," answered Miss Jane, "but we do not contemplate leaving Downside for the present. We have dismissed our servants with the exception of our faithful attendant, Susan, who insists on remaining, and though we may be occasionally pinched, it is only what our poorer neighbours constantly are, and we should be ashamed not to bear it as well as they do."

"My good cousins, you are indeed wonderful women," exclaimed Lady Castleton. "I suspect that had such a misfortune happened to us, we should have broken down completely."

"You see we know in whom we trust, and He supports us," remarked Miss Mary. "You would find the same support were you to seek it."

Lady Castleton did not quite comprehend her cousin's remark. Her heart, however, was softened by her son's loss, and feeling compassion for her cousins, she frequently drove over to see them, and sent presents of fruit and vegetables, believing that she was thus affording them all the assistance in her power. It did not occur to her to limit her own expenses, and thus have the power of offering them more substantial aid. Julia, however, was anxious to do so, but her own allowance was small, and she found that she had saved so little that she was ashamed to offer it, especially as she doubted whether her cousins would accept the gift.

May carried out her intentions as far as she could. Miss Jane would not let her work as hard as she wished, and she herself and Susan attended to the household affairs, while they left May to take charge of Miss Mary.

May, with the numerous duties which now employed her time, was unable to get down as frequently as formerly to see Dame Halliburt and Adam, though the dame never passed Downside on her rounds without leaving a dish of fish for the ladies' acceptance.

When May, at Miss Jane's desire, expostulated with her, the good woman replied—

"Tell them it's they do Adam and me a favour, and it's no loss to us, for Adam generally catches more fish than we can sell, and if we were to send them a dish every day for the next hundred years, we could never repay them what we owe; so just beg them, with our respects, never to say another word about the matter."

As may be supposed, this constant supply was really very welcome, and contributed to keep down Miss Jane's weekly bills. Thus, although their means were greatly straitened, the ladies still hoped to pay the rent of their pretty cottage.

Their lives were spent in a daily routine of duty. Miss Jane visited the poor as she had been accustomed to do, although she had much less to give them than formerly, and May took her daily walks with Miss Mary, and read to her as much as usual, finding time notwithstanding for her other duties.

As soon as Sir Ralph returned to Texford, Lady Castleton and Julia spoke to him about their cousins' loss of property, and expressed their wish that some means could be taken to increase their now very limited income. Sir Ralph listened to them with more attention than they had expected.

"You are both very kind and charitable ladies," he remarked, in a tone they did not like. "I will ride over and call on our cousins."

"Let me accompany you, papa," said Julia. "I can take a stroll with May in the garden, while you are discussing business matters with the elder ladies."

"I do not wish you to be on intimate terms with that young person," answered Sir Ralph; "and as my visit will be on business, I must beg to be favoured with your company when I ride elsewhere."

Julia felt grieved at her father's reply.

Sir Ralph rode to Downside. Miss Jane received him with her usual frank and kind manner. She hoped that Algernon's death might have softened his heart. He sat and talked for some time, addressing Jane and Miss Mary, but, except the formal bow which he gave on entering, not noticing May, though he now and then turned an involuntary glance at her—a tribute to her beauty.

At length he said—

"I must confess, my good cousins, I came over to have a little conversation on business, and if you will afford me your attention in private for a few minutes, I will explain my object."

"We have no secrets from our dear May," answered Miss Jane.

"That may be," said the baronet, "but I wish to address myself to you alone."

May rose as he spoke, and left the room.

"I have no doubt you have ample reasons for the regard you entertain for that young person," he began in his most bland tone. "She may be very estimable, and her beauty is, I own, of a high order."

"It is the least of her excellences, Sir Ralph," observed Miss Jane, resolved to meet the baronet in his own style.

"That may be," he answered, with a bow; "it is the quality, however, which has probably attracted my son Harry. You must be aware, my good cousins, however much he may fancy himself in love, I naturally object to his marrying a person of unknown birth and destitute of fortune. I objected when he was my second son, and since he has become my heir, I am doubly opposed to the match, as I wish him to marry a lady of rank and fortune who will contribute to his advancement in life. I am thus candid, that you may understand my motive for the offer I have come to make."

"We are happy to listen to anything you may have to say, Sir Ralph," answered Miss Jane, bowing, "though I cannot promise that we shall be ready to accept your offer."

"You will at all events hear it before you decide, my good cousin. Not to keep you longer in suspense, I will at once place you in possession of my intentions. You have, I understand, lost a considerable amount of your property, which, if I am rightly informed, you had left by will to the young person of whom we have been speaking. Now, I am willing to make up your loss to you so that you may leave her as well provided for as you intended, on condition that she signs an agreement not to marry Harry, and to refuse ever again to see him. He is somewhat of a headstrong character, and it is the only security I can have that he will not on his return to England induce her to become his wife."

"Is that the offer you have to make?" asked Miss Jane, in a tone of mingled surprise and anger. "I speak for myself and my sister. We certainly cannot accept it, and I am very certain that nothing would induce our dear May to sign such an agreement. She has already refused to marry Harry should you and Lady Castleton withhold your consent. She did so, confident of Harry's love—in the belief that you would in time relent. But you might as well plunge a dagger in her breast as ask her to abandon the hope which now supports her of some day becoming his wife. I beg, therefore, that you will not expect us to make so cruel a proposal."

"Very well, my good cousins. I must take other means of preventing Harry from marrying the girl, and you will lose the advantage I have offered," answered the baronet.

"We at all events shall have the consciousness of having acted rightly," observed Miss Jane.

Sir Ralph, who was courteous under all circumstances, rose as he spoke, and gracefully putting out his hand, bowed low and quitted the room.

"Abominable," exclaimed Miss Jane, "he must have formed a strange opinion of us."

"He holds, I fear, a low opinion of his fellow-creatures generally," said Miss Mary, "and the sooner we try to forget what he has said, the better."

The ladies agreed not to let May know of Sir Ralph's insulting offer as they justly considered it. Miss Jane's only fear was, that he might, under the belief that she would be induced to consent, make it to May herself. She determined to be on the watch to prevent him, if possible, from doing so.

He did not, however, again appear at Downside. The great event which occurred to break the monotony of their lives was the arrival of a packet from the East containing Harry's enclosure to May. With what eagerness and delight she read it, what pleasure she felt in being able to give one from Jacob to the dame. May's heart throbbed as she read Harry's account of the capture of the French ship. Her woman's heart was gratified too, when he told her how completely he had loved her for herself alone, and that he had only just discovered that she was not, as he had supposed, a fisherman's daughter, but might some day be found to be as well-born as himself.

"I cannot help hoping that such will prove to be the case, and then the only bar to our happiness will be removed, dearest May," he wrote. Other letters came describing the voyage of the *Thisbe* through the Indian Seas, and then month after month passed by and no more were received. The roses began to fade from May's cheeks, even the Miss Pembertons became anxious. Neither had Julia nor any of his family heard from him.

Julia told them that Sir Ralph had obtained permission for Harry to return home, and that possibly being on his voyage he had thought it unnecessary to write; but this would not account for the long interval between his last letter and the time when he could have received the Admiralty's orders.

Whenever Julia went to Downside, she had to give the same answer—"no news from Harry."

Sir Ralph himself had become anxious, and made frequent visits to the Admiralty to hear whether his son had been heard of. The only information he could gain was that the *Thisbe* had been sent to the Indian Archipelago and had not returned to Calcutta.

At length news was received that she had arrived after encountering a terrific hurricane, and that she had captured a prize, in which one of her officers and several of her men had been lost.

"But the officer's name," asked Sir Ralph of the clerk who was giving him the information.

"I shall find it shortly, sir. Yes, as I feared, it is Lieutenant Castleton." Sir Ralph staggered out of the Admiralty. At the door he encountered General Sampson.

"I have just come to enquire about my gallant friend, Captain Headland, and your boy Harry," exclaimed the old soldier, taking the baronet's hand. "Why, you look pale, Sir Ralph, what is the matter?"

"He has gone, lost in a hurricane," answered Sir Ralph, with a groan. "I do not believe it; cannot be the case; he would swim through fifty hurricanes," exclaimed the petulant old general. "The clerks here never have the rights of the story. Come back with me, we will have a look at the despatches. We manage things better at the War Office, I flatter myself."

"The account was very circumstantial though," said Sir Ralph, with a sigh. "I wish I could believe there was a mistake."

"Of course there is a mistake, very sure of it. Come along, and we will soon set it to rights."

The general dragged Sir Ralph back into the building. The clerk looked somewhat offended at the general's address.

"I understand that you have told Sir Ralph Castleton that his son is lost. You should be more exact, sir, in the information you give. Just let me see the despatch."

The clerk hesitated, on which the general desired his name to be taken in to the secretary. He was admitted, and the despatch placed in his hand. His countenance fell.

"Still I do not see that it is certain," he observed. "The ship was not seen to go down, and if she had, some of the people may have been saved: people often are saved from sinking ships, and there is no proof positive that she did sink. Though the *Thisbe* may have been in danger, and I am sure if Captain Headland says she was, it must have been of no ordinary character, that is no reason that the prize might not have weathered the hurricane. He speaks of her, I see, as a recapture, and in all probability an Indiaman, and those hulking tea-chests will float when a man-of-war will go down."

"I trust, general, you are right," observed the secretary: "I will not fail to inform Sir Ralph directly we receive further information."

Notwithstanding all the general had said, Sir Ralph felt so greatly dispirited, that, writing to Lady Castleton, he gave her no hopes of Harry's having escaped.

Unable to speak, she placed the letter in her daughter's hands. As Julia's glance fell on the name of the *Thisbe*, and the words "all the people are lost," a sickening sensation came over, and her eyes refused to convey to her mind the meaning of the letter. It was dropping from her trembling hands when, by a great effort, she recovered herself, and at length was able to decipher the writing. She read on. The *Thisbe* and Headland were safe. Poor Harry was lost. She blamed herself for selfishly feeling that this was a relief. Then May, crushed by the agony of her grief, rose before her.

"This blow, sweet creature, will break her heart," she thought.

"Oh, mother, this is very very sad," she said aloud, "can it be true?"

"Your father speaks as if he had no hopes; he would have expressed himself differently had he entertained any."

"Mother, I must go and break this sad news to our cousins and that poor girl; it might kill her were she to hear of it suddenly."

"Grief never kills in that way, though it may by slow degrees," said Lady Castleton, with a deep sigh. "It will, however, be kind in you to do as you propose; will you drive or ride over to Downside?"

Julia determined to ride; the air and exercise would nerve her for the trying interview.

Why had not Headland written though? probably he had been prevented by his professional duties.

Attended by the old coachman who generally accompanied her with one of the carriage horses, she reached Downside. May hurried out to meet her. Julia could scarcely restrain her agitation, or keep back her tears, as May, with an inquiring glance, led her into the drawing-room where Miss Mary and Miss Jane were seated.

"What has happened?" asked May, in an agitated voice, taking Julia's hand, who sank into a chair.

"I will speak to cousin Jane first," said Julia, as she rose. Unable longer to restrain her feelings, she threw her arms round May's neck, and burst into tears.

"What has happened?" exclaimed May, her voice trembling as she spoke. "Oh tell me, has Harry been wounded? is he in danger?"

Julia's sobs prevented her from replying. Miss Jane believing the worst, led May to the sofa as if she considered that Julia's information most concerned her.

"We must all live prepared to say 'thy will be done,'" said Miss Jane, seating herself by May's side, and taking her in her arms.

The colour forsook May's cheek, and she gazed at her with a glance that showed she was unable to comprehend what was said.

"Where is Harry? is he ill?" she gasped out.

Julia feeling that it would be best at once to speak, told May the contents of Sir Ralph's letter.

"Let me see it," she said at length.

Julia, who had brought it, put it into her hands.

"I cannot, I will not believe that he is lost," she exclaimed; "your father himself is not certain. He will come back, I know he will, and he must never, never go to sea again. How cruel in those who have thus written to say that he is lost when they cannot know it;" and poor May laughed hysterically.

Julia forgot her own grief in attending to her. Miss Jane did her utmost to restore her to herself. She succeeded at length, and May was able to speak calmly of the contents of the letter. She even inspired Miss Jane with the hope that Harry and his ship had escaped destruction.

Julia rode back to Texford with her own mind greatly relieved. May had borne the intelligence much better than she had expected, and she trusted that her father had too readily believed the report of Harry's loss. She resolved, at all events, not to credit it till she had heard directly from Captain Headland, and she fully believed that she should ere long receive intelligence from him, which would either contradict the report altogether, or strengthen their hopes that Harry, though he might have been in danger, had escaped.

Week after week went by and still no letter arrived from Headland. Julia frequently went over to Downside, and was surprised to find May so calm and cheerful, attending regularly to her various duties. She was paler, it is true, than usual—no longer was there the beaming smile on her countenance, nor did she ever give way to that joyous laugh which seldom failed to inspire those who heard it. Sometimes Julia was almost inclined to doubt whether May could be so much attached to her brother as she had supposed, but then if his name was mentioned there came an expression on her countenance which at once convinced her that the young girl loved him with a devotion as true as ever woman felt for man.

The report of Lieutenant Castleton's death soon got abroad in the neighbourhood of Texford, and Dame Halliburt being among the first to hear it, feeling naturally anxious about Jacob, hastened up to Texford to ascertain its truth. She found Mr Groocock in his office. He could only assure her that nothing had been said about Jacob, that he knew Miss Julia entertained the idea that Mr Harry was still alive. Since Sam's death she had become more anxious and nervous than was her wont, and she made up her mind that Jacob must have accompanied Mr Harry, and that if he was lost her son was lost also. She expressed her fears to others, though she endeavoured to restrain her feelings in the presence of May to avoid wounding her: for the same reason she appeared to be more cheerful than she really felt when talking to Adam, who, accustomed all his life to the dangers of the sea, did not allow himself to be influenced by the reports he heard, and declared that Jacob was just as likely to come back again safe and sound as ever.

Still it was generally believed among the Hurlston people that Lieutenant Castleton and Jacob Halliburt had been lost at sea, and sometimes it was reported that the *Thisbe* herself had gone down with her gallant commander, Captain Headland, and all hands.

Chapter Forty Six
A French Professor

Miles Gaffin had long been absent from Hurlston, though he still retained possession of the mill, which was kept going under charge of Dusty Dick. The lugger, however, had not again made her appearance, and it was supposed by some that she had been lost, but others asserted, and among them Adam Halliburt, that during the war time she had plenty to do in procuring information from France, as well as in carrying it to that country from England, for Jacob had told his father of the papers Gaffin had shown him, and Adam saw no reason why he should keep the matter secret. If such had been Gaffin's occupation, it for some reason or other came to an end; probably both parties found that he could not be trusted, and he, to avoid being hung or shot as a spy, thought it wise to abandon it, and to betake himself once more to smuggling.

He again appeared one morning at his mill. No one knew whether he had arrived by land or by water. It might have been supposed from his manner, when some grist was brought to be ground, that he had never been absent.

"He will soon be at his old tricks again," observed Adam, when he heard of his arrival. "He has come here for no good."

The observation was repeated by the dame to Mr Groocock.

"I will tell you what it is, he won't be here long at all events. His lease is up in a few months, and though the law won't let us turn him out, it cannot compel us to keep him there longer than we like," observed the steward. "He will cease at Michaelmas to be the tenant of Hurlston Mill, and if we cannot get a more honest man to take it, it will certainly be hard to find a greater rogue. I have never been quite satisfied in my mind that he had not something to do with the attack on Mr Harry."

Gaffin soon made himself acquainted with all that had been going on in the neighbourhood. Harry's supposed death which he heard as an undoubted fact, gave him great satisfaction.

"As there is no longer a rival in the case, my son may now have a better chance than formerly," he said to himself. "I will write and get the fellow back; girls don't wear the willow all their lives, and though she may mope and sigh for a time, she will be ready enough to take a presentable young fellow when he offers himself."

Miles had been left in France, where he was among those who had been detained when the war broke out. His father, however, knew that he should have no difficulty in getting him back. Meantime, he found him useful in obtaining and transmitting information, though the young man ran no small risk. He had, in the meantime, in his own opinion, become a polished gentleman, with all the graces and airs of a Frenchman.

Gaffin accordingly wrote for his son to return, though a considerable time elapsed before he was able to get on board the lugger which had put in to receive him. At last, he one morning made his appearance at the mill. The lugger had not come empty, her cargo having been landed during the night, and stowed away in the vaults. It was not long before Gaffin found an opportunity for re-opening his favourite project. It was evident that he had private information relating to May, but of what nature even his son dared not ask, although his curiosity was more excited than his enterprise. Gaffin now spoke with the more vehemence, having been so long frustrated in his purpose, and he hinted that nothing must now be allowed to stand in his way. Young Miles was startled by his violent language, and felt the courage oozing out at his palms. He declared that he did not want to run the chance of putting his head in a noose for any girl alive, whatever her fortune, but his father's taunts, as well as the glowing pictures which he drew, stimulated him to make another venture. The plan arranged by the smuggler and his son need not be described.

Young Miles appeared so completely changed in appearance and manners that there was little risk of his being recognised by the inhabitants of Hurlston.

The day after his interview with his father, a post-chaise which had come from the neighbouring town, drove up to the Texford Arms. A Frenchman descended from it. He stated that he was a Royalist who had been some little time in the country, and that he wished to take lodgings in the village, his object being to give instruction in French to the families in the neighbourhood. He was told that there were no lodgings, but that he could be accommodated at the inn. Saying that he wished to be quiet, he persisted in searching for them, and after many enquiries he found that Mrs Brown, whose son sailed as mate of the *Nancy*, could take him in. She had a neat little room looking out on the sea, with which he was perfectly satisfied, and at once had his portmanteau removed to it. His name he told her was Jules Malin. She was afraid he would not like her English cooking, but he assured her that he should be perfectly contented with anything she could provide, for that in making his escape from France he had been inured to so many hardships, he found himself in a perfect paradise in her quiet cottage.

He seemed somewhat disappointed on hearing that there were but few families in the neighbourhood likely to take advantage of his instruction. Some of the better class of farmers might wish their daughters to learn French. There was also, Mrs Brown said, a young lady at Downside who might be willing to take lessons, and possibly Miss Castleton, at Texford, might also become a pupil, although, having had a French governess she probably understood the language.

Monsieur Malin set out at once with a packet of cards and called on several of the farmers. His terms were very moderate, and they were glad of the opportunity of having their daughters instructed in French. Miss Castleton, at Texford, after speaking a short time to him, asked him whether he was not a German, and on his assuring her that he was not, she informed him that as she did not admire either his pronunciation or idiom, she could not recommend him as a master.

Not in anyway abashed, he made a low bow, and shortly afterwards appeared at Downside. Miss Jane received him very politely, and begging him to be seated in the dining-room, said she would take counsel with her sister on the subject.

"As May has never had the opportunity of speaking to French people, although she, I doubt not, understands French thoroughly, it will be a pity not to give her the advantage of receiving instruction," she observed to Miss Mary.

May was grateful to her friends for their kind intentions, and was perfectly ready to take lessons. The young Frenchman seemed highly pleased, and was ready to begin at once.

Miss Jane was present. He behaved with great respect, though May was somewhat astonished the way he set about giving instruction, for he seemed to understand nothing about grammar, and she suspected that his pronunciation was far from correct.

"He may nevertheless be of assistance to you," said Miss Jane, after he had gone, "and as I promised to let him come to-morrow, we will see how he then gets on."

And so it came about that the audacious Miles again found himself in the presence of innocent May. He was so elated by the success of his first lesson that he could with difficulty maintain his assumed character, and more than once he inadvertently dropped the French accent and addressed his pupil in English. May's suspicions were gradually aroused, and as he grew more familiar in tone she attentively examined his countenance. Suddenly recognition seemed to flash upon her, and rising quickly she darted out of the room.

"I have been and made a mess of it again," he muttered to himself, "still I will try and calm the old lady if she says anything, and set matters to rights."

Miss Jane was not so easily deceived. May told her her suspicions. She entered with a stern brow, and the sum she had promised to pay for the lessons in her hand.

"I do not enquire who you are, but I have to inform you that the young lady does not wish to receive further lessons, nor do we desire again to see you here," she said, giving the money.

The pretended French master endeavoured to expostulate, but Miss Jane only pointed significantly to the door.

At last, finding that he was not listened to, he took his hat with an ill grace which further betrayed him, and hurried out of the house.

The next day he called intending to apologise, but Miss Jane refused to admit him.

"But will not Miss Halliburt see me just for one minute?" he asked, offering Susan half-a-guinea. "They don't pay you very high wages here, I guess."

"Take yourself off, Master Gaffin, and your money too," exclaimed Susan, indignantly, putting her hands behind her back. "Do you fancy we don't know you with all your pretended French airs and gibberish. Let me advise you not to show your face inside those gates again."

Miles sneaked off without attempting to reply. Recovering his audacity on his return to his lodgings he for several days made attempts to see May, who, fearing to meet him out-of-doors, was kept a prisoner within the grounds.

Miles, foiled in his plan, determined to consult his father, but, not wishing to be seen near the mill in daylight, he took a stroll on the Downs, intending to make his way there at dusk.

He had gone some distance, when suddenly the tall figure of Mad Sal, rising as it seemed out of the earth, stood before him. He started back and would have hurried away, recollecting her appearance when he had assisted in the outrage on Jacob Halliburt.

Though others might not have recognised him, she, it was evident, did so, from the way she addressed him.

"What have you done with the hapless lad I saw you bear away over the salt sea, salt sea?" she exclaimed. "I have waited long, but in vain, for his return. Have you sent him wandering far from home and country, or is he fathoms deep beneath the salt sea, salt sea?"

"I don't know of whom you speak, old dame," answered Miles, mustering up his courage. "I am a stranger here, and know none of the people. You mistake me for some one else."

"I take you for the son of the miller of Hurlston," she exclaimed, laughing loudly. "Go and tell him that I have watched his doings. I know his goings out and his comings in, and ere long the ministers of justice will track him down, and consign him to the fate he so richly merits."

"What have I to do with the miller of Hurlston? He would be a bold man who would speak to him in that way," answered Miles, trembling with fear.

"It's false, it's false," shouted the old woman. "You are even now on your way to him. I saw you leave his door not many nights ago, when you thought no one was near. Go, tell him to beware of the fate which will ere long overtake him. Go, I say, go," and she waved her staff wildly round, compelling Miles to retreat before her. He, at last, having nothing with which to defend himself, and not daring to seize the staff whirled about his head, turned round and fled across the heath followed by the shouts and shrieks of the unhappy creature who seemed to triumph in his discomfiture. He did not stop till he got out of her sight, when sitting down to rest, he tried to recover himself before venturing to enter the mill.

Miles Gaffin listened to his son's account with a contemptuous sneer on his lips. Another subject was at that moment occupying his thoughts. He had just received notice from Sir Ralph's steward to quit the mill the day his lease expired.

"It is old Groocock's doing," he told his son. "Sir Ralph takes no charge of such matters, though I should expect no favour from his hands. We are old foes, and though he does not know me, I know him. I would be revenged on him, and I would burn Texford over his head without compunction, had I not good reason for preserving the place. Had you succeeded with Maiden May as she is called, the way would have been smoother. Fool as you are, you can keep counsel. Now listen. The *Lively* will be here again ere long with all her old crew, and a few other bold fellows we have picked up of late. We will make sharp work of it—first embark all the goods stored here, then with a strong hand push on to Texford, take my revenge on Sir Ralph and his chattering old steward, then set fire to the mill, and get on board the lugger before half-a-dozen men can collect to oppose us. I think I may trust you meantime with another piece of work. You shall have half-a-dozen fellows, and you can surround Downside, and may bring on board either of the ladies you like. As the girl is supposed to be hard-hearted, you may secure one of the old ones; I leave that to you."

"Trust me for the one I'll lay my hands on," answered Miles. "If you will give me the men, you may depend that I will not let her slip this time."

"Well, I think you have got sense enough to do that, and the *Lively* will not be here many hours before our plan has been carried out, and we are away from Hurlston."

Chapter Forty Seven
A Warning Voice

Poor Maiden May, as her loving friends still delighted to call her, waited day after day, anxious at not receiving a contradiction of the report of Harry's loss. True it is that "hope deferred maketh the heart-sick;" her cheeks lost their bloom, her step its elastic tread; still she performed her wonted duties, her voice was as melodious as ever when she read to Miss Mary, and she endeavoured, as she led her about, to speak with cheerfulness, and to describe, as she used to do when a young girl, the progress of the vegetation in the garden, the fresh flowers blooming, and the birds and insects as they flitted about among the trees and bushes. How eagerly she looked out for the arrival of the postman at his accustomed hour of passing the house, and her heart sank with disappointment as day after day he went by with no letter for Downside.

Julia, too, surrounded by the luxuries of Texford, was not less to be pitied than May. She, too, was waiting in expectation of receiving a letter, and no letter came. Sir Ralph was angry at her objecting to come up to London, and he informed her that he intended inviting several gentlemen of fortune and position to the Hall, adding, "now understand, Julia, should you receive an offer of which I approve, I must insist on your accepting it. I am resolved never to sanction your marriage with the man who so presumptuously aspired to your hand, and as I shall take care to convince him of this, he will abandon any hopes he may have entertained. As, in consequence of the death of your poor brother, the baronetcy will cease to exist, I am doubly anxious to see Texford possessed by a man of family, who will take our name, and be able, from his wealth, to obtain the title."

Still Julia did not despair. She felt that no one was more worthy to become the possessor of Texford than Headland, or was more likely, from his merits, to win the title her father wished his son-in-law to obtain.

One morning May saw the postman approaching to put a letter into her hand; it bore only an English postmark, and was addressed to Miss Pemberton. It was from Mr Shallard. He hoped to have the honour of calling on the ladies the following day on a matter of business connected with their ward, as he might venture to call her. They wondered, naturally, what he could have to communicate; it could scarcely be that he had made any discovery regarding her birth, he would have said so had such been the case.

May tried to overcome any curiosity she might have felt, indeed one subject only could interest her. Was he likely to bring her tidings of Harry?

He came at the appointed hour.

"I fear that the matter which has brought me here must prove painful to that young lady," and he bowed to May, "and, at the same time, to those who have her interest at heart, it cannot fail, in other respects, to be gratifying. Before Lieutenant Castleton went abroad he executed a will, in which he left the whole of his property in trust to you two ladies and myself for the benefit of that young lady, whom I have been very careful to designate in a way which may preclude any mistake, though from the rough notes he drew up, I found that he was under the idea that she was the daughter of Adam and Betsy Halliburt. As Sir Ralph is convinced of the death of his son, I have proved the will, and as the money is invested in the Funds, your signatures only are required to obtain the dividends, when the amount, which I calculate to be about 500 a year, including that arising from the Texford property, will be paid over."

"Oh, he is not dead, I cannot receive it," cried May, in a tone of grief which went to her hearers' hearts, as, hiding her face in her hands, she sank back in her chair, and would have fallen, had not Miss Jane and the lawyer sprung to her assistance.

"I deeply grieve to have wounded your feelings," said Mr Shallard.

"Oh, do not tell me he is dead, do not," cried May again.

"My dear young lady, had not his father been convinced of the fact, I should not have ventured to interfere in the matter. He, I trust, may have received wrong information, and I hope Lieutenant Castleton may really be alive, and that he may bestow his fortune on you in a far more satisfactory manner. I have only taken a precautionary step in case the will should be disputed."

The lawyer knew enough of the female heart to be aware that his remarks were more likely to be beneficial to the interesting young girl than any expressions of condolence he could have uttered.

May looked up with a smile of hope.

"Yes, he will come back, I am sure he will. No one saw the ship go down."

The lawyer, however, induced Miss Jane to accompany him to the dining-room, and to sign the necessary papers, observing—

"I trust the young gentleman may appear, but it is always right in these cases to be on the safe side. If he reappears, I am sure he will be much obliged to us for acting as he would have wished had he been lost."

Miss Jane took the opportunity of mentioning to Mr Shallard the arrival of young Miles Gaffin in disguise at Hurlston. The lawyer listened to all she said.

"I will have the gentleman looked after," he answered. "Information has been laid against the father, and he, in all probability, will be implicated. If it can be proved that he assisted in carrying off young Halliburt, we can lay hands on him at once. If his father gets an intimation of our intentions, we shall require a strong force, as he has a number of desperate fellows at his back, and would certainly protect his son, and endeavour to rescue him."

"But if so, do you think that we here are safe from his atrocious designs. It never occurred to me before," said Miss Jane, in some trepidation, as the idea entered her mind, "that he may possibly make some rash attempt upon this house. It is not easy to fathom his motives, but there must be something behind which we do not yet understand."

"I cannot say that I think you are quite safe," observed the lawyer. "If I have your authority for stating that you dread an attack from the smugglers, I will apply for a body of revenue officers to be sent to Hurlston, and as we have a body of sea-fencibles at Morbury, I will get my friend, Captain Shirley, to send over a few to support them. A ruffian, such as this Gaffin undoubtedly is, must no longer be allowed to continue his career if the law can lay hands on him."

The arrangement Mr Shallard proposed greatly relieved Miss Jane's mind. She had not mentioned her fears either to her sister or to May, and probably they weighed more on her mind on that account.

Mr Groocock had, in the meantime, received authority from Sir Ralph to use force in expelling Miles Gaffin from the mill should he refuse to give it up, and the steward had taken steps effectually to execute his orders. He also had applied for the assistance of the military to carry them out.

The day was approaching when Gaffin's lease of the mill would terminate.

Mr Groocock thought he had kept his arrangements secret, or he would scarcely have ventured to ride about the country by himself.

Gaffin was now constantly at the mill, and the steward knowing the man's desperate character, might justly have feared that he would revenge himself on his head. He was one evening returning home later than usual on his steady cob, when passing through a copse not far from the Texford gate, his horse pricked up its ears, and moved to the other side of the road, as if wishing to avoid an object it had discovered. Never since he bestrode it had it been guilty of shying.

"What is the matter, old steady?" he said, patting his steed's neck.

Suddenly the question was answered by the appearance of mad Sal's tall figure emerging from the copse.

"Old man," she said, "I come to warn you that danger threatens your life. You are kind and generous to those in distress. You have cared for and pitied me while others mocked and scorned me, and refused the bread I asked. He who has turned me from his doors with curses and scorn when I asked a crust at his hands, is plotting the destruction of you and those you serve. He thinks that he has been unobserved, but I have dodged his footsteps when he knew not I was near. I have been within the walls of his abode when, had he discovered my presence, he would have strangled me without compunction. I tell you this, lest you think the poor mad creature, as people call her, is talking folly; but I charge you, as you value your own life, and the honour and the liberty of those you serve, to let the officers of justice lay hands on him before he has done the mischief he contemplates. I leave your master to his doom. From me he deserves no favour, but for his hapless wife and daughter I feel as woman feels for woman, as they, too, have lost him they love in the cruel salt sea, salt sea. Be warned, old man, be warned."

Before even the steward could speak mad Sal had retreated within the shelter of the copse. He had, as she acknowledged, compassionated her forlorn condition, assisted her with food and money; indeed, through his means, and that of other charitable people in the neighbourhood, she had been enabled to exist. He was, therefore, convinced that she had not warned him without cause, though he wished that she had given him more exact information on which to proceed.

He hurried home determined to communicate with Mr Shallard the next morning, and to obtain a sufficient guard at once for Texford, in case Gaffin should really venture to attack it.

Each morning May rose with the hopes that a letter would come from Harry, and not till the postman had passed did her fond heart grow sick again with hope deferred.

The usual hour of his coming had arrived, and as she heard his step on the gravel walk she hastened out to meet him. He held a letter in his hand. It was directed to Miss Pemberton. She gazed at the handwriting.

"Yes, yes it is from him, he is alive," she exclaimed, with an hysterical cry as she sprang up the steps, and flew into the drawing-room.

Fortunately Miss Jane made her appearance with the required sum to pay the postman.

"Read, read," cried May, standing trembling in every limb as she gave the letter to Miss Jane, who, tearing it open, handed one to her, directed "to my beloved Maiden May." Her eyes swimming with tears of joy, she could with difficulty decipher the words. Yet she saw that Harry was alive and well, and in England.

"He would be at Downside the next day, or in two days at furthest. He had met with many adventures. He knew that she must have been anxious at his not writing, but it had been impossible. He had been wrecked, and lived long on a desert island, and finally made his escape on board a slow sailing merchantman, which, after running many risks of capture, had safely reached England. What he considered the best news he had to communicate was the discovery not only of the person who would serve as the missing link by which his friend, Captain Headland, hoped to trace his father; but of that father himself, who was thoroughly prepared to acknowledge his friend as his long lost son. There is some mystery about him," he added, "but he is so evidently a man of refinement and education, that I am sure there is nothing of which my friend will have cause to be ashamed; I suspect, indeed, that he is a man of title, or the heir to a title, which he, perhaps, may have reason to think will be disputed. I am delighted, too, to find that the *Thisbe* has been ordered home, and her arrival is every day looked for, so that I hope Headland's long cherished wish will be accomplished, and he will find that he belongs to a family to which even my father cannot object. And I trust, too, dearest, that this happy event will soften my father's heart, and that he will no longer object to our union."

Much more Harry said to the same effect. May, indeed, had full reason to believe that he loved her as devotedly as ever.

Chapter Forty Eight
Saved from the Wreck

We must return to Harry and Jacob on board the prize. The young lieutenant well knew the dangerous position in which the ship, now under his command, was placed. All that he could then do was to keep her before the wind, and to try and take in the remainder of the canvas. Few of the Frenchmen seemed inclined to exert themselves, appearing utterly indifferent to their fate. Harry urged the French officer to induce his men to work, for their own sakes as well as his; but he shrugged his shoulders, and declared that he had lost all command over them.

On the ship flew, the hurricane every instant increasing in fury. The topgallant-masts were quickly carried away, and the canvas which had not been taken in was soon flying in shreds, which lashed themselves round and round the yards.

To clear away the wreck of the masts was no small danger. Jacob and two of his companions going aloft accomplished the task. A few of the French crew were shamed into assisting them.

The ship required all his energies and attention, and he had scarcely time to look round to see what had become of the *Thisbe*. When he did so, he could only just see her dimly far away astern. He knew, however, that if possible Headland would follow and endeavour to lend him the assistance he might require.

Harry now found that the prize was the *Culloden*, an English ship homeward-bound, which had been captured by a French privateer, and was on her way to the Mauritius. Her officers, with most of the English crew, had been removed on board the privateer.

There was no time, however, at present to visit the passengers who had been left, as all his attention was required on deck. He had at first hoped that the threatened gale would prove of an ordinary character, but it was soon evident that it was to prove a hurricane. Every moment it increased in fury, while the sea got up its white-crested billows, hissing and roaring on either side as the ship clove her way through them.

He had had no time to disarm the French crew, and he could not help fearing that they would rise on him, and retake the ship. As long, however, as the *Thisbe* was in sight they would not make the attempt.

Fortunately there were several Lascars who had before belonged to the ship, and they were more likely to side with him than with the French. The knowledge of this probably kept the latter in order.

Harry's difficulties were increased by discovering that the *Thisbe* was no longer in sight. To bring the ship to the wind, and wait for her was impossible. His only chance of safety consisted in running before it.

The French officer was a young sub-lieutenant, evidently not much of a seaman. Harry pointed out the danger in which the ship was placed, and demanded his word not to attempt to retake her.

"If you give it I will trust you, and you shall be at liberty, but if not, I must be under the necessity of placing you in confinement," he added.

The Frenchman shrugged his shoulders and replied, "that he would comply with the English officer's request, though he could not be answerable for his men."

"I will look after them," said Harry, and, calling Jacob, told him to keep an eye on the French crew.

He sent for the Lascar boatswain, and obtained his assurance that he and his men would remain faithful to the English. This gave him rather more confidence.

The cabin-steward, who was among the English prisoners, came to announce that dinner was ready. Leaving two of his best men at the helm, and inviting the French officer to accompany him, Harry hurried into the cuddy to snatch a few mouthfuls of food.

The passengers, who were all civilians, crowded round him eagerly asking questions. They had kept below, afraid of the risk on deck from the spars or blocks falling from aloft. They expressed their satisfaction at the recapture of the ship, not appearing to be aware of the danger she was in. Harry, taking them aside, told them that he must depend upon their assistance should the French crew attempt to retake the ship.

"Very little chance of that," was the answer.

"It is as well to be cautious, however," he observed.

He was told that there was another passenger ill in his cabin, out of which he had not made his appearance for several days. Harry, however, unwilling to remain longer than was absolutely necessary from the deck, could not then visit him.

The *Culloden* drove before the hurricane which now blew from one quarter, now from another. Harry had no one on whom he could depend for keeping a correct reckoning. The binnacle had been knocked away, and the other compasses on board were out of order. It was impossible to ascertain in what direction the ship was driving. The *Thisbe* was nowhere to be seen. A leak was sprung, the pumps were manned, but the water gained on them. The French crew threatened to mutiny, and were with difficulty prevented from breaking into the spirit-room. By the strictest vigilance were they alone kept in order. The Lascars, however, who had belonged to the ship, remained faithful, and readily obeyed Harry's commands. Day after day went by, the hurricane rather increased than lessened. The masts went by the board, and the *Culloden* remained a helpless wreck on the stormy ocean. The sea through which she was driving was but little known, but numberless dangers, many of them as uncertain, were marked in the chart. In spite of his anxieties, however, Harry kept up his spirits. He could venture to take but brief intervals of rest, but he could rely on Jacob who took his place when he was below. By great exertions a jury-mast was secured to the stump of the foremast, and a sail was set which kept the ship before the wind, and prevented her from being pooped. Still, should danger appear ahead, it would be insufficient to enable her to avoid it. Several days had passed, the gale had decreased, but the ship was still running on before it. The night was very dark, Harry was on deck. He hoped on the return of daylight to get an after jury-mast rigged, and to heave the ship too. All hands were at the pumps. By keeping them going alone, they well knew, could the ship be prevented from foundering. Suddenly there came a cry from forward of "Breakers ahead." It was followed by a terrific crashing, rending sound. The next sea lifted the ship to strike with greater force. Several of the passengers who rushed from the cabin, and many of the terrified crew, were carried away by the following sea which swept with resistless force over the deck. Harry and Jacob, with the rest of the Englishmen, clung to the stauncheons and bulwarks, and escaped. The ship still drove on till she became firmly fixed in the rocks. Land could dimly be discerned over the starboard quarter at no great distance, but a foaming mass of water intervened. Some of the Frenchmen and Lascars on discovering it began to lower a boat. Harry in vain ordered them to desist. Before she had got a dozen yards from the ship, the boat and all in her were engulphed. No other boat remained. Still Harry hoped from the way the ship remained fixed that she would hold together should the sea go down, and that in the morning he might be able to establish a communication with the shore.

Finding that nothing more could be done on deck, he made his way to the cuddy to offer such consolation as he could to the passengers.

They thanked him for his exertions, aware that it was from no fault of his the ship had been wrecked.

He went to the cabin of the invalid gentleman. The occupant was sitting up dressed.

"What, wrecked again!" he exclaimed, as Harry appeared. "Is the death I have so often escaped about to overtake me at last?"

"I hope not," answered Harry, and he expressed his expectation of being able to reach the shore in the morning.

"I ought to be grateful to you, sir, and will endeavour to feel so," said the invalid. "But bereavements and numberless misfortunes have made me indifferent to life."

On his return on deck, hoping that the island might be inhabited, Harry ordered a gun to be fired, and blue lights to be burned. As the latter blazed up they cast a lurid glare over the ship and the wild rocky shore, tinging the sheets of spray which still flew over the deck, though the wind had gone down and the sea had much subsided. For a considerable time no answer was returned to these signals. At length a light was seen, and presently a fire blazed up on a spot directly opposite the ship. Still it seemed impossible to carry a rope across the seething cauldron which intervened. Jacob volunteered to make the attempt. Harry, though unwilling to let him risk his life could not refuse his offer.

The fire threw sufficient light on the rocks to enable him to see his way. Fastening a line round his body he lowered himself down and made for the nearest rock. Now the sea appeared to be carrying him away, now he bravely breasted it, till at length the rock was gained. Next instant a sea washed over it, but he clung fast, and as soon as it had passed, he sprang forward and reached the next. Sometimes he was hidden altogether from sight, then again the glare of the blue light showed him still either tightly clinging to a rock, or making his way onwards.

He at length had passed the most dangerous portion. Three men had at first only been seen near the fire, a fourth now appeared, it was Jacob. A loud cheer showed him that his shipmates were aware of his success.

A hawser with another smaller line was then made fast to it, and taxing to the utmost the strength of the four men, hauled at length on shore.

A cradle was next rapidly constructed and fitted with ropes for hauling it backwards and forwards along the hawser. The desired means for conveying all on shore was obtained.

This task had occupied a considerable time, and the rising wind and increased violence of the sea made all on board anxious to gain the shore.

Harry's men wished him to go first.

"No, my lads," he answered firmly. "I will see all in safety before I leave the ship."

The passengers and the greater number of the crew had reached the shore in safety, when Harry recollected that the invalid passenger had not made his appearance.

Having ordered the two men who remained, to secure a large block, and to reeve a rope through it, by which means, when on shore, they could still communicate with the wreck, he hurried into the cabin, where he found the gentleman seated at the table, with a book in his hand, endeavouring to read by the light of the cuddy lamp.

"I was waiting till I was summoned," he said calmly. "Trusting to your assurance, that there was no danger, I was unwilling to expose myself to the wetting spray longer than was necessary."

"I was mistaken, there is no time to be lost," exclaimed Harry. "I must beg you to come without delay," he exclaimed. "At any moment this part of the ship may break up, as the bows have already begun to do."

The gentleman leaning on Harry's arm, proceeded with him on deck. Even in those few minutes the danger had increased. Only one man remained.

As Harry with his charge reached the side, he was surprised to hear Jacob's voice.

"I came back by the last trip, to lend you a hand, sir," he said. "If you will take charge of the gentleman, I will wait on board till you are safe on shore; he cannot go by himself, that's certain."

There was no time for expostulating, Harry, therefore, securing the gentleman in the cradle, placed himself by his side, and those on shore began hauling away on the line.

Scarcely had he left the wreck, than a heavy sea washed over it. He still, however, could distinguish Jacob clinging to the bulwarks.

The cradle seemed now to taughten, now to be lowered so much, that he and his charge were nearly submerged by the foaming water. He dreaded every moment that the wreck would part, and his faithful follower be washed away.

At length the rock was reached, and his companion was lifted out of the cradle. The cradle was quickly run back to the wreck. The darkness prevented them seeing whether Jacob was still there. A minute of intense anxiety elapsed. At length a tug at the rope was given, the signal to haul in. His shipmates gave a loud cheer when Jacob, by the light of the fire, was seen in the cradle as they dragged it to the shore.

"All right, Mr Castleton," he exclaimed, "though I did think, as I was stepping into this basket, that I might have had to take a longer cruise than I bargained for."

"Castleton," exclaimed the invalid gentleman. Harry, however, did not hear him speak, as at that moment the three strangers introduced themselves.

They had been long living on the island, they said, having been wrecked some years before, since when no ship had come near the spot. There was water and wood in abundance, and fish and birds could be caught. This was satisfactory news.

"Well, my friends," said Harry, "the first thing we have to do is to get up shelter, and in the morning, if the ship holds together, we must try and obtain provisions. In the meantime, if you will take the gentleman I brought on shore, with some of the other passengers, who can least stand exposure, to your hut, I shall be obliged to you."

"It is some way off, sir," answered the man who had spoken, "but we will do our best to look after the gentleman."

Though the invalid expressed his readiness to walk, Harry believing that he was ill able to do so, had a litter constructed with two light spars and a piece of a sail which had been washed on shore; and Jacob and three of the other men carried it. Most of the passengers accompanied them.

The daylight soon afterwards broke and Harry set the men to work to collect whatever was washed up by the sea. He was chiefly anxious to obtain provisions, the bales of rich silks and other manufactures of the east were of little value to men in their situation.

The wind had again increased, and sea upon sea dashing with terrific violence against the wreck, she in a short time broke up, her rich cargo being scattered far and wide over the waters and cast upon the beach.

A number of casks of provisions, bags of rice and other grain, and a few cases of wine, some chests of tea and other articles, were however saved.

The islanders, as the men found on the island may be called, now returned and advised that the stores should be removed from the bleak and rocky bay, in which the ship had gone on shore, to the more genial situation, where they had formed their settlement.

Harry shouldering a heavy load, the men followed his example, and the stores were soon conveyed to the settlement.

It was a picturesque spot at the head of a valley extending down to the sea, with a stream of water running through it, descending from a high hill which rose in the centre of the island. On one side was a grove of trees, and on the other where the ground was level, the men had cultivated a garden of considerable size with a field of Indian corn.

A suitable spot was selected on which the party set to work, to put up huts formed partly of pieces of the wreck and some sails which had been washed up; and partly of the branches of trees which were cut down for the purpose.

Harry had been struck by the superior intelligence and activity of one of the islanders. He showed from the first especial skill in erecting huts and the other men soon learned to follow his directions. Harry enquired of Jacob if he had heard anything about the man.

"Not much, sir, except that he is a man of war's man. His mates call him Jack and that's all I know, except that he is a right sort of fellow."

Harry had had as comfortable a hut as could be erected arranged for the invalid gentleman who had hitherto remained in that of the islanders. He had also designed a larger hut for the other passengers; he himself having slept under such temporary covering as the canvas which had been saved afforded. He found however on his return from an excursion to the scene of the wreck that Jacob and Jack had erected another hut.

"You have been only thinking of us sir," said Jacob, "but Jack and I thought of how you ought to have a house to yourself, so we took the liberty of putting it up, and we hope you will find it comfortable. The Lascars and Frenchmen have been building others for themselves, and as soon as we have finished this we are going to turn to and get one up for ourselves, and then we shall all have palaces like kings."

With the aid of some mattresses and the bales of cotton and silk which had been saved sufficiently comfortable bedding was arranged for the invalid gentleman as well as for the other passengers. He seemed grateful, and appeared mostly to mourn the loss of his books.

At length the first arrangements for their residence on the island were completed. A flagstaff was put up on a neighbouring height, and an English flag was hoisted as a signal to passing vessels.

Harry had now to consider the means for obtaining food for the settlement and for giving occupation to the inhabitants.

Chapter Forty Nine
Sailor Jack

Harry had gone to his hut after the labours of the day were over,—and was about to lie down and rest when Jacob appeared at the entrance.

"Beg pardon, sir," he said, "may I speak a few words with you."

"Yes," answered Harry, "what are they about?"

"Why, sir, I have been having a talk with Jack, and he has been asking me questions which I can't answer, but which I've a notion you can; and if you'll let him he'd like to see you, sir."

"What is it about, Jacob?" asked Harry.

"Why, sir, he was telling me how he was serving on board a man-of-war, how the boat he belonged to was cut off by the savages and every soul on board killed except himself; and how after he had been for several years made to work like a slave he escaped and got on board a Dutch merchantman. He was working his passage home in her when she was cast away on this island, and only he and two other Englishmen were saved. But that's not what I was coming to. When I happened to be talking of Captain Headland he seemed wonderfully interested. 'Why Jacob,' he said, 'that's my name.' I then told him that he and you, sir, were old shipmates, and that you knew much more about him than I did, sir. Jack asked me if I would come and speak to you, for he is just like a man out of his mind, he is so eager to know who the captain is."

"Tell him I shall be glad to speak to him at once," said Harry, much interested in what he had heard, and Jacob hurried off to call Jack.

Jack soon reached the hut, showing his man-of-war's-man manners by doffing his hat and pulling one of his long locks. His countenance, though burned and bronzed almost to blackness, and somewhat frizzled by age and exposure, wore the same honest, kind expression which Headland had described.

"Sit down, my friend," said Harry, giving him one of a couple of stools he had manufactured. "Halliburt has been telling me that you wish to hear about Captain Headland."

"Ay, that I do, sir, and if you knew how my heart is set on him, for I am sure it must be him, you would not wonder that I make bold to axe you. I never had a son, but if I had, I could not love him better than I did that lad, whom I watched over ever since he was a small child just able to toddle about the decks by himself. I took charge of him when there was no one else to see that he did not come to harm, and I may say, though there is nothing to boast of in it, I saved his life more than once when he would have been drowned or burned to death, or carried away by the savages. It was a proud day when I saw him placed on the quarter-deck with a fair chance of becoming an admiral, as I am very sure he will be, and there was nothing so much went to my heart when I was made a prisoner by the rascally Malays as the thought that I could no longer have an eye on him, and maybe help him a bit with my cutlass in boarding an enemy or in such like work. And then, when I at last got away from the Malays and was coming home to hear about him again, as I hoped, it was just the bitterest thing that could have happened to me to find myself wrecked on this desolate island without the chance that I could see of getting off again. And then, after all, to have some of his ship's company and his greatest friend, as Jacob tells me you are, sir, cast ashore here to tell me about him, almost surpasses my belief and makes my heart jump into my mouth for joy."

"I will not ask if you are Jack Headland of whom my friend has spoken, and for whose faithful care he has expressed the warmest gratitude, for I am very sure you must be," exclaimed Harry. "He has told me all the circumstances you have described and nothing will give him greater satisfaction than to find that you are alive and well. He is more than ever anxious to discover his parents, and you are the only person alive that he knows of who is able to help him to do so."

Harry then gave a brief account of Captain Headland's career from the time since his faithful friend had been parted from him.

"Thank you, sir, for telling me all this," exclaimed Jack. "I have often and often puzzled my head to call to mind the name of the craft aboard which I first saw him, and the place she sailed from; do you see, sir, I had no learning and was a thoughtless lad at the time, and I never asked questions about the place we had come to, and all I remember is that the name of the craft seemed pretty nigh to break the jaws of all who attempted to speak it. Still, where there's a will there's a way, maybe somehow or other it will come back to me."

"At all events I am sure you will do your best if we can manage to get away from this place; and Captain Headland will certainly not leave these seas without looking for us," answered Harry.

The conversation was so interesting that it was not till a late hour that Jack returned to his hut in which Jacob had been invited to take up his quarters. The two warm-hearted sailors had so many qualities in common that they had been especially drawn to each other, though they probably were not aware of the cause. Utter freedom from selfishness was the chief characteristic of them both. No sooner had Jacob Halliburt discovered Harry's love for May than he was ready to sacrifice even his own life if it were necessary for May's sake, to preserve that of his lieutenant, without a thought about the destruction of his own vain hopes, while honest Jack's whole soul was wrapped up in the boy he had preserved from so many dangers.

The invalid gentleman had recognised Jacob as the seaman who had returned on board the wreck, and had assisted in his escape by placing him in the cradle. Jacob had since then been attending to him and looked in every now and then to enquire if he wanted anything: he had besides helped to fit up his hut. He had not from the first associated with the rest of the passengers who professed not even to know his name. Some pronounced him proud and haughty, and others expressed their opinion that he was not right in his mind; although, except that he had kept himself aloof from them, he had done nothing which would warrant such an assertion.

Jacob was attending on him the first day he had occupied his hut.

"Is there anything more I can do for you, sir?" asked Jacob, who had brought him his share of the evening meal cooked at the general fire, for Harry had established a system by which all shared alike.

"Thank you, my man, there is nothing more I require; but as your appetite is probably better than mine, if you will wait a few minutes you can carry off some of my rations," answered the gentleman, looking at the mess with the eye of an invalid, as if it was not especially to his taste, "I fear I have no other means of repaying you for the trouble you are taking on my account."

Chapter Fifty
Mr Hastings

Jacob had from the first constituted himself the attendant of the invalid gentleman, and daily brought him his food from the common stock.

"By-the-bye, my man," he said, looking up at Jacob, "I heard your officer spoken of as Lieutenant Castleton, do you know to what Castletons he belongs?"

"I don't know exactly what you mean, sir, but I know that his father is Sir Ralph Castleton of Texford, because I come from Hurlston, which is hard by there; and mother lived in the family of Mr Herbert Castleton near Morbury, so you see, sir, I know all about the family."

"Ah, that is remarkable," observed the gentleman, as if to himself. "Has Sir Ralph Castleton been long at Texford?" he asked.

"Let me see, it's about a matter of three or four years since he came there, when his uncle Sir Reginald Castleton died. There was an elder brother, I have heard mother say, Mr Ranald Castleton, who was lost at sea, so Mr Ralph became to be Sir Ralph and got the estate."

"Has Sir Ralph many children?" enquired the gentleman, who appeared much interested in Jacob's account.

"Yes, sir; besides Mr Harry there is his eldest son Mr Algernon, and their sister Miss Julia, a young lady who, I have heard mother say, is liked by everyone in those parts."

The gentleman asked whether Lady Castleton was alive, and made many other enquiries about Texford, and its neighbourhood.

"If you will give me your name, sir, I will let Lieutenant Castleton know what you have been asking, as he can tell you more about the family than I can."

The gentleman made no reply and for some minutes appeared lost in thought.

"Yes," he said at length, "you may inform him that my name is Hastings—that having once known some members of his family, on hearing his name, I was curious to learn whether he was related to them, and that I shall be happy to see him at any time he has leisure to look in on me."

Jacob delivered the message, and next day Harry paid Mr Hastings a visit. He found him, as his appearance betokened a man of education and refinement, but his spirits appeared greatly depressed. He received Harry in a friendly way, and soon threw off the formal manners he had at first exhibited.

Harry, though naturally somewhat curious to know more about him, afraid of appearing inquisitive did not venture to question him in the way he might otherwise have done.

"I fear, sir, you feel greatly the misfortune that has happened to us," observed Harry, "it must have been a bitter disappointment indeed, when you had every reason to hope that you would, after we had retaken the ship, been able to proceed on your voyage to England."

"My young friend, I am inured to misfortunes and disappointments," answered Mr Hastings. "For years past I have been accustomed to them. I have been deprived of all I held dear in life. I had resolved long ago to return to Europe, soon after the last war with France broke out. I was on my way to England, when the ship in which I had taken my passage, was captured by the French and carried into an island in the Indian Ocean, with which no English seaman was acquainted. Here I with many others was detained a prisoner. Some were liberated, every means being taken to prevent them from becoming acquainted with its position. I unfortunately was known to have ascertained it from some observation I had been seen taking, and I was therefore detained till the termination of the war. My health gave way and I had given up all hopes of recovery, when I was taken to Batavia. Here I remained till long after the commencement of the present war, but was at length, however, allowed to sail for Bencoolen. I was again detained till the arrival of the *Culloden*, on board which I embarked, and she, as you know, was captured by a French frigate, and it seems to me that my prospect of reaching England is as far off as ever."

Harry endeavoured to cheer the unfortunate man, assuring him that he felt certain Captain Headland would, as soon as he possibly could, come to look for the *Culloden*, and that he would without fail visit their island.

"I wish that I possessed your hopefulness, my young friend," answered Mr Hastings, with a look of melancholy.

Harry after this conversation with Mr Hastings often visited him, and was always received with a warm welcome. Instead of having suffered from the exposure to which he had been subject on the night of the wreck, he, from that day, appeared to gain strength, and was soon able to walk about, and to visit different parts of the little island. Whatever he might have appeared to the passengers he showed no haughtiness when, as was frequently the case, he entered into conversation with the men. He never failed, when he met Jacob, to have a talk with him, and make more enquiries about Texford and Hurlston. At last one day Jacob said:—

"I think, sir, you must know the place."

"You forget, my friend, that you have already told me so much about it, that I might easily describe it as well as if I had been there," was the answer.

By Harry's judicious arrangement, good discipline was maintained among the community over whom he was called to govern, while he induced them to add to their stock of provisions by fishing and snaring birds, and by collecting eggs among the cliffs, and shell-fish from the rocks. Fortunately a cask of hooks had been saved from the Dutch ship, as also a box of seeds. The islanders had cultivated a considerable plot of ground which produced vegetables of all sorts, and this was now much increased by the new comers.

Every evening after their return from fishing and bird catching, the men collected round the common fire which had by general consent been lighted in the middle of the village. Here they employed themselves in cooking and eating the fish and birds they had caught. It soon became the general meeting place of the whole community. At first the passengers had kept aloof, but by degrees they were induced to come and listen to the seamen's yarns, and to join in the conversation.

Harry and Mr Hastings sometimes came near to the fire and joined in the conversation, though they more frequently sat at a little distance, listening to what was going forward, and often not a little amused by the remarks of their companions.

They were thus seated when the evening meal having been served out, the men as usual amused each other by narrating their adventures. Jack was appealed to, to give his, for he was supposed to have gone through more than the rest.

"Do you mean, mates, how I got away from the Malays, and was wrecked on this island?" he asked.

"No, no, Jacob has been telling us that you were wrecked long before that time, and had to live among savages ever so long," answered one of the men. "Can't you begin at the beginning; let us hear all about yourself since you first came to sea."

Jack at first modestly apologised for talking about himself, but in a short time Harry heard him giving an account of his early days when he first found himself on board a ship, knowing no more about the sea than did one of the sheep of the flock he had been wont to attend. He went on exciting the interest of his hearers till he arrived at that part of his history which he had already given to Harry.

"You see, mates, as I wanted to part from the skipper, and the skipper wanted to part from me, I was not sorry to ship on board another craft, little thinking what was about to happen to her. She had a strange name, had that craft, so strange that neither I nor any one else, I should think, could manage to speak it."

Jack then went on to describe how the little boy had been brought on board, how the mate seemed to have especial dislike to the child, and then how the vessel was wrecked.

Mr Hastings who had before been lying down, sat up, and bending forward, listened with the greatest attention to what Jack was saying.

Suddenly he exclaimed in a tone of the deepest interest, rising and coming up to Jack, "Was the name of the craft you sailed in the *Bomanjee Horrmarjee?*"

"That was the name, sir," exclaimed Jack, "and if you are not the gentleman who brought the little boy aboard, you are just like him, though to be sure as a good many years have passed since then, that would make the difference."

"I am the person you suppose, and the father of the little boy; and tell me, my friend, was he saved from the wreck? Is he still alive? What has become of him?"

"This is indeed wonderful," exclaimed Harry, who had accompanied Mr Hastings. "I can answer your questions. Your son has long been my most intimate friend, and is now my captain. He commands the *Thisbe*, and I trust before many weeks are over that the earnest desire of his heart will be fulfilled, that he will have the happiness of meeting the father he has so long desired to find. When I discovered Jack Headland, the faithful guardian of his early days, I congratulated myself that the only existing clue, as I supposed, on which my friend could depend for tracing his parents had been found, though I little thought that it would be so rapidly followed up. I can assure you, sir, that you will have every reason to be proud of your son, for a more noble and gallant fellow does not exist; and that he is your son I have not the shadow of a doubt."

Mr Hastings, begging Jack to follow, retired to his hut accompanied by Harry, that he might learn from the honest seaman fuller particulars of everything relating to the boy he had brought up.

Jack seemed to rejoice as much as he did, and to be fully convinced that he was right in his conjectures. Jack at length retired, leaving the two gentlemen alone.

"It is, indeed, wonderful, Mr Castleton, that you and my son should thus have been brought together, and I trust that whatever may occur, your friendship will continue as warm as ever."

"There is little doubt about that, sir;" answered Harry, "especially as I hope we shall some day become nearly related, as my friend is engaged to marry my only sister, though my father objects to the match on grounds which I consider very insufficient—his ignorance of his parentage; but now I trust that will no longer be an impediment."

"If my son is really attached to your sister, I have very little doubt when I plead his cause that your father will give his consent," said Mr Hastings, in a tone which somewhat puzzled Harry. "It maybe a satisfaction for you to know that my family is in no way inferior to yours. More I need not say, as I have reasons for not entering into particulars."

As may be supposed, Harry was now doubly anxious for the arrival of Headland, contemplating the joy and satisfaction the discovery of his father would give him, and he longed also to be able to write to Julia to tell her the news which would, he knew, tend so much to banish her anxieties for the future.

Still day after day went by, and no sail appeared to cheer the sight of the shipwrecked party.

Chapter Fifty One
First Greetings

Day after day passed by, and Harry and his shipwrecked companions began to despair of escaping from the island. If Jack Headland had lived there so many years without seeing a ship, it was possible that they might have to continue an equal length of time unless they could build a vessel in which to make their escape; but no wood was procurable, nor did they possess tools fit for the purpose.

A gale of almost equal violence to that which wrecked their ship was blowing, when Jacob, who had been on watch at the hill, rushed into the camp with the intelligence that a sail was visible in the offing. Most of the party hurried up to have a look at her. The general opinion was that she had made out the island, and was endeavouring to give it a wide berth.

"I am afraid that is more than she will do," observed Jack. "She is fast driving towards the shore."

"Can she be the *Thisbe*?" exclaimed Jacob.

"I think not," observed Harry, "her canvas has not to my eye the spread of a man-of-war."

As the stranger drew nearer, most of the party agreed that Lieutenant Castleton was right, she was certainly not a man-of-war.

Their flag blew out distinctly in the gale.

Their anxiety for the ship's safety were at length set at rest. She weathered the outermost point of the reef, but now they began to fear that she would pass by and leave them to their fate.

Scarcely had she cleared the reef, however, than the sound of a gun gladdened their ears: their flag was seen, and the ship hauling her wind stood along the shore till she gained a shelter under the lee side of the island.

The gale had by this time considerably abated, and it was hoped that a boat might be sent on shore. They hurried across the island.

Just as the beach was reached a boat was seen leaving the ship. She soon landed with the first officer, who no sooner heard Lieutenant Castleton's name than he greeted him with a hearty welcome. It had been feared, he said, that he and his boat's crew had been lost, for that the *Thisbe* had herself been in great danger, and had with difficulty, after suffering much damage, got back to Calcutta. He added that his ship was the *Montrose*, homeward-bound, and that after touching at Bencoolen, she had been driven by the hurricane out of her course, when the island had been sighted in time to weather it, though no one on board was before aware of its existence.

As the wind might change, the captain was anxious to be away as soon as possible, and the whole party therefore hurried on board.

Fortunately, soon after the *Montrose* got into her proper course, she fell in with an outward-bound fleet, and by one of the ships Harry sent a despatch to Captain Headland, which he hoped might prevent the *Thisbe* from sailing in search of him and his companions. In it he also communicated the important information of his discovery of his friend's old protector Jack Headland, and of his wonderful meeting with Mr Hastings on board the *Culloden*. Mr Hastings also wrote a private letter to Captain Headland, the contents of which he did not allow Harry to see.

"From the high character you give of your friend, I have spoken to him of matters in a way I should not otherwise have ventured to do, and which I do not wish to make known to any one but my son," he observed to Harry. "That he is my son I have not the slightest doubt, and I feel confident that I can convince your father of the fact."

The Montrose continued her homeward voyage. She was fortunately a good sailer, and a bright look-out being kept she escaped the enemy's cruisers, and arrived safely in the Downs. Here Harry and Mr Hastings with Jack Headland and Jacob, landed and proceeded at once to London.

Harry knowing how anxious Adam and the dame would be to see their son, sent Jacob off immediately by the coach expecting that he would reach Hurlston soon after the ladies at Downside had received a letter he had written from Deal.

The captain and passengers of the *Montrose* had pressed on Harry and Mr Hastings the loan of as much money as they would accept, so that they had no difficulty about their expenses.

It was late in the evening, when after rattling through the ill-lighted streets they drove up to the Golden Cross, then the principal inn in the West end of London.

"I will remain here while you go and announce your arrival to your father, Mr Castleton," said Mr Hastings. "As many years have passed since I travelled by land, I am weary with my journey, though I shall be happy to accompany you to-morrow, to renew the acquaintance which existed between us long ago, and for my son's sake I am anxious to do so. I must beg you however not to mention my name, or if you do you can tell your father that you have reasons to believe it is an assumed one and that with my real name he is well acquainted."

Harry had gone into the coffee-room while waiting for a coach which he had directed the porter to call for him. He was walking through the centre when a person started up from one of the stalls and grasping his hand exclaimed.

"What, Harry my boy, is it you, sound in limb and present in body instead of being buried fathoms deep beneath the ocean wave? I said so, I was sure of it, I knew we should see you again. I am heartily delighted, my dear boy."

Harry having recognised in the speaker his old friend General Sampson, briefly explained what had happened and said that he was on the point of starting to see his father.

"I will save you the trouble then; he left town this morning for Texford, where he has invited me to join a party of friends—three or four marrying men high born and wealthy; but between ourselves I suspect that their visit will be in vain as far as the object the baronet may have in view is concerned.

"Well, it is fortunate I fell in with you, as I have saved you a long drive and a visit to an empty house. I was just taking a chop before going to see the great stars of the theatrical world John Kemble and Mrs Siddons act Macbeth and his wife; but I will give up my intention for the pleasure of passing the evening with you unless you will accompany me."

Harry confessed that even those great performers could not attract him, and begged the general to come to his private room, being assured that his friend Mr Hastings would be happy to make his acquaintance.

"I left him about to retire to his chamber to rest, but I daresay he will join us during the evening. In the meantime I have a matter of much interest to talk to you about," he added as he led the way upstairs.

"I never believed that you were lost, though your father and all the family went into mourning for you," said the general, as they proceeded. "Your sister never gave up hopes of seeing you again, nor from what she wrote me, did another young lady who is interested in your welfare. Mr Shallard as in duty bound proved your will, but I understand she would not consent to touch a penny of the fortune you left her. If however you have a fancy for making her take it, all you have to do is to go to sea again and get killed or drowned in reality."

"Thank you for your advice, general," answered Harry laughing. "I trust that I may find a more satisfactory mode of settling the question."

"I hope so, my boy, and I promise you I will lay siege to your father, and it will not be my fault if I do not compel him to surrender at discretion should he refuse to capitulate on honourable terms."

As soon as they were seated, Harry told his old friend of the various occurrences with which the reader is acquainted.

The general was delighted.

"For my part I believe that any man would be glad to claim your friend as his son. But I am doubly pleased at the thought that your father will no longer object to Headlands marrying your sister."

The general was still rattling on asking Harry questions and describing late public events when Mr Hastings entered the room. Harry introduced the general as a friend of his and Captain Headlands.

"I am happy on that account to make General Sampson's acquaintance;" said Mr Hastings, "perhaps indeed we may have met in our younger days."

"Very likely we have," said the general. "Your features and figure are familiar to me. In fact, I could almost swear that I knew you, though upon my life I cannot tell where it was."

"Perhaps you may have met me in company with Sir Ralph Castleton; indeed I am sure of it, as I confess that I recollect you. I say this as you are his friend, and, that should you have a suspicion who I am you may be careful not to express it to others." While Mr Hastings was speaking, the general was scanning his countenance with a look of the greatest surprise. The former continued, "As Lieutenant Castleton has begged me to come to Texford, perhaps if you are going there you will favour us with your company on the road. I should wish to set off to-morrow, but as I require longer rest and have some matters to settle in London, I must defer starting till the following day, if that will suit you."

"It will exactly do, sir," answered the general. "I promised Sir Ralph to go down on that day, and will join you here in the morning. At what hour do you propose leaving London?"

"We must not start later than six, and shall then scarcely reach Texford till some time after nightfall," answered Harry.

"No indeed," observed the general, "I always take two days, for I have no fancy to travel in the dark, and run the risk of being ordered to 'halt and deliver.'"

The general at a late hour wished his friends good-night, and returned to his lodgings.

Mr Hastings drove out the next morning alone, and was absent for most of the day. He also paid a visit accompanied by Harry to Captain Headland's agent, who, without hesitation shewed the locket and other articles which had been deposited with him. Mr Hastings at once recognised them. "Had I entertained any doubts, these would have convinced me that their owner is my boy," he said turning to Harry. "And I am convinced from what I know of you, that you will assist him in obtaining his inheritance."

"That I will most gladly," exclaimed Harry, "though I do not see how I can help him except with my purse."

"More than you may suppose," answered Mr Hastings significantly.

Harry had during the day called at the Admiralty, to report his return to England. He heard that the *Thisbe's* arrival was every day looked for. He left a letter for Headland, urging him to ask for leave, and to come directly to Texford. "Mr Hastings would wait for you," he wrote, "but he seems anxious on your account to see my father without delay, and as you may not arrive for some weeks he does not wish to defer his visit."

At the appointed hour the general appeared at the inn, and the three gentlemen set off on their journey, in a coach and four, with Jack Headland on the coach box, not omitting to provide themselves with firearms.

Chapter Fifty Two
Visitors

Sir Ralph Castleton arrived at Texford in the middle of the next day after he left London. He was surprised to see his servants in their usual liveries, and still more so when Lady Castleton and Julia came out to greet him in coloured costume, instead of the black dresses they had lately worn.

"What means this?" he exclaimed. "You show but little respect to the memory of our boy by so soon discarding your mourning."

"We have no reason to mourn for him," said Lady Castleton, "he is alive and well, and will be here in a day or two at farthest."

She then briefly gave the account Harry had written from Deal. Sir Ralph expressed his satisfaction, though his words sounded cold to the ears of his wife and daughter.

"Let me see the letter," he said, "I can scarcely even now believe what you tell me."

Lady Castleton very unwillingly produced Harry's letter. A frown gathered on Sir Ralph's brow as he read it.

"I thought a few months would have cured him of his infatuation; but he still speaks of that girl as if I were of so yielding a character that I should ever consent to his committing so egregious a folly. And I see, Julia, that he alludes to Captain Headland. Clearly understand me that if he returns to England I must prohibit his appearance at Texford. I have every reason to believe that you may become a duchess if you act wisely; and I cannot allow a penniless adventurer to stand in the way."

Julia had learned that 'a soft answer turneth away wrath,' or, that if that cannot be uttered, 'silence is the best.' She adopted the last resource, and left her father and mother alone.

"I am thankful our boy has escaped, and I can only hope that he will be induced to act with wisdom and discretion. I am placed in rather an awkward position with regard to the Duke of Oldfield. Under the belief of Harry's death, I have arranged to forward a match between the Marquis of Underdown and Julia. The duke assured me that he admired her greatly when they last met in London, and believing her to be my heiress, he was ready to sanction his son's offer, because he frankly told me that the Marquis must marry a girl of fortune, though he should object unless she was of good family. Underdown will arrive here to-day, and Sir John and Lord Frederick, and the other men I asked, were merely to act as foils, though I should not object to either of them, should the Marquis fail; but I believe that a ducal coronet will carry the day with any girl not excluding our daughter Julia."

"I never venture to oppose your wishes, Sir Ralph, and my earnest endeavour has been to secure Julia's happiness," said Lady Castleton humbly. "I fear, however, that her affection for Captain Headland is too deeply rooted to allow even the Marquis any prospect of success."

"But when the marquis finds that Harry is alive, his prudence will probably make him beat a rapid retreat, or at all events the duke will recall him," remarked Sir Ralph, with a sneer. "You will thus see my wisdom in asking the other gentlemen, and I must insist that you use every effort to induce our daughter to give up this naval officer, and accept either of them who comes forward. We must at all events manage her, though we may find Harry more obstinate than his sister."

"I can only do my best," said Lady Castleton, endeavouring to suppress a sigh.

Sir Ralph enquired about the Misses Pemberton, and hearing that they were at Downside, remarked—

"I wish they with their ward could be induced to go away again, they have been thorns in my side since I came to Texford. It would have been wiser had we at once ignored their existence, and Harry would have had no excuse for visiting them."

The expected guests arrived, and were cordially greeted by Sir Ralph, who watched the countenance of the young marquis as he was informed of the fact of Harry's existence. From its expression the keen man of the world argued that the young nobleman would not long honour him as his guest.

Julia, who was in very good spirits, received the visitors with her usual frank and easy manner. She had greater difficulty next day to maintain her composure, as she was looking forward to the arrival of Harry and his mysterious companion, the father of Headland.

Lady Castleton received in the morning another letter from Harry, which he had written that she might show it to his father. He stated what he had already done to Julia, adding that he hoped Sir Ralph would give a warm greeting to his friend, who assured him that they had formerly been well acquainted.

"Who he can be I have no conception," exclaimed Sir Ralph. "I wish Harry had told me. We must ascertain who he is first. It is possible he may be some impostor who has discovered his anxiety to find a father for his friend. I shall be very careful how I trust him."

Chapter Fifty Three
Attacked

Mr Groocock, afraid of alarming the ladies, had not informed them of the warning he had received, but as soon as he had an opportunity of speaking to Sir Ralph he told him what had occurred; and of the precautionary measures he had taken.

"I suspect the old mad woman has practiced on your credulity," observed Sir Ralph. "However, do as you think fit, it may be as well to be prepared, in case that fellow Gaffin should venture on so daring a deed. With so many gentlemen in the house, backed by the servants, he will not think of attacking the hall."

"I suspect, Sir Ralph, that desperate as he is, there is nothing he would not dare to do."

The steward, fearing that some mistake might occur had ridden over to Morbury, to beg that Mr Shallard would see that the men he had applied for were sent in time. It was fortunate that he went, for Mr Shallard had been away from home though expected back every minute. Mr Groocock anxiously waited his return. He arrived at length, when the steward explained his object, and asked if he had not received a letter he had sent about it. Mr Shallard found it on his table with several others.

"Here is also a requisition," he said, glancing at another letter, "from the Misses Pemberton to obtain protection for Downside. She has been warned as you were, by an old mad woman, and she assures me that she feels confident the warning should not be disregarded. Though I have no great fears on the matter, my gallantry compels me to ride over there at once to afford the ladies such security as the presence of a gentleman can give; and I will beg that a body of fencibles may be sent to arrive soon after dusk. If no more men can be spared, we must obtain a few cavalry, as fortunately some troops arrived here a few days ago, and are to remain a short time to obtain recruits in the neighbourhood. I will see their commanding officer, and take care that they are sent off in time to reach Texford by dark. You may go home, therefore, Mr Groocock, with your mind at rest on the subject. They will soon be at your heels, and you will, I daresay, look after them and see that they are provided with a supply of good cheer, such as soldiers expect under the circumstances."

"No fear of that, Mr Shallard," answered the steward. "I must no longer delay, for I am already late, and with my own good will I would rather not be out after dusk, considering the sort of people likely to be abroad."

"By-the-bye, I have not congratulated you on Lieutenant Castleton's safe return. I received the news from Miss Pemberton just as I was leaving home yesterday, and nothing has given me greater pleasure in life. A fine young fellow your future baronet, and I heartily wish that all difficulties in the way of his happiness may be overcome. He will prove a worthy successor to his excellent uncle. I have no doubt about that, though neither you nor I, Mr Groocock, can properly wish him to come into possession for many years."

"I wish that all were like him. He will make a kind master whoever serves him, but my head will be laid at rest before then," answered the steward, with a sigh. "However, I must be on my journey," and Mr Groocock, shaking hands with the lawyer, mounted his cob and rode back towards Texford.

The family at Texford were assembled in the drawing-room. Dinner had been put off, as they were every minute expecting the arrival of Harry and his friends, and Sir Ralph, usually so calm, kept moving about the room, frequently expressing his surprise that they had not come.

"I hope nothing has happened to them," he said to himself. "Is it possible that they can have encountered that fellow Gaffin and his ruffian crew?"

Julia in vain endeavoured to understand what the Marquis and Lord Frederick were saying to her, but could only give the vaguest of replies.

The window of the back drawing-room, which looked towards the park, was open. Sir Ralph had looked out several times in the hopes of hearing the carriage wheels. He rang the bell, and a servant appearing, he ordered dinner to be served.

"By-the-bye," he asked, "has Mr Groocock returned from Morbury?"

"No, Sir Ralph," was the answer.

"Let me know when he comes," said the baronet.

At that instant the sound of a shot was heard; it came from the direction of the park gate. It was followed by several others.

"What can that mean?" asked most of the gentlemen in a breath.

Sir Ralph, without answering, rang the bell violently, when the butler hurried into the room with a look of alarm.

"Tell the servants to get their arms, and have the shutters of all the lower rooms closed. Gentlemen," he added, turning to his guests, "if any of you have firearms or swords, pray get them. I received a warning that the house was to be attacked by a desperate gang of smugglers, but took no notice of it, though I fear from these sounds I ought to have done so."

Most of the gentlemen, who had fowling-pieces or pistols with them, hurried off to get them ready. Lady Castleton sank on the sofa, another lady fainted, and two shrieked out in their terror, believing that the next instant they should see the ruffians breaking into the house. Julia endeavoured to calm her mother and their guests, while Sir Ralph went to the front door to see that it was bolted and barred. At that moment he heard carriage wheels rolling at a rapid rate up the avenue. Again several shots were heard much nearer than the first. He ordered the door to be opened. The horses, panting and foaming, were pulled up by the postillion, and Harry sprang out of the chaise, followed by General Sampson. They both turned round to assist out another person, while a fourth leaped from the box.

"Drive round to the coachyard, and tell the grooms to close the gates," cried Harry, while he led the stranger up the steps. On seeing his father he greeted him affectionately.

"We were fired on by a band of ruffians, but as we returned their salute briskly, they did not venture to come to nearer quarters. They may, however, be following, and we should be prepared for them." Sir Ralph was on the point of giving some further directions to the servants, when General Sampson and his companion reached the hall. Sir Ralph started, and gazed with a bewildered look.

"Who are you? Speak. I well remember those features," he exclaimed.

"And I remember yours, Ralph," said the stranger, stepping forward and taking his hand. "However, we will say no more on the subject at present. Your son and General Sampson know me as Mr Hastings; let me retain that name till we can converse in private. In the meantime, continue your preparations to receive the ruffians, who are close at hand. Thanks to the speed at which we were driving, the volley they fired did us no harm."

Sir Ralph seemed scarcely to comprehend what Mr Hastings said, but continued gazing in his face without replying.

General Sampson, at once comprehending the state of affairs, took upon himself the command of the garrison, and ordered the servants to see that all the other entrances to the house were closed. He then requested those who had firearms to load them with ball, and to be ready to make use of them if required. Scarcely had he done so than a thundering knock was heard at the door, and a man from the outside announced himself as a sergeant from the — Dragoons, who had been sent over from Morbury with a party of fifteen men to guard the Hall.

On this the door was opened, when a fine soldier-like fellow appeared, who requested to know where he should post his men.

"My orders are to remain here if Sir Ralph Castleton wishes it, but if not, to proceed to Downside Cottage, at Hurlston. As the smugglers, or whatever they are, caught sight of us just as we entered the avenue, they are not likely to attack this place."

Harry, who had just been receiving his mother's and sister's embraces, heard what was said.

"Let some of your men accompany me, and I will show them the way to Downside," he exclaimed; and he directed one of the servants to bring a horse round without a moment's delay.

"Where are you going, Harry?" exclaimed Sir Ralph, recovering himself, on seeing Harry hurrying down the steps. "The troopers will look after the ruffians."

"To assist those who require protection," answered Harry. "There is no time to be lost."

"Just like him," cried General Sampson. "The ruffians won't stand a charge if he leads it. I'll be after you, Harry. One of you get me a horse."

"Thank you, general," exclaimed Lady Castleton, "We cannot tell what these desperate men will venture to do, and you may be of the greatest assistance."

"I must not wait though for you, general," said Harry, mounting. "What is the matter?" he asked of the groom who assisted him on his horse.

"Oh sir," said the groom, "there has been murder, we fear, already. Mr Groocock's cob has just galloped in from across the park with blood on his saddle, and it's too clear that the steward has been killed, or the animal would not have come home without him."

"This is terrible," said Harry; "poor old man. Go some of you and search for him. I must not delay." Turning to the sergeant, he added, galloping on—"Do you and your men accompany me."

The sergeant mounted his horse and followed him. The troopers were found drawn up at the entrance of the avenue, while in the distance were seen a large band of wild-looking fellows armed in a variety of ways, some on horseback, and others on foot, apparently watching the movements of the soldiers, by whose timely arrival they had been prevented from entering the park.

The sergeant ordered his men to follow.

"Those are the fellows who fired at the carriage, and were nearly overtaking it when we came up, I can swear to that," he said.

"We must seize their leader, and as many as we can get hold of, or they may still attack the Hall," answered Harry.

"The sooner we are at them the better, though I fear they will not stand us," cried the sergeant. "Charge, my lads, and get hold of the fellow on the black horse. I saw him fire two shots."

And putting spurs to their horses, they dashed on.

As they were galloping along, and before they had gone many paces, Harry, to his grief, saw the apparently dead body of the steward lying close by the road-side, where he had, it seemed, fallen when shot. He could not stop to ascertain whether he was dead or alive.

The smugglers still held their ground not two hundred yards off. Harry recognised Miles Gaffin, who, by his actions, was evidently endeavouring to induce his followers to advance to the encounter. As the well disciplined little band drew near them, the ruffian's courage gave way. The men on foot rushed off on either side. The horsemen stood a moment longer, and at Gaffin's command fired a volley, but directly afterwards, though superior in numbers, knowing well how ill able they were to resist the charge of the troopers, they wheeled round their horses, and galloped off in the direction of Hurlston. Gaffin was the last to turn. He quickly overtook the rest, and pushing through them on his fleet and powerful horse, soon took the lead. Though vastly superior in a charge, the troopers' horses were ill able to come up with the active steeds of the lightly-armed smugglers. The latter kept well ahead, though Harry urged his companions not to spare the spur. As openings occurred free of trees, first one of the smugglers rode off, then another, others following, some going on one side, some on another, till a small band only held together, led by Gaffin, who had, however, distanced them considerably. Believing, probably, that he was going to desert them, the remainder, swearing loudly at his cowardice, following the example of the first, began to disperse, several throwing themselves from their horses, and making their way through the thick brushwood, where the troopers had little hopes of overtaking them.

HORSE AND RIDER DISAPPEARED OVER THE EDGE.

HORSE AND RIDER DISAPPEARED OVER THE EDGE.

"Keep the fellow on the black horse in sight," shouted Harry. "He is the man, I doubt not, who murdered the steward. Let some of your men accompany me, and follow him with the rest."

The sergeant gave the order as Harry requested, and half the men continued on with Harry towards Downside, while Gaffin was seen to be making by the nearest road for the mill. His object apparently was to take shelter within it, and to sell his life dearly, or he might hope to conceal himself till he could make his escape by some secret passage, or by other means with which he alone was acquainted.

The thickening gloom of evening rendered all objects indistinct. The sergeant and his men, however, kept the smuggler in sight till they saw him reach the downs on which the mill stood, where his figure was distinctly visible against the sky. It was but for a moment, for at the same instant, a party of the sea-fencibles who had been concealed behind the mill, started up, and several shots were fired at him. It was not seen whether any had taken effect; the horse and rider disappeared, at it seemed, over the edge of the cliff. The troopers expected as they reached the spot to see him dashed to pieces on the sands, but he had reached the bottom in safety by a pathway which a desperate man alone would have ventured to take. They caught a glimpse of him as he galloped along the sands towards the south.

"We must follow him, my lads, or he will escape after all," said the sergeant, though, as no one dared descend the path Gaffin had taken, the troopers were compelled to take their way round by a circuitous road till they could gain the level of the beach. By that time the daring smuggler was lost to sight.

In the meantime, the foot soldiers hurried along the top of the downs to stop him should he desert his horse and attempt to escape by climbing up the cliffs and make his way across the country.

The sergeant and his men made comparatively slow progress over the sands. They discovered too that the tide was rising, and had good reason to fear that they might be caught under the cliffs, and be carried off by the sea which was rolling in with a sullen roar.

The sergeant at the same moment fancied he could discern the figure of a horseman at some distance ahead, close under the cliffs, and already surrounded by water. The steed was plunging and rearing, while the rider in vain endeavoured to urge him forward. Presently, both together disappeared, overwhelmed by a sea which rolled in, and broke in masses of spray against the foot of the cliff. Not far off a dark object, which might have been a boat, was seen.

However, the advancing sea warned the sergeant that he and his men must beat a rapid retreat, or run the risk of losing their horses, if not their lives. They had, indeed, to plunge through the sea up to their horses' girths before they regained the end of the cliff, where they were once more in safety.

Chapter Fifty Four
Surprises

Since we last met Adam Halliburt the *Nancy* had shared the fate of other craft; her stout planks and timbers gradually yielding to age, she had become too leaky to put to sea, and had been broken up for firewood. Adam having no sons to help him, had taken to inshore fishing in a small boat which he and a lad could manage. The dame's baskets were, however, still well supplied with fish.

Honest Jacob, to his parents' joy, had arrived at home. Adam was about to set out on his daily fishing.

"I will go with you, father," he said; "maybe with my help you will sooner be able to get back."

The dame, glad that Adam should enjoy his son's company, was willing to wait till their return, to hear all Jacob had to tell them.

They stood away under sail to the south, where the best fishing ground lay.

Seldom had Adam been so happy as he was listening to Jacob's account of his adventures, and not often had he been more successful in making a good catch of fish.

The evening was drawing on, and it was time to return, when the wind shifting, headed them, and they were compelled to take to their oars, Jacob and the boy pulling, while Adam steered. They kept close in shore to avoid the tide, which was running to the southward. The wind increased too, and they made but slow progress, so that night overtook them before they had proceeded half the distance.

There was still light sufficient to enable Adam to see a man on horseback galloping along the beach under the cliff, the water already reaching up to the animal's knees.

"What can he be about?" exclaimed Adam. "He must be mad to try and pass along there; he will be lost to a certainty if he moves a few fathoms further on."

Adam shouted at the top of his voice, and waved his hat, but the horseman neither saw nor heard him.

Presently, as Adam had anticipated, the horse began to struggle violently in a vain effort to escape from a soft quicksand which prevented it either from swimming or wading. The next instant a sea rolling in washed the rider from its back. He struck out boldly, making a desperate effort for life. Jacob and the boy pulled with all their might towards him, but before they could reach him a sea had dashed him against the cliff. By a mighty effort he got clear of it, when a receding wave carried him towards them. Before the boat reached him, however, he had ceased to struggle, and was sinking for the last time when Adam caught him by the collar, and with Jacob's assistance hauled him into the boat. Jacob had at once to resume his oar, for they were so near the cliff that the boat might, in another instant, have been dashed against it. They got clear, however, but the tide had drifted them to the south.

"He is still alive," said Adam, "but seems much hurt, and I fear will die if we don't soon get him before a warm fire. We are just under Mad Sal's hut, and the best thing we can do will be to carry him up there."

"It will be a hard matter to land though, father, won't it?" said Jacob, "and we may risk the loss of the boat."

"Worth risking it for the sake of a human life, even if the man was our greatest enemy. There is a little creek in there, and if I can hit it, the boat will be safe enough. Stand by to jump out when I tell you."

Jacob and the boy pulled on, and in another minute a sea lifted the boat, and though the surf broke on board she floated on, and dropped down safely into a pool, where there was no danger of her being carried away. Adam and his companions jumping out, hauled the boat up on the beach. Leaving the boy in charge of her, he and Jacob then carried the man they had rescued, and who was still insensible, towards Mad Sal's hut, which could just be distinguished on the side of the ravine by the glare of light coming through the chinks in the window and door.

Adam knocked loudly.

"Who comes to disturb me now?" exclaimed the old woman from within. "Is my solitude constantly to be broken in upon by strangers?"

"We bring you a well-nigh drowned man, who will die if you refuse him your aid, good dame," said Adam. "In mercy do not keep us outside."

The door was opened.

"What! another victim murdered by the cruel salt sea," exclaimed old Sal, as she saw the burden Adam and Jacob carried.

"We must have off his wet clothes, and warm his hands and feet, or he soon will be dead," said Adam, as they carried the man into the room.

The sight seemed to calm instead of agitating the old woman, for she set about attending to the man in a more sensible way than might have been expected. While Adam and Jacob took off the man's wet clothes, she brought a blanket that they might wrap it round his body. She then, kneeling down, assisted them in chafing his hands and feet. A deep groan showed that their efforts were successful, and the man soon opened his eyes, and gazed wildly at them. The old woman threw some sticks on the fire, which blazing up now for the first time, revealed his features more clearly than before.

"Why, father, he is Miles Gaffin," exclaimed Jacob.

"I knew that," answered Adam, "when we hauled him into the boat."

"Miles Gaffin," cried Mad Sal, "the bloodthirsty and wretched man shall not live out half his days; yet, as the sea refused to keep him, we must not be more cruel."

Gaffin made no answer, but continued to glare wildly at the faces bent over him. He occasionally groaned and muttered a few unintelligible words.

"He seems to have lost his senses," whispered Adam to Jacob.

Such, indeed, was evidently the case. Several times he tried to sit up, but he had received some severe injuries, and each movement made him shriek with pain.

What now to do was the question. Adam was unwilling to leave him alone with the poor mad woman, yet he was naturally anxious to return home. The sound of the wind, which howled and whistled up the glen, warned him that he could scarcely hope to continue his voyage.

Telling old Sal that they would speedily return, Adam and Jacob went down to the beach, and made safe their boat and fish. Then they sent the boy quickly to Hurlston, with instructions to tell the dame that they hoped to be home in the morning. The lad being warned to keep away from the edge of the cliff, set off without fear. Adam and Jacob, carrying up a few fish and some bread, returned to the hut.

As they entered they heard Gaffin's voice raving incoherently. Mad Sal stood like a statue, the light of the fire falling on her pale features, gazing at him with a look of mingled astonishment and dread. They stopped to listen to what Gaffin was saying.

"Who are you?" she exclaimed at last, gasping for breath, and advancing towards the unhappy man.

"Who has a right to ask me that?" he shrieked out. "Martin Goul I was once called. They tell me I broke my father's heart, that my mother threw herself from the cliffs, and that the only being I ever loved was laid in the cold grave. So I went forth to do battle with the hard world, to live in hopes of revenging myself on those who had scorned and wronged me. Each time, though I missed my aim, I thought the day of vengeance would come at last, but again and again have I been mocked by the cunning devil who deceived me."

"Martin Goul! who speaks of him," exclaimed the old woman, moving a step nearer the man.

"Let me be at peace, old hag; why torment me with questions?" shrieked out Gaffin.

"Young Martin Goul has long been fathoms deep beneath the ocean wave; and you tell me that you bear that name," said Mad Sal, in a hollow frightened voice.

"No one else would dare to claim it," cried Gaffin. "When my son marries the heiress of Texford, I will shout it out to all the world. She will be his bride before many hours are over, and then those who have scorned me will have to ask favours at my hand. They did not know that I possessed the secret of her birth, that it still lies locked up in the chest guarded safely in the vault beneath the mill, and that it will be beyond their reach before to-morrow. Ah! ah! ah!" and he broke out into a cry of maniac laughter.

The old woman passed her hand across her brow, and took another stride which brought her close to where Gaffin lay.

"Answer me, I adjure you; again I ask you, are you the Martin Goul who years gone by was pressed and carried off to sea?"

"Yes, I am that Martin Goul, the pirate, smuggler, spy, murderer," he shrieked, out raising himself. "There are no deeds I have not dared to do. I, by forged letters, kept Ranald Castleton from his home, and willingly would I have allowed his innocent child to perish. Now I have answered you, what more would you learn from me? Ah! ah! ah!" he shouted out, as if impelled by an uncontrollable impulse to utter the very things he would have desired to keep secret.

"It's false, it's false," cried the unhappy woman. "My son was wild and extravagant, but he could not have been guilty of the crimes you name. I was the mother of young Martin Goul; he was the only being on earth I loved. Oh the salt, salt sea."

"You my mother, you," shrieked out the wretched man, and he again burst forth into a fit of hideous laughter, which froze the hearts of Adam and his son. "Begone, old hag, begone, begone," he shouted, and endeavoured to raise himself up, but his strength, from some internal injury, was fast giving way. The effort produced a paroxysm of pain. He shrieked out, and sinking back on the bed no longer moved.

The old woman gazed at him like one transfixed. Suddenly the fire sent up a bright flame, which fell on his face.

"Yes, yes," cried the unhappy creature, "I know you now, you are my son, my boy Martin." But the person she addressed no longer heard her. His spirit had fled to stand before the Judge of all men. She waited as if expecting him to reply, then suddenly she became aware of what had happened, and lifting up her hands fell forward over his body.

Adam and Jacob sprang to assist her, for they feared from the force with which she fell that she must have injured herself. She neither moved nor groaned. They endeavoured to lift her up.

"Poor creature, she is dead!" said Adam. She had survived but a few moments her unhappy son.

Adam and Jacob placed her body by his side, and closed the eyes of both. As they could no longer be of assistance they would gladly have set off for their home at once, but the night had become very dark, the storm raged furiously, and as they had their fish to carry, they would have found it difficult to make their way over the downs. They therefore agreed to wait till daylight.

Adam had noted what the dying man said with regard to the chest and the little girl.

"Could he have been speaking of our Maiden May, and how came he to call her the heiress of Texford?"

"He did call her so, there is no doubt about that," observed Jacob. "He cannot tell us now, though, what he meant."

"But the chest may. I was always sure that Gaffin had visited the wreck, and carried off something of value, but little did I think all the time that he knew who our Maiden May was," said Adam.

"If we can get the chest we shall soon know all about that father; and it will be the thing of all others that Lieutenant Castleton will like to know, and I shall be glad to help him find it out."

As neither Adam nor Jacob felt disposed to go to sleep after the scene they had witnessed, they sat up discussing the subject till dawn. The wind having shifted, and the sea gone down, they launched their boat and sailed before the wind for Hurlston. As they passed close under the mill they saw a vessel cast on the beach, which they recognised as Gaffin's lugger. They afterwards discovered that having been left with only two or three hands on board she had been driven on shore, and, like the *Nancy*, having seen her best days, had been quickly knocked to pieces by the heavy sea which had for a short time broken on the coast.

Young Jack had arrived safely, and delivered the message Adam had sent the dame, so that she had not been anxious about them. But she had a terrible account to give of the events which, according to report, had taken place at Texford and Downside, and which had caused her the greatest alarm, and she was only waiting their arrival to set off to ascertain the truth.

Adam agreed to accompany her, as he wished to give Lieutenant Castleton the information he had obtained, and thought it probable that he might be at Downside. He had besides to give notice of the deaths of Martin Goul and his mother.

Chapter Fifty Five
On the Defence

Harry and the dragoons after Gaffin's escape galloped rapidly to Downside. He would soon have distanced them had he not feared that they might lose their way. He kept urging them to spur on with greater speed. The gate was opened, and as they approached the house a thundering sound was heard, and he caught sight of several men endeavouring to burst in the front door. The noise they were making prevented them from hearing the approach of the horses. One of them turning, however, caught sight of the dragoons, when, he shouting to his companions, they let the log fall and rushed down the steps, two or three of them as they did so firing the pieces they carried. The soldiers fired in return, when two or more of the gang were wounded. Their companions, however, dragged them off, and scrambling over the hedges, they made their escape before the dragoons could overtake them.

Harry announced his arrival.

"Stay, it may only be a trick," he heard Miss Jane observe.

"Oh, I am sure it is Harry. I know his voice. I am not afraid of opening the door," exclaimed May.

The bars and bolts were quickly withdrawn, and the next instant Harry pressed May to his heart. He quickly narrated all that had happened, and Miss Jane and Miss Mary were very grateful for his coming so opportunely to their rescue.

"And I, too, am glad to greet you, Mr Castleton," said Mr Shallard, stepping forward. "It is far more satisfactory than having had to act as your executor; indeed, this young lady most obstinately, as I thought, refused to allow me to do so."

Much more to the same effect was said, when the lawyer remarked that he must go and look after the dragoons.

"You maybe surprised at our calmness," he observed, "but the truth is, I expected every moment the arrival of a party of the sea-fencibles, and fully believed that they would come in time to stop the ruffians in their attempt to break into the house, and to capture the whole of them into the bargain. Till they appear, it may be prudent to retain the dragoons."

Harry willingly allowed Mr Shallard to do as he proposed.

Shortly afterwards a party of the fencibles arrived, who by some mistake had been sent to the mill instead of coming first, as was intended, to Downside. The dragoons were then sent down to the Texford Arms.

Though Harry felt that he ought to return home, he could not leave the cottage while there was a possibility of the smugglers rallying. He was not sorry at having a good excuse for remaining.

Miss Jane, on hospitable thoughts intent, was much troubled at being unable to offer beds to her guests, but they both assured her that they should prefer sitting up, that they might be ready for any emergency.

Susan having recovered from her alarm, set to work to get supper ready, and, in the meantime, Miss Jane declaring that she and her sister had business to settle with Mr Shallard, left May and Harry in the drawing-room.

Those were joyous moments to the young lovers. The clouds had not entirely cleared away, but they both saw, they believed, the dawn of a brighter day.

Harry and Mr Shallard sat up as they had proposed, though the lawyer very soon fell asleep, with outstretched legs, long before the young sailor closed his eyes.

Nothing occurred during the night to disturb the household.

The dragoons had started at daybreak to scour the country, but did not succeed in capturing a single smuggler. They had discovered, however, in a cottage, a man dying from a gun-shot wound, and from the description given of him, Harry had little doubt that he was young Gaffin.

May appeared at breakfast, looking as bright and fresh as ever. As soon as the meal was over, Harry and Mr Shallard, assured that the ladies were in no further danger, were on the point of setting out for Texford, when Adam and Dame Halliburt arrived.

After the dame had expressed her joy at seeing May and the ladies safe, Adam described to Harry and Mr Shallard the events which had occurred on the previous evening, and gave them the information he had obtained from the dying man. May listened with breathless eagerness. Was indeed the secret of her birth to be at length disclosed? The heiress of Texford! That seemed impossible. It must have been a fancy of the dying smuggler. She might, indeed, be proved to belong to a noble family, and Sir Ralph's objections to her might be removed; or, on the other hand, her birth might be such, that still greater obstacles might arise, or the proofs, had they existed, might have been removed. Fears and hopes alternately gaining the mastery, she in vain endeavoured to calm her agitation. Miss Mary stood holding her hand, her sightless eyes turned towards the speakers, listening to all that was said; while Miss Jane every now and then threw in a word, gave her advice, or cross-questioned Adam with an acuteness which won the lawyer's admiration.

As they were still speaking, a dense wreath of smoke, with flickering points of flame rising beneath it, was seen in the direction of the cliff.

"The mill has been set on fire," exclaimed Mr Shallard. "Men ought to have been stationed to guard it. We may yet be in time to save the chest. Not a moment, however, must be lost."

The gardener having been despatched with an order to the fencibles to hasten to the mill, the lawyer, with Harry and Adam, set out in the same direction.

"Oh, Harry, do not run any risk in searching for the chest; far rather would I let the secret be lost," exclaimed May, as Harry sprang down the steps to overtake Mr Shallard and the fisherman.

They met the fencibles on their way to the mill. As they reached the neighbourhood, they found a number of fishermen and others collected round the burning building. There appeared, however, but little prospect of saving it. The flames had got possession of the interior woodwork, and the long arms of the sails were already on fire.

"Never mind the mill," cried a voice from the crowd. "It is the house we must look after," and Jacob appeared with several young men carrying a heavy piece of timber.

A few blows burst open the door, and, in spite of the clouds of smoke rushing out, and the masses of burning wood which came crashing down, breaking through the roof already in flames, Jacob and his party boldly dashed in, still carrying their battering-ram. Harry with others followed. They were attacking an interior door. That quickly gave way.

Then suddenly, in the midst of the confusion, several men were seen emerging with a heavy chest, which they carried between them.

"We have got it, Mr Castleton, we have got it," cried Jacob, as several of the bystanders sprang forward to his assistance.

In another minute the whole house was in a blaze, and the rafters which supported the vault catching fire, the tall mill fell with a loud crash, and a huge fiery mass alone marked the spot where it had stood.

Enquiries were made for Dusty Dick. No one had seen him issue from the mill, and it was generally supposed that, following his master's orders, he had set fire to it, and perished in his attempt to escape.

"If you will restrain your curiosity for a short time, Mr Castleton, we will have the chest carried up to Downside, and examine it there," said Mr Shallard. "It will be a fitter spot than the open Downs."

Plenty of bearers were found, and the old lawyer had some difficulty in keeping pace with them, as, followed by half the population of Hurlston, they bore it up to the Miss Pembertons' cottage.

Chapter Fifty Six
Sir Ranald Castleton

Harry, as he galloped off from Texford with the dragoons, had left the party in the house in a state of considerable anxiety.

Several of the other gentlemen had hurried out on foot towards the park-gates, near which they found General Sampson dismounted, and bending over the steward.

"He is alive, I am thankful to say," said the general; "and as I shall have no chance of overtaking Castleton and the dragoons, I shall be of more service in looking after this worthy man."

Mr Groocock was accordingly carried to the Hall by the general, the two noblemen, and Sir John, a footman who had followed them leading the former's horse.

"Oh, is it Harry?" cried Julia.

No sooner had she uttered the words than Lady Castleton started forward, and would have fallen fainting to the ground had not her husband and Mr Hastings supported her.

Julia's alarm for her brother's safety was soon set at rest by the arrival of the party, but it was long before Lady Castleton recovered.

A groom was in the meantime sent off for the surgeon. The general having examined the steward's wounds, pronounced them not likely to prove serious.

The attack of the smugglers, and the pursuit, had aroused Sir Ralph Castleton's keenest interest, but the presence of Mr Hastings still more disquieted him. There was something in his presence which made a more intimate conversation imperative, and now the baronet, who was unusually pale and agitated, had invited his guest to meet him in his study.

What transpired during the conversation was not known.

The surgeon arrived sooner than expected, the groom having fortunately met him on the road. He corroborated the general's favourable opinion of Mr Groocock's wounds.

"The old man seems highly flattered at the way he was brought back to the house by the general and his friends, and I believe it will contribute greatly to his recovery," he observed, smiling.

Lady Castleton appeared, however, much to require the surgeon's attention. She had remarked the agitation Mr Hastings' appearance had caused her husband, and dreaded the effect it might produce on him. She frequently inquired whether he had yet come out of the study, and Julia could with difficulty prevent her from attempting to get up, and join him there.

The general, who had been bustling about the house, giving directions to the servants, and trying to entertain the other guests, at length entered the drawing-room to which Lady Castleton had been conveyed. There she lay, still unable to move, on a sofa.

"Oh, General Sampson, who is that terrible man?" she exclaimed, catching a glimpse of the general, who, not aware that she was there, was about to retire.

"They tell me that he is a ruffian called Gaffin, but my friend Harry and the dragoons will soon give a good account of him, I suspect," answered the general, not understanding her question.

"The person who is now with Sir Ralph," cried Lady Castleton; "he called himself Mr Hastings."

"I beg your ladyship ten thousand pardons," answered the general. "I had no idea of whom you were speaking. There is nothing terrible about him; he is a most gentlemanly refined person, has evidently mixed in good society all his life. He tells me that I knew him in our younger days, and he is certainly an old acquaintance of Sir Ralph's."

Julia was perfectly ready to believe the general's account, and assisted him at length in sufficiently calming her mother's fears to induce her to retire to her chamber.

At last the hungry guests, whose dinner had been so long postponed, assembled in the dining-room, where they were joined by the master of the house and Mr Hastings. Sir Ralph still looked nervous, and instead of exhibiting his usual self-possession, his manner was subdued, and his mind evidently distracted, as he appeared frequently not to have heard the remarks made to him. He treated Mr Hastings with the most marked attention, while he seemed almost at times to forget the presence of the marquis and his other titled guests. Julia excused herself from coming downstairs on the plea of having to attend to her mother.

The general tried to make amends for Sir Ralph's want of attention to his guests, and talked away for the whole party.

"I hope, Mr Hastings," said the general, drawing him aside after dinner, "you have convinced my friend Sir Ralph that your gallant son is a fit match for his fair daughter, Miss Julia. I should like to be able to give the young lady a hint to calm her anxiety on the subject."

"I think, my dear general, that her father will no longer object to the match; but I have agreed to retain my incognito till the arrival of my son, whose ship was announced as having reached Spithead yesterday evening, and as I obtained leave for him at the Admiralty, he will come on here at once."

The general, who was as much at home at Texford as at his own house, found means to communicate with Julia, and to give her the satisfactory intelligence.

He was too good a soldier to neglect placing sentinels on the watch during the night, which, however, passed without any appearance of the enemy in the neighbourhood of the Hall.

Next morning the marquis and Lord Frederick, who had not been unobservant of what was taking place, though somewhat puzzled, were prepared for the hint which the general conveyed to them, that the heart and hand of Miss Julia Castleton were engaged. Regretting that their stay should have been so short, they paid their respects to the master and mistress of the house, and took their departure, much to Sir Ralph's satisfaction.

Julia, who had become somewhat alarmed at not hearing of Harry, was much relieved during the course of the morning by receiving a message from him, saying that he was at Downside, and hoped shortly to return to Texford. She hurried to Lady Castleton to inform her, and then went to Sir Ralph, who was alone in his study, engaged in writing. He was so absorbed that he scarcely noticed her entrance. She had to repeat what she had said.

"Foolish boy!" he exclaimed, without expressing any satisfaction. "If he knew the position in which I am placed, he would see that I have greater reason than ever for objecting to his making that match. If a proper pride, and a sense of what is due to his family no longer restrains him, let him understand that his father is a mere beggar, dependent on the will of another, though you have nothing to fear, as I may tell you that he acknowledges your lover as his son, and insists on my sanction to your marriage."

"My dear father," exclaimed Julia, "I had hoped, indeed, that all impediments to my happiness would be removed, but how can that affect you or Harry?"

"You shall know all in time," answered Sir Ralph, gloomily. "Till the arrival of Captain Headland, I am prohibited from saying more. Leave me now, only if you have any feelings of affection and duty you will use your influence with Harry. I do not wish to make an enemy of my only son, but tell him while I live I will never be a party to his committing the rash act he contemplates. Go, girl, go," and Sir Ralph waved his daughter from the room.

She returned to her mother, who had sufficiently recovered to come downstairs. The guests had gone into the grounds with the exception of Mr Hastings and General Sampson. The general came hurrying into the drawing-room from the hall, exclaiming—

"A post-chaise is driving up the avenue," and taking Mr Hastings by the arm, he added, "I do not know whether you or Miss Castleton should be the first to greet the occupant; I must leave you to decide."

"Let my future daughter have that happiness," answered Mr Hastings, by a violent effort calming his evident agitation.

He imprinted a kiss as he spoke on the young lady's brow.

"Go and bring my son to me when you have exchanged greetings. Do not detain him long."

Julia hastened to the ante-room, scarcely daring to hope that the general was not mistaken. From the window she saw the carriage approaching. She had not long to wait. Captain Headland sprang from it, followed by another person whom her eyes, from the mist which stole over them, failed to recognise. She heard his step in the hall. In another minute he was supporting her and listening to the account she had to give. She led him into the drawing-room, where Mr Hastings was seated alone.

"I require no one to tell me you are my son," he said, embracing them both.

They spoke for some time. Julia would have retired to leave the father and his son alone, but the former detained her.

"For your sakes alone should I desire to resume my name, and take the title which is lawfully mine," he continued. "I am your father's elder brother, my dear Julia, but I know that when you become my son Ranald's wife, you will endeavour to console him and your brother Harry for the loss of an empty title of which I may be compelled to deprive him. But I am happily able to leave him in possession of a fortune equal to that which he at present enjoys."

"Believing that you did not desire to hold the baronetcy, I would gladly have resigned my future right to it in favour of Harry," said Headland. "As, however, you gave me leave to consult any friend in whom I had confidence, I at once went to my old captain, Admiral Fancourt, who, of all people, as my uncle's brother-in-law, was the most capable of giving me advice. I placed the whole matter before him, and he assures me that should my uncle desire a baronetcy, Government will readily grant him one for his political services, so that he will consequently not be deprived of the rank he prizes. Having known me from my early days, and being convinced of the truth of the account I gave him, he accompanied me here that he might satisfy my uncle's mind, and assist in arranging matters."

As Headland, or rather Captain Castleton, ceased speaking, the door opened, and Admiral Fancourt entered the room. He at once recognised Sir Ranald Castleton, as Mr Hastings was henceforth to be called, and expressed his satisfaction at his return, assuring him that he would have no difficulty in establishing his claims.

Lady Castleton shortly afterwards joined the party, and having been introduced to her brother-in-law, warmly welcomed her nephew.

Headland received a still more enthusiastic welcome from the old general, who quickly made his appearance.

"And here comes Harry and another gentleman galloping along the avenue as if the fate of the kingdom depended on their speed," he exclaimed.

Julia and the captain went out to meet them, and in another minute returned accompanied by Harry and the lawyer. Harry could scarcely speak. Julia knew by the way he embraced her and his mother, that his heart was bounding with joy.

"She can no longer be looked upon as unworthy of marrying a Castleton, for she is a Castleton herself, though all my May desires is to bear my name," he exclaimed at length; "but Mr Shallard will explain the discovery we have made more clearly than I can. Our good cousins promise to bring her here as soon as a carriage can be obtained."

Sir Ranald, as may be supposed, listened to this announcement with the deepest interest, as he did to the account given by the lawyer.

Mr Shallard, after briefly describing the discovery of the chest which had been so long hid by Martin Goul in the old mill, then went on to state that, having examined the documents in it, he had no doubt whatever that the little girl who had been rescued from the wreck on board which the chest had been found, was the child of the long lost Ranald Castleton. This was corroborated by the locket with the initials of M.C. which she had on, and with the dress which had been carefully preserved by Dame Halliburt, while several of the articles in the chest had the Castleton arms and crest.

The eyes of those who knew Sir Ranald were turned towards him.

"Through the mercy of heaven my two children have been restored to me on the same day," he exclaimed. "I had embarked for England after her mother's death, with my little daughter and her native nurse. While we were still in ignorance that the war had broken out, we were captured by a French privateer. A heavy gale was blowing at the time, and I, with other passengers, had just been removed, when all further communication between the ships was prevented by the fury of the wind and sea. I was almost driven to despair when I found that the ships had separated during the night. It was the opinion of our captors that only a few men having been put on board, the crew had risen and retaken the vessel. They searched in vain for her. It was believed, with savage satisfaction by the French, that a wreck we fell in with two days afterwards, which went down before she could be boarded, was her. I had no reason to doubt that they were wrong in their suspicions, and mourned my child as lost to me for ever."

All listened with breathless interest to what Sir Ranald Castleton was saying. Harry's satisfaction can better be imagined than described.

"I am very sure that you are Sir Ranald Castleton; those who doubt it have only to examine your picture in the study. Though I recognise you, I doubt not so will the old steward, Mr Groocock, and many others who knew you in your youth," said Mr Shallard, as Sir Ranald warmly greeted him as an old friend.

Harry, after a satisfactory interview with his father, could no longer restrain his eagerness. He set off again for Downside. He had not to go far, however, before he met the carriage. Returning with it, he had the happiness of handing out his beloved Maiden May, and introducing her to her father and brother.

Two weddings shortly afterwards took place by special licence at Texford Hall, Sir Ranald and Sir Ralph giving their daughters away.

A fête was held in honour of the occasion in the park, to which the Miss Pembertons came, where Adam and Dame Halliburt, with their two sons, for Sam had just returned from sea, were among the most honoured guests.

"I knew our Maiden May was a real young lady, though little did I think she would one day be Lady Castleton," said Adam.

Sir Ranald, who the dame had at once recognised, insisted on settling an annuity on old Adam and his wife.

Honest Jack Headland, the only one now of the name, not unwilling to remain on shore, was appointed to a post at Morbury, suited to his taste, though the comfortable income settled on him by Sir Ranald Castleton, might have enabled him to enjoy a life of ease and idleness to the end of his days.

Though the young officers, while the war continued, again went afloat, they did not object to being employed on home service, and Harry, who had purchased Downside on the death of his cousins, spent a portion of every summer at the place which was so endeared to him and his beloved and still blooming May.